SAVED *by the* PILOT

ANNE M. SCOTT

Anne M. Scott
Visit my website at www.amscottwrites.com/romance

First Printing: Jan 2025

Version 1.0
Lightwave Publishing LLC

To survivors of family betrayal—you are loved and
wanted.
Stay with us.

Contents

Content Warning

The main female character in *Saved by the Pilot* is an attempted sexual assault survivor via forced child marriage—a horrific practice that is still too common. This is not a condemnation of arranged marriage among consenting adults—if they are truly in agreement without undue outside pressure.

This novel also contains:

- Gun violence

- Sex trafficking, attempted sexual violence (unsuccessful, **on page**) and physical violence (**on page**)

- An evil enemy; the tone of this novel is darker than *Saved by the Airman*

- Family betrayal (and found family)

- A strong protective hero

- A determined, capable heroine

- Thrilling wilderness survival

- Closed door scenes

I hope you enjoy!

Chapter 1

Holly Bose strolled the perimeter of the posh hotel ballroom, casting casual glances at the massive mahogany double doors. Her stomach churned, but she maintained her calm, composed, emotionless appearance. The overpowering scent of expensive perfume and cologne mixed with huge floral centerpieces intensified her nausea. But the worst part was being alone in the hostile crowd.

He'd promised to join her at the dance because if her parents knew she had a boyfriend, they wouldn't have let her come. But their high school graduation ball was—she glanced at the clock for the four-thousandth time that night—halfway over. Sharp sneers, nasty laughs, and cutting comments shot from the mouths of her classmates and got louder each time she circled the room. She should have remained skeptical and kept turning him down because it seemed their year of dating was an elaborate joke after all.

Her super-rich, elite, and famous classmates would love to see her, the poor scholarship student with the best grades in the class, crash and burn. These petty people called the Bose family "immigrant trash" to her face. Determined to push back, she shoved her heritage in their bigoted faces, wearing her mother's beautiful red wedding sari to the dance. Ice princess was the nicest of the many names they called her, a title she happily embraced, letting the word spears slide off. Her mother was right—keeping her emotions from showing was a very useful skill.

The ballroom doors whooshed open and a tall, beautiful blonde woman Holly didn't recognize swept inside. She paused, hip cocked, a seductive and superior smile on her face, wearing a gorgeous gold gown Holly had seen on the Academy Awards red carpet. And she'd accessorized perfectly, clasping Lukas Sevrason's tuxedo-clad arm.

Gasps sounded across the room, followed by tinkling laughter. Heads swiveled in synchronization, staring at her. She forced her body to turn away, toward the band, like he didn't matter. As if she'd known all along.

But the agony of betrayal and rage tumbled together like knives in a dryer, sharp and piercing. She clenched her teeth, keeping the small serving of cake she'd eaten down. She wouldn't give them the satisfaction of seeing her pain.

He introduced his date to their classmates surrounding him like adoring fans. As the couple sauntered through the crush, his sardonic smile didn't waver, and he didn't cast a single glance her way.

Holly meant nothing to him.

She'd been such a fool. Her heart dropped like a rock from the top of the Washington Monument, shattering forever. But she wouldn't let him or anyone else break her. She took a deep breath, strengthening her spine.

Holly Bose didn't belong with these nasty, small-minded, entitled people. She gathered her wrap and walked out the door, head held high. She'd attend the graduation ceremony to please her parents and smear her summa cum laude status in her classmate's arrogant faces. Then she'd never have to see any of them, especially Lukas Sevrason, ever again.

One year later...

"Holly, your orders are getting cold! Hurry up!"

Holly hustled, loading plates on her tray, and ran to the swinging door. Pushing through, she slowed to a walk, projecting the calm and unhurried poise the Cliff House insisted on. The attitude was second nature—hiding her emotions behind a mask of serene calm was one of her earliest lessons. Serving the six-top table, she checked on all her others. Fortunately, the diners were happy. Back in the kitchen, she stretched her aching back, picked up a dessert, and returned to the dining room, despite her sore feet.

After finishing their long, tough shift, Holly left with her roommate. Cathy, who was usually a golden retriever in human form, groaned. "What a night! Way too many kids at my tables, and all the parents drinking. I hate to think what might be on my skirt right now." She brushed at the black material. "I should bring a change of clothes with me. That would keep my car seats clean, and I wouldn't have to go home before I meet Vincent at the bar."

While Holly couldn't wait to collapse on her bed, Cathy only wanted to party with her boyfriend. Hopefully, her tips were better than Holly's. "I got elderly people tonight. But not nice ones. No, I got crotchety old people who don't think tipping is important. I've got to find a better way to pay for college."

Cathy jangled her keys. "College is overrated. Come out with me. It's been ages! There's a great band later, and I want you to meet my friend Ronnie. I think the two of you might really hit it off." Cathy smiled with a raised brow, the picture of hope.

Holly almost groaned but kept it inside. "It's late, and I have a paper due on Monday. I can't stay out all night." She was already burning the candle at both ends; melting the middle was asking for trouble. She had to keep the few scholarships she had.

Cathy pulled the band from her messy bun, shaking her blonde hair loose. "You don't need to stay out all night. Just come meet Ronnie. Then you can go home and study. Please?"

Holly kept her smile in place, even though she wanted to scowl with a resounding no. Cathy's boyfriend had too many loser friends and wasn't far from total loser territory himself. But Cathy was wonderful; she'd helped Holly survive her first weeks in Tacoma, completely lost and bewildered. And Cathy got her the job allowing her to pay for the University of Washington, Tacoma. Plus, Cathy kept loneliness from consuming Holly's life. She owed Cathy. And maybe Ronnie would be a good guy after all, even if he wouldn't be gorgeous and rich. But she only needed decent—wealthy and entitled was a recipe for disaster. "Okay. I'll come for a while, but I really can't stay long."

Cathy squealed and hugged her. "You won't regret it! Let's go."

At home, they showered and dressed, then walked to Cathy's favorite bar, The Hot Spot. The funky little joint had the best local bands, decently priced beer, and delicious pizza. At the door, metal rock hammered her ears while a cloud of hot cheese and bread aroma made her mouth water. Cathy spotted her boyfriend and sprinted through the crowded tables to jump on his lap. Holly followed, slower. The theater-style lighting reflected off the hardware, decorating Vincent's face.

Surprisingly, the man sitting next to them and rolling his eyes didn't look like most of Cathy's friends. He had very short blond hair, a decent pair of shoulders, no piercings or obvious tattoos, and a friendly smile. Looks could be deceiving, though—he was obviously checking her out.

She pasted a friendly, but not too friendly, smile on her face and held out her hand. "Holly. How are you?"

He grinned. "Hey. I'm Ronnie and I'm great now that you're here."

Sitting, Holly didn't let her grimace show. The pizza better be worth the hassle. "Right. Nice to meet you. What do you do?"

His chin lifted. "I'm studying computer engineering at UW in Seattle."

That was surprising and interesting. "Really? I'm trying to get a degree in electrical engineering, but I can't afford UW." She could barely afford the satellite campus in Tacoma, and working all the time meant she didn't have time for side projects to impress scholarship donors.

Ronnie frowned. "Cathy said you're smart. Don't you have scholarships?"

She shrugged, slightly offended, even though she shouldn't be. "I've got some, but it's not enough to pay for Seattle."

His brows lifted. "If you're smart enough, you could do what I did—join Rot C."

She had to have misunderstood what he said. "Rot C? What's that?"

He frowned at her. "What rock did you grow up under? You've never heard of R-O-T-C?" He spelled out the acronym slowly, like she couldn't hear or understand.

"No, or I wouldn't have asked." She kept a friendly smile pasted on her face, rather than scowling. If there was a way to pay for school, she'd put up with his condescending attitude.

"It stands for Reserve Officer Training Corps. The military pays for college, then you serve as an officer for a few years. I'll spend five years in the Navy, and I'll get a huge bonus when I go in because I'm going for nuclear submarine engineering." He shrugged one shoulder. "After those five years, I can get out or stay. I'm not a huge fan of all the marching and orders, but I'll put up with it for the money. All the services offer the program."

Five years was nothing if she could get college paid for. "Are they full-ride scholarships?" She'd learned to ask a lot of questions—if it was too good to be true, it probably wasn't real.

He held up his hand and waggled it back and forth. "Some of my friends only have partial scholarships, but if you want to study electrical engineering, your grades are good, and you do good on the test, any of the Services will give you a full ride, no problem."

"So what's the catch?" There was always a catch.

He wagged his finger at her. "You are smart. The biggest one, I told you about. You have to stay in the military for four to eight years after you graduate depending on your career specialty. You take ROTC classes during the year, wear a uniform, and do a four-week training course in the summer between your sophomore and junior years." He grinned. "It's a pretty sweet deal if you don't come from money."

Holly snorted. "I definitely don't come from money. Thanks, I'll check it out." Hopefully, she wasn't too late, since she was in her sophomore year. She offered Ronnie a real smile, grateful for the information. If she could get in, not only would she pay for college, but she'd have a safe, secure career far from her family and the rich idiots she'd survived in high school. Lukas

Sevrason and the rest of them wouldn't be caught dead in a military uniform.

Ronnie grinned, scanning her body. "Sure. Want to dance?"

Chapter 2

Holly, nine years later, on vacation,
Marcus, Montana

Holly left the living room of Amy Stone's Montana house, caution warring with unwarranted hope. Her friend Amy was amazing, but her height, analytical attitude, and military rank made a lot of men uncomfortable. Plus, Amy's horrible former boss smeared her reputation, calling her a promiscuous troublemaker. But despite that handicap, Amy had recovered and become a true leader. Holly liked to think she and her best friend, Kristen, had helped, both through direct encouragement and by testing Amy's potential dates. If a man responded to Holly's looks or

Kristen's blatant advances—and most them did—he was written off forever.

But she was worried. Amy's behavior was very out of character. She'd invited a stranger to join her while backpacking, and then she brought him home, where the two of them would be alone. Under most circumstances, Amy and Rex were more than capable of fending off an aggressive man, but she seemed to take Sergeant Hall at face value. His story of about a friend who was supposed to pick him up from a remote trailhead in the middle of nowhere, Montana, seemed unlikely.

However, when Kristen made a play for Sergeant Hall, he'd immediately turned her down, chastising her as a bad friend, and bluntly answered Holly's invasive questions, including the fact that he was enlisted. Since Amy was an officer, a romantic relationship between them was forbidden—they'd get kicked out of the Air Force. They claimed a temporary friendship built on necessity, but their mutual attraction was crystal clear. Even though both were fairly reserved, they practically had heart-eyes every time they looked at each other. And that happened constantly.

Plus, Hall was good looking, confident—and even taller than Amy. It seemed like a match made in heaven, but unless one of them got out of the military, it was a cruel trick. At least it wasn't deliberate—simply fate.

After using the bathroom, Holly washed her hands. Knowing her luck, Hall's friend would be just as great—and just as enlisted. She chuckled almost silently. Not that it would matter because Kristen would have any guy twisted around her finger in two seconds. Very few men resisted her charms or tried. Besides, Holly's life was complex enough without a man.

Rex barked, and she jumped. Meeting new people, especially men, was never fun. Which made her job, working mostly with men, difficult. But Chris Hall seemed like a legitimately good guy. Surely his friend would be a decent person. She put a polite smile on her face and padded down the short hallway to the living room, and stopped.

No.

It couldn't be. Not him.

Holly clamped her open mouth shut and, with immense effort, plastered a polite smile back on her face. Lukas Sevrason was the last person she'd expected in Amy's living room. Or a friend to anyone not in his social-economic class, or in the military, especially an enlisted man.

Chris waved his hand toward Amy. "Major Amy Stone, meet Major Luke 'Revlon' Sevrason. He's a pilot with the air refueling wing on Fairchild. That's Captain Kristen Lake."

Major? Lukas Sevrason, the wealthy heir to Sevrason Aerospace, had joined the military? No way. It had to be a prank. But Chris had no reason to play jokes on her; they'd just met.

Kristen rose, sauntering toward the men. "Well, hello, handsome."

Holly wanted to run but kept her feet frozen to the floor. She would NOT make a scene. She waited for Chris to turn to her, then cut him off. "Luke. I'm surprised to see you. Please excuse me." She spun on her toe and walked up the stairs, letting her feet go faster with each step. Out of sight, she sprinted to the bedroom door, dove inside, and shoved it closed. The bang made her jump; she hadn't meant to slam the door.

Kristen would know something was wrong; Holly had to regain control. Dropping to the bed, she put her face in the pillow and silently screamed, beating it with her fists. She indulged for five seconds, then sat up, shaking out her hands and relaxing her jaw muscles. Her mother's lessons were deeply embedded and would pay off again. Never show emotion was rule one and had allowed her to succeed in a male-dominated profession. Ignoring that rule, even with her closest friends, would do her no favors.

That didn't keep questions from bombarding her brain. What was Lukas Sevrason doing in the Air Force? He came from money—tons of it. His father had expected him to join the family business after Luke finished college. And that college wasn't a state school, no, only Harvard would do. He'd planned to major in Business Economics, with a minor in Government Administration. If he didn't join Sevrason Aerospace, he'd get a law degree, then run for office and steer business to his father's company.

And Mr. Sevrason had made it clear that Luke had to find the "right" woman while he was at Harvard. Holly Bose wasn't acceptable even for a high school fling. Luke needed the American equivalent of royalty—a Kennedy, a Bush—to enhance his political chances.

Remembering her introduction to Luke's father made her fists clench with rage again. First, he'd leisurely scanned her head-to-toe and then refused her outstretched hand when Luke announced she was on a scholarship. Luke had glared at his father and pulled her away. Stupid little girl Holly had believed Luke was protecting her. But after dumping her so publicly, she'd reassessed all their interactions. Clearly, Luke was simply falling in line with his father's plans, removing the undesirable girl from his father's presence.

Major Lukas Sevrason made no sense. Even with his pedigree and connections, he'd be useless to his father as a line pilot at an air refueling wing in eastern Washington State. Even in the Pentagon, a major would have zero influence. Since he was a major already, he must have entered the military right after four years of college, probably through the ninety-day Officer Training School, rather than ROTC like she had. Between survival and the years before getting a full-ride scholarship, she'd been older than average when she entered active duty. Once again, money smoothed the way. But the idea of Lukas Sevrason as a military pilot still seemed wildly unlikely.

The door opened and Kristen marched in. Holly straightened, smoothing her expression. "What's wrong? How do you know that guy?" She fanned her face. "He's hot. Supernova hot. But if he's a jerk, it doesn't matter."

Holly wasn't sharing her secret with anyone. Not even her best friend. She shrugged. "I knew him back in high school. You know I was a scholarship kid. He definitely wasn't. I never expected to see him again, especially in the military. There's no deep, dark secret." Kristen's brows wrinkled in a skeptical expression.

Holly got up, grabbing her toiletries to avoid answering more questions. "I'm going to brush my teeth. It's been a long day."

Leaving the door open behind her, she entered the bathroom and prepared for bed. She'd avoid memory lane—it was over and done. She was a successful captain in the Air Force with a great career and steady income, not a poor girl wearing second-hand uniforms and eating homemade lunches, desperate to join the rich kid's club. She took long, slow, steady breaths, pushing the memories of that foolish girl away.

She wasn't going back to those awful days, especially not for Luke Sevrason. Even if he had grown from good-looking into a truly gorgeous man. His shockingly green eyes hadn't changed, but the planes of his face had sharpened and his severe military hair cut enhanced his features. His tall, lean runner's body had filled out, stretching the shoulders of his designer polo shirt, and his legs below the khaki short were strong and muscular.

But his mouthwatering model-like looks were a wrapper, a pretty shell—the inside was rotten.

Luke Sevrason and his kind weren't part of her life. Amy couldn't have a relationship with Chris, so there was no reason she'd ever have to see him again. Holly could shove him back into the dusty recesses of her memories, where he belonged. On the trash heap with the rest of her old life.

LUKE

Luke strangled his steering wheel, leaving his best friend and the small house behind, even as he longed to turn around. Holly Bose had drawn him like a magnet back in high school, but as an adult, her unexpected appearance struck him like lightning. For years, he had tried not to think about her, knowing she'd been married off by her family. But every woman he dated came up short in comparison, so he could never truly forget her.

Obviously, the marriage hadn't happened, or she'd gotten divorced. He'd never considered she'd end up in the Air Force. But then, few could believe he'd joined either.

So many questions and thoughts churned in his head that it was basically impossible to think. And then there were the visuals. She'd been stunning in high school, but as an adult? He really couldn't think of the right term. Absolutely drop-dead gorgeous, beautiful, exquisite—none of the terms did her justice. If she didn't get married, then why wasn't she in Hollywood? Or New York City on a runway?

She was too short to be a model, but still, she'd be incredible on a stage. Her petite, sexy body, her soft caramel skin, deep brown hair cut in a shiny, thick cap framing her big, slightly tilted velvet brown eyes in a rounded oval face all came together to stun him senseless. And the voice of an angel too. All of that, along with her natural poise, would shine so brightly on a screen.

As he kept driving, he gradually recovered from the shock and awe—and got his body's reaction under control. Then he realized—her supposed marriage was another Machiavellian scheme created by his father. One more lie in the long list of them, one more attempt to twist Luke into his mold. Luke snorted. That wasn't going to happen, and the sooner Daddy Dearest figured that out, the better.

As he neared his family's "Montana cabin"—and wasn't that a ridiculous misnomer for the huge timber-framed mansion—he forced his questions, wants, and needs to take a back seat, just as if he was on a mission in his jet. All that mattered right now was his half-sister, Susan. To get through this latest medical crisis, she needed caring, considerate parents. If only one of them was there, poor Susan would be ignored, as usual. But with both of them present, they'd compete for her attention. And if that took selling Father a bucket of prop wash, that's what he'd do. She wouldn't suffer the way he had.

HOLLY

With Sevrason gone, Holly enjoyed her too-short Montana vacation with Kristen and Amy. Chris was supportive, kind, and unusually tolerant of Kristen's over-the-top plans and mannerisms. But that didn't change the fact that Amy and Chris were headed for heartbreak or career suicide. And Amy could protest all she wanted, but despite all the trouble she'd had, she loved being an Air Force officer.

Holly understood; she loved her career, too. But she'd never, ever give up her occupation for a man. She'd rather deal with heartbreak because she knew how to survive that. She tried to convince Amy that was true, but as they drove away, Holly was pretty sure her warnings had fallen on deaf ears.

Kristen smirked at her from the driver's seat. "No deep, dark secrets, huh? Still doesn't look that way to me." She was determined to get the full story, and she had a seventeen-hour drive to do it in.

"Really, Kristen. I knew Sevrason back in high school. His father owns Sevrason Aerospace." Holly shrugged deliberately. "I was a scholarship kid. I knew him, but not well." And that was truer than her high school heart wanted to admit. "I never thought he'd go into the military, not in a thousand years. Why would he? He's rich." Calm, cool, collected. She repeated it like a mantra. Her stomach spun like a tilt-a-whirl, but there was no reason to show it.

"Interesting." Kristen pursed her bright red lips. "I've heard of Sevrason Aerospace but never worked with them on a contract. I wonder if they're playing a long game?"

Holly considered the idea. "That makes more sense than anything I could think of. The son makes general and gets to know all the important people, pushing them towards the company, but he's not in a direct position to influence a contract. It might work."

"That's a long time to wait and kind of risky." Kristen shrugged. "Luke's a pilot, plus smart and gorgeous. But he's not a fighter pilot, which I believe is Sevrason Aerospace's main customer base. Even with all his advantages, there's no guarantee he'd make general or have any influence over those contracts."

"But let's face it, looks matter." Holly sniffed, half amused, half annoyed. "We know that."

"Sure do. A good-looking guy has a better chance at everything than an ugly one. And there's no downside for men like there is for us." Kristen snorted. "A handsome guy has to prove he's stupid, where a beautiful woman is assumed to be dumb." She mockingly fluffed her blonde hair. "Although we've both used that to our advantage more than once."

Holly held out her fist, and Kristen bumped it. "You bet we have, and we will again." There'd been more than one contractor shocked by her analysis of whatever they were selling. She enjoyed being underestimated but hated the almost-constant leering and unwanted advances.

"I'm worried, though." Kristen twisted her hands on the wheel.

Incredulous, Holly turned in her seat. "About Luke? Why?"

Without looking away from the road, Kristen smacked Holly's thigh. "No." She shook her head. "You're thinking a lot about this guy, no matter what you say. Anyway, I'm worried about *Amy*." She emphasized the name.

Holly let Kristen's comment about her go. She'd done it to get a rise, but Amy was the important person. "I am too. She can say they're just friends all she wants, but she's got it bad."

Kristen nodded, her face unusually glum. "She does, and it's nothing but trouble. She's had enough of that with the Air Force. A relationship with an enlisted man, no matter how hot, thoughtful, and kind, is a death knell for her career. And Amy doesn't hide anything well, we both know that."

"Yeah." Holly couldn't agree more. "But I don't know what we can do about it, other than support her when she sets off the mines and blows up her life. Because it will happen."

Kristen nodded but didn't say anything more, letting Holly stew about Amy's issues. But it wasn't long before Holly remembered how badly her life had gone after Luke dumped her so cruelly. There was only one conclusion. Men were trouble.

But dwelling on the past was stupid, and she wasn't. She lifted her phone. "How about a podcast? I downloaded a couple."

"Excellent idea." Kristen smiled. "No reason for us to be all gloomy about something that hasn't happened."

Holly hit play, and the comedian's distinctive voice filled the car. But despite that, Holly had to keep bringing her attention back to the podcast and away from the memory of piercing green eyes.

Chapter 3

THREE WEEKS AFTER THEY'D returned from their Montana vacation, Holly met Kristen for lunch at the Space Force headquarters cafeteria in Colorado Springs. The food wasn't bad, but the view sold it. The wall of windows revealed the majestic Front Range and Pike's Peak. Snowy mountains glistened in the blue sky, framed by the sleek silver and blue of the building. She and Kristen were trying to catch up; eating in the building saved them a lot of time. And Amy could join them on video, too.

Amy grinned and waved from Kristen's phone. After they shared the latest in their lives, Amy held up her hand. "Before I forget, I've got big news and a favor to ask."

She rarely asked for anything, so Holly didn't hesitate. "Just let me know and I'll do it."

Kristen waggled her brows. "Hopefully, it involves a handsome, single man."

Amy smiled at Kristen but sobered when she glanced at Holly. "You're in luck, Kristen. I'm sure you remember Chris's friend, Lukas Sevrason? Luke's just been assigned to the 13th Air Operations Squadron. It's an Air Force unit that supports the Army, located on Fort Carson. I'm sure he'd appreciate a tour of the area and help finding a house."

The food in Holly's stomach solidified into an indigestible lump, and she pushed her tray away. Luke living in Colorado Springs was a disaster waiting to happen. "He's all yours, Kristen."

Kristen flashed a frown at her. "Yeah, right." She returned to Amy. "But I am happy to help. Especially a pilot on an Army post. That's going to be a difficult transition."

"Maybe. I guess Luke's deployed with the Army before. That's why he got selected. Plus, he volunteered for the position to avoid his father." Amy shrugged. "He wouldn't say anything more about that, but I guess his dad has pressured him to move to the Pentagon so he can help Sevrason Aerospace. Like a major or even a lieutenant colonel has any clout there." Amy smirked. "Speaking of colonels, Kristen, there's one sitting behind you, glaring. It's kind of shocking. Don't you have all the male officers in the building twisted around your little finger?"

Kristen turned and wiggled her fingers at the lieutenant colonel sitting near the exit. When she smiled and batted her eyes, his glower deepened. "That's Colonel Lee. He's the intelligence division commander—I've worked with his people on a couple of projects. And when the husband of a friend got injured downrange, he was super helpful with status and updates."

Holly also smiled at Colonel Lee and got a sharp nod, but he returned his gaze to Kristen quickly. "I think he might be a fan, Kristen, but maybe he doesn't want to acknowledge it?"

"Maybe." Kristen shrugged. "Plenty of fish in the sea. This one is too senior for me, anyway."

Kristen's nonchalance fell a little flat. But she was right—a captain dating a lieutenant colonel, even well outside of her chain of command, was a stretch. And Colonel Lee was a commander—he had to exceed the standards.

Amy tilted her head. "True, but that's never stopped you. Hey, Wiz is calling. I've got to go. Stay safe out there while you're having fun without me."

Holly smiled. "Have some fun yourself!"

Kristen laughed. "With that hot man coming home every night, she's got all the fun she can handle." She waved her hand in front of her face. "But don't worry about us. Holly's taking the group mom role seriously."

Amy ended the call. Kristen stood and looked down at Holly. "I'll see you Friday night for dinner and drinks, right?"

"Sure. Wherever you want." She'd enjoy time with her friends before Luke showed up and ruined everything.

"I'll text you. Good luck with your presentation." Kristen headed toward Colonel Lee's table, but he'd already gotten up to leave.

"Okay." Following Kristen out, Holly returned to her cubicle, lost in thought. Her minimal social life was about to come to a screeching halt. She'd hung out with Kristen since their first duty assignment together, but if Luke became part of their group, she'd have to find new friends.

She plopped into her chair and scowled at her blank computer screen. No, she couldn't accept that. Luke wasn't taking anything else from her. She was keeping Kristen, Amy, and Chris. In a group setting, Luke would get polite responses only if absolutely necessary. He didn't deserve even that, but she wouldn't make everyone uncomfortable. And if that made their conversation awkward now and then, she was sure Kristen and Amy would forgive her. That's what friends did.

Three months later

Holly and Kristen entered Old Chicago's, the classic downtown pizza joint in Colorado Springs. The scents of yeasty bread, toasted cheese, and sharp hops wafted on the air, while the bedlam of a hundred different conversations assaulted her ears. The restaurant served a mix of trendy influencers, college students, and military members all looking for a good time while drinking an around-the-world beer tour. They wound through the crowd toward tables in the back, Holly dragging her feet in Kristen's wake. She couldn't wait to see Amy and Chris again, but Luke would be there, too.

Kristen pointed. "Hey, there they are. Looks like they saved us a prime spot. Good thing they're both tall, or I'd have missed them."

Too bad. If Kristen hadn't seen them, Holly wouldn't have to deal with Luke. When they arrived, Amy bounced on her toes, her arms open wide. Kristen squealed and hugged her, then pulled Holly in, too. "I missed you two!"

"Missed you, too." Kristen grinned. "Holly's more fun when she's not designated driver."

Holly ignored her. "I wish we lived closer." Amy was more of a sister than her blood sisters, by a long shot.

"Yeah, me too." Amy's nose wrinkled. "But C Springs is too crowded for me. I like Spokane, but Montana is even better."

Chris tugged Amy into the semi-circular booth next to him. "Won't be long before Montana is home full time."

Amy leaned into Chris. "And I can't wait."

Despite Holly's best effort, Luke sat next to her—the very last place she wanted to be. She scooted closer to Kristen, but Luke's muscular shoulder pressed into hers. His addictive scent, a peppery citrus underlaid with sharp cedar, made her remember all the stolen moments they'd had. But those days were long gone. He'd stolen much more than moments.

Amy waved her hand across the table. "You can all visit us and we'll hike, float the river, fish, and do all the fun things. Or ski in the winter. Erin and Ryan, our friends in Marcus who own Coffee and Cars, promised to show us the best runs. The local ski hill is way less expensive than Colorado."

"We should plan a ski and board trip for this winter." Luke sipped his dark beer. "But maybe here in Colorado on a holiday weekend so we don't have to take leave." He motioned to Holly and Kristen. "Although that means you'd have to, Chris."

He shrugged. "A little less terminal leave won't kill me."

Everyone pulled out a phone and looked at their calendars. Holly sipped her water. No matter how much she loved to ski, she wasn't going—an evening was fine, but overnights were out. No way she'd spend that much time with Luke.

The server came, and they ordered drinks and pizza. Calendar discussions continued as the drinks arrived.

Chris tapped his phone. "The middle of February looks pretty good for me and Amy. It might be cold, but that's okay. We can always do a run, go have a drink, do a run, right?"

"Perfect." Kristen fluffed her hair. "I'm more of a ski bunny, anyway."

"Yeah, right." Amy shook her head. "If by bunny you mean hare, screaming down the mountain at warp speed." She faced Holly, her brows wrinkling. "Holly, you haven't said anything. Don't you want to come? You love skiing."

Holly forced a smile. "Sure, I'll come. Count me in. It's just that my schedule is pretty open right now. I can go whenever." And the week before, she'd get a cold or schedule a meeting in DC. Better to lose money than live with Luke.

"Luke, I'm assuming we can't sneak under the radar and use one of your family homes, right?" Chris asked.

Holly didn't roll her eyes, but she wanted to. Poor rich boy with all those vacation spots to pick from.

"No, sorry." Luke grimaced. "I don't want to run into Daddy Dearest. Now that my original eight-year commitment is up, he's been sending emails and leaving me phone messages non-stop about returning to DC." He scowled.

Chris chuckled. "Doesn't he know you've added a year's commitment by accepting the new assignment?"

Luke grinned, a sharp, predatory grin. "He doesn't even know I've moved. And the leadership back at the squadron agreed not to volunteer anything if he calls. I leaned hard on the possible conflict of interest. Plus, they're grateful. They've been trying to fill my position with the Army for a year. Besides, he's not on my emergency notification lists or life insurance—so he has no legal right to know anything about me."

Kristen whispered in Holly's ear. "Wow, I can't imagine cutting ties to my family like that, can you?"

Holly smiled, hoping it looked genuine, but pain stabbed her through the heart. "Will you all excuse me? I need the restroom."

Luke let her out of the booth. She pushed her way across the jammed room to the bathroom. Being short made crowds even worse, and the chatter was deafening. She finally made it, closed the stall door behind her, and held back a sob. Kristen hadn't meant to hurt her; she didn't know Holly had left her family behind a long time ago. Sometimes, being with friends made her feel even more alone.

Odd that Luke was in the same boat. In high school, Luke had been respectful and obedient to his father, except when it came to her. But in the end, he'd obviously given her up without regret. No wonder he'd agreed to keep their relationship secret. Her tears dried and her fists clenched.

But something must have come between Luke and his father during college, or he wouldn't have joined the Air Force. Back in high school, Luke had planned to get his degree and work his way up at Sevrason Analytics, his father's very successful defense lobbying firm. Or go to work for a competitor.

Holly snorted. More than likely, he'd decided flying would be more fun. He got control of his trust fund after college graduation, so he didn't have to live on a military salary. Why work in a boring office when zooming through the sky was an option?

But Luke's rich-kid problems weren't hers. Avoiding him was the issue. She washed her hands and checked her makeup, reinforcing her cheerfully bland expression. Leaving the bathroom, she narrowly avoided colliding with a man standing outside the door. She stepped aside. "Excuse me."

Hands clenched her upper arms, spinning her to face an angry stranger. The man looked a lot like her Uncle Raj, with deep-set dark brown eyes topped by thick, black brows, his glare carving deep lines into his umber skin. The stench of unfiltered cigarettes made her choke. "Holiday Bose. I've finally found you."

Holly twisted, trying to break his grip. "Who are you?" Not that it mattered. She didn't let anyone manhandle her. Not after she left home. She brought her right leg back, ready to kick him between the legs.

His lip curled. "You should recognize me. You were signed, sealed, and supposed to be delivered as my wife." One hand reached for her chin.

She spun out and away. "Keep your hands off of me, or I'm calling the cops!"

The man stepped to the side, an ugly sneer on his face. "Now that I've finally found you, I'll get what I paid for, one way or another. You'll regret running for the rest of your life."

"Don't threaten my friend!" Amy loomed over the man, raising her fists. Holly jumped; she'd been so focused on the stranger, she hadn't seen Amy. Amy's voice was ice cold. "I've killed one would-be rapist. Do you want to be next?"

The man held up a hand. "Do not speak to me. Women should know their place." Without looking at Amy, the man turned and walked away.

Holly stared at the man's back until he disappeared. She jumped again when Amy put an arm around her shoulder, pulling her through the crowd. "Come on, we're getting out of here."

She shook violently, hanging on to Amy, terror and anger clouding her thoughts. At the table, Amy leaned forward. "Are any of you carrying a weapon?"

"Not in a bar." Luke leaped to his feet, standing on Holly's other side, facing the crowd. "What happened?" Kristen and Chris joined them, crowding close.

"Some guy just threatened Holly. Kristen, can you run down the bill and get some to-go boxes? We'll get her to the car." Amy tugged Holly around to face the door. Luke got in front of them, head turning back and forth while Amy and Chris bracketed her, walking her outside.

At her Subaru, Amy pushed her into the back seat. Luke squeezed into the seat nearest the bar, his back pressing into her shoulder as he searched out the window. Chris reached under the car's front seat, pulling out a semi-automatic handgun. He remained standing at the driver's side door until Kristen joined them, hands full of pizza boxes. She got in next to Holly, handing her a few of the boxes. The warmth melted some of her icy disbelief.

Amy joined Chris. "I'll drive, you guard. Where to?"

Luke said, "My place. It's close; just a few blocks away." He gave Any directions while watching out the windows.

Holly looked at her pizza boxes on her lap, stunned and incredulous. She should have been safe after all these years. What were the odds of discovery at a bar in a town half a country away from home?

The car stopped on a tree-lined side street next to a huge Western Victorian. Christmas lights twinkled from the eaves, and bright garlands wrapped the graceful porches. Luke got out. "I've got the top floor. Straight up the stairs. Wait here until I'm armed." He sprinted away, opened the door, and reappeared with a weapon in his hand before Holly could slide off the seat.

Amy took the pizza from her. "Come on, let's go." She led the way up the stairs, and they squeezed past Luke, entering a large living area with dark leather sofas and an enormous screen filling the one solid wall. Modern shades hid the windows surrounding them.

Doorways led to a kitchen and a hall. The apartment was graceful and gorgeous, but modernized enough to live in. Holly hadn't even looked in Old Colorado City, knowing everything was well out of her price range.

After Chris entered, Luke locked the door. "Have a seat. I'll grab plates, glasses, and drinks." He entered the kitchen, Kristen on his heels.

"Holly, are you okay?" Amy bent, frowning in her face.

She shuddered the encounter away. She had to regain control. Nothing had actually happened; she was fine. "I'm fine, thanks. Let's have pizza. We don't want it to get cold. There's nothing to worry about." She plopped into the nearest chair, unable to hold back a shiver from the cold leather.

Luke and Kristen returned, bearing beer, soda, water, plates, and silverware. Amy and Kristen distributed slices. Chris and Luke placed their guns on the coffee table, glancing at the door.

Holly accepted a plate and took a bite. But the pizza was dust in her mouth. She set the plate on the coffee table and rubbed her sweaty palms on her jeans. Both hands shook, and she gripped her knees so it wouldn't show. Her friends exchanged speaking looks.

After a few bites, Amy put her plate down. "Holly, you've never said anything about your family or your past, and I've never asked. It wasn't my business if you didn't want to share."

Of course, it would be Amy. She never hesitated to do the right thing. Holly gripped her legs hard enough to bruise.

Amy took Holly's right hand, squeezing gently. "But now, I think you're going to have to explain why that man said he would get what he paid for and that you'd regret it. Was that your father?"

Holly laughed, but despair dropped her heart into her stomach like a piece of space junk sucked into Earth's gravity. She absolutely did not want to talk about her family, but there was no way they'd leave without knowing the story. Making up a believable tale on the fly was beyond her, too. She sucked in a big breath. Her friends wouldn't laugh or abandon her. Luke might, but he wasn't a friend. "No, he's definitely not my father. I've never seen him before and I don't remember his name. But I can guess who he is from what he said."

She swallowed heavily and then took a drink of water. Hopefully, she'd get through this without breaking down. "At the end of high school, I ran away from home. My mom dropped me off for the graduation ceremony, but instead of filing into the auditorium with everyone else, I ditched my gown and got on a bus. I went to a women's shelter across town." Her mouth drying, she sipped more water. Right before the ceremony, her father demanded her presence in his office. Since that never happened unless she was in trouble, and she'd behaved perfectly for the last year, she'd thought he was congratulating her on graduating. Instead, he'd shoved a pen in her hand and told her to sign a marriage contract or she'd never leave the house again. "My father arranged a marriage to a man I'd never met." She shuddered, then controlled her reaction. She had to remain calm. "My father had received the bride price already. The wedding was supposed to happen the next day. I'd thought all the preparations were for one of my sisters, but no. It was me."

Curses flew, but Amy held up her hand. "You'd never even met the guy?"

Her friend's incredulous fury made it easier to continue. "No. It's normal in my family. My grandparents were from the old country. Marriages are arranged. There's no romance or love. It's a way to bind families for political and monetary gain. My sisters and cousins think it's great—they didn't have to deal with dating and Mother made sure the men were appropriate. It seemed to work out for them. Mostly." She grimaced. Her sisters' husbands were just as old-fashioned as her father, but they had treated their wives decently. "But my mother got breast cancer at the beginning of my senior year. Treatment cost a lot of money, and she had to focus on herself. I'm sure Mother thought that the smart youngest daughter was at an expensive American school, and making connections, so she'd be fine." Holly shrugged. Mother had never been particularly demonstrative, and the cancer made her a shadow of her former self.

She stood and walked to the windows, unable to face her friends. "I signed a formal contract. I knew the name on that document. His previous wife had been abused, and even though the family tried to cover it up, she'd committed suicide. I'd learned a lot more than my father realized at school, and I wasn't going to be sold into slavery to a monster." She looked at the ceiling for a moment to keep from screaming, then made herself continue. "For the graduation ceremony, I wore half of my dowry—the traditional gold chains. Just before we left, I stole my father's copy of the contract." She moved the shades to peek outside, but all she saw was her father's study and the ornate walnut desk containing her doom—and salvation. "I got away and got some cash from selling the dowry. I was still under age, so I ended up in the foster system. But the women's shelter helped me file a sealed emancipation case so I wouldn't be legally under my father and mother's control. Since I got away before the marriage, the state investigators said child abuse charges probably wouldn't stick. But the contract is a part of the official court record and the main reason the judge ruled in my favor. The prosecution wanted to file charges against my father and husband-to-be, but I refused to testify—I just wanted to leave. The shelter helped me move across the country. I know that my family probably suffered because I broke the contract, but that's why I left half of my dowry."

"Your family deserves to suffer. They tried to sell you!" Luke's hands were clenched, his face white, and his jaw was so tight she wondered if he'd grind his teeth to dust.

She shrugged and turned away. His fury was too late. And fake. He didn't care about her. "They see it as giving an unruly, over-educated daughter a stable man to guide her into her proper role in life. And I'm pretty sure they needed the money after my mother's bills."

Kristen threw her hands up, then let them drop into her lap. "I can't believe things like that still happen in America!"

Holly shook her head. Kristen was sheltered. "Arranged marriages are nothing, even ones that twist the traditional monetary exchanges into outright sale. Thousands of girls and boys are taken, bought and sold by traffickers in this country, both Americans and kids from overseas. It happens all the time. People just don't want to believe it. And I'm sure you've heard of honor killings? Those don't just happen in foreign countries; they happen here too. We're just better at tracking down the killers and prosecuting them, if someone reports it, which doesn't happen very often." The community-wide pressure to keep quiet was immense.

"There's not much we can do about the past, or all those other people, right now. But we can do plenty to make sure nothing happens to you." Amy joined her, taking her hand and tugging her back to the sofa. "You'll be coming to the range this weekend with me and Chris. Get some practice with a firearm. You'll stay with Kristen until we figure out who this guy is, where he lives, and if he's really a threat. And you'll be making a formal report of a threat, with me to back you up, so the police can get a case started and get surveillance from the restaurant."

Kristen nodded. "After we tell your boss and security forces, we'll get you pepper spray and permission to bring it with you on base and into the office. And you'll be coming with me to self-defense classes. You're strong, so a little technique is all it will take."

"I think you should have someone with a concealed carry permit escort you whenever you're off base." Chris grimaced. "If you weren't military, I'd tell you to quit and move in with us. But you can't do that."

Holly had already thought about resigning. She had little commitment left, but she liked the military. Despite the tedious administrative tasks and the huge number of regulations, military acquisitions was challenging. And important—Space Force's assets affected the lives of all military members. Plus, it offered a level of protection against her family. If she disappeared, the military would look for her. But maybe it was time to move on to something new.

"I don't have a permit here yet, but it shouldn't take me long." Luke pointed at her with his elbow. "Or you. I have a weapon you can have. It's too small for my hand, but I never bothered to sell it."

Holly held up her hand. They didn't need to get involved in her family drama; it was her responsibility. "Wait a minute. I told you all what was going on because I knew you wouldn't believe me if I said it was nothing, but this isn't your fight. It's my family, my problem."

Protests came from everyone, but Amy stood and held up her hand, quieting the group. "Not our fight? You are family." She swept her hand across her body, indicating all of them. "We're family. Yours doesn't deserve you."

"Of course this is our fight!" Luke scowled, his face dark as a storm cloud. "This should have been my fight from the start. Why didn't you tell me?"

"Tell you?!" Fury burned through Holly like rocket fuel. She clenched her fists, widened her stance, and glared at the arrogant liar. "Slime ball! You got what you wanted, and then you dropped me like a rock! Why would I ever trust you? You used me!"

Luke's head jolted back and his mouth hung open, like he was the injured party. Which was ridiculous. He'd repudiated her publicly, flaunting the proper kind of girl in her face. He was putting on a show for her friends.

Then she realized Kristen and Amy wore stunned looks on their faces, while Chris glared at Luke. Her stomach sank. She'd lost control. If she hadn't reacted, they'd never have known the depths of her humiliation. She had to regain her unemotional state—quickly, or the group might fall apart.

Amy glanced between her and Luke several times. "Seems like you've got some unfinished business. Shall we leave you two alone? No, wait, take it down the hall. We're not leaving until we get the security situation ironed out."

Luke grabbed her hand, trying to tow her away. Holly twisted, wrenching out of his grip. "Don't touch me!"

He held up both hands. "Sorry. This way, please." He led her down a short hall and turned right, into a bedroom. A huge, cherry wood mission-style bed took up most of the room, the matching dresser and nightstands leaving a narrow path to the closet and bathroom. A forest green comforter with coordinating pillows in dark red and old gold invited sleeping, and his signature scent hung heavy in the air. He turned to face her, his lips compressed, and put his hands behind his back, standing at parade rest.

She glared but closed the door behind her. Amy was right. They had unfinished business. "How dare you—"

Luke held one hand up, his face blank. "My father told me you weren't attending the graduation dance.

You were with your fiancé. The fiancé I knew nothing about." The muscles at the back of his jaw jumped. "Then I saw you. That's when I realized just how much he lied to me."

"Right." Holly sniffed. "That's why you dropped her at the punch bowl and came to find me." He'd strolled around the room with that woman, laughing and joking, ignoring her entirely.

"Brenda latched on tighter than a tick." He shook his hand like he was flinging something nasty away. "I tried to get rid of her, but she stuck to me like a barnacle." He grimaced. "Looking back, I'm sure she had instructions to keep me away from you. By the time I scraped her off, you were gone."

"Uh huh." She crossed her arms. Even in high school, Lukas Sevrason could be ruthless. He'd made no effort to get rid of his gorgeous date.

He grimaced and ran a hand through his almost too-long, black, shiny hair. Holly remembered how soft those strands were, but expensive products were all it took. He sighed. "Hindsight being twenty-twenty, I should have pushed her away when I spotted you. But I thought there would be time to explain at graduation the next day."

Holly glared at him. Surely, he realized she wasn't stupid. She'd have turned her back to him at graduation, and he knew it.

Luke turned in a small circle, running his hands through his hair. "This is ancient history. We need to keep you safe from this guy."

Holly spun and opened the door. "I'll keep myself safe. If I need help, I've got friends."

"Holly, I know there's a lot of turbulence between us, but I am your friend." Pain and desperation coated his voice.

He knew how to lie with the best of them. "No. You aren't." She walked away. She couldn't be alone with him for one more second. He'd learned to play others early; a necessary skill at his social level. If she stayed, eventually, he'd talk her into believing him. But she knew better.

In the living room, Holly faced Amy, the leader of their group. She had to defuse the situation. It was her problem, not theirs. And while she might not be an actor of Luke's caliber, she'd learned a lot in the intervening years. "I think we're all overreacting, me the most. Yes, it was a shock hearing that ridiculous line from that nasty man." She rolled her eyes and huffed. "But he's a fat old guy who smokes." She wrinkled her nose. She wasn't faking her reaction to that stench. "I can kick him into next week. Not only that, but I've got the law on my side, and if I disappear, the military will look for me."

Amy stepped close, jabbing her finger into Holly's chest. "I thought Blake wasn't a real threat. I almost got Chris, my dog, and me killed!"

Holly blinked. The situation obviously terrified Amy. But Holly's...intended wasn't deranged, just certain of his rights under his cultural norms. That would fall apart under legal scrutiny, especially ten years later.

Chris wrapped his arm around Amy. "Holly, I understand your point of view. But Blake was a fat old guy, too, and law enforcement was actively looking for him. We came too close to dying. The police won't do anything about your problem, other than take a report. Let's get a plan together. Even if it doesn't end up being necessary, we'll be prepared."

If Chris was concerned, Amy would never give up. Despite Holly's surface exasperation, deep down, she was grateful. The years alone after she'd left home and during college had worn her to the bone. Constant vigilance was exhausting. "Okay. Operation Bubble Wrap is a go."

"There's no bubble wrap here, honey." Kristen hugged her. "We're going to make sure you can fight back and get law enforcement on our side." She stepped away and grinned. "We'll be roomies for a while. It'll be fun!" Despite her words, Kristen's worry was crystal clear.

Luke stepped in front of her, holding out his hand, a semi-automatic pistol not quite covering his palm. "Here, it's unloaded. See if it fits."

Holly picked up the weapon without touching him. She ejected the magazine and checked the chamber. It was clear. Then she wrapped her hands around it, properly, aiming it at the bottom of the front door, slid the magazine back in, and worked the action. Most semi-autos were too big; she could barely qualify with the military issue 9mm because it was hard for her to properly grip. But Luke's gun fit her hand perfectly. "It's good." She didn't want to take anything from him, but her friends were right—she needed a weapon.

"It's a .380 Ruger LCP, meant for concealed carry. It's not going to take down a bear, but it'll slow down a person. It's not a distance weapon—seven yards at most." Luke walked back toward his bedroom. Holly kept her eyes on the gun. She didn't need to watch him.

Amy said, "I've got one just like it. It's not what I used on Blake—that was a .45 I borrowed from Mrs. Murphy—but you put all those rounds into the center of his chest, he's going to feel it. We'll take it with us to the range this weekend."

Holly gripped the weapon tight, aiming it toward the door. She'd need ammunition and a holster.

Luke returned with two boxes and a thin, black magazine. "Here's an extra magazine and two boxes of practice ammo. We'll get some hollow points tomorrow. And a small safe for storage at your home."

Kristen chimed in. "I've got a gun safe."

"You do?" Holly was surprised.

"Sure. I might act silly sometimes, but I'm not a fool." She held up her purse, opening the side. "I occasionally carry concealed, but not at a bar or a bank, of course."

Holly held up the weapon. "Thank you for the gun, Luke." She forced the words out. "I'd like to practice, and I can stay with you, Kristen, tonight. Let's reassess in the morning." Then she could go home, sort through all her emotions, and lock them down. She'd keep her friends and family apart.

"Please humor us." Amy grasped her shoulder. "We can't lose you."

"You won't." Holly had escaped her family as a child. They certainly couldn't threaten her as an adult and a military officer. That nasty old man wasn't a problem.

Chapter 4

AFTER A LONG WEEK of even longer days, Holly rode home from work in Kristen's passenger seat. "Before we go to your house, can we stop by my place? I need a change of clothes." She had plants to water, too. Plus, the threat had to be over. No one had seen the guy. Not base Security Forces, not the Colorado Springs Police, not her boss, and definitely not her. She could return home.

"Sure, that's easy enough. Is living with me really so bad?" Kristen mock pouted. "It's like old times!" She took a left at the next light, rather than a right.

Holly smirked. "Rooming together was fun back then. But your place isn't really big enough for two of us long term." They'd had a fabulous time as brand-new second lieutenants, but Holly missed her bed and adequate bathroom space. Kristen's makeup and hair products took up every inch of counter space in her one-bedroom apartment. Her pullout couch wasn't horrible, but it wasn't great, either.

Kristen pulled into Holly's driveway. Holly rented half of a duplex rather than an apartment like Kristen. A bright green note flapped on her dark brown front door. She got out of the car and pulled off the "delivery attempted" notice from the Post Office.

"Did you order something?" Kristen stepped up next to her.

"No, I don't know what this is." Holly stuffed the card into her purse. "The Post Office is closed by now. We'll get it tomorrow." She glanced around her neighborhood but saw nothing out of place. "Let's do all of this tomorrow."

Kristen returned to her vehicle. "Good idea. We need guns before we go in your house."

The next day, Kristen drove her to the Post Office. After she signed a delivery card, the postal worker handed her a certified letter. In the car, she opened it. Kristen leaned over, not even pretending to give Holly some privacy.

> Holiday Bose,
> You will return home immediately. You have family obligations to fulfill and the family has suffered because of your failure. If you do not comply, further
>
> actions will be taken.
> Gafur Bose

Kristen scoffed. "Seriously? So last century. But I guess we'd better get this to the cops."

Holly took a picture and emailed it to her assigned contact at the Colorado Springs police department. "I can't believe my father thinks this will work."

"It's probably just to cover his bases." Kristen pulled out of the parking spot and spoke in a gruff tone. "See, I am trying, but she's not paying attention. So sorry."

Holly shook her head. "I've never heard my father admit he was wrong. He's certainly never apologized for anything." She'd pushed much of her childhood out of her mind, but the memories were returning. Her life had been so small, so limited, and looking back, terribly toxic. Abusive, even. She'd never been hit, but expectations of perfection were impossible, especially for a child. Even when she'd done everything right, it was never enough for her father. He was never happy with her. "You know, I think part of it was he desperately wanted another boy. I was the last child and there went his legacy, because my brother was awful." She wouldn't be surprised if he was in prison for fighting or drugs, or both.

"At least you know why he was always disappointed." Kristen frowned. "Maybe you can put it behind you." She wrinkled her nose. "You should probably see a therapist."

Holly chuckled. "You're undoubtedly right there. Probably should have a long time ago. But it's not going to be today. Let's go get my stuff."

Kristen pointed to her feet. "Then we're giving each other pedicures. Pretty toes make everything feel better."

"Sure do." Holly grinned, and for once, she didn't force it. She had real friends who had her back and didn't let her hide away from the world. And pedicures were a great reason to avoid Luke's latest lunch invitation. He kept texting and leaving messages for meals, events, and anything else he could think of, but she was done.

She never wanted to see his piercing green eyes again.

On Monday, her boss's secretary sent her an appointment notice. The subject read personnel issues. She didn't have anyone working for her, she wasn't due to move, and no one had complained about her. Or maybe that sleazy contractor who kept asking her to dinner had said something. Even if she'd been attracted to the man, he worked on the government contract she oversaw, a clear conflict of interest. Besides, he was obviously married. The signs were so clear. If he'd made a complaint, she'd fire back rather than ignoring the issue. She returned to clearing her email inbox.

Five minutes before the appointment, she left her cubicle and walked to Colonel Haywood's office. His secretary, Alice, showed her in and shut the door behind her. She relaxed slightly. If it was a disciplinary matter, Alice would have told her to formally report in with a salute. Even though she'd been sure, Holly's steps past the casual seating area were lighter. She stood in front of the Colonel's desk, but not at attention. A tall, slender man with graying light brown hair, he was always professional. Calm under pressure, made necessary decisions without drama, and he never even swore. The perfect role model of a military officer.

"Have a seat, Captain." He kept typing.

That confirmed it wasn't a disciplinary issue. "Thank you, sir." She took a seat and waited, relieved.

Colonel Haywood removed his reading glasses and rubbed the bridge of his nose. "Captain Bose, a Gafur Bose, who says he's your father, has made a written request to the Air Force Personnel Center to have you released from your military service to fulfill family obligations. He wasn't more specific than that. They were confused because you don't have a commitment at this point. Do you know what this is about?"

Holly squeezed her eyes shut. The nerve of that man! "I'm sorry, sir, I can't believe this." She sighed. "I told you about the man threatening me, so I could carry pepper spray on base." Her fists clenched, then she released them, one finger at a time, trying to regain her calm, cool demeanor. "Which I appreciate. I'll have to tell you the whole medieval story. I'm so sorry. I never dreamed they'd go so far." She told him the entire story and ended with what she and her friends were doing to keep her safe.

"You didn't think it was important that I know about this, Captain?" He stared at her without any emotion she could read. No one could conceal their feelings better than Colonel Haywood.

"Sir, I just thought it would go away." She shook her head. "I've been gone for over a decade. I can't believe this guy is still trying or that my family would come after me. But I should have told you right away."

"Yes, you should have." He stared at her for a moment, then his mouth flattened in a frown. "I'll tell Personnel to ignore any communication from your family. Since Mr. Bose wasn't on any of your official paperwork, they didn't reply. And I'll give Security Forces his name and bar him from entering the base. No sense in taking chances." He tilted his head. "Who is on your emergency notification list?"

Holly smiled. "Captain Lake and retired Major Amy Stone, sir."

"And your life insurance?"

"The women's shelter in DC that helped me escape." They could certainly use the money; she sent them what she could, but it wasn't much.

He nodded. "Very good. Did you report the emancipation on your security clearance paperwork?"

"Yes, sir, I did." When she'd applied, they'd warned her not to leave anything out, even sealed records. Since she didn't care if the Air Force knew, it was an easy decision.

"Excellent." He frowned slightly. "Does anyone know the name of your so-called fiancé?"

Holly shook her head. She'd tried so hard to wipe the horrible events out of her mind. She'd been too successful. "Sir, the contract was part of the emancipation court case, so it's in the record, but the police aren't having much luck getting it. The court is willing to hand it over, but they haven't found it, and it hasn't been scanned. They weren't using electronic records for sealed cases back then." Even Amy's boss, Wiz, hadn't found it and she was an expert hacker. "I'm not calling my father to ask." The idea sent a chill down her spine.

He shook his head, his lips pursed. "No, any kind of contact would be a very bad idea. I believe you're doing everything you can. Keep being smart and don't let down your guard." He leveled a piercing look at her. "I can tell you're annoyed by what you feel is over-protectiveness. I agree with your friends—you need people around you twenty-four seven. Individuals aren't always predictable. Even you don't know much about your family anymore, do you?"

He was right. Ten years later, they would have changed, maybe as much as she had. "No, sir, I really don't. I'll be careful. Thank you, and I'm sorry I didn't tell you. I should have."

"Yes, you should have, but I can understand why you didn't. Have a good day, Captain Bose." He turned back to his computer.

"Thanks, sir." Holly escaped to her cubicle and dropped her head into her hands. That wasn't the brightest move she'd ever made. Amy and Kristen had told her she needed to talk to him, and she'd agreed and then ignored it, which wasn't like her at all. The pursuit, her family, Luke—the entire drama was messing with her head. She needed to straighten herself out.

The next day, her office phone rang. "Captain Bose, COMSAT Requirements," Holly answered.

"Holiday Bose, you will return home immediately. There will be no second chance."

Holly hung up without saying a word. She hadn't heard her father's voice since the night of the graduation ball, and she never wanted to hear it again. The phone rang again, and this time she checked the caller ID. She let it ring.

By the end of the day, she had five messages from her father, all with increasingly vitriolic language and tone. She made copies and emailed them to the police. With recorded threats against her safety, the locals could ask the police to visit Mr. Bose and perhaps find out the name of the man who'd threatened her. She forwarded the email to Colonel Haywood, Amy, and Kristen, too. She wasn't going to make the same mistake twice.

Even though she'd done everything she could, working was impossible. She couldn't pay attention to what she was doing. When quitting time came, she was grateful it was gym day, needing the release of a workout.

Kristen met her in the lobby, looking almost as grim as Holly felt. They left the building, walking through the vast parking lot with five hundred other people all trying to leave at the end of a long duty day. Halfway across the blacktop, the scent of harsh, unfiltered cigarettes wrinkled her nose. She examined the people surrounding her. She'd never smelled that kind of cigarette on base and the people who worked here knew better than to light up before they were in their cars. She saw the usual mix of uniforms and business casual, with a few in workout clothes.

A short, heavyset man with dark hair above a dark suit walked in front of them, smoking a cigarette. She nudged Kristen with an elbow and pointed, discretely. "Kristen, I think that might be him?"

"Him who? Oh, him!" They slowed, but remained behind the man. "He's glancing back a lot. When we reach my car, get in the back seat. I'll drive by the guy and you try to get a picture. Or video."

"Good idea, let's go." They moved to the left and sped up, weaving through cars rather than remaining on the main walkway. Holly got in the back seat, and they returned to where the man should have been. "There he is!" Holly snapped photos and then took video. Cars blocked her view much of the time, but hopefully, it would be enough to identify the man. If it really was him. Holly wasn't positive, but the smell combined with the man's build certainly rang big bells in her head. She flopped back in the seat, grateful beyond measure that Kristen was with her.

Just before Christmas, she got a call from Detective Brown, the officer assigned to her case. "Captain Bose, we've made some progress. The police sent a detective out to interview your father, and he identified your former fiancé as a Mr. Ravana Das." The name shot a shock of recognition through her like a knife to her gut. "Mr. Bose denied any kind of monetary arrangement but said there was a written contract because that's how marriages were arranged in your family. He also said that the contract had been written with your consent and knowledge and that since you got cold feet at the last moment, that it had been voided and destroyed many years ago." He paused.

She didn't have anything to add, but hearing that name chilled her to the bone.

"Mr. Bose also claimed that while there was a loss of prestige on his family's part, that no one would have forced you to go through a wedding you didn't want. The family obligations he mentioned are simply that he and his wife are getting old and that, traditionally, an unmarried daughter must take care of her parents." His tone was desert dry.

"It's a nice cover story that fits the apparent facts," Holly said. "And a lie."

"Plus, he threatened you on the phone. If the courts can find your file, then we'll have proof of a contract for sale."

Her stomach sank. She'd tried to remember the details, but she'd been so furious when she read it. Her emotions wiped away the facts. One more reason to always be in control. "Detective, I didn't read the whole contract and I can't remember much of it. I'm not sure the monetary part is spelled out—it may just be implied."

"That would make a legal case for trafficking minors more difficult. But we can still make a case for a restraining order based on harassment and attempted threats on your life. But first, I have some potentially bad news that takes precedence. We ran the name, and while there are many men named Ravana Das, only one is the right age, has base credentials, and lives in the DC area. And he works for the Inspector General of the Secretary of the Air Force."

"Oh. I'll talk to my boss. Thanks for your help." She put the phone down, her hand shaking. Ravana Das worked for the IG. Her stomach sank along with her mood. He could certainly make trouble for her. Just opening an investigation, even if they found absolutely nothing, could smear her reputation forever. And not just hers. She picked up the phone to call Colonel Hayworth's secretary—he needed to know immediately.

Chapter 5

After the big revelation, Holly could only hurry up and wait. Being in the military, she should have been used to that, but the uncertainty weighed heavily on her. Her case was a low priority compared to the pre-holiday spike in domestic violence. Amy's boss, Wiz, had done what she could, but Das had no social media presence, and Wiz didn't hack private information unless a life was at risk. Colonel Haywood had thanked her for the warning and told her to leave it to him. Despite her best efforts, worry simmered, upsetting her stomach. She lost weight because she couldn't eat.

Fortunately, keeping busy helped, and she had plenty to do. Her co-workers, higher headquarters, and contractors all wanted to clear their desks before the holidays, so she worked long hours to keep up. Colonel Haywood rewarded the entire branch, giving them most of the holiday period off without using leave if they remained in the local area.

Kristen held a Christmas brunch for their single friends, and they skied twice at Monarch Mountain, a smaller area to the south of Colorado Springs. She'd heard from Amy that Luke joined her and Chris in Montana for a few days, then spent January at an undisclosed location, training.

Meanwhile, the February group ski trip loomed. Holly had warned everyone that her car needed major repairs soon—not a lie—and with lodging and lift tickets, a ski trip was out of reach. Kristen and Amy had immediately offered to pay her share, which she refused. Relying on other people's money meant losing control of her life and she couldn't do that, ever.

After another week of living with Kristen and no sign of Das or her father, Holly returned to her house. Kristen worried, but Holly was tired of being in her way, and she hadn't received any more threats. The police visit would have scared her father and he would have told Das. If Das worked for the IG, then he'd know better than to draw legal attention. He'd lose his clearance and probably his job.

Two weeks later, Holly turned on to her street after a long day at work. Two women stood at her front door. She drove past her house, peering at them. Both women had long, dark hair and wore knee length black coats. Full, bright-colored skirts showed below the coats, covering them to the ankles. She didn't quite recognize them, but they looked familiar. Very familiar. Two blocks away, she pulled over and called Kristen.

"Hey, what's up? Want to get dinner?"

"Are you busy right now?" Holly tried to keep her tone level, but she spoke too fast.

"Nope." Kristen's breathing picked up. "Wait a minute. What's wrong?"

Holly released the lower lip she'd bitten. "There are two women on my front porch. I think it's two of my sisters. They're not a problem, but if their husbands are here, that might be trouble. Or maybe my brother." She shuddered. "Or my father." Anger and fear battled for dominion, but she pushed the emotions away. She was a military officer, and while the chances of her being under enemy fire were slim, she'd been trained. She could handle her family. "You know what? Never mind. I got this."

"No, you don't!" Kristen snapped. "Wait for me. Where are you, anyway?" Keys jingled, and a door slammed.

"I drove past my house and parked a couple of blocks away." The two women still stood on the porch. At the curb, a small silver economy car waited. Two more people could easily fit inside, so there might be a real threat.

"Wait for me. I'll park across the street from your house. Do you want to talk to your sisters? Cause I can tell them to go pound sand." Kristen practically snarled the classic military insult.

Holly snort laughed. "Thanks, but I got it. I'm not really worried. Even if my brother or father are there, what can they do? Kidnap me? That would be stupid."

"Wait for me anyway. I'll stay in the car until you go inside. Then I'll check your backyard, see if anyone is there, and let myself in. You won't see me unless there's a threat."

Holly sighed. "And what can you do about that?"

"Call 911, of course. I'm armed, and I've got pepper spray and a taser, too."

Holly pulled her pepper spray from her backpack. Good thing Kristen had reminded her. "I've got pepper spray, but I'll wait for you. Thanks."

"Got your six. See you soon."

Holly tried to calm her nerves while she waited for Kristen to arrive. She hadn't seen her older sisters for over a decade. They hadn't been close even when Holly lived at home. Kristen arrived, parking across from her duplex.

Holly turned around and pulled into her driveway, then got out of the car. She'd leave the garage closed. If there was another person nearby, she didn't want to get trapped. She took in a deep breath, then let it out and crossed the yard. Both women had deeply lined faces, probably from worry and stress, looking older than their years and uncannily like Mother.

"Holiday?" the woman with the hot pink skirts asked. Both women frowned, seemingly unsure about her identity.

She probably looked significantly different than they remembered, wearing her dark blue Space Force uniform coat and pants, with short hair under a blue flight cap. "Yes, it's Holly. May and June?" Her mother wanted her girls to have very American names, but English was her second language. So each girl was named for the month they were born in, or an event in that month. If they'd been Christian, she undoubtedly would have been named Christmas. She thanked all the little gods for small favors.

"Yes. It's good to see you after all these years. May we come in?" June's expression was solemn.

"Sure. Are your husbands here?" As Holly unlocked the front door, she clenched the pepper spray tight. She opened the door and swept her arm out, inviting them to go first.

"No. This is Bose business, not their business." June raised her nose and entered the house.

Holly locked the front door, then followed them into the living room. "Have a seat. Can I get you something to drink? Coffee, chai, water?" She put her backpack on the proper hook but kept her coat, keys, and pepper spray. She probably didn't need them, but she'd remain wary.

"Some water would be very nice, thank you." The corners of May's mouth rose slightly.

Holly filled glasses with water. Kristen waved through the glass on the back door. Holly unlocked and opened it while the water ran. "Thanks."

Kristen gave her a thumbs up, then pulled her close. "Record the conversation."

"Smart." Holly found the voice recorder on her phone and activated it, then carried the water to her sisters. "How is everyone?" She set her phone down on the coffee table behind the candle centerpiece and handed out the water, sitting on the chair facing her small couch.

May perched on the edge of the couch. "Everyone is in good health, except Mother. She is failing and would like to see you."

She'd had a hard life and borne a lot of children. But it might be ruse. "She isn't that old. What exactly is wrong?"

June waved her hands. "Women's troubles. Too many children, and now she's having problems. She can't afford a doctor."

Their family business had been successful; insurance was expensive, but not out of reach. "Why not?"

May shook her head slowly. "The penalty for your broken marriage contract was very expensive. They had to take a second mortgage out on the house, and they are having trouble making the payments." She was clearly disappointed Holly didn't let her father sell her off.

Holly deliberately scowled. "Really? I left most of my dowry behind. That should have paid for it."

June shook her head. "No, they got a very good bride price for you. You were so beautiful and a virgin."

Holly couldn't help laughing. The archaic customs were disgusting. At least she'd been in love during her first experience, even if the latter betrayal sullied the memory. "Well then, sisters, it's a very good thing I ran away." She kept snickering, although there was nothing to laugh about.

The two women looked at each other again, seemingly shocked. "Shame on you. Despite that, you still have an obligation to our family." June scolded her with a shaking finger.

"No. I don't. I signed that contract under duress. Father threatened me. I wanted nothing to do with that abusive old man." Holly met June's gaze. "In case you have forgotten, we live in America, and selling people is called trafficking or slavery. It's been illegal for a very long time, and I will certainly not be a party to trafficking, nor will I support its continuation, and I will do everything in my power to bring this to light, so it ends." She swept a hand down her uniform, then tapped the silver captain's bars on her shoulder. "I took an oath to support and defend the Constitution of the United States. And making slavery illegal is a part of that Constitution, in case you don't remember." At least she could get confirmation of the man's identity. "By the way, what was my so-called fiancé's name anyway, since I don't remember?"

Both women scowled. May stood, clenching her fists. "His name is Ravana Das, and he has ruined our family, you evil child! How can you put anything above your family?"

Holly relaxed in her chair, gripping the pepper spray. "The family that tried to sell me into sex slavery? And is still trying? I don't owe that family anything."

June stood and attempted to loom over Holly. "Ravana Das works for the government. He has a lot of power, and he will make life very difficult for you, as you have done to us."

"He can certainly try." Kristen leaned against the doorway to the kitchen, shaking her head with a slight smile on her face. She still wore her uniform, too. "I don't think the military will allow a civilian to threaten an officer."

May and June both jumped at Kristen's appearance but recovered quickly. "You have no say in this matter." May marched to the door, June following. "You must return to your family and fulfill your obligation, Holiday, or it will go badly for you and us."

Time to get to the issue she actually cared about. "Sisters, is Mother really sick?"

At the door, they turned back. "Yes, she is. Father will not let her see a doctor. He believes American institutions are evil. He's gotten worse over the years, and the police asking questions angered him." May hunched, like she was avoiding a blow.

Her father was a horrible person. Her mom hadn't protected her, but she didn't deserve to suffer, either. "Find a decent doctor and I'll pay the bill. But I will not return to that house." She had one more chance to make her point. "Do you want your daughters sold to mean old men?"

May looked at her feet. June frowned and her mouth twisted. "We will tell Father you refuse to return and why, although I suspect that will make things worse." She sucked in a big breath, then let it out and nodded. "We will find a doctor and tell Mother you are paying. We won't tell Father about that." She glanced over at May, who nodded. "Despite your refusal, we wish you happiness and blessings."

Holly smiled. "I wish you both happiness and blessings as well. Travel safely."

Kristen crossed the room and opened the front door. Her sisters left. Holly stopped the recording on her phone, smiling grimly at the device. "I think I'll send this recording to the Defense Criminal Investigative Service as a matter of national security. Ravana Das has messed with the wrong woman." She grinned at Kristen, feeling triumphant. "I bet DCIS will find my emancipation records. Then they'll take away Das's security clearance and he'll be out of a job." She dusted her hands together. "No more trouble." There was more than one way to fight back. She'd use every legal means at her disposal, and some slightly shady ones, like recording without consent, too. Fortunately, it wouldn't have to stand up in court.

"You are an evil child!" Kristen grinned and held up her hand for a high five, which Holly gladly gave her. Kristen shuddered. "That whole conversation was so awful. And awkward. Like strangers on a reality TV show."

Holly nodded, agreeing. "I didn't know May and June all that well. I wasn't even ten years old when they were sold into marriage." At the time, the marriage ceremonies—elaborate, week-long affairs—had been so exciting, she hadn't even considered if her sisters were truly happy.

"That's so crazy." Kristen shook her head. "I mean, okay, if everyone agrees to the arrangement. But forcing it is so wrong."

Holly sighed. "I know. I hope they get Mother to a doctor right away. Looking back, I think she tried to protect me. At graduation, I'm pretty sure she was supposed to stay with me until we walked into the auditorium. But she told me she had to go to the bathroom, and she'd left the car unlocked, which she never did. That let me grab my backpack when I ran." Her poor, downtrodden mother, watching her husband sell off her girls to nasty old men, must have decided the last one was worth the risk. Holly could repay a small part of that with some medical care.

Kristen grimaced. "A little passive, but still, she tried. And now you're trying to help her. Karma can be good."

Holly laughed. "Hopefully it's terrible for Daddy." She sneered the title the man didn't deserve.

LUKE

Luke's office phone rang. "Major Sevrason, 13th ASOS, Training."

"Major Sevrason, you and I have a mutual interest." The man's voice was rough and raspy, with a slight accent.

Caller identification indicated a military number, from the Washington DC area. He didn't recognize the number, but the SAF/IG declaration was clear enough. The call had to be connected to Holly. His heart rate picked up, but he ignored his physical reaction, entering military mission mode. "And you are?"

"You won't recognize my name, but I am Ravana Das with the Secretary of the Air Force Inspector General's office."

Luke held back a snort. No sense in helping the enemy; he'd play dumb. "What can I do for SAF/IG today?"

"It's more of what can I do for you, Major, than the reverse." Das sneered his words.

He forced a puzzled tone. "Okay, but I don't know what that would be."

"It seems your father may have the attention of the IG." Smug arrogance rang in his tone.

"That has nothing to do with me. I don't work with or for my father. I know nothing about his company's dealings with the Air Force."

"I don't expect you to know anything. But you don't want him investigated or charged with criminal offenses, do you?" Das's tone conveyed certainty.

Under enemy interrogation, short answers were best. "No." Surprisingly, it was true. He didn't have much respect for his father's methods, but he didn't want the man hurt, either.

"Now we get to the part where you and I can help each other. While I can't prevent an investigation, or charges, I can misplace the data I've found."

"Okay." Luke scrambled for a pen and paper. He didn't want to miss anything. Too bad he couldn't record the conversation, but he was fairly certain his cell wouldn't pick up Das's words. "Why would you do that?"

"I believe you know Captain Holiday Bose, correct?" Das sneered Holly's rank.

Finally, they were getting to the interesting part. Luke had to play his part, keeping his focus on the potential official investigation. "Yes. But she's in Space Force. She doesn't have any dealings with Sevrason Aerospace either."

"I know that. But I need to talk to her."

Luke huffed and put some incredulity into his voice. "Call her office and make an appointment. I'm sure she'll be happy to accommodate the IG. Do you need her number? I don't have it, but I can find it quickly."

"I have her official number. I need to speak to her on a personal family matter. Alone. Not on base."

He had to play dumb. "Again, I don't know what this has to do with Sevrason Aerospace."

"Nothing. Unless you refuse to help me. I'm merely asking for an opportunity to speak with her, one on one, off base. After that, the data goes missing."

The arrogance of the man was infuriating, but Luke remained calm. "I see. If you're planning to harm her, or any other military member, then no deal. I won't put a company ahead of an individual."

"No harm will come to Holiday while she speaks to me."

But two seconds after the conversation, Das would use a taser or something, and she'd be in a world of hurt. "I see. I don't know Holly very well anymore, but I'm sure I can arrange a public meeting spot."

"Very good. I will send you an email with a place and time. Do not betray me." Das hung up.

Luke replaced the handset and took a few deep breaths. Fury at the man tightened his entire body, but he could react later. He had to tell Holly, and he had an obligation to report the conversation. Picking up his cell, he put a summary of the conversation in their group chat, and followed it up with up his intention to speak with his commander immediately. Everyone in the chat agreed, and Holly added that she'd share his information with her commander, too.

He trotted down the hall to his boss's office. So much for working on his training plan; the situation would take a while to run all the way up the flagpole.

Luke had vastly underestimated the time commitment. For the seventh workday in a row, he and Holly sat in a small, stuffy conference room in Space Force Headquarters. Every day brought a new set of investigators and organizations. Civilian law enforcement was already involved, plus the Air Force Office of Special Investigations and the Department of Defense Inspector General. A jurisdiction fight got the FBI involved. Plus the myriad of organizations involved in military security clearances and acquisition fraud.

He'd gone over and over the conversation he had with Das. Holly had explained her situation and played her recording even more. Sometimes they were interviewed together, sometimes apart. Each investigator had spoken to Chris, Amy, and Kristen too, along with Holly's co-workers and chain of command.

Lieutenant Colonel Mikells, Luke's squadron commander, must regret hiring him. Luke and Holly couldn't even work while they waited because outside electronics weren't allowed in the secured conference room. They couldn't even pass the time playing mindless phone games. After the first day, they'd both brought paperbacks. Luke considered bringing cards, but Holly remained distant. They exchanged greetings, but Holly shut down any attempts at conversation.

Unfortunately for him, simply being near her increased his longing. Particularly when she reluctantly spoke about her escape from her family and the circumstances that led to that. Her determination and intelligence were inspirational.

After all the interviews, conferences, and organizational arguments, Luke believed the FBI was winning the lead investigator role. But he wasn't sure why they were so heavily involved.

The phone on the table rang, and Holly picked it up. "Captain Bose." She nodded. "Be right there." Standing, she jerked her head toward the door and picked up her bag, sliding her book inside.

Grabbing his things, he followed her down the hall and into the larger space. A long wood conference table could seat twenty, and seats around the exterior of the room held more. Earlier, every seat had a uniformed officer or a suit occupying it, but only a few people remained. Luke plopped into the chair next to Holly's at the end of the long wood table. At least the chairs were more comfortable.

FBI Special Agent Ness stood at the head of the table. The silver strands in his blond hair almost glowed under the bright lights, and his off-the-rack dark blue suit was creased. "Major, Captain, we've investigated the allegations you've made. Captain Bose, we retrieved your sealed emancipation case file. Ravana Das is the name of the man to be married, yours is the name of the woman, and your father is named as the representative of the Bose family. The document specifies five hundred thousand dollars and other considerations, including political support and mutual business support. It also spells out penalties, which include return of the money plus fifteen percent.”

“They should have been able to pay that easily.” Holly leaned forward, anger warring with confusion in her voice. “The gold dowry I left behind should have paid the penalty.”

Ness nodded. “From your description, I agree. Unfortunately, the settlement amount had already gone to help pay your father’s debts, which are quite large and to some very unpleasant people.” He gave her a raised brow look of irony and understanding. “Your father has a gambling problem, and he’s deeply in debt to organized crime.”

“That—” Holly clamped her lips shut. Fury carved lines into her gorgeous face, and she clenched her hands tight, turning her knuckles white. If her father had been there, Luke would put his chances of survival at next to nothing.

He put his hand on her shoulder and squeezed lightly, then let go, not wanting to raise speculation among the security folks. Too bad there was nothing to raise.

“It appears that every time Mr. Bose got desperate, he sold a daughter.” The agent’s face twisted. “Disgusting.” His shoulders rose and his head shook slightly. Then his expression cleared, and he met Luke’s gaze.

“Major, Sevrason Analytics has been involved in some questionable dealings in the past, but now, they’ve moved into provable crimes. The company raised campaign funds for a few select congressmen, who have ensured earmarks—you know, the so-called 'pork projects'—favorable to Sevrason Analytics and other defense contractors. Most of these military projects are lucrative for the companies involved, but the Department of Defense gets next to nothing out of the deal." He gave them a tight smile. "Sevrason Analytics has also branched into small time shipping for their partners, who don't want to be bothered with mailing a single washer or a single bolt at a time. The item is generally worth less than a dollar, but the shipping charges? Those are in the hundreds of thousands." He scowled.

Surprise jolted Luke. "Lobbying I can easily believe, but shipping fraud seems awfully sloppy for my father. I can't believe he'd stoop to outright theft. He's always preferred to deal in influence." Easier to get away with than most crimes.

Ness sniffed. "His influence seems to have run a little thin, and he's lost some big customers recently. The company is teetering on the edge of bankruptcy."

Something didn't add up. Father wasn't stupid. "This doesn't make sense. It's too obvious, too easy to catch." Next to him, Holly nodded.

The corners of Ness's mouth rose, but Luke didn't think he was amused. "It would be, except he has a friend, who happens to work in the financial analysis section of SAF/IG."

Suddenly, Father's decision made sense. Luke sighed. "Let me guess. My new best friend, Ravana Das."

"Exactly, Major." Ness tapped his forefinger against his nose.

Holly sat back in her chair, crossing her arms. "You wouldn't have told us this unless you wanted something from us." Her expression was blank. All that fury packed away—someday, a nuke was going off. He hoped he wasn't the target.

"Very smart, Captain Bose." Ness nodded. "We want both of you to play along with Mr. Das and Mr. Sevrason. We believe that Mr. Sevrason will contact you, Captain Bose. While their current mutual aid agreement works well, they've become suspicious of each other. We think Mr. Sevrason wants his son, and Mr. Das wants his promised wife, and by going after each other's subject, they think they'll avoid suspicion. And they'll have a mutual blackmail point until they can trade." He looked back and forth between them.

"You aren't seriously suggesting we allow ourselves to be abducted, are you?" Luke wouldn't allow them to put Holly in that kind of danger.

Ness held up both hands. "No, just play along with the planning. And abduction may be too strong a word. Mr. Sevrason wants Major Sevrason to work for him, just as he planned. Mr. Das hasn't said much about Captain Bose, but he's definitely interested. He's been researching your career through official and unofficial channels."

He focused on Luke. "We don't think they're planning an immediate abduction. If we see such activity, then we'll arrest them both. By then, we should have enough evidence to convict. We could arrest them both now, but the charges would be much less severe than they deserve. Mr. Das has hidden evidence very effectively, including the bribes Mr. Sevrason must be sending his way. We've put together a list of recommendations for SAF to fix the problem. But they can't implement it until this is over, and we need to find what he's hidden. Will you help?" His brows rose.

Asking seemed rather insulting. Of course, Luke would help.

"Will this be publicized after it happens, or swept under a rug, or classified?" Holly asked.

Once again, Holly proved she had the brains between the two of them. If the arrests weren't public, there was less reason to take the risk. He would, anyway, but he'd be unhappy.

Ness smiled at Holly. "The arrests will be public. There aren't any classification issues, and neither of these gentlemen have enough political clout or money to cover this up. They'll be an object lesson, actually."

Holly nodded slowly. "Thank you for not denying money and clout can cover things up. Count me in. I'd like to make sure the role of bride-selling as human trafficking is emphasized. Maybe another father will think twice about continuing the practice. Publicizing human trafficking in this country is an excellent idea too. Denial isn't helpful." Holly scowled, an unusual show of emotion in public.

Ness nodded once. "We can tip off certain reporters—they'll love that angle. Especially if they can get an interview with you and put a personal spin on it."

Holly nodded. "Absolutely."

She was so brave. Luke could only try to match her and protect her if things went wrong. And they probably would. "What do we need to do?"

Ness sat down. "The email you've been waiting for has finally come in, without a specific date or time. He claims unforeseen schedule conflicts. To prepare, we want to tap your cell phones and work phones. Do you have any burner phones, satellite phones, or additional work phones?"

Luke didn't. "No." Holly shook her head.

Ness nodded. "We'll also monitor your unclassified work and personal emails and your social media accounts. We'll need user names and passwords. We'll give you very small recording devices with GPS trackers, and we'll put trackers on your vehicles. Agents will watch you everywhere but work, so don't do anything you don't want to see in a court record." One corner of Ness's mouth rose. "For now, don't do anything different. Go to work, go out on the weekend. If you're going out, text the agents your destination and expected route. You can brief Captain Lake, Ms. Stone, and Master Sergeant Hall; we know you'll tell them, anyway. We'll brief Colonel Haywood and General York and Lieutenant Colonel Mickells about the operation. And we'll tell the Colorado Springs police department. Anyone else must be approved by us. Don't leave the local area."

"So much for the ski trip." Holly shrugged.

Ness's brows rose. "Were you going together?"

"Yes." Luke wanted to make that trip happen. If he could get some quality time with Holly, he might make some progress.

"If you're together, that's not a problem. Let me check if I have enough agents who ski to follow you during the day. I don't know if Das or Sevrason ski. We'll track their travel plans, too." Ness turned toward one of his other agents who took a few notes.

Maybe offering Ness information would help. "Father doesn't ski, but he owns a house in Beaver Creek. We were going to stay in Frisco or Dillon—it's a lot cheaper."

"You're not using the family house?" Ness frowned.

"No." He didn't want to run into his father, but that wouldn't matter to Ness.

Ness's frown deepened. "That might make Mr. Das suspicious. He seems to think you are very close to your father, otherwise he wouldn't be making these threats."

Luke shrugged. "Or he thinks I just care about the money." Like his father.

"I'll talk to our analysts. It might be better to use your father's house." Ness's assistant took more notes.

Luke grimaced. "Only if you want my father showing up. And me taking a shot at him when he's rude to my friends."

Ness shook his head slightly. "And if it's necessary for you to be polite to make this plan work?"

Luke sighed. That was the last thing he wanted to do, but if it took that to keep Holly safe, he would. "Then I'll do it, but my acting skills aren't that good."

Holly snorted. "Yes, they are."

Ness frowned. "Remember, your friends' lives could be relying on your acting ability."

"Noted." He did not want to play nice with his father, not one little bit. But Holly's safety came before his comfort. He'd fall at his father's feet and beg for a job, if he had to. Then laugh in the man's face later.

A little petty revenge would be a great bonus.

Chapter 6

LUKE WAITED IMPATIENTLY, BUT there was nothing more from Das or his father all week. Ness said the men were avoiding each other. The only bright spot in the week was getting the green light for the ski trip. But his mood soured when the feds insisted they use his father's Beaver Creek house.

At the end of the week, they gathered at Luke's house. Dark circles betrayed Holly's sleepless nights, but his pasty-white skin signaled his were just as bad. He ordered pizza, then sent Chris and Amy a video request. Maybe chatting with their friends would cheer Holly up. The women talked about their week while he and Chris texted sarcastic comments. His new squadron contained good people, but he missed his best friend. Besides, he couldn't tell anyone else about their situation.

"You know what I don't get?" Holly asked abruptly. "I don't get what Luke's father gets out of having Luke abducted." She aimed her comments at Amy and Chris; she'd been avoiding him all evening. "If Das kidnaps me, he can get revenge, but abducting Luke would make him fight harder. And if he's officially absent without leave from the military, he can't be a lobbyist or do anything public. It just doesn't make sense."

Luke wrestled his fury down; an angry outburst wouldn't help Holly. His lack of control might increase her distrust. "Any threat to you, Holly, would effectively control me." He snorted derisively. "Until we figured out how to rescue you. Then they'd both regret it." They'd both be dead, but he wasn't stupid enough to say that when the FBI had his phone under surveillance. But he wasn't sure why she'd brought it up; the FBI said they weren't at immediate risk. Maybe she didn't believe them.

"What stops either one of you from just killing your captor?" Kristen asked. "You can both take those two old men down."

Holly grimaced. "Neither of them are stupid, and they're not going to act alone. I'm strong, but injury, drugs, dehydration, and starvation would make it difficult to defend myself, let alone attack." She shrugged, seemingly calm.

Amy said, "You're right. I'll send you some information on survival, resistance, and escape tactics."

Luke had endured the Air Force's survival, evasion, resistance, and escape course before Amy's assignment to the SERE training group. She'd have the latest and best information. But the thought of Holly suffering the kind of techniques they'd experienced in training—and been briefed on even worse—made his fists and jaw clench with rage. If his father was in front of him, he'd beat the man just for the possibility. "I wouldn't hesitate to kill my father if he threatened Holly."

Amy shook her head. "Not if he tells you that Das must get a coded message from him every day or something horrible happens to Holly."

Needing an outlet for his anger, Luke stood up and paced. "I'd still kill him, then find Holly. Das wants her; he's not going to kill her. We'd track him down." And then beat him to death.

Chris said, "Yeah, but in the meantime, she'd be suffering, and if this guy is clever, he'd have someplace off the books that's hard to find." He paused, then continued. "I don't think it will be quite so easy as you think to kill your own father, Luke." Chris's voice dropped to its lowest register on the last phrase. He and the women laughed.

Obviously a joke, but not one Luke recognized. "What's so funny about that?"

"Don't you know Star Wars?" Kristen grinned. "I'm your father, Luke."

From her low tone, that had to be a quote. "No, sorry. Pilot, remember? More Top Gun, less space geek."

Amy broke through Holly and Kristen's objections to the term geek. "Luke, despite the bad jokes, Chris is right. Killing someone isn't easy, even when you're defending yourself."

Chris put his arm around Amy's shoulder. "It's true. Up close and personal is a lot more difficult to live with."

They'd know. "Sorry, I didn't mean to bring up bad memories. But if my father threatened Holly, I'd do whatever it took to escape him and turn him in, if I didn't kill him. Holly's a survivor. She'd make it until we found her."

Amy held up her hand. "Think back to your SERE training, Luke. Anyone can be broken."

"That's true, but I'd break him first." Luke stared at Holly, while she stared at Amy and Chris.

A knock on his door interrupted him. Kristen bounded from her seat. "Pizza! I'll get it."

Luke turned to Holly. "I promise. I'd find a way, no matter what it took." She still didn't look at him, but it didn't matter. His vow didn't depend on her returning his love; he'd save her even if she hated him forever.

On Monday, Luke accepted an invitation for a classified video conference that afternoon from Holly's official email. The FBI was taking advantage of Space Force's extensive classified capabilities. Not driving across town would save him a lot of time and make his boss happier. He'd rather waste time on the road and see Holly in person, but his happiness wasn't anyone's priority. Five minutes before the meeting, he entered their small conference room and logged in.

At Space Force headquarters, Ness sat at the end of the table, Holly next to him, and Ness's admin on the other side. "Thanks for joining us. We'll have status calls every Monday, unless we need more. We haven't seen anything concrete from Das or Sevrason, but trust seems to be eroding. We have a plan to push them along."

"Is pushing them smart?" No matter what they wanted, Holly's life was more important than a criminal conviction.

Ness's mouth twisted for a moment. "We don't have unlimited resources and this isn't my only case. If we don't see action soon, we'll have to pull back to monitoring the situation. My analysts believe that evidence of a relationship between the two of you will speed things up."

"What? No." Holly's voice could cut steel.

But a tendril of hope rose in Luke; if he could spend more time with Holly, he'd have a better chance of winning her back. And more importantly, protecting her.

Ness turned to face Holly. "Without any sign of a romantic relationship, neither Das nor Sevrason are sure that threatening pain to the other will work. That's eroding their mutual pact. Major Sevrason, you told Das that you weren't close with Captain Bose, which reinforces the problem. If you act like you're in a relationship, that will reassure the two that their scheme will work. They'll make a move and we'll arrest them."

Holly thudded her fist against the table, an unusual display of emotion. "Can't you just arrest them now?"

"No." Ness grimaced. "They've been very careful. If we arrest them now, the charges would be minor, the case would be circumstantial, and they'd still be a danger to you. We're positive that Sevrason isn't Das's only, or biggest, fraud client. We've got to find his hiding places and money transfer methods."

Luke considered Ness's words and followed to the logical end, anger rising. "You were lying about not allowing an abduction. Holly's capture allows you to track the money." They'd get Holly killed—or worse.

Ness raised his hands. "I'm sure we'll be able to arrest them before anyone pulls a gun or coerces you into a car."

"How?" Luke's fists clenched. "You need a money transfer."

Holly turned to Ness. "I don't think you can, either. But I'm not pulling out. I want my life back." She returned to the camera, her caramel eyes burning into his. "We'll have our first date on Wednesday night, at the little Italian place downtown. Meet me there. Next one, you'll have to pick me up."

Luke huffed his frustration. He wanted that date, but not if it risked her life or her freedom. "Holly, this could go very badly. Das isn't stupid. My father didn't build a company by being dumb." Luke pointed at Ness. "If these guys are just a little slow, or less than brilliant, you could be at that man's non-existent mercy for days, weeks, months or longer." Luke didn't trust the FBI. They wanted the arrest more than they wanted to protect Holly.

Holly glared at him. "If we pull out, that could still happen and no one would be looking for us. How is that better?"

Luke closed his eyes for a second, trying to find a good argument and failing. "It's not. I hate this. I can't stand thinking of you in that situation."

"Well, stop." She jabbed her forefinger in his direction. "Pull yourself together and get your emotions under control. This is an operational mission, and the winning part is never in question. Understand?"

"Ma'am, yes ma'am!" He followed up with an ironic salute. "But Ness, I think this is a very bad idea."

"Yes, we understand that, Major Sevrason." Ness's tone was desert-dry. "We'd much prefer to arrest them now, but it would be a waste of time. We don't like working with untrained personnel. But we know that both of you can act to some extent. Are you willing to follow our analyst's suggestions?"

Luke sighed. "Yes." He'd do whatever it took to keep Holly safe.

Holly said, "Whatever will get this done faster."

"Excellent." Ness nodded once. "Don't move too quickly. Go out on some dates, show affection in public, gradually get closer over the next two weeks or so. That ought to convince them that you are effective leverage against each other."

Luke held back a growl. "Holly could be used as leverage against me now. Just because we aren't a couple doesn't mean it wouldn't work."

"Understood, but they don't believe that." Ness shrugged. "It wouldn't be true for either of them, so it can't be the case for you."

At least he'd get time with Holly. "Okay, agreed on the Italian place, but I'm picking you up. Father would expect me to try and get you drunk." He smirked at her.

She rolled her eyes. "Fine. Pick me up at seven, and don't be late."

Luke huffed. "I'd never be late for a date. Who do you think you're talking to?"

She raised her eyebrows and cocked her head. "A whiny, reluctant, over-emotional pain in the ass."

He smiled, slowly. He'd rather see her annoyed than get nothing. "With that attitude, I'm not too sure your acting skills are up to the challenge."

She narrowed her eyes and jabbed her finger toward him again. "Just watch me, Sevrason. You'll believe I'm totally in love with you in three weeks."

"You're on." He smiled. He'd take this opportunity and run with it.

Ness stood. "Great, we're done here." The screen went dark.

Luke walked back to his desk. His triumph faded into jitters like adrenaline after an aborted mission. Maybe he had a second chance, but the FBI and the circumstances didn't help him other than forced proximity. Holly promised he'd believe she was in love with him, not that she would fall for him again.

But he had a chance to get to know her, for real, as an adult, rather than a stupid, hormone-driven boy. He'd make the best of his break.

And if it didn't work, there were always plenty of deployments.

HOLLY

Holly wanted to pace or fidget, but she remained on the couch. Calm and serene, that was the plan. It wasn't even a real date; it was a tactical mission, part of an operation.

Despite her pep talk, she fidgeted with tension, despising her weakness. Dates didn't make her nervous because she had low expectations. Most men expected too much too fast. Three dates weren't enough to trust someone, and most men wouldn't stick around past that without a physical relationship. Even when she paid for the rare second date.

She'd had two serious relationships since high school, but neither one lasted more than a couple months. The first guy had become possessive and controlling after a month; she'd broken it off immediately. If she'd wanted that, she would have married at her father's command. The next guy said he felt like he'd never really gotten to know her, just the surface she showed everyone.

He'd been right. She'd never quite trusted him enough to let him in emotionally. In hindsight, she shouldn't have kept dating him, but she'd been so lonely at that point that she'd gone against all her rules. He'd been kind, which was more than her stupidity deserved.

She had to be a whole lot smarter with Luke Sevrason. And the whole operation.

She sat, outwardly calm on her living room sofa, inwardly dreading his arrival. Luke had known her better than any man. And she couldn't deny the attraction existed. Lying to herself wasn't conducive to survival. But he was charming, and knowing her background, he could use that knowledge better than any other man could.

But high school was a long time ago, and she'd changed a lot. At the very least, she could act confident and self-assured even if she didn't feel that way inside. And she knew him, too—she could pull his strings better. Confidence reinforced, she smiled. She'd win their war.

The doorbell rang. Grabbing her purse and coat, she opened the door and couldn't breathe. Even with an open door, Luke sucked all the air out of the room. He scanned her with a wicked little smile on his face, his gaze leaving heat behind. Wearing a perfectly fitted dark gray designer suit, he looked like a fallen angel; all he needed were the wings. Big, black, glossy ones, to match his thick, dark hair. The intensity and heat in his sparkling green gaze took her breath away. And thud—there went the confidence, dropping like a rocket's first stage into the ocean.

"Ready?" He took her coat off her arm and held it for her.

Holly slid into it and turned away, trying to minimize physical contact. "Sure, just let me lock the door." She fumbled a bit with the key. He was smoking hot—she had to get him out of sight for a few moments and get her breath back.

After a deep breath, she turned back, polite face firmly back in place, faking confidence for all she was worth. He held out his arm, and she took it, feeling his warmth through the fine material. They walked to a copper-colored coupe at the curb arm in arm. He opened the door and waited for her to buckle up before closing the door. Her heart beat faster, so she concentrated on breathing slowly through her nose.

She needed a neutral subject before she lost control. The black leather seat under her hands was buttery soft and supportive, and the control panel was highlighted with copper LEDs. "Nice car."

"Thanks. Father had it delivered to my house while I was deployed last year. By the time I got returned to the states, they wouldn't take it back, so I kept it. I'd returned a couple others before that and one six months ago. He just doesn't know when to quit."

The car fit his personality, but she would expect a darker color. "Is this what you'd pick for yourself?"

"No." Luke looked in the rear-view mirror and pulled onto the road. "Sure, a Mercedes AMG Coupe is a great car. But I prefer my SUV because I can easily go off road." He drove fast, but not aggressively, while constantly checking the mirrors and his surroundings.

"An SUV would be better in the snow, too." Every winter, she swore she'd get an all wheel drive, but she never did.

"This has a fancy traction control, but yes, I'd much rather drive the SUV in the snow." He smiled wryly. "Less expensive to fix if I get hit, too."

They arrived at the restaurant. He came around to open her door and escorted her inside, opening each door and pulling out her chair when the hostess seated them. He had exquisite manners. But then, so did she. All around them, couples murmured and ate, while openly displaying their affection—it must be lovers' night.

After the server took their drink orders, Luke smiled at her. "What shall we talk about?"

She faked a smile and glanced around again, trying to avoid his intent gaze. "I'm not sure it matters if we look happy. Like everyone else here."

"Probably true." His smile faded as he focused on her like a laser. "I'll pick this time. You pick the next."

"Okay." She shrugged one shoulder.

He lowered his head and captured her gaze. "Will you tell me what happened after high school? I'd really like to know."

She broke his stare and watched the flickering candle in the middle of the table. She didn't owe him that miserable story, but she could share the highlights, just to get it over with, because he probably wouldn't stop asking. "I guess." She grimaced, then remembered they had to look happy. "Just make sure you keep smiling." She forced her lips to curve up. "I left the graduation ceremony and took a bus to a women's shelter across town. Since I was underage, they had to call the police, but I got lucky. The foster family they placed me with already had two other teenage girls, and they were a lot of trouble. The mom was thrilled to have someone responsible and self-sufficient, so I had a lot of freedom. The women's shelter kept helping me, too. They found me a lawyer, and she filed for emancipation from my parents. Then they got me financial aid for college and some scholarships. They also bought me a bus ticket across the country and handed me off to a shelter in Tacoma, Washington." Her throat drying, she sipped water, then continued when Luke didn't say anything.

"I got a job waiting tables in a fancy restaurant, found a roommate, went to school, applied for ROTC, and got a three-year scholarship, then graduated from the University of Washington. My first assignment was at Wright-Patterson in Ohio. I met Kristen on my first day—we became roommates—then we both got assigned to Los Angeles Air Station. Then we came here." Amazing that she could sum up that terrifying time in just a few sentences. And equally amazing that she'd survived.

"I can't believe you got through all that on your own. You're so strong, so resilient. I'm incredibly impressed." Luke shook his head a bit and smiled at her, like he was proud of her. Their server stopped at the table, and he nodded. "Go ahead, Holly."

They ordered. Distracted by Luke's admiration, she picked the first chicken dish on the list, not caring what it was. Attempting to get them back to less emotional territory, Holly changed the subject to facts about Colorado Springs and fun places to go. Luke played along, and before long, her smile was real; he could charm everyone.

Luke paid the check and escorted her out. After driving for a few minutes, he broke the silence. "I appreciate you telling me what happened, even if you told me the grade school fairytale version. I'm sure most of the time you were terrified and stressed. But it doesn't surprise me that you survived and thrived, because you're tougher than anyone I know."

She shouldn't be shocked he'd seen through her storytelling. He was intelligent, and part of his charm was his listening skills. But the sincere compliment was surprising. "Thanks. I just do what I have to do."

"That's what I mean. You're more than a survivor; you're driven to succeed. I'm sure that if I'd been in your shoes—" he glanced at her feet, "which are smoking hot, but I'd break an ankle—I wouldn't have been so successful. I'd still be waiting tables and going on cruises, dancing with little old ladies for my room and board."

She couldn't hold back her bark of laughter. "Lukas Sevrason, male escort? Not a chance. You're just as determined as I am and way more ambitious. Besides, if you were doing something dependent on your looks, you'd be an underwear model." She clamped her lips shut.

He laughed, then turned to her, his expression softening and heating. "At least you admire my body." He reached across the console and picked up her hand, running his thumb across her palm, the caress sparking heat and desire. "Determination got me through pilot training. My greatest ambition was to avoid working for my father without destroying our relationship. But I'm not tough like you." He shook his head. "If I was, I would have cut the man out of my life a long time ago. But he's done that for me now." He pulled into her driveway and turned off the car, pinning her with an intense stare. "I don't care about him or my career anymore." He got out.

Released from his gaze, she shivered, then jumped when he opened her door. He held out his hand, and she placed hers in his, letting him help her out, even though she knew touching him was dangerous. When she was steady on her heels, he twisted his hand around hers, walking her to her house. His big, calloused hand wrapped hers in warmth, and the certainty of security followed. At the door, she turned and leaned against it, sliding her hand out of his, mourning the loss. She desperately wanted to invite him in, but that was asking for big trouble. Despite knowing it was a mistake, she asked. "What do you care about?"

He put an arm on the doorframe above head and leaned in close. "You." His lips barely touched hers in the lightest kiss. Then he spun and jogged to his car. She tried to breathe. In his car, he pointed at her house, waiting until she was inside before backing out of the driveway. When his taillights disappeared, she collapsed back against the door again.

She felt fragile, not tough. Hope was a double-edged sword.

Chapter 7

THE NEXT WEEK, LUKE took Holly and Kristen out to lunch on Tuesday, then just Holly on Thursday. He chose restaurants popular with military members, hoping that Das and Sevrason would hear about their relationship. But if Holly let it become real, he wouldn't care what either man thought. After that tiny kiss at the end of their dinner, sleep was impossible. He'd worked out half the night, then tossed and turned until morning, and he'd struggled all week. Fortunately, the guys in his squadron invited him to a shooting competition that weekend, keeping him busy. He came in fifth, a respectable showing with a borrowed rifle.

The constant contact didn't help. If they were in uniform, they couldn't make any obvious personal displays of affection, but he seized every opportunity to touch Holly. A hand on her back to escort her through a door, leaning his shoulder into hers, or a stroke down her arm after helping with her jacket. Each touch ramped his desire higher.

She smiled and thanked him but showed no sign that his touch affected her. Nor did she try to touch him. The lack of reaction shouldn't disappoint him—it was consistent with her restrictive childhood. And their fake relationship.

But it wasn't fake for him. Despite everything, he wanted her more every day. Yearning, fear, and frustration battled for supremacy, kept him from sleeping. The FBI made it worse by refusing to keep them fully in the loop. Day after day, they said nothing had changed.

At the end of the next, never-ending week lightened only by a single lunch with Holly, Luke took Holly and Kristen out to dinner at a popular Mexican restaurant downtown. He ordered a pitcher of margaritas, asking the server to make them half strength. While they ate, Kristen provided the entertainment. Man after man approached their table, trying to join them or buy them drinks. Kristen turned each one down, some less politely than others. If it was someone she'd met before, she'd share the backstory. Too often, the so-called man in question was a player, too aggressive, or a cheater.

After dinner, they went dancing at an exclusive, expensive nightclub. Luke claimed Holly for the whole night, glaring at every man who came near. Letting her go at the end of each song got harder and harder. He wanted to keep her next to him for the rest of the night—and the rest of his life. Beautiful women and men surrounded them, but no one compared to Holly.

After a breather at their table, he escorted her back out onto the floor and pulled her close, but not tight. He tried to respect her discomfort with their charade. But she fit him perfectly, nestled against his heart, where she belonged. After a few moments, she relaxed, but not completely; tension tightened her shoulders and back. Making her suffer wouldn't help his cause. "Are you okay?"

She kept her head on his chest. "I'm fine."

He knew that meant the opposite. "I know you don't want to be here and wouldn't be near me if it wasn't for the threats." He loosened his arms again—thinking about her leaving made him hang on harder.

"True. But on the scale of good to bad, dancing with you is way better than being married to Das." She kept a serene smile on her face, but her muscles tensed.

"There's some faint praise. But thanks anyway." He had to stop thinking about her and consider the mission. It was the only way she'd get free, and her safety was paramount.

The song ended, and she jerked out of his arms, still smiling. "Let's go home. I'm tired."

"Sure. Let me find Kristen." He left her at the table and cut in on Kristen's date without a second thought for the protesting man. "Holly's had enough."

Kristen put her arm through his and pulled him off the floor, dropping into a seat next to Holly and whispering in her ear. Holly shook her head at Kristen and rose, sliding her jacket on while Kristen laughed. Then he escorted both women to Holly's car. He frowned at the small hatchback. Even in the dark, he could see she needed better tires to handle the snow and ice.

Before she could get in the car, he pulled her into his arms and kissed her, but not hard. He didn't want to make things worse, but he had to show her how much he cared. She responded, but barely—just enough to fool an audience. He pulled away and looked down at her, but she wouldn't meet his gaze.

"See you later, Luke." She got in the car and started it. As they drove away, he watched, but she never looked back.

His walk home was cold and lonely.

"Wow." Kristen fanned her face. "That was one hot kiss! That man wants you." She shot a glance at Holly. "Forever."

Holly gripped the steering wheel tighter so she wouldn't strangle Kristen. That kiss was exhilarating and terrifying. If only their fake relationship was real! But that kind of thinking was dangerous because when the dust cleared, he'd be gone. He'd be dating some fashionable blonde who fit into his moneyed world and rise the ranks to general, or get into politics, or some other high-flying position.

No matter what Kristen thought, she couldn't see Lukas Sevrason, heir to an aerospace firm, settling down with Holly Bose, of no name, no money, and no fancy career. She was just a girl ready to run when trouble came—and it would. Even when the current crisis was over, if it ever was, she'd still have a messed-up family. Siblings begging for money, sisters needing help to escape their marriages and avoiding arranged marriages for their kids. Plus, her father would never give up. Dread tightened her stomach. Unless he was killed. She might despise him, but she didn't want him dead.

She had nothing but baggage and Luke couldn't overlook that. Even if his father's money was gone, he'd make his own. He was going places, while she was just surviving. "He wants this ridiculous situation to be over with, that's all. And he's a very good actor. That's one reason he ruled our high school."

"You're fooling yourself, Holly." Kristen shook her head. "Don't cry when someone snaps him up and I say I told you so."

"I don't cry." And she didn't. Crying did nothing but make everything worse.

The next evening, Luke picked her up just before seven. She turned away, locking her front door and hiding her flush of desire. His custom designer suit enhanced his perfect build. He should be on a fashion runway or a billboard, not taking her out on a covert mission. When he politely handed her into the car, the seat was toasty—he'd turned the heater on for her. Gorgeous and thoughtful—keeping her head was almost impossible. But she had to—he was performing, not sincere.

They drove across town in silence. It wasn't exactly comfortable, but Holly wasn't breaking the ice. She kept her breathing even, remaining calm and cool and not thinking about Luke Sevrason. But hints of his expensive scent sent an arrow from her head to her heart. Avoiding his gorgeous looks, she gazed out the window, but she was surprised when they reached the restaurant—she'd been so lost in thoughts of him, she hadn't seen a thing.

As they entered the restaurant, his hand heated the middle of her back, undoing all her pitiful efforts at calm and shoving cool out the door. After Luke talked to the host, they followed to a small, dimly lit booth in the corner.

Luke held out his arm. "After you. Don't forget, it's your turn tonight."

"My turn for what?" She slid into the burgundy leather booth, grateful that her dark complexion hid her blush.

Luke sat next to her. His knees bumped hers, then their shoulders rubbed. "To pick the subject we talk about, remember?"

"I'd forgotten." She blew out a breath and tried to recover by inspecting their surroundings. Classy, old-world ambiance, with tiny booths circling the room and widely spaced dark wood tables in the center. The walls held old-gold curtains partially obscuring flocked floral wall paper above dark wood paneling. Once again, the restaurant was full of lovers.

They ordered drinks and dinner while she wracked her brains for a conversation starter that wouldn't lead to the wrong places. The easiest solution was to ask the same question he had. "Why don't you tell me how you ended up in the Air Force. Didn't you go to Harvard? They don't have ROTC."

Luke grimaced. "It's actually a kind of stupid story." His grimace turned sheepish, an unusual look for the confident pilot. "Okay, the story isn't stupid. I was. I had just finished my sophomore year at Harvard, and I was hanging out with a friend for a couple of weeks in the Atlanta area. We were at a big street festival, and my friend's big brother was buying us beer, so we were pretty drunk." He shook his head. "The Air Force recruiters had a flight simulator, and it looked like fun. Even drunk, I was good at it, and the sergeant manning it told me I should go take the real test and see how I did. I said 'sure, why not?' and before I realized what was going on, he had me signed up with a time and place and everything."

"I'm sure that made you happy." She snickered. Privileged Luke Sevrason, suckered into a military testing station.

"I was happy that day, not so much the next." He grimaced. "Especially with a killer hangover. When I pulled the appointment card out of my wallet, I was going to throw it away, but my buddy wouldn't let me. He'd signed up for the test too, sure that my win on the sim was a fluke." He shrugged one shoulder and flashed a grin. "Long story short, I tested very high on the pilot portion, and my buddy basically flunked. I already knew I didn't want to join Father's firm, and I had zero interest in continuing a political or business dynasty—way too boring. When they told me that pilot training came with an eight-year commitment, that was eight years of telling my father to go pound sand." He flashed a grin. "Besides, being a pilot looked a lot more fun that sitting in an office someplace, doing spreadsheets or managing projects or even worse, selling insurance." He shuddered. "So, I applied for Officer Training School and got in right after college. Ninety days later, I was off to pilot training and the start of an awesome career." He chuckled. "And a better life out of my dad's clutches."

Holly did the math. "But you've been in at least ten years, right?"

"Yes, but you know every move adds a year, and I added on more commitments, rather than trying to avoid them. Besides, I was right." He grinned. "It's a lot of fun to fly. The rest of the military paperwork and training can be a drag, but flying a refueler is great. Most days, I can't believe I get paid to do this. A lot of pilots don't like tankers because you spend a lot of time burning holes in the sky, and you don't get the attention the fighter pilots do. But it's perfect for me."

He seemed genuinely happy, but that didn't add up with the boy she'd known. "I can see where flying would be fulfilling but not very lucrative."

He frowned at her. "Why do you think I want money? My needs are pretty simple. I don't need a fancy car, or half a dozen houses, or designer clothes. I have some of those things, but I don't need them."

Rage swept through her. "You say that now, but you've always had a safe fallback. If you ever had nothing, you'd feel different." Living with constant fear was horrible—the fear of other people taking everything, attacking physically, the uncertainty of not having a home, no one to care if something happened—it was exhausting and terrifying. Even though she was careful to keep her face and voice emotionless, something must have tipped Luke off.

He enfolded her hand in his. "I'm sure that's true. I'll never be in the position you were in. I wish you'd never been there, and I deeply regret my part in that horrific experience. I'll make sure you're never there again."

And the arrogance was back. She yanked her hand out of his. "*I'll* make sure I'm never there again. I don't need anybody else to look out for me, especially you." He was the same as the rest of those superior rich people they went to school with, sure that money fixed everything and they could run over everyone in their way.

He held up his hands. "Holly, I didn't mean to offend you. I know you can take care of yourself—we discussed this last week, remember? But having a wingman is important, because no matter how good or careful you are, sometimes you can't do it all. Maybe I phrased it badly—you make my protective instincts kick in, and I really am sorry if it offends you—but I just wanted you to know I've got your six, whether you need it or not."

"Kristen and Amy and I have been looking out for each other for a long time now. I've got wing women. I don't need you." He was too tempting, and he'd leave, probably at the worst time.

Luke sighed. "You can never have too many people watching out for you, Holly. Quite frankly, I'd appreciate it if you'd return the favor. Even if you want nothing to do with me romantically, we're going to be together a lot because of Chris and Amy. Besides, we all need multiple people watching our sixes—there's just too many other things out there that can launch a missile into your blind spot when you least expect it. Very few of us have supportive blood relations—we both need as many other people as possible." The corners of his mouth rose, but he wasn't happy.

Holly closed her eyes. There was the crux of the problem—Amy and Chris were mutual friends. She had to get over her little crush quickly. It was just physical attraction—he had a great body and a pretty face—and that usually wore off quickly. "Fine. You're right. We'll all look out for each other. But still, you can't deny you had it easy because of your family money."

He frowned. "I've never denied that. My point is, I don't *need* my father's money. A major with flight pay isn't poor. My flight pay has always gone straight to investments, along with my deployment pay, and I max out my Thrift Savings Plan. While I bought my first house with my trust fund, I've bought one or more at each base I've been stationed at with my own money. I rent them to other military members for a secure income stream. I'm doing pretty well all on my own. I can't afford a chartered jet or a vacation home, but getting away to a hotel a couple of times a year is easily in reach."

Keeping the conversation on money was easier than feelings. "Flight pay would be nice." It didn't seem fair that pilots got extra for something most of them would pay to do, but she'd had a scholarship, so maybe it evened out.

"But it doesn't last forever." He sipped his water. "That's why I invested. And not in some fancy fund that one of my father's so-called friends recommended. Nice, solid index funds and some bonds and blue chips."

He was smart to stick with the basics. "I've always maxed out my retirement fund, too. I don't own my place, but I'm looking. Real estate is a little pricey around here, but I've got a few leads."

He smiled, a real smile. "I can help you look. I picked up a few things, especially after I'd already bought."

"That's a nice offer." No way she was house hunting with him. It would give him the wrong impression entirely. She was not going down that rabbit hole, not with Luke Sevrason.

"I mean it, Holly. I'm not just saying it to be polite." He reached across the table to squeeze her hand.

"Okay. Thanks." That was a spectacularly bad idea.

He smiled. "Did you want dessert?"

"No, thanks." Her stomach barely tolerated the main meal. "Let's go. I've got the check this time."

He grinned at her and snatched the folder, sliding a card inside and handing it to their server. Her stupid heart thumped again. "No way. Daddy's getting these checks. I've had one of his credit cards for a long time and never used it, but since he's causing the problems, he can pay for the solution." He shrugged. "He'll never notice; his financial managers pay the bills."

Holly chuckled at the poetic justice. "Nice. I like it."

When the server returned the card, Luke stood and offered her a hand. "Ready?"

Reluctantly, she took his hand and tried to ignore the warmth radiating from him. They drove back to her house in silence. She'd run out of polite topics and was too worried about the next step to make meaningless small talk. Luke pulled into the driveway, handed her out of the car, and they walked to the front door.

She unlocked it and turned to him. "I guess if we're selling this story, you should probably come in."

He took one of her hands, rubbing it gently. "Holly, I don't want to make you more uncomfortable than you are already. This is your house, and I'm not going to invade your sanctuary. I doubt there's anyone but the feds watching, anyway."

Holly held back a grimace. She didn't want Lukas Sevrason in her home. It would lead to all the wrong things. But their dating story had to move along. "So we prove our acting ability to them."

He shrugged. "All right, I tried." He followed her in, his spicy, citrus scent invading along with his warmth.

The snick of the front door's deadbolt thumped like a doom bell in her heart. She pointed at the couch. "Have a seat. Do you want anything to drink?"

"No, thanks." He sat in the corner of the couch, relaxed, confident, and sexy, with one arm across the back of the cushion next to him, inviting her to cuddle. And that would feel so very, very good.

And be so very, very dumb. Holly kicked off her high heels and sat in a chair across from him. "What do we talk about and how long are you staying?"

He looked at her feet. "I'll only stay a few minutes. I can just hang out here if you want to go brush your teeth or something. I don't mind."

Her upbringing would never allow such an action. "I may not like the fake dating scheme, but I'm not rude."

"It's not rude, Holly, just practical." He frowned. "I understand you're not romantically interested, but a friend wouldn't care that you're getting your jammies on."

Even sweats wouldn't be enough armor against him. "Luke, I'm sorry, but I can't do that."

His brows pinched. "Because you don't trust me. I understand why you felt betrayed, but that was a long time ago." He stood, fists clenched. "It was high school! I'm not going to attack you physically."

"Luke—" Telling her that did no good. She'd nurtured her anger and fear for so long that it was a part of her. And that wary skepticism had kept her safe for a long time.

He ran a hand through his hair and looked at the ceiling, then returned to her gaze. The anger was gone, replaced by sadness. "Never mind. It doesn't matter. You'll never really trust me." He walked out the door, closing it quietly.

Holly locked her door, then flopped back into her chair. Separating the pain of his duplicity from her family's betrayal and all the subsequent actions and emotions was practically impossible. That twenty-four hours of emotional trauma was cemented in her brain as the starting point of her entire adult life. Her *precarious* adult life, although she had a lot more certainty as a military officer. But her lack of trust wasn't entirely Luke's fault.

She didn't trust herself. Luke truly was a friend—his current actions proved his sincerity. But she wanted more than friendship. Luke said he wanted a relationship, but what kind? Eventually, she wanted it all; husband, kids, and a pet. He might not want anything so formal and she wouldn't settle for less.

She stood and paced. The potential for a catastrophic heartbreak was imminent. Luke was an accomplished actor; it went hand in hand with his charismatic charm. Foolish girl Holly had believed everything he said, so eager to fall for him completely. Adult Holly was older, but not necessarily wiser. She'd been alone for so long, and she desperately wanted love. Luke's love, more specifically.

But she just couldn't, wouldn't, trust him. Despair hit her hard, right between the eyes. She dropped her head into her hands and cried for the first time since that long, horrible, lonely bus ride across the country all those years ago.

LUKE

On Monday afternoon, Luke sat alone in his squadron conference room, joining via secure video from Space Force headquarters. The FBI lead, Special Agent Ness, briefed the status of each target and the subjects, namely he and Holly. Seeing his daily activities summarized so succinctly and publicly was a little disconcerting—evidently, Luke Sevrason was one boring guy. Holly's life was equally bland. He'd like to convince her they'd have more fun together, but that seemed improbable.

Das and his father circled each other for assurances, although they'd gotten word of Luke and Holly's relationship. Das was angry that his fiancée was with another man but also reassured that his leverage would work. Father was harder to read, but the FBI analysts thought he was mostly relieved that Luke would be easier to control. The two men sniped at each other whenever they met.

Ness looked into the camera. "Major Sevrason, we've been trying to figure out exactly what Mr. Sevrason wants with you. Since the emotional reasons don't make sense, we decided to follow the money. It's taken us a while because he has some excellent financial advisers and lawyers. As you probably knew, he has a lot of offshore accounts that go through a dozen different shell companies. But some of the easier to find accounts are in your name."

That made no sense. "News to me. I have a credit card from my father, but I never used it until this whole thing started. I haven't willingly taken a penny from him since college."

Ness smirked. "We know you don't know anything about these accounts. Mr. Sevrason set them up as joint accounts many years ago, some while you were still in college, and then, about three years ago, he made you the primary or solo holder. For the past two years, you've been drawing a salary from his company, too, gradually increasing as if you were getting promotions."

Curiosity mixed with dread tightened his shoulders. "Shouldn't the IRS be knocking on my door?"

Ness held up his forefinger. "To hide the money from you and everyone else, he made you the CEO of a limited liability company, sub-contracted to a minor subsidiary of his company. You've just started to earn some money, but it's via a contract with his company, not a salary. It's reported via 1099, not a W-2, and the paperwork goes to Sevrason Aerospace. The Sevrason Analytics

CFO has paid all the taxes owed by the company, so it made no difference to your taxable income, or the IRS would be asking questions already. If it wasn't for this investigation, you'd be getting a sternly worded letter from the IRS in about a year and no idea why."

Luke listened, his disbelief quickly growing to fury. His father had been harassing him about joining the company, but that was fake. He was being set up.

Ness held up a hand, undoubtedly reading Luke's expression. "Making matters worse, also a year ago, those same accounts received large, single deposits, timed with quarterly earnings reports. Your salary increased substantially, too."

Luke controlled his anger. An outburst would do no good. But he couldn't hold back an annoyed huff. "I guess it must be nice to be me." He gave Ness an ironic look.

"Evidently, Mr. Sevrason has finally realized that you may not comply with his plans for a political or commercial dynasty and decided to use you anyway." Ness stopped smiling. "Bluntly, he's setting you up as a fall guy."

Luke nodded, keeping his emotions under wraps. "Pretty obvious. And typical. He always gets his pound of flesh one way or another." But it still hurt, knowing his father chose to stick a knife in his back.

Ness continued. "Of course, there are problems with this attempt. First, Major Sevrason is an Air Force officer assigned to operational units. Your movements are easily tracked. A cursory look at you makes the senior Sevrason's narrative unbelievable. Second, there's a lack of physical evidence. There is nothing tying you to the accounts Mr. Sevrason set up. It's difficult to open accounts and be a CEO when you're deployed and every electron is monitored."

Luke nodded. Ness had mirrored his thoughts. "So how will he make it look real?"

"We believe he planted some evidence, but we haven't found it yet. Or maybe it's ready to be planted but not in place. But we believe he's going to offer a fall guy who can't defend himself. Then the law might not look a gift horse in the mouth."

"You think his own father will try to kill him?" Holly sounded enraged.

Hope rose, then crashed. She'd be upset about anybody getting killed, especially to cover a crime.

Ness held up his hand and tilted it back and forth. "Yes and no. We don't think Mr. Sevrason would kill personally, but hire, coerce, or persuade someone? Absolutely. We believe that's why Sevrason is taunting Das about your relationship. Das believes you should have been faithfully waiting all these years just for him. He's becoming delusional when it comes to you, although he isn't showing signs of overall instability."

"Becoming delusional?" Luke knew that law enforcement spoke in hypotheticals, but Das was way off the flight path. "Sounds to me like he's there. Why does he think a military officer can disappear without anyone looking for her? We need to call this off. It's too dangerous for Holly." Relationship or not, she'd get used to him being around, no matter how much she hated him. That tango wouldn't get a chance at taking her.

She frowned at him. "Your father is trying to kill you! You're in more danger than I am."

"I don't think that's true." And even if it was, her safety was way more important to him.

"Why? Because you can protect yourself better?" Holly rolled her eyes. "I don't think you're bullet proof." She glared at him.

Maybe she felt something for him after all. Hope rose unbidden.

Ness cleared his throat. "I don't believe the danger to either one of you has increased substantially. We just know more about the type of danger. We will inform you if either one of the men makes any attempt to come to this area physically, or if they send someone, and increase our protection details significantly if that is the case. Neither man seems ready to commit physical violence. That's why they're still negotiating and taunting each other—neither one will cross the line to violent criminal acts. The psychologists believe it will take some sort of catalyst to move them that far."

"What kind of catalyst?" Holly asked.

He wanted to know that, too, and avoid it. He had to keep Holly safe.

"Proof that you are in a permanent relationship, like an engagement, might do it for Das." He held up a hand to stop any questions. "No, we aren't suggesting you do that. For one, it's too fast, and two, we don't want to push that hard. We need Mr. Sevrason to reveal more of his plans and find more evidence against both men before we do anything drastic." Ness leaned forward. "Because of that, we definitely don't want you doing anything that implies a physical relationship, like spending the night together.”

"Thank Vishnu for small favors," Holly muttered.

Luke sagged in disappointment, then his brain kicked in, and he realized they'd have a very awkward and uncomfortable night. Better to wait until she trusted him a little more, then he might have a chance. He snorted internally. He was kidding himself.

Ness's mouth twisted. "We may suggest that later, but not yet. Anyway, that's where we are right now. Are you still planning on a ski trip in a couple of weeks?"

"Yes, we are." Luke wanted more time with Holly, even if it was with a group. Besides, he could use a wingman. "I haven't made reservations anywhere."

Ness nodded. "We don't have a consensus among the psych staff, but most of us think you should use your father's house. That would reassure him that you're still interested in luxury and the trappings of vast wealth. We don't think he'll come out and confront you because he's going to want to distance himself if you're going to be an effective fall guy. And Mr. Das doesn't participate in winter sports, or any sports at all, although I certainly wouldn't be surprised at any move he makes."

"Great, we'll cruise along, waiting to suck up a missile." Luke grimaced. "Sitting duck decoy—my favorite." And a great way to get dead when alone and unafraid.

But even if the FBI let them down, he'd have Holly's six, no matter what it took.

The next week was a repeat of the last. On Thursday, Luke had to visit the Air Force personnel office on Peterson. A perfect excuse to drop in for lunch. The guard at the Space Force Headquarters front desk called Holly for permission, gave him a visitor's badge, and told him to wait for an escort. Kristen's blonde hair stood out in the mass of uniforms and suits heading out for lunch.

"Hey, Luke, didn't expect to see you today." Kristen beckoned him to follow.

In her second-floor cubicle, Holly typed, peering at her computer. "Just a second. Got to finish this thought."

"No problem. I can easily wait for such beautiful ladies. Especially when my alternative is lunch with a bunch of sweaty guys." He winked at Kristen.

"Funny." Holly's fingers flew on the keyboard, typing notes on a presentation. "We don't have time to go out today. Do you still want to join us? The death star cafeteria isn't exactly fine cuisine." She didn't even glance at him, her voice full of cool disinterest.

He held back a reaction shiver. "Better than the Army's chow hall. Or fast food." He shrugged. "Besides, it's new to me." Even when she was cold as ice, he'd rather be with Holly.

"Come on, then." Holly hit save and grabbed her purse and Kristen's arm. "I'll get yours. No need to get your purse." Kristen turned to him and rolled her eyes but stayed with Holly.

They led him upstairs to the cafeteria. In the food line, he copied them, getting the special of the day—lasagna and salad—and followed them to the dining area.

A wall of windows displayed the front range of the Rockies on the west and a view of the town to the north, too. "Hey, this is pretty sweet. Way nicer than anything on post." The Fort Carson Officer's Club was elegant but crowded with retirees.

"Shhh." Kristen put her forefinger to her lips. "It's a big secret. The food is decent and the view is gorgeous. In the summer, you can sit out on the deck. It's a nice perk when you don't have time to leave the building."

Holly looked at a man sitting alone near the north-facing windows, her brows wrinkling. "Kristen, Lieutenant Colonel Lee is glaring at you again. What did you do this time?"

"I don't know." Kristen's shrug and pout seemed overdone. "I haven't seen him for a while. I think he dislikes me on principle, which is too bad because I'd like to play teacher to his principal, if you know what I mean." She patted her blonde hair and batted her eyes.

"Kristen! No wonder he glares at you. You're incorrigible!" Holly was trying to hold back her laughter.

"Not most of the time, but I could be with him." She stared at the lieutenant colonel, who very obviously avoided looking at her.

Luke wasn't sure how to feel about Kristen's play for a senior officer. But when in doubt, the right answer was staying quiet. He knew better than to get involved in someone else's love life. He had enough trouble with his own.

"He doesn't seem like your type." Holly shook her head. "He's good looking, the glasses are kind of hip geek, and you can tell he works out, but he's not some super stud like most of the guys you date." Her mouth twisted. "Not to mention the rank gap. Captain and a lieutenant colonel are a bit far apart."

"The studs ask me out." Kristen clamped her lips together for a moment. "But they're usually as thick in the head as they are in the chest. I like the brainiacs a lot more, but they're usually too intimidated to ask me." She shrugged, then went back to staring at Colonel Lee.

Luke shook his head, not buying Kristen's act. "Even if you dress like it, we're not in the 1950s anymore. You can ask a guy out these days. They'd be flattered."

"Normally I would." Kristen sighed. "But we're two ranks apart, and not just two ranks, but company grade to field grade. And he's in a command position. That's a big leap for little ole me to try." She shook her head, pouting again.

Holly snorted. "Kristen, somebody who doesn't know you might buy that 'little ole me' bit, but not me. Besides, the rules have never stopped you before, especially unwritten ones."

Kristen grimaced. "All that glaring is hard to get past. I don't think he likes me much."

From the covert glances, Luke was fairly certain the opposite was true. "Or maybe too much." He recognized the look of a man who wanted someone he couldn't have. The same look was on his face every day. He stood, implementing the best or worst idea ever, and crossed the room, holding out his hand. "Hello. I'm Lukas Sevrason, Chief of Training at the 13th ASOS on Fort Carson. You're the Intelligence Director here, right?"

Lee stood, shaking his hand solidly but without challenge. "Nice to meet you. Anything I can do for you?"

Luke shook his head. "No, not right now. But you never know what you might need in the future. We have to rely on intel from our Wing, which isn't local, and the Army, who has different priorities. Plus, we have mutual acquaintances." He tilted his head toward Holly and Kristen. "And Holly and I are causing the loss of your facilities, which I imagine is annoying. If I could do something about that, I would, but I can't."

Lee held up both hands. "Not a problem. I'm always happy to assist federal agencies."

Luke didn't hold back his frown. "In the same way I am, I'm sure." Kristen had helped him, so he'd help her. "Since you're by yourself, want to join us?"

Lee jolted in his seat. "Umm..." He glanced around, a slightly desperate look in his eyes that Luke recognized.

"We don't bite." Luke laughed internally at the colonel's expression. "At least I don't. Can't promise for the ladies, but it's just lunch."

Lee grimaced but grabbed his tray, following Luke to the table. He sat next to Kristen, the only open seat, since Luke was next to Holly.

"Hello, Colonel Lee." Kristen's voice was low and throaty.

"Hello, Captain." He turned to Holly. "How are you holding up, Captain Bose?"

"I'm doing okay. Not like I have a choice." Holly grimaced.

Lee nodded. "There's always a choice, but sometimes, none of them are optimal. I'm in the loop on your situation, so if you need to talk, come see me." He turned to Luke. "That goes for you, too, Sevrason."

"Thanks. I'm fine." Holly should take that offer, but suggesting it would be dumb.

Lee turned back to Holly, handing her a card. "Don't hesitate. My schedule is always busy, but I take the time to come here and look at the mountains, so I can certainly make time for you. I'll let my secretary know to give you priority."

Holly took his card. "I appreciate that, but I'm doing okay. And you have more important things to do. I see the weekly briefs and I know you're working impossible hours."

Lee shrugged. "The perils of command, but my offer remains. Intel always works long hours because we never have enough people. We're in high demand downrange. And I'm shorter than a lot of units because this is a headquarters, and more of my folks are higher ranked. They're short of intel supervisors downrange, so percentage-wise I get hit harder. And for longer tours." He shook his head and tried to smile, but it came out as a grimace. "Sorry, don't mean to whine."

"No, it's interesting." Kristen frowned slightly. "Most of us in acquisitions and space operations never deploy, but you guys are gone all the time. It hardly seems fair."

He shrugged. "You're not trying to avoid deployment; it's just the nature of the business. Your position is critical. Without worldwide communications, our job is impossible."

Kristen tilted her head, gazing at Colonel Lee. "I've thought about volunteering for a deployment that they'll take anyone for. I'd like to be in a more military-like role at some point in my career."

Colonel Lee huffed. "You're the last person who should deploy, especially to the middle east, Captain."

Luke couldn't help but agree with him and nodded vigorously. Beautiful and vivacious, she'd be targeted.

"Why?" She scowled at Colonel Lee.

He raised his brows. "Because you'd offend the majority of the local male populace just by being you, let alone with your normal attitude."

She raised her brows in an ostentatiously offended look. "Oh really? And just what attitude is that, Colonel Lee?"

He frowned, then raised one brow. "This will get me in trouble, but I'll be blunt. You're a gorgeous flirt. You'd be a liability."

She glared at Lee. "I can be serious and professional with the best of them."

Luke knew he'd regret it, but he had to save the colonel from himself. "He's right. Blonde and beautiful? You'd be a huge target, and not just for the bad guys. You'd have to be incredibly careful, and that might not be enough." Too many women ended up attacked by the men who were supposed to be on their side, and Kristen would be an irresistible target to those kinds of so-called men.

She glared at him and Colonel Lee. "Over-protective much, gentlemen? Somebody's got to show those women how to stand up for themselves. I'm not a pushover."

Luke shook his head. She wasn't stupid, either, and even though he was treading in dangerous waters, he had to continue. "If you really want to go, go as part of a unit, so you'll have backup. Most of the positions you're talking about are out there flying alone and unafraid." Being downrange was bad enough, but without a squadron, it could be horrible for women and men.

"He's right." Colonel Lee nodded sharply. "If you insist on going, and I really wish you wouldn't, go as part of a unit."

"That's not likely to happen. And on that note, I have a meeting to get to. See y'all later." Kristen stood and sashayed her way out the door.

"There goes trouble." Colonel Lee watched her walk away.

Holly snorted. "You hardly know her, but you're right. No wonder you're always glaring at her."

"I am?" Lee looked shocked.

Luke started to laugh, but he recognized the signs of a man overcome by desire. His impulse died quickly. "Sorry, but you do."

Lee looked at the table. "Oh. I didn't realize…" He fiddled with his tray.

Luke took pity on him. "Come on, Holly, we need to figure out this weekend's logistics."

"Sorry, I've got a meeting too. See you later, Colonel Lee." Holly carried her tray toward the exit.

Luke followed, putting his tray in the proper place. He walked back to her cubicle, letting his arm brush hers. "Call me and let me know where on Friday?"

"Sure." She picked up a notebook and walked away.

He left, dropping off his visitor's badge and driving to his squadron, depressed again. It didn't even help to know that Lee was in a worse position than him.

Chapter 8

LUKE WAITED UNTIL A week before the trip to call Ms. Varchenko, his father's property manager, about the Beaver Creek house. If his father had lent the house to someone else, he'd ruined the trip, but he couldn't give Daddy Dearest more notice than necessary. His friends would forgive him, even if the feds wouldn't. Fortunately, Ms. Varchenko said the place was available. She'd notify the cleaning service to check it and if there was enough time, have it stocked with groceries. He told her not to bother, they'd bring what they needed. He didn't think Chris and Amy would appreciate caviar and Cristal, his father's favorites, although Kristen might.

He drove Holly and Kristen up on Sunday, making good time, since they were opposing most of the traffic. Federal agents tailed them in a typical black SUV. They'd stay in a rental house just down the street.

During the drive, Kristen kept the conversation flowing easily, starting with how much she was looking forward to seeing Amy. Luke equally anticipated hanging out with Chris, far away from a military environment.

At the house, the excitement of reconnecting with their friends covered any awkwardness between him and Holly. Then they focused on snow sports, restaurants, and group activities, so they hardly spoke to each other. On the hill, the snow wasn't great, but snowboarding with Chris was always fun—they pushed each other to excel without the stupid stunts of their younger days. Amy was graceful and precise on skis, and Kristen was surprisingly competitive, beating all of them down the runs. Holly was the most tentative, sticking to the less-extreme hills, but she improved rapidly. Rex seemed to enjoy his time at doggy daycare, the staff reporting he played almost non-stop.

Every morning before he got out of bed, Luke checked his phone to see if his father had made travel arrangements. The first three days, the answer was no. So they skied, went out, partied a little, and generally ignored the feds following them. Unfortunately, their fun didn't last. The FBI told them Wednesday night that Mr. Sevrason had a rented corporate jet, arriving late Thursday afternoon.

They decided Thursday was a non-skiing day, giving them a break and the FBI time to prepare. They slept in, made brunch, and just lazed the morning away in front of the fire, drinking coffee and cocoa. Agents slipped in and out of the house, rearranging surveillance.

After lunch, Kristen asked, "What do you want to do now? It's too early for trouble to be here yet."

"Figure it out without us." Chris rose, holding out a hand to Amy. "I think Amy needs a nap. Got to be careful of her medical condition, you know." Chris winked and pulled her up off the big leather couch. "Right, love?"

Amy smiled softly at Chris and followed him out of the living room. "Of course."

Luke stared down the hallway long after they were out of sight. If only…but Holly would never trust him enough to really let him into her life. He was trying to juggle feathers behind a blasting jet engine. He should just give up, but he couldn't. Even when he'd thought she was married off and out of reach, he'd never found anyone to match her, and after their current adventures, he wouldn't even try. Not until there was some other guy's wedding ring on her hand, a thought that made his entire body clench with jealous despair.

Kristen bounded to her feet. "No sense in hanging out here. Let's go do something fun. Meet you back here in thirty, okay?" She grabbed Holly, towing her out of the room.

"Sure." Luke took a quick shower and changed into jeans and a sweater. There was no telling what kind of fun Kristen would find. In the living room, Kristen and Holly wore their ski clothes. "I thought we weren't boarding?"

"We're not, but you'll want the same gear." Kristen winked and grinned.

Trepidation made him frown. "All right, but I'm not sure I want to be part of whatever it is you're planning. That smile is scary." He changed and grabbed his keys, then escorted the ladies to his SUV. "Kristen, where are we going?"

"Back to our childhood," Holly said from the backseat. Kristen plugged in her phone, sending directions to his navigation unit.

"Childhood?" He'd rather not. His wasn't fun, and he was sure Holly's was worse.

Kristen bounced in her seat. "We're going sledding! On giant inner tubes. It will be a blast!"

"You've got to be kidding me." Sledding was for kids.

Holly leaned between the seats. "When was the last time you did something completely silly?"

He shrugged. "Yesterday."

She blew a raspberry. "Snowboarding at your level isn't silly. You and Chris are way too competitive."

"Live a little, Revlon!" Kristen caroled, pointing at a parking lot. Beyond the parked cars, a hill was covered with groomed lanes, and huge, brightly colored plastic tubes filled with kids careened down them.

He hated that callsign. "Tubing? Looks like there's nothing but kids out there." Luke parked. He had to admit, the kids were having a lot of fun—the squeals, yells and jumping around proved it. Maybe a return to the childhood neither he nor Holly had was a good idea. He'd sledded a few times as a kid, but it had been a run or two on snow days, sneaking over to Chris's house to borrow a sled. His father didn't approve of fun without a purpose. He hadn't learned to snowboard until college.

He paid for tickets, and they each received a tube, then they walked to the starting platform. Sledding had changed a bit since he was a kid. No need to walk up the hill—sitting on a tube and getting towed was far easier.

As he went up, he inspected the layout. Every rider rode down alone in separate lanes. Too bad—half the fun was running into each other. Still, he bet he could game the system at least once—calculating lead and speed was second nature to a pilot. He grinned. Might get him kicked out, but with the right hit, it would be worth it.

The first few runs, he played it straight—nice and safe. He videoed Holly and Kristen racing and took more while he flew down the slope. It was fun, but he had something better in mind. Anticipation brought a grin to his face.

Handing his phone to Kristen, he bent to whisper in her ear. "Make sure you get this." She quirked a brow at him but brought his phone up. He bowed to Holly. "You first, milady."

She grinned, her eyes sparkling. Happiness suited her. He had to make sure she had more opportunities, even in the middle of their current mess. "Okay. Whoo-hoo!"

The lane guard waited, then said, "Next!"

Luke sprinted down the icy lane and jumped on the tube, ignoring the guard's shout, keeping his body flat to minimize his wind resistance and gain speed. He closed the gap between them but wasn't sure if he'd catch Holly before the lane ended. It would be close...he grinned, feeling like a little kid again. As Holly slid down the lane, she spun slowly. When she spotted him, her eyes opened wide, and she yelled, but he couldn't understand the words. Her hands grasped the tube handles as she turned back to face him.

His tube slammed into Holly's—her wide-eyed, open-mouth expression was priceless—and then he launched from his tube to hers. He landed on her tube, not Holly, and bounced once, trying to expend some of the energy. Then he dropped on top of her, wrapping his arms around her and twisting to the side to take his weight off. He snuggled her in close and laughed like a maniac, having the time of his life and winning the very best prize.

Holly smacked his chest with her open palm. "You idiot! Are you trying to kill me?" She tried but failed to hide her laughter.

He held her tighter and kept laughing. They slammed into the end barrier and he rolled on top of the tube, keeping her close, so she ended on top of him. He couldn't stop laughing, and neither could she. Her eyes sparkled, and her mouth curved in a big open grin, tempting him to close it with a kiss.

He raised his head and swallowed her laughter, teasing her with light kisses. She responded, and he deepened the kiss, their tongues twisting together and hands gripping tight. Heat rose from his belly, but he didn't want to stop kissing Holly.

"You're out of here! Give me that ticket!" a voice yelled above them.

Holly startled and jerked away. He released her and let her roll off. Too bad the guy couldn't hold off a few more minutes. He sat up and bounced on the tube to stand up. "Yeah, sure. Cool your jets." He reached down and helped Holly up, then turned, holding the ticket attached to his jacket up so the employee could clip it off.

Kristen slid in, bouncing against their tube, and almost knocking all of them over. Luke pulled Holly out of the way. The employee cursed, his face turning bright red. "You're all out of here!"

Kristen laughed and accepted Luke's hand. "That was awesome! Got the whole thing on video!" She bounded to her feet and gave his phone back. "Come on, let's go. We can't win this battle."

As they walked by, the kids in the tow line clapped and cheered. Luke took a bow. "Kids, be sure to try that at home, not here!" Leaving the fenced area, he put his arms around the women's shoulders and walked to the car, unable to stop grinning. "We're branded criminals now, ladies, so what's next?"

"I think this calls for a drink!" Kristen bumped him with a hip.

"Great idea." Although he'd rather lock lips again with Holly, her silence didn't bode well. "We'll go back to the house and take a ride share." He opened the doors for Holly, then Kristen, and jumped into the driver's seat.

Just after he pulled onto the freeway, Kristen stared at her phone, then blew a raspberry. "Get back, fast." She sounded furious. "Your daddy showed up and kicked Chris and Amy out!"

True to form—his father was awful. Luke stepped on the gas, putting the all-wheel drive to the test. As they pulled up, Chris and Amy were putting luggage, skis, and boards into the back of Chris's truck, Rex dancing around their feet.

Kristen jumped out before he could turn his SUV off, Holly right behind her. Luke took the time to make sure his vehicle was secure before joining them.

"Luke's father showed up and ordered us to get out, even though he remembered me." Chris scowled, then turned and winked. "Seems nobody told him we were using the place." Amy rolled her eyes.

Luke's anger grew. First the man set him up, and then he made it worse, being rude to his friends. "That's not true. I went through Ms. Varchencko. He knew."

Holly rose on her tiptoes, trying to peer over into the back of Chris's truck. "You got Luke's stuff out too, right?"

"Of course." Chris smirked. "Not stranding my wingman."

Luke appreciated that. "Thanks. I'm surprised he let you."

Amy snorted. "He didn't know. Chris kept yelling at him about being kicked out and Rex stayed with me." She laughed. "He seems allergic to dogs. Or maybe he's just allergic to Rex's teeth. Rex doesn't like him."

Luke grinned and scratched behind Rex's ears. "Good boy, Rex. Too bad Mom didn't let you bite the bad man." He helped load the rest of their stuff. They could sort it out later. "Let's blow this popsicle stand and get dinner. I'm buying. Chris, you and Amy can stay at my house as long as you want, or you can head home tomorrow. Up to you." They decided on a restaurant in Frisco. At the last second, Kristen jumped into the truck with Amy, leaving Holly with him.

As they drove away, Luke's anger waned with the relief of avoiding his father. After they pulled on to the freeway, his phone rang. The vehicle screen displayed his father's number. "Sevrason."

"Lukas, where are you? I thought we'd have dinner and discuss your future." His father's tone held an undercurrent of anger.

Luke kept his eyes on the traffic surrounding them but couldn't help gripping the wheel tighter. The man's arrogance knew no bounds. "Why would I want to talk to you after you treated my friends so badly? You know Chris, and you know we're friends. You had no reason to kick him and his wife out."

Holly's phone chirped. She made a circular motion with her hand and mouthed, "FBI. Keep talking."

"I had no idea that they were here." His father's usual arrogant anger returned. "Ms. Varchenko didn't tell me you were using the house."

Luke sighed. "That's strange because I checked with her a week ago, and she assured me that she would let you know. I have an email from her confirming the cleaning and stocking, and it was sent to you as well."

"If I got it, I didn't pay any attention to it. I didn't know I was coming here until last night."

Luke held back another sigh. "Why are you here? You don't ski."

"No, but some of my associates do. They'll be here tomorrow, and they're bringing some lovely, well-connected young women eager to meet a brave pilot."

Luke's lip curled, but he kept his tone even. "I only had one more day before I'm due back, so they wouldn't meet me, anyway." He wasn't sorry at all to miss the kind of woman his father would attract.

"Surely your commander would extend your leave for a day or two." The words might be a question, but Father's tone made it a command.

Luke had stopped responding to his father's commands years ago. "I have tried to explain that the military leave system isn't very flexible, but as usual, you choose to not believe me. And I didn't drive up here on my own. I need to get my fellow military members back, too." He'd avoid using their names, even though Father knew.

"I can certainly get you back to Colorado Springs, Lukas. The jet can make a stop or I'll have a limo take you back."

Luke held his anger in check. "You could, but you won't. You don't care much about military needs or timelines."

"That is a ridiculous statement. My company is built around the needs of our brave military men and women. Stop being so childish."

Luke gritted his teeth to keep from retorting. "You care about military needs for your company, but not the needs of my military service."

"You're just one boy. I think they can do without you for a few days."

So much for holding back his anger. "I'm the Chief of Training. What we do saves lives. I have a full week ahead." He used short, snappy statements to keep from ranting.

"Your loss. Meet me for dinner later this week, probably Thursday or Friday."

"Sure." It was still the last thing he wanted to do, but he would for the feds.

"I will let you know when and where." The phone call ended.

Luke relaxed his grip on the steering wheel. He'd practically strangled the thing.

Holly's phone chirped. She read the message. "Good job. We'll strategize tomorrow."

He grimaced. "I guess if the FBI scripts my conversation, we might have something to talk about, rather than sitting in uncomfortable silence."

Holly chuckled. "Sounds like conversations with my family. I'm sorry, Luke. It's not fun when your family sees you as nothing but a means to an end." She reached out and squeezed his forearm.

He slid his hand off the wheel and grasped hers. "You've lived with that a lot longer than I have, without money to make life easier. But thank you. I appreciate your support." That sounded awkward, but hopefully, she heard his sincerity.

She smiled and turned to look out the windshield but left her hand in his. He held on and hoped. He had to find a way to forever with Holly, or life wasn't worth living.

On Monday, Luke sat alone in his squadron conference room again, listening to the feds speculate. These meetings would be better if he was sitting next to Holly, rather than watching from across town.

Special Agent Ness tapped the table. "Major Sevrason, Mr. Sevrason's actions surprised us. We think he's making one more attempt to bring you into the company for real. Part of the bait is the bank accounts he's setup for you."

Luke shook his head. His father, setting him up on a lose/lose scenario. So typical. "How do you want me to play this? Pretend that I'm thinking about it, or shut him down?"

"We still haven't found any physical evidence tying you to any of the fraud he's committed, so if you turn him down flat, it might force his hand. We'd rather you lead him on a bit. We believe that if he's unsure of your intentions, he might set one or two pieces of evidence, but not all of it. That would make it easier to find more evidence against both of them."

"I see." Luke understood the feds' motivation, even if he desperately wanted to tell his father to go pound sand. "I'll tell him that I'm thinking about getting out because I hate not flying and working with the Army. But I can't right now because I have a year commitment from accepting the new assignment."

A small smile graced Ness's face. "Exactly. Add in a few things about Captain Bose. You could provide a better life for her and any children you might have, that kind of thing."

Luke snorted. His father was the definition of an absentee father. But that didn't matter; Holly did. "If he's trying to bring me in, where does that leave Holly and Das?"

"We're sure that Mr. Sevrason thinks you need a politically advantageous relationship, so he'd just as soon see Captain Bose with Mr. Das. We don't think he'd try to make you help Mr. Das, but he might make it look like you did, so if things go wrong, you'll be blamed for anything that happens to her. That would increase his leverage over you."

"Typical." Father was a selfish jerk, but clever.

"He's not stupid, but he does have some blind spots, and one of them is definitely you. But that makes him underestimate you, too."

"Nothing new there. What is Das doing?" They should have started with Holly. Ness and company wouldn't want to hear it, but there was no contest between Holly and his father. Holly would always come first. Das was dead last. Ness seemed reluctant to talk about Das, which made Luke very suspicious.

Ness paced the front of the room, not looking at either of them. "Right now, he's continuing to hide Mr. Sevrason's dealings, and they are negotiating timelines for action. Mr. Das wants to move now, but Mr. Sevrason has successfully reminded him that even a small mistake means getting caught. We think that if Mr. Sevrason can bring Major Sevrason on board, he'll then help Mr. Das." Ness stopped.

"How, exactly?" Holly asked before Luke could.

Ness grimaced. "Mr. Sevrason will give general tips to the police. Not enough to find either Das or Captain Bose, but enough to take the pressure off him. He'll claim that Mr. Das was manufacturing all the evidence against him, and we think he'll make sure Mr. Das can't testify." Ness's face was expressionless.

Dragging every word out of him was getting old. "And how is he going to do that?" He stared hard at Ness. The man had better stop stalling and start talking.

Ness stopped pacing. "He's exploring a number of options. He's told assistants to research poisoning, fatal car crashes, fatal home fires, and other such things, supposedly to protect himself. He's also been tentatively sounding out associates about less-than-legal people they may know, but he moves in the wrong circles for that. He hasn't asked about hitmen or anything that drastic."

"He's not stupid." Just selfish and delusional.

"Stupid criminals are much easier to catch." Ness grimaced again.

Luke scowled. Ness was still holding back. "Let me sum up. If Das gets his hands on Holly, not only is she in danger from him, she's also in danger from my father. Because my father will see her as nothing but a loose end."

Ness waved dismissively. "Yes, but he won't get the chance."

An optimistic FBI special agent seemed unusual. Maybe it was misplaced over-confidence. Either way, Luke would shoot him down. "Ever heard of Murphy's Law?"

Ness slashed his hand through the air in front of his body. "We have a lot of resources on this case. There are millions of dollars in fraud here and a potential political impact. It's a high priority for the Bureau and the Department of Defense."

"Right." Luke didn't believe him. "You're not telling us everything and Holly's life is on the line. We need to know."

Holly nodded. "So is Luke's. So tell us."

Ness glared. "We've shared everything we know and all useful speculation. If Mr. Sevrason contacts you about dinner, you need to join him. Don't commit to getting out of the military, but complain about your current job, say you're stuck, the kind of whining most military people know how to do so well. We're sure he'll buy it."

Luke glared in return. "Special Agent Ness, I don't appreciate the general condemnation of me or my fellow military members. I don't remember seeing any of you downrange for months in the sand. I suggest you check your privileged attitude at the gates next time. Now, I'd like to know why Das hasn't contacted me. I'm sure someone in your organization has speculation about that." He raised a brow, deliberately challenging Ness.

Ness's expression blanked. "We are surprised that Mr. Das hasn't contacted you again. We thought he would want to move ahead with his plans, with or without Mr. Sevrason's cooperation. However, his real job has been demanding, and he's dealing with a family obligation, so all of that may be slowing him down."

"I see." Luke never wanted to hear the man's voice again, but his silence was nerve-wracking.

"This a good thing, Major. It's easier to concentrate on one issue at a time." Ness forced a smile. "We'll see you next week."

The video went black. Luke left the room, wondering what Das's family obligation was and why Ness didn't want to talk about it. Or anything else. Alarm bells were ringing—Ness might be setting him and Holly up for a fall. They had to talk, because they were going to need each other to get through the coming trials.

Father's secretary sent him a Friday night dinner invitation. Luke accepted; they'd meet at an upscale restaurant downtown. Luke chose a navy Armani suit paired with a Harvard tie and an Air Force tie tack. He stuck the FBI microphone under the lapel near the empty boutonniere slot and carefully tucked his smaller semi-auto into a concealed holster at the back of his waist.

Checking the mirror, he saw no trace of the weapon unless he drew both arms forward. Since he wasn't going to hug his father, it should remain concealed. Drawing from behind his back wasn't easy or fast, but if he had to use it, everything had gone wrong. Leaning against the weapon wasn't comfortable, but he expected dinner to be uncomfortable, anyway. Overall, it was better to be safe than sorry.

He stepped into the restaurant lobby three minutes before seven. As expected, his father was sitting at the best table in the place. He handed the hostess a small gratuity. "I'll seat myself, thanks." He pushed past her.

As he reached the table, he held his hand out to shake his father's. "Good evening, Father."

He stood and shook. "How are you, Lukas?"

"Just fine. How are you?" Luke sat and repeated the "keep calm and carry on" slogan. He had to tolerate every awful word from the horrible man sharing his DNA. Showing any emotion might be fatal.

"Doing as well as can be expected, I guess." He met Luke's gaze. "I would do better if I had someone to share the burden of leading my company."

Loading up the guilt before drinks was unusually direct. "You have lots of talented people working for you. Plus, two leaders can make contradictory decisions. It's a bad idea."

Father jolted back and scowled. "I would be in charge, but I'd be able to train you and then retire."

Luke laughed without faking it. "I don't see you retiring anytime soon." His father would never let anyone else control his company, especially the son who was only useful as a fall guy.

"Not soon. But training a CEO takes time. It's an entirely different world than the military." He turned to the waiter who'd walked up during his speech. "Pappy Van Winkle on the rocks."

The waiter nodded. "And you, sir?"

"The same, but neat, please. Thank you." Luke waited for the man to leave, then returned his attention to his father. "I can't imagine there's any real rush. You're clearly doing well and enjoying yourself."

"Thank you, I am." He nodded. "But I want you to join me. I'm not getting younger." He shrugged slightly.

"None of us are." Luke mirrored his shrug. "I can't get out anytime soon. I have a commitment to get through."

"Are you still enjoying it?" Father toyed with his napkin. "I can't imagine why."

Luke ignored the insult. "Flying is great. My current job isn't my favorite because I'm not flying and the Army can be... challenging. But it's extremely important work. Saving lives is a great feeling." That was one hundred percent true and his father should have heard his conviction.

"I can understand that. You're young. Being a hero is important." He met Luke's gaze again. "When you get a little older, you understand the nuances better. Sometimes, indirect actions can save more lives in the long run."

"I'm sure." The man couldn't be more condescending if he tried.

The server returned with their drinks and took their orders. Father grimaced when Luke ordered a soda, rather than sharing his wine. Before he could make another pointed remark, another server brought salads.

Despite the FBI's list of topics, Luke struggled to find something to discuss. Back to the usual awkward silence.

Father sipped his expensive red wine. "Are you seeing anyone special?"

So much for neutral. Even though he despised the idea of mentioning Holly to his father, not saying anything would be suspicious. "Funny you should ask.

I've run into an old friend from high school. Do you remember Holly Bose?"

"Holly Bose? The scholarship girl? I thought she was married off by her family. At least that's what they told me." The look of surprise on Father's face was patently false.

"They told you that?" In turn, he was careful to show some surprise. Hopefully he was a better actor than his father.

"Yes." Father played with his utensils for a moment, probably searching for the right twist to his story. "The night before your high school graduation ball, her father called me and told me that she wouldn't be attending. He'd arranged a marriage with a suitable man for the day after graduation." He frowned. "I thought it was barbaric, but I certainly couldn't argue with him, especially when I hadn't known you were *dating*." His lip curled, then he continued. "That's why I called my friend and arranged for his daughter to be your date for the dance." His chin lifted. "A much more suitable choice."

Luke controlled his anger. His father's story was plausible and on-brand, except there was no way Holly's father could have known they were together. "She never told anyone we were dating, so I don't know how her father knew."

"Kids talk. I'm sure it was one set of parents telling another, and then word gets around." He waved a hand dismissively.

Luke shook his head. "I doubt it. The Bose family wasn't in our social circle. Or anyone's at the school. And we kept it quiet."

He scoffed. "You thought you kept it quiet. But I didn't know until Mr. Bose called me that night."

"I distinctly remember introducing her to you, and I had her over to our house more than once to study. I thought you'd assume I was dating her." He'd known his father would never speak to Holly's family, even before he'd been rude to her during that introduction.

"That girl? I assumed you were actually studying. Why would you date her?" He shook his head, a mournful look on his face. "I was gone too much, and missed too much. I didn't give you enough guidance. It's one of the biggest regrets I have. If I hadn't been so focused on work, perhaps we would be closer now."

Luke held back his anger and forced a conciliatory response. "Perhaps." Not a chance; the man was too selfish.

"It doesn't help that you look so much like your mother. She was beautiful, the love of my life, and losing her so soon was difficult." He blinked like he was holding back tears.

That was pushing it. For one, Luke was almost a copy of his paternal grandfather. Two, he remembered the screaming fights, including the accusations of cheating on both sides. Most of all, he remembered how little time passed between his mother's death in a car wreck and his father bringing another, much younger woman home. Fortunately, the entrees showed up and he didn't have to say anything.

"Next time I come out, be sure to bring Ms. Bose along with you." He was back to his oily smile.

"It's *Captain* Bose." It wouldn't hurt to remind the man he was taking on two military officers. "I don't know if it will last, but she's also a friend of my best friend's wife."

"That seems overly complex." He sipped wine and looked at his phone. "I asked you to join me for another reason." He looked up. "My doctors are a little concerned about my heart. Nothing terribly serious." A little shrug and dismissive wave of his hand followed his pronouncement. "They've put me on a cholesterol-lowering drug and a blood pressure medication, and a few other things like that. But it drove me to update my will and living will. You are still my executor, and the original documents are stored with my attorney. I've brought you his card just in case you lost it in your move." He held it out across the table.

Luke took the card. "Are you sure this isn't anything serious? Maybe you should see a specialist?"

"I have seen a specialist as a precautionary measure. He said that I'm doing well, but I may need bypass surgery in the next few years." He spun his fork in the creamy pasta sauce. "I'm on weight-loss drugs, too. I'm excited to see the results." Typical—the man was sure he could beat any system without any effort. Even his salad had been covered in high-calorie dressing.

Luke held back a snort. "Father, that's not doing well, that's dangerous. Are you exercising and watching what you eat and your stress levels?" His concern wasn't fake, even though he didn't want to feel anything for his DNA donor.

"It's not dangerous yet, merely something to keep an eye on. And yes, I am exercising. I do yoga three times a week, which lowers my stress levels. It doesn't hurt my heart to look at all those lovely young ladies while I'm doing it." He winked.

Luke snorted to keep from shuddering. "Of course you needed an additional reason to exercise."

"Certainly." He smiled smarmily. "Effort requires incentives."

The server joined them. "Gentlemen, can I interest you in one of our fabulous desserts?"

Luke shook his head. "None for me, thanks. Father?"

"No. Just the check." He was back to fiddling with his phone.

"Of course. Here you are." The man put the folder on the table.

Father shot a sad smile at him, then dug for his wallet. "I would like to stay and talk, but I have a very early flight. The time zones aren't in my favor."

"I have an early day myself tomorrow. Thank you for dinner. It was very good, and it was nice to see you again." *Let's not repeat it.*

"Always wonderful to see my only child. And, son?" He quirked a brow.

"Yes?" Guilt trip incoming in three, two, one...

"Do think about joining me and the company. I'd make it worth your time. It could be yours sooner than you think." He nodded once.

"I hope not!" Luke didn't want the fallout dropped in his lap.

Father smirked. "I'm not dying, but there are other things to do with life when you get to be my age."

"I'll keep it in mind." He finished his soda to keep his mouth shut.

After the bill was paid, they left the restaurant. Luke held out his hand.

His father shook and pulled him into a one-armed hug, patting him on the back. "We must do this more often." The smile was patently fake.

"Have a safe trip home." They both nodded and walked off in opposite directions. As he started his car for the short drive home, his phone rang and he hit the answer button on the steering wheel.

Agent Ness's voice came through the speakers. "Excellent job, Major Sevrason. I think you assured him that you have no idea what he's currently doing and kept everything else sufficiently vague. We wish you'd been a little more enthusiastic about your relationship with Captain Bose, but on the other hand, keeping him guessing isn't bad."

"It's no secret that I'm not happy about Holly's involvement in this, Special Agent Ness. I thought that saying nothing about her would be a dead giveaway, but I'm not going to be the one to endanger her more."

"I can understand that, Major Sevrason. I'm not sure she'll be so understanding, but that's not my problem." He hung up.

He was right. Holly wasn't going to be very happy with him. But angry was better than dead.

Holly found Monday's meeting interesting and boring. Boring, because they went over the Sevrason family reunion in excruciating detail, analyzing each and every sentence for nuance. Interesting, because she hadn't known anything about Luke's mom. He never talked about her. The information about Das was even better.

Ness pointed at a map displayed on the screen. "Mr. Das has been quite busy. He's been looking at remote Colorado homes. We assume it's to stash Captain Bose, at least temporarily. He's also searching for a hold over Major Sevrason, other than a threat against his father. Unfortunately for him, there's nothing to find."

Holly couldn't hold back a sniff. "Luke always played the good boy. Never rocked the boat, never disobedient, never talked back to the teachers. Guess that hasn't changed." Luke smirked at her, but didn't say anything.

Ness continued. "Mr. Das is digging deeper into Mr. Sevrason's company. Luckily for us, he's found some of the so-called evidence against Major Sevrason. Mr. Sevrason set up email addresses with Major Sevrason's name on them, forwarded emails to those addresses, and then tried to edit them to look as though they'd originally gone directly to Major Sevrason. Some of the emails are from congressional staffers and junior executives of companies that Mr. Sevrason has assisted. No direct ties to congressmen or company CEOs—only people that a lower-level executive would be expected to work with." He sniffed derisively. "Fortunately for us, Mr. Sevrason is too paranoid to ask for too much help, and he doesn't understand the concept of metadata. His editing is a joke. We know exactly where those emails originated."

That was good news. But Holly wanted to know when Das or Sevrason would make a move.

He looked into the camera. "Major Sevrason, you should hear from Mr. Das soon. Please play along with whatever he wants—we want him to think you're tired of being in the military and want the good life."

Luke's expression was grim. "Copy that. If he asks me to abduct Holly immediately, do I stall him?"

"Yes." Ness nodded. "A classified exercise with a local Army unit that you can't miss would be ideal. He couldn't easily check, and with a little time, we could probably get the Army to make it look real. Try for a date a week or two away."

"I'll do my best." Luke grimaced.

"That's all we can ask." Ness paced. "Mr. Das has tried to create a case for incompetence against Captain Bose. But since your last project just finished, and the launch failure was proven to be a rocket manufacturing problem, there isn't much he can do. He may go back farther and try to discover something earlier in your tenure with the program, or a program you've worked on in the past, but the farther he goes back, the harder it is to adjust things. And he doesn't have the technical background to make any accusation stick." Ness sniffed. "No offense, but a captain doesn't have enough power to make big financial decisions, so he can't alter anything in his field of expertise. He was attempting to create an embezzlement, but Captain Bose doesn't have any access to the accounting side of the contracting world, just the writing of requirements and testing of results."

"All true." She'd never been more grateful for the ridiculous complexities of government acquisitions in her life.

"Even if he comes up with a plausible scenario, we'll make sure everyone knows it's fake in the end." Ness nodded.

"Thank you." Not that it would help, because retractions and rebuttals were always assumed to be cover-ups. But she had options. She had a degree, and she could do something else for a living. Avoiding Luke Sevrason for the rest of her life was a bonus. She ignored the sadness that followed her thought; a left-over longing from childhood.

The meeting finished shortly after, and she retrieved her phone from the lockboxes outside the classified area. Luke had sent a text.

> You'd make it through just fine. You're a survivor.

Holly killed the burst of warmth from his approval. She didn't need a man's admiration; she knew her self-worth. But she couldn't hold back the pleasure entirely.

AFTER A WEEK OF no contact with Das, Luke was ready to hunt the man down and shake or strangle him. While he sipped coffee at his desk on Monday morning, the office phone rang. "Major Sevrason, training. Can I help you?" He sat up in the ancient metal chair, reaching for a pen, and winced at the ominous squeal.

"Captain Sevrason, this is Ravana Das. I'd hoped to speak with you earlier, but the Inspector General's office has been too busy."

He picked up a pen and focused. Even with the conversation being recorded, he didn't want to miss anything. "It's been busy here, too."

"Quite. Anyway, on the subject we spoke of earlier, have you discovered a way to get Holiday alone?"

Luke would tell him as little as possible, while still giving the man something. "Yes. We've dated a few times, and she trusts me." She didn't, but she could fake it.

"Do you think you could get Holiday to take a short trip with you?"

Das was getting to the point. "Depends on where, when, and how long. And what I get in return."

"I have successfully quarantined the data that I have on your father's company. If you deliver Holiday to me, I will give you the data on a thumb drive, and you can do whatever you'd like with it."

All Das needed to complete his villain profile was a thin mustache to twirl. "How do I know this is the only copy and you won't double cross me?"

"Unfortunately, with computers these days, it's very difficult to prove anything is gone. But if I double cross you, I would expect you to come after me personally. Since I'm much older than you, I expect you would make me very uncomfortable at the least." He didn't sound very concerned. Probably counting on his father making him a fall guy and unable to do anything but rot in prison.

"That's a mild way of putting it." Thinking of Holly in Das's hands, Luke snarled the words.

"Do we have a deal?"

"I need to make one thing crystal-clear." Luke put every bit of his officer's training into his voice. "I won't be a party to injuring or killing someone, especially a fellow officer." Hopefully, that didn't scare the delusional Das off, but if it did, he didn't care. He wanted to pound Das into a bloody pulp just for thinking about Holly as his.

"I certainly have no intention of killing or injuring Holiday. Resorting to violence is distasteful."

Luke snapped the pen he was holding in half, sending black ink spraying across his hand. He had no doubt that Das would resort to more than distasteful to accomplish his mission. And Holly would receive plenty of abuse in that man's hands. Luke dropped the broken pen in his garbage can and shook drops of ink off his hand. "All right then, we have a deal. When and where?" He spoke deliberately, to keep his fury from showing in his voice.

"A few weeks from now. I'll contact you."

"I'll need warning. The Army doesn't conform to a standard work week. They like to hold exercises over weekends, and sometimes we don't get any warning. I can't miss those." That was absolutely true. Mikells would kill him personally.

"I will give you as much time as I can."

The guy was a real piece of work. "I'm not going absent without leave for my father's screwups. Going to jail for being AWOL wouldn't help any of us."

"I understand. I will text you a time and place." The phone clicked off.

Luke sat, shivering from adrenaline, and tried to clean the remaining ink from his hand. He needed a shower, or a drink, or both. He was seconds away from losing his breakfast at the thought of Holly in Das's hands.

His cell phone buzzed with a text from Ness.

Good job.

At least the feds were happy. Hopefully, Holly would be too, even if the discussion infuriated him. He sent Das an email with his cell phone number and washed his hands, trying to recover his normal calm demeanor. But he'd felt better after a failed mission. He gave up and headed for the minimalist squadron gym—he needed to sweat the fear and anger away.

That Friday night, he joined Holly and Kristen in the Peterson Air Force Base Officer's Club. The Lieutenant Colonel promotions had been announced, and according to tradition, the selectees were buying drinks. Not knowing anyone on the list in Colorado Springs, he sent congratulations to those he knew on other bases and arrived a little late. It didn't take him long to find Holly and Kristen; they'd collected quite a crowd.

He slid in next to Holly and bent to whisper in her ear. "You heard?"

"Finally. I can hardly wait for this to be over." She took a small step forward. "I've got more good news. Colonel Haywood is getting me an ops assignment!"

Kristen bounded to Holly, hugging her. "That's awesome! Congrats!"

His stomach sank. She could be sent to a remote assignment, and he'd lose any chance to make things right, let alone foster a relationship. He forced a smile. "That's great. Where and when?" He wasn't the only one to ask.

"With the 3rd Space Operation Squadron at Schriever. I'll start next September." She grinned and clasped her hands, an unusual show of emotion for Holly. "I'm so excited! I'll actually get to do command and control on communication satellites. When I come back to acquisitions, I'll have a much better idea of what the control interfaces should look like."

Relief shot through him. He waited for all the others to congratulate her, then pulled her into a quick hug. "That's great, congrats."

"Yes, congratulations, Captain Bose." Lieutenant Colonel Jason Lee stood behind Holly. "Good things happen when the people buying the stuff have to use it."

Holly pulled away from him, turning to Colonel Lee. "I agree!" She grinned. "By the way, since you said you don't get out much, I've been meaning to invite you to our Friday dinners. I can send you a text with the location."

"Thanks for the offer, but I'm usually working." He smiled at Holly and carefully didn't look at Kristen.

"Friday nights are for fun!" Kristen's tone was outraged.

Luke held back a laugh. She was a couple of years younger than he and Holly, and sometimes it showed.

"Not for directors." He turned, very slowly, toward Kristen, looking like a man headed for his doom but wondering how much he'd enjoy the journey. Luke recognized his expression.

Kristen gave him a blatantly sexy smile, cocking her hip. Every man in the area turned to look at her. Luke had zero interest in Kristen Lake but still paid attention, wondering how she did that voodoo. "Wow." She shook her head, wagging her finger at Lee. "You need to get out more. Come on, buy a girl a drink, will you?" Kristen hooked her arm into Lee's and dragged him toward the bar.

Kristen's skill and guts were impressive. The male officers surrounding them watched longingly and slowly dispersed.

"I guess she decided to go for what she wanted." Holly laughed.

Luke caught Holly's gaze. "Sometimes you just have to call 'fight's on' and commit to the target." Once this mess with the FBI was over, he wasn't waiting. The fight was on, and he was going to win.

A week and a half later, Luke's cell phone buzzed on his ancient scarred steel desk.

> Wilkerson Pass Rest Area, Saturday, 1100.

Notice on a Tuesday afternoon; far less than the week he'd asked for. He'd wait for the feds to reply, since they'd have gotten the text when he did. He tapped his keyboard, updating his training plan for the coming exercise, but couldn't keep his eyes off his phone. As he waited, the minutes dragged, each one taking an hour.

A text from Ness buzzed.

> Agree with his plan.

Luke blew out a breath of relief and replied to Das.

> Copy, Wilkerson Pass Rest Area, Sat 1100.

Don't be late.

Ness sent another text.

Meeting this afternoon. Don't change your routine, but come to Peterson at 4:00 pm.

Those orders were contradictory, but he knew what Ness meant. He emailed Mikells, telling him he'd have to leave early for the meeting, then saved his training plan, because he wasn't working on that anymore. He had more important planning to do.

He'd driven by that rest stop on Highway 24 during the Beaver Creek ski trip, but he'd never stopped there. A commercial mapping program would give him a general idea of what the area looked like. Then he'd find airspace maps, terrain maps, and see if training imagery was available here at the squadron. He'd be prepared for anything and everything by the meeting time.

Holly arrived at the conference room early. She was jittery, but that might just be the extra coffee. Most likely, it was anticipation. She couldn't wait to get her life back. When she entered the room, she found Luke pacing along the far edge of the conference table.

He paused for a second when she came in, then resumed walking. "You heard?" He glanced at her, wearing his usual grim, this-is-a-bad-idea face.

She went to her usual seat but didn't sit. "Just the place and time."

"That's all I've got." He kept moving. Luke's display of nerves was unusual.

"Aren't you happy that we'll get this over with and get back to our real lives again?"

He didn't stop. "Sure. *If* it goes as planned."

They had the might of the FBI on their side, and she'd seen no sign that Das or Luke's father were brilliant. "Why wouldn't it, Luke?"

He stopped and frowned at her. "Aren't you the one who just had a rocket launch fail? Millions of hours, millions of dollars, and still things blow up." He brought his hands up and spread them, miming an explosion. "A plan only lasts until first contact with the enemy."

"That's why we make lots of alternative plans. Sure, sometimes things go catastrophically wrong." She scowled, thinking about the rocket failure. "But even when everything blows up, there's usually a bright side or a way out. As a pilot, I'm sure you've had things go bad, but you've survived." They were stuck with the current circumstances. She wasn't going to worry about what couldn't be changed.

"I've gotten spectacularly lucky more than once. That's why I'm worried." He crossed his arms.

Two FBI agents entered the room. Luke smoothed his expression and joined her, pulling her chair out. She nodded her thanks and sat.

More people in suits and business casual entered the room wearing visitors' badges. It would be standing room only, but she wasn't giving up her seat. Even the four-star general's executive officer showed up, sitting in a chair at the back to monitor the meeting. Holly appreciated the show of interest and support.

Special Agent Ness started the meeting, displaying the text exchange between Das and Luke on the screen. "Ladies and gentlemen, we have our starting point." He clicked a remote, and an aerial photo of the rest stop and highway appeared, a big arrow pointing at the rest stop. "Here is the Wilkerson Pass rest area on Highway 24. There's only two ways in and out. East on Highway 24 back toward Colorado Springs, or west across South Park to Highway 9. Once you get across South Park, you can then go to Breckenridge and Frisco, and possibly Interstate 70, or get on Highway 9 to Canon City, or stay on Highway 24 to Salida or Leadville. But there are a lot of miles across a lot of open ground before any real turnoffs going east or west. Makes it easy to stop a vehicle." He paused.

A voice came from behind her. "What about flying?"

Ness nodded. "There isn't a legal landing zone at the rest area at Wilkerson Pass, but we'll have a State Patrol chopper up just in case." A man in a Colorado State Patrol uniform raised his hand but said nothing.

"There are a lot of miles of dirt roads out there, too. What about those?" the same voice asked. Holly turned but couldn't tell who was asking.

Ness frowned. Was he annoyed by the interruptions or by the questions? "Another reason to have a helicopter. Chase vehicles can stay far back, then move in when necessary."

Luke slapped his hands on the table, rising halfway from his chair. "Wait a minute. I thought we weren't going to go through with any abduction?"

Ness's head reared back, like he was offended. "Certainly we're not planning on that. But mistakes happen. We plan for all contingencies."

"Then let's have a proper operations briefing. Go over the ideal plan, then the contingencies. Questions come at the end." Luke shot a scowl behind them, then sat. Luke was very unhappy and made sure everyone knew it.

Ness, on the other hand, looked quite pleased about Luke's interruption. "Agreed, Major Sevrason. I'd prefer to do this the right way. Please hold your questions." He scanned the room, then brought his attention back to her and Luke, while bringing up the next page of his presentation. A detailed diagram of the rest area appeared, and Ness picked up a laser pointer. "Since it's winter, the lot is officially closed, but we'll have the gate opened and stage construction equipment as an excuse. On Saturday, Major Sevrason and Captain Bose drive to the rest area in an undercover vehicle we'll supply. You'll park here, at the southwest end of the parking loop. Major, back into the parking slot."

Luke nodded.

"We'll have two sniper positions and undercover units here and here and here." Ness pointed to locations across the highway from the rest area and parking places spread out around the loop. "We believe he'll park next to you and either ask you to transfer Captain Bose to his vehicle or get in yours. Either way, do nothing until you receive the USB drive and confirm the information on it. We'll give you a laptop for that. He must pass real information to you. We believe he'll try to give you nothing. Be ready to drive away at the first sign of a weapon. If you're outside the car, make sure Captain Bose is with you and keep a vehicle between you and Das. Tell him to toss the USB to you. Do not let him get close. If we see a weapon, we'll move in no matter what information is or isn't passed. You two just duck. The vehicle will be bullet resistant." He shrugged, seemingly unconcerned with their safety. "If he does give you the USB drive, and the information looks real, then say the words, 'It's real,' and drive. We'll move in."

They should have instructions for her, too. "How am I supposed to react during this? The guy threatened me. That's how all this started, remember?"

Ness nodded. "Assuming it's Das who comes to the pass—and there aren't any guarantees it will be him—react how you normally would."

Holly scowled. "Das might not be at the pass? He's got people working for him on this? That's information you should have led with." She held up a hand to stop his explanation. "If it's some stranger, I'll just sit there. If it's Das, I'll yell at Luke that this guy threatened me, and we need to get out of there." She'd almost certainly feel that way. It was easy to be brave sitting in a conference room on base, a lot harder out in the real world. She'd survived so far by running—fast feet were the best survival tactic.

"Understood. Major Sevrason, you tell Captain Bose that you're making a business transaction, and it will only take a moment. Then the next move will be up to Das or his representative."

Luke's scowl had become permanent. "Why would I talk to anyone but Das?"

"Because Das thinks you're interested in your father's money. Play along." Ness frowned at Luke, then looked at her. "If there's a weapon, we'll move in immediately. We won't take chances with your safety." Ness lifted his chin. "Otherwise, you'll follow the same procedure. If the information is real, then say, 'it's real' and drive away. We'll arrest that person and get them to turn on Mr. Das."

Despite his words, Ness didn't care about their safety. But his plan was stupid. "If they don't turn, will I have to watch my back for the next twenty years? I want this over with and done. What do I have to do?" The situation had to end, or she'd have to run again, which was impossible while in the military.

Ness looked outwardly concerned, but she got a distinct feeling of satisfaction. "There's certainly an option for you to play along, but since you aren't trained special agents, I'd rather not do that."

Ness might be saying the right words, but Holly was pretty sure he didn't mean them. "I'm not an agent, but I am an officer, not a shrinking violet." Whatever Ness's motivations were, she wanted Das out of her life. She'd do whatever it took to get there.

Luke put his hand on hers. She pulled away, uncomfortable with the public display of affection in uniform, especially in front of so many officials. "Holly, you haven't had survival training, let alone the evasion, resistance, and escape parts of SERE. Captivity is no joke."

Ness broke in before Luke could continue or Holly could retort. "The plan is to take anyone showing a weapon down immediately. We'll also have you two outfitted with the latest in surveillance and tracking equipment. Major Sevrason, your cover story for Captain Bose is that you're going sledding. That way, you'll be equipped for cold conditions."

"If things do go tango-uniform, and we end up abducted, where is the guy taking us?" Luke asked.

Ness frowned, then his expression cleared. Probably figured out that the phrase "tango-uniform," meant "go horribly wrong." "He's been exploring properties online, but he hasn't bought or rented anything with the accounts we've found. He could have found an empty house that he could break into and use for a night or two. We're checking everything he or his associates have looked at in that area. We're tracking their internet use closely."

Holly asked the obvious question. "Who are these associates?"

"Neither he nor Mr. Sevrason have contracted professional help, but Das has a large extended family. Several of the men have been in the military, some even in special ops. But they're all in his age range and haven't been active for years."

"You don't forget how to do that kind of stuff," Luke growled.

Luke was right. It seemed odd that Ness had delayed telling them about these additional people.

"No, you don't, but you do get out of practice and out of shape." Ness shrugged, seemingly dismissive. "His extended family owns dry cleaners and restaurants. Five male family members traveled to Colorado this week, staying in a Denver chain hotel. They've done little but eat, smoke, and watch TV and movies."

Holly could see tons of holes in Ness's so-called plan and wondered what else he'd hidden. But in the end, she wanted to get the whole thing over with more than she cared about Ness's dubious motives. "Back to the basic plan. If there's no weapon involved and Das refuses to give Luke the USB drive unless I get in his car, what do we do?"

"Major, just keep telling him that Holly isn't leaving your car until you get the USB drive and check it." He raised both hands. "Play on the 'I'm an officer and I'd never lie' concept, so he trusts you."

Luke glared at Ness. "And if he insists I won't get anything until she's in his car?"

"Drive away. Or you both get into the car." Ness spread his hands in a helpless shrug.

"And if he pulls a weapon then?" Luke practically bit out the words.

"Use the duress word. It's 'harmony' for this operation."

"Harmony?" Luke asked dubiously. "Duress words are supposed to be obscure, but that's ridiculous."

Holly had the solution. "That will work. 'Hey, can we all live in harmony, please?' or 'let's have some harmony,' or something similar. I'll sound like a pacifist. I don't talk like that, but my sisters do. He'd never know the difference." She'd hardly spoken to the man.

Luke shook his head. "Then he's got two hostages, with the feds surrounding the car. That never turns out well for the hostages."

Ness scowled at Luke. "We have an excellent track record with hostage recovery. But it's better if you resist.

If Das drives off without giving you the USB, then you drive away, too. Go the opposite direction Das goes. We'll get another chance."

"You've got a wiretap, right? Maybe Das will get pissed off and vent to one of his guys, and then you'll have him." Luke raised both brows.

Ness shook his head. "He doesn't vent. He never discusses, just gives orders. He's very controlled. The only break in his behavior has been his obsession with Captain Bose. If it wasn't for that, neither of you would be here. He's also not stupid. If we have him surrounded, he is smart enough to know how hostage situations end. He's shown no risky behavior or any sign of a death wish." He looked at Luke. "Do you have a feasible alternate suggestion, Major Sevrason?"

"No," he snapped.

"We'll have you fitted with the latest gear and weapons. But we don't think you'll need it. It's precautionary." Ness rolled into specifics, giving each agent a position and making sure the legal team had the appropriate search warrants.

Holly couldn't keep all the agents' positions straight, but her part was pretty easy. React normally, run if needed. Soon it would all be over forever and she could have a real life, not one hidden in the shadows. As he went through contingency plans, Holly was relieved Ness was more prepared for trouble than it had seemed initially.

When the briefing ended, Luke and Holly stayed behind with Ness. "You two have a date Friday night at Captain Bose's house. We'll put a couple of agents inside the house before you arrive and outfit you with clothing and equipment. I need your sizes. You can note your preferred styles, too." Ness handed Luke a notepad. "Do you both have good boots? Something you can run in, not bulky snow boots. Waterproof hiking boots and wool socks are ideal."

"I've got hiking boots and gaiters." Luke wrote on the notepad, then handed it to her.

Holly wrote her sizes on the paper. "Me too."

"That should work." Ness took the notebook back.

"Am I supposed to cook for everyone Friday night?" Nervous excitement was running through her body—cooking was the last thing she wanted to do. She doubted that would change on Friday.

"No." Ness waved away her concerns. "We'll keep monitoring Das and Sevrason and keep you up to date. We'll see you Friday night."

"Wait a minute, Ness." Luke held up his right hand. "You forgot a very important contingency."

Ness turned to him, brows raised. "What's that?"

"The contingency where something happens and we're on our own." Ness opened his mouth, but Luke held up both hands. "Don't tell me it can't happen because it can. And whatever you say doesn't matter—I'm telling you what we're going to do, and that's run. I'll get Holly, and we're going into full enemy territory escape and evasion mode. Is that clear?" Luke stared at Ness.

Ness held Luke's gaze and nodded once. "Absolutely. I would expect nothing less. If everything goes wrong, extract yourselves from the situation." Ness's expression was blank, but the tension in his shoulders said he was angry. "Anything else?"

Luke shook his head no, his jaw clenched so tightly the muscles popped.

Ness turned to her. "Captain Bose?" She shook her head no, and Ness walked out. Holly followed Ness. Finally, the end was coming. She'd get all this over with and go back to her normal, safe life.

Luke put a hand on her arm, gently pulling her to a halt. "Holly, wait a minute, will you?" He grasped her hands. "Are you sure about this? I'm worried, especially for you. The feds are approaching this much more casually than I'd like."

"You're worried for me, but not for yourself?" She tried to pull away, but he gripped her hands tighter.

"I'm not the one in the hot seat." Luke grimaced.

"I wouldn't be so sure. Das could decide the handoff isn't worth the trouble and shoot you in the parking lot." She realized she was clenching his hands and forced them, and the rest of her, to relax.

He shook his head. "Too big a risk. There are cameras in that parking lot."

"It might not be Das. One of his family members might not be so concerned. Or smart. They might just shoot both of us."

Luke shook his head again. "That wouldn't do anything for Das. He needs both of us alive, but he's planning an ugly revenge on you. I am not going to let that happen."

She glared. "If it's a choice between you getting shot and me getting assaulted, assault is survivable. And there are opportunities for escape. Dead is done." Survival was all that mattered in captivity. He ought to know that from his SERE training.

His eyes widened and his head reared back. "When did you get so grim and fatalistic?"

She snorted. "Luke, I've lived a lot of years since high school, and some of them haven't been easy. It changes a person. Plus, one of my best friends is an expert on survival. Amy's taught me and Kristen some good stuff." She tugged her hands out of his.

He released her, sliding his fingertips across her palms. "You've changed since high school, but then, so have I."

His words cooled the warmth his fingers had created. "I'm not so sure." Privileged, wealthy, charming, handsome; all those things made his life so much easier than hers. He still had a distinct advantage over her; he was a pilot and they ruled the Air Force. Holly's career was solid so far, but one bad decision could change that in an instant.

He frowned. "I don't take anything for granted, and I take life more seriously. Making life and death decisions tends to do that." He folded his arms across his chest.

Holly shrugged. "You're more serious; I'll agree with that, but you're still the same basic person. Back then you were an arrogant, but smart, jock. Now you're a pilot. Same attitude." She put her hands on her hips and raised her chin in a superhero pose. "I'm the best and you peons know it!"

"Oh, come on." He chuckled but frowned. "I was never that bad."

Holly laughed. "No, you weren't. If you had been, you wouldn't have bothered with me, unless it was a bet or something."

Luke glared. "I loved you. I thought we'd date during college, even if it was long distance. Hearing you were getting married to some guy you didn't even know was horrible. I didn't want to go to that stupid dance, but Daddy Dearest insisted on keeping up appearances. I wish I'd told him to go pound sand." He turned away.

She'd meant it as a joke, not an accusation. "Luke, wait!" She grabbed his arm. "I'm sorry. I wasn't throwing shade at you. It was a bad joke."

Luke didn't turn and his fists clenched. "I overreacted. Sorry. I'm just on edge."

"I think we both are. Let's get dinner." Maybe Kristen was still around. She could smooth things over.

He sighed and held the door open. "Sure. Let's go."

Walking to her cubicle, Holly had plenty of time to regret her words. They had so much history, so much bad blood. Even innocent remarks came out ugly, and some of hers had been mean. She had to do better. They couldn't trust Ness. They had to work together and watch out for each other, so she needed to get over her childish feelings of betrayal. Especially when Luke's part was so small and so long ago and her father was to blame. He'd organized the emotional blow on purpose, ensuring she had nowhere to turn, so she'd comply with his demands. He'd never dreamed she'd have the guts to leave on her own.

But she had. She'd been brave and determined, and it had paid off. No matter what happened, she'd survive. But making it through her current problem would be a lot easier if someone was watching her back.

Even if she couldn't trust Luke with her heart, she had to truly forgive him, or neither of them would ever move on.

Chapter 10

Holly's work week dragged, but she had a long, boring but important document to read, keeping her busy. Friday afternoon, Holly flew out the door and bounced in her seat as she drove home—she couldn't wait to get the whole thing over and done.

At her house, Luke waited at the front door. She hugged him for any watchers, then tugged him inside. In the hallway upstairs, a male and female flashed FBI IDs at them, the male agent steering Luke toward Holly's guest room. Good thing she'd cleaned.

The woman led her into her bedroom. "We've outfitted a ski coat and pants with voice-activated recording equipment and trackers. I've got more for your boots." She picked up the jacket. "We've placed a thin stiletto knife, a vial of pepper spray, and a common handcuff key along the inner forearm seams. They unravel when you pull the small tab just beyond the cuff. You should be able to reach that with your hands cuffed behind you." As the agent spoke, she turned her jacket to demonstrate, then handed it to her. "We chose a slalom racing jacket, so the outer forearms have plastic guards, meant for bashing poles out of your way." The agent brought her forearm up in front of her chest, then pushed it away to the side. "We replaced those with thicker, harder panels, in case someone comes at you with a knife, and layered flat batteries behind them for the trackers. The jacket is waterproof but thin, though, so wear lots of layers."

Holly looked at the seams, but she couldn't tell they'd been modified. The forearms of the jacket were stiff and heavy, but unless a pat-down was extra thorough, the weapons wouldn't be noticeable.

The agent picked up the pants. "We've done the same in the pants lining, down here on the inner calf seam, with a different, but still common handcuff key. There's a pepper spray that looks like a lip moisturizer in your left pants pocket. It's named 'Hot Stuff', so you don't use it accidentally." She handed the pants to Holly. "Captain Sevrason will bring a weapon, but you're not supposed to know what's going on, so you shouldn't bring a firearm." The woman frowned. "Unless you carry concealed all the time?" Holly shook her head, and the woman nodded. "We've placed chemical hand and foot warmers in your pockets and a pack of matches and a lighter."

"Great. Can I bring some food?" She always carried food, water, and cash, plus a pre-paid credit card and silver and gold coins in her backpack. The agents had zero idea how paranoid she could be.

"Absolutely." The agent nodded. "Whatever you would normally bring." She turned toward Holly's bed. Clothing with a winter camouflage pattern covered the comforter. "We've placed recorders, trackers, tiny icepick-type knives, and handcuff keys in the seams of your long underwear in the same places, inner calf and forearm. The knives have a sheath over the tip, so you can't stab yourself, but you should be cautious. And these recorders have a lot less power and memory, so try to keep your outer wear with you."

"Okay." They'd thought of everything.

"Now, we'll attach an even smaller emergency tracker and recorder to the underside of your upper arm and just above your ankle with padded flesh-colored latex. I hope you're not allergic?" The woman raised her brows.

"No." And even if she was mildly allergic, it would be worth the irritation.

The agent worked on her ankle and wrist in silence—it didn't take long, and the sharp chemical smell of the adhesive quickly dissipated. "There you go. You can shower in the morning, just be gentle in those areas." The woman handed her a tampon; the tip was red. "Put this in place in the morning. There's a tiny folding knife and a tracker in there. Don't worry, it's been sanitized and there's no chance of getting cut until you open the knife. The tracker is extremely short-range, almost useless, but the tech insisted. I think she wants to test her design." She shrugged.

"It's clever." Holly chuckled. "I guess there's an advantage to being a woman."

The agent winked. "We didn't give Major Sevrason the equivalent, so yes." She sobered. "Also, if you tell an attacker you're on your period, it might give you some protection. That doesn't work with everyone, but it will with some."

Holly nodded, her excitement dimming with the serious threat. "The men are my father's age, so they might have religious taboos."

She nodded. "It might anger them more, though, so be careful." She grimaced. "If they strip you to your skin, activate the tracker/recorder by pressing straight down for two seconds on each one." The agent pointed to the latex-covered flat disk glued under Holly's arm, about two inches above her elbow. The other was on her inner calf, concealed by a boot sock; neither was easy to see or free. "They don't have much power, so wait until it's necessary. Do both if possible. If you're cuffed behind your back, you can usually lean on the arm tracker and activate it. If your feet are tied, it's harder, but usually possible. If they search you, hold your arms away from your body to minimize the chance of them feeling that arm tracker, even though the coating makes it difficult to notice. By the way, swallowable trackers are a myth. They need too much power for safety. Any questions?"

Holly shook her head. The overlapping tech seemed very complete. "Not that I can think of. Thanks very much for your help."

"No problem. The safer you are, the easier our job." The agent left Holly's bedroom. "We'll show ourselves out. Pizza should be delivered soon. Good luck." The two agents trotted down the stairs and out the back door.

Holly followed them down and collapsed on the sofa. "Wow, I feel like I'm in a James Bond movie."

"Yeah, or a Tom Clancy novel." Luke sat next to her but didn't say anything else.

Holly was on an emotional rollercoaster. Scared, excited, worried, and happy it would all soon be over. Talking it over would probably be healthy, but she didn't want to, especially with Luke.

"I'm starving. Stress makes me hungry." Luke's smile flickered, then disappeared.

"The agent told me pizza was coming soon." Holly smirked at him. "How do you stay in shape and stress eat when you fly all the time?"

Luke shook his head. "Flying isn't stressful."

"Not even combat?" The possibility of being shot out of the sky was scary.

He shrugged. "Generally, refuelers are well behind the lines and we've got fighters protecting us. Missiles are always a threat. But we plan for that, and I never think about the risk until I'm safe on the ground."

He had a point. "I guess that's true for me, too. I'm good during a crisis, then I fall apart afterward."

"Our training tends to reinforce that reaction." Luke grimaced, then sighed, and glanced at her.

Something was bugging him, but he'd decided not to tell her. "What?"

"Are you sure you're ready for this?" His face scrunched like he'd bitten something sour.

She snorted. "Ready or not, it's here and I'm doing it. I want it over." Saying the words hardened her resolve and made her feel more confident. But Luke didn't seem to feel the same.

"I guess I can understand that." He turned toward her. "I'm worried. I don't think this operation will go well." He grimaced. "Would you mind if I held you? Just that, nothing more." Luke's expression was pinched, something she'd never seen before.

Holly stared at him. He'd admitted being scared for her, but his concern seemed greater than that. She couldn't deny him the comfort of a hug, especially when she wanted that, too. She scooted over on the couch and snuggled next to him.

He took in a breath like he was going to speak, but he didn't. He pulled her in tight, wrapping his arms around her. She nestled close, loving the warmth, security, and reassurance. After a few wonderful moments, he pulled her onto his lap, nestling her against his hard chest and putting his chin on the top of her head. "You feel perfect."

Holly put her arms around his waist and her head against his shoulder and held him tight. "Yeah." She could barely get the word out. He felt perfect, too, like coming home after a long absence.

Luke's arms tightened, and he trembled. Holly held on, sharing the comfort she had to give. After what could have been hours, Luke's grip on her relaxed, but he didn't let go. "Thanks, that helped."

"My pleasure." And that was absolutely true. Holly wasn't sure if she should slide off his lap or stay. Being held, secure and safe, was comforting. She'd missed hugs. Getting to the endgame was exciting, but she was just as worried. There were too many things that could go wrong. But his presence held her fears at bay. She refused to worry about anything while she felt so good.

After a few more minutes, his fingers stroked, then his hands slid up and down her back, and his lips dropped to her neck. Heat rose in her body and pooled where she snuggled on his lap. His arms tightened, and he kissed up her neck, across her cheek, and to her mouth. His lips were soft against hers, giving her quick little kisses, with plenty of opportunities to pull away.

And she should, but she couldn't. Not when it might be the last time. She responded, and he pressed a little harder. She opened her mouth, bringing her tongue in to twine with his.

He accepted her invitation, deepening the kiss. She moaned into his mouth, the sound wrenched from her.

The doorbell rang. They both jumped. Holly slid off his lap, rushing to the door. She huffed a laugh and squeezed her eyes shut. She'd forgotten everything but Luke. Not a good idea, especially in the middle of a mission. She checked her doorbell camera, opened the door, and accepted the pizza. She'd been stupid to get lost in him.

Luke stepped up next to her, offering the driver a tip. She took the pizza to her small dining room table and got out plates and glasses. She had to keep her head. They were the subjects of an FBI sting, lives were at risk, and she'd been down the road to romance with Luke before. They'd crashed and burned. Getting involved with him was not a good idea.

They ate in silence, both of them shooting glances at each other, but Holly wasn't willing to speak first. Luke evidently didn't want to, either.

After they ate, she packed up the remaining pizza. Without being asked, Luke scrubbed the plates and silverware by hand. After he finished, he dried his hands. "I'll grab my clothes from your spare room and get going." A smile flickered. "Thanks for letting me stay for dinner." He trotted upstairs, and when he returned, he went straight to the door.

Holly opened the door. "See you tomorrow."

"Tomorrow." He kissed her cheek, then left.

She went to bed, but sleep eluded her. Thoughts of the mission tangled with the passion of his kisses into a huge confused mass that left her reeling and bewildered and searching desperately for her normal, serene attitude. It was exactly the wrong time to lose the one thing that helped her survive all these years. She turned over again and attempted a meditation mantra—it hadn't worked the last dozen times or so, but try, try, try and she might succeed.

The next morning, Luke picked her up in a large, black SUV. All the windows, including the windshield, were coated with one-way film. The vehicle's interior was mostly standard, except a couple of empty brackets. The infotainment system had additional options, all cryptically named. "Interesting vehicle. FBI?"

Luke pulled out. "No. It's a sanitized Secret Service motorcade support vehicle. One broke down last time the president visited, and it's been sitting in the base motor pool ever since. The feds commandeered it for us. It's four-wheel drive, of course, plus bullet resistant glass, armor plating, run-flat tires, traction control, automatically deploying tire chains, and a modified suspension that should let me drive it like a race car." He laughed. "Since I haven't had the official defensive driving class, I've been told to stick within the legal limits." He huffed. "Like I'll care if the chips are down."

"No kidding."

He flashed a smile at her, but it died quickly. "They can hear every word we say, by the way."

"I figured as much." Holly tried to think of a neutral conversation topic but eventually, settled for watching the miles roll by.

The closer they got to Wilkerson Pass, the more nervous, eager, and nauseous she got. She tried to stay calm and not fidget, but she must not have been successful.

"Nervous?" Luke continued scanning the road in front of them and the mirrors.

She grimaced. "A little. Are you?"

"Yes, like before a mission." He chuckled. "Don't worry, once we get there and things get started, you'll be fine."

"Promise?" She desperately wanted to regain her normal control.

"Yes." He winked. "You'll be great. And I'll be right here, keeping you safe."

She turned toward him in her seat, grateful for his help, but she could take care of herself. "I'm glad you're here, but please don't do anything stupid for me. Don't forget, Das is just an old man who smokes like a chimney, not a Ranger or a SEAL. He startled me before, but I'm ready. I'll take him down myself."

As they passed the sign for the rest area, Luke laughed. "I'm sure you will. Most likely, we'll get enough evidence right there in the parking lot and he'll get hauled straight off to jail." He made the turn into the almost empty parking lot, driving around a temporary barrier with a sign that read, "Rest Area Closed for construction." The feds must have decided to limit collateral damage by closing the lot but not using the big metal gate that normally secured the area. That would have been difficult to get around in the large SUV.

"Spooky." Three cars were parked around the lot, and orange traffic cones were stacked near the stairs to the restrooms. Orange plastic fencing blocked access to the restrooms.

Luke shrugged one shoulder. "You wouldn't think so if you didn't know what was supposed to happen." He drove to the pre-planned location and backed into the slot, leaving the vehicle running.

Holly tried to laugh but gave up. "You're probably right. I guess we wait." She tried again to sound unconcerned, even if her heart rate was elevated. "With the restrooms closed, what's your excuse for stopping here, making me wait before our sledding date?" She put a little outrage in her tone.

Luke laughed. "So sorry about that, love. The next person who borrowed the Beaver Creek house from my father found something I left there."

"He couldn't mail it?" A couple at the far end of the lot, dressed in active winter clothes, fussed with their backpacks. Snowshoes rested against the rocks behind them. Obviously one of the undercover teams.

Luke hummed. "It's a weapon?"

"That's almost plausible. Except that very few military people would ever be that careless with a weapon. Where were we going sledding?" Keeping her movements casual, she searched the rest of the area. Two people stood near the restrooms, looking at a phone, and two more sat in a third car. Their backup was in place. She didn't look for the snipers.

"We weren't sledding. We're going to a romantic hotel. I'm buying plenty of spiked hot chocolate and taking advantage." He waggled his eyebrows wildly.

Holly couldn't hold back a laugh. She was sure his story was designed to lighten the mood. Then an older, white, four-door sedan pulled into the parking lot.

"Go time." Luke unfastened his safety belt. "Take a deep breath, hold, and then release, letting out all the tension."

She did and then smiled at him. His was as strained as hers. The car pulled in on Luke's side, leaving a space between them. It wasn't Das, although there was a certain resemblance, probably one of his relatives. Holly's mood sank, but her nerves disappeared. She unfastened her seat belt, made sure her gloves were in her pockets, and put one hand on her small backpack.

Luke left the vehicle running and got out, leaving the door slightly cracked. Cold air cooled her warm face.

The driver got out, standing in his open door. "Major Lucas Sevrason?" A pistol handle showed above his belt.

Holly could barely hear him. But the threat was clear enough.

"Correct." Luke nodded. One of his hands gripped his pistol in the holster.

The man held up a USB drive. "Here."

"Toss it over and let me check it." Luke let go of the pistol. "Where's Das? The agreement was I get the information and he gets to talk to Holly."

The driver tossed the drive to Luke. "After you confirm the information, follow me in your vehicle."

Luke stopped with his hand on the back door. "That wasn't the plan. I get the information; Das talks to Holly. That was the deal." He put just the right amount of anger into his statement.

"The deal has changed. You bring the girl; you get the last copy." The man leaned back against his car.

Luke opened the back door and pulled out a laptop, inserted the USB drive, and scrolled through what appeared to be pages of data. "This looks real. But if he's changed the deal once, he'll do it again." He put the laptop on the seat and turned, pulling his weapon but keeping it pointed at the ground. "In a remote area, you could just kill me, so why should I?"

Holly clamped her mouth shut. No matter how much she wanted to get it all over with, Luke was playing his role.

The man flipped his hand dismissively. "Killing an active-duty officer would bring too much attention. You'll live. Follow me."

"And what do I tell Holly about this change of plans?" Luke slid the laptop back into the case, placing it on the floorboards, then slammed the back door.

"You planned a surprise. Trust me, it will look perfect."

Luke scowled. "This is a surprise all right. If you double-cross me, you'll regret it. I've got friends in higher places than Das does." He practically snarled the words.

"Right. Follow me." The man got in his car and backed up without waiting.

Luke closed the back door and climbed in the front, putting his seatbelt on. "I knew this would happen. I think Ness knew it too. He was just spinning his plan for his boss and ours. He wants a big splashy op. Probably needs the attention for a promotion or something." He pulled out, following the man.

Holly sat back and pulled up the mapping program on her phone. They got back on the highway, heading east, but they didn't stay on it long, pulling off on a country road going south. "Luke, do you know what's down here? I can't get a location on my phone."

Words appeared on the infotainment screen.

> You're headed towards Eleven Mile Reservoir. Use the navigation program on here.

She tapped the home screen button, then the nav program chimed. A map popped up, displaying them as a blue dot on the typical green map background. "We're headed towards Eleven Mile Reservoir. I think there are a bunch of summer cabins there." She'd searched for lake shore rentals for a vacation last year.

The white car took a right, then parked at the end of the dead-end road. White, snow-covered fields surrounded them. Holly shivered at the emptiness. That man could pull a gun and kill them when they got out of the car. Or kill Luke and take her. Her guts tightened, and dread slithered down her spine. *Try* to take her. She'd fight them to the end.

Luke pulled his weapon, leaving it on his lap. "I don't like this. Let's stay in the car and make him come to us."

Holly nodded. "I guess we keep playing this as if you're taking me on a surprise trip, right?"

The console displayed a message.

Yes, play along.

"The feds agree. Guess we're making this up as we go." Holly sucked in a deep breath, then let it out slowly.

The man walked up to them, and Luke rolled down the window partway, keeping his finger on the button. "Why are we stopping here?"

He crooked a finger. "We have another form of transport coming."

"Are we coming back here? I borrowed this car." Luke looked worried. He probably wasn't faking that at all.

"Don't worry. You'll be back very soon." The man waved them to come along.

A thumping noise drew her attention, then it appeared. "A helicopter? Oh, Luke, how exciting!" That wasn't in any of the contingency plans. But Ness had a helicopter, too, so they'd be okay. The agents would be right behind them.

"Yes, a helicopter. I'm glad you like it." He turned toward her and mouthed "no."

She glared a warning, then put a happy smile back on her face. She wanted this done, and if they arrested this guy now, they wouldn't get Das. They couldn't even make an abduction charge stick, since they weren't technically being coerced. They might make a bribery charge, but it would be minor.

The helicopter landed, creating a mini-blizzard, the thump of the rotors deafening. Holly got out, grabbing her pack and putting it on. Luke followed on her heels. The man led them to the door, opening it and pointing to seats behind the pilot and co-pilot. They hopped in. Holly took off her backpack and buckled up. The man closed the helicopter door and returned to his car.

Holly forced a grin and yelled, "Where are we going?" She hugged her backpack close.

A man in the right-hand front seat leaned toward them. "It's a surprise. No cell phones. They interfere with navigation." He turned forward.

Luke put his cell in his coat pocket. Holly smiled and hoped it looked real. A helicopter definitely hadn't been in any of the plans. They weren't offered headsets, so they didn't know what the pilot was saying. Luke gave her a grim look, then stared out the window.

They flew for a long time. Holly's stomach soured, and she couldn't help fidgeting, unable to suppress the nervous movement.

Luke put his hand on her thigh gently and smiled. "See, I told you it would be fun!" Then he turned back to the window, intensely focused. He must be looking for landmarks, which was smart.

She watched the ground, too, but since she wasn't familiar with the terrain from the air, nothing stood out. Just mile after mile of snow-covered fields, with the occasional group of trees and bare fences. Roads appeared, then vanished in the snow.

They finally descended, with nothing but trees and snow-covered fields in sight. She craned her neck. A minivan waited nearby. They landed, snow blowing again. A man in winter clothing opened the helicopter door, motioning them to follow him to the van through the mini blizzard and then waving them in. No one showed weapons. Das wasn't in sight. Holly's stomach sank, and dread weighed her shoulders down. But she was a military officer, not a little girl. A true survivor, and she'd make it through, no matter what.

They climbed into the minivan. The middle seats were gone, so they sat in the back. The windows were almost blacked out; it felt like climbing into a mine shaft. She wiped snow from her face and clothing.

The man who'd opened the helicopter door got in the passenger seat and turned to them. He looked like one of Das's relatives, too. "Relax, and we'll be at our destination shortly." His smile was insincere and oily.

Holly shivered a little, but she had a role to play. "Luke, I thought we were going sledding. Where are we going?"

"Don't worry, Holly, it will all become clear shortly, right, gentlemen?" He took her hand and squeezed.

"Yes, it's a surprise." The man's tone was menacing.

Holly turned her hand up, clasping Luke's. She might be wary of his intentions, but he was on her side and those men weren't.

The van took them along the snow-covered roads, twisting and turning, the trees getting thicker and taller. They entered a valley; the mountains rose higher on both sides, and Holly lost all sense of direction.

Luke stared intently out the window and held her hand firmly.

They turned onto a narrow, bumpy road that twisted and turned through a dark, sinister forest for what felt like an hour. The air in the van became heavy, her mouth drying, leaving a metallic aftertaste. Finally, they pulled up in front of a large log house with an attached garage. When the van door opened, Holly could breathe again. But the dread stayed with her. They'd traveled a long way from Wilkerson Pass.

The man who'd opened the van door jerked his head toward the house. "Come inside." They followed, entering a small foyer. "There's a hook for your coats." Ski parkas hung on most of the hooks already. By the number of coats, there were a lot of men inside.

Holly wrapped her arms around her waist. "I'm still kind of chilly. I'll just keep it." A bead of sweat rolled down her back, making her shudder, lending authenticity to her story, even if it was for the wrong reason.

The man shrugged. "Up to you. Come." He walked away. The driver was at their back, probably to make sure they came. Holly followed, with Luke following on her right.

They followed the man into a large, high ceilinged room, huge timbers crisscrossing the space above them. To her left, a kitchen, and in front of her, Das and Luke's father stood with drinks in hand near a mission-style sofa and two chairs. A sliding glass door led to a smooth, snow-covered surface. Two men with rifles blocked the patio door. Holly stopped at the edge of the carpeted living room. They were outnumbered and outmaneuvered.

Luke took a half-step in front of her. "Father? Why are you here?"

"I wasn't expecting you." He turned toward Das.

Das laughed. "Did you really think I trusted you? Now I can ensure your cooperation."

Das was so close to a supervillain mua-ha-ha laugh, it wasn't funny. Holly's stomach sank. This wasn't going according to plan at all.

Mr. Sevrason shook his head. "His presence is completely unnecessary. You hold all the cards here."

"I do now." Das smirked.

Holly remembered she should be shocked. "What is going on?" She frowned and took a step back. "Never mind. I'm going home. Luke, you haven't changed. Your surprises aren't fun." She spun on her toe. The van driver grabbed her shoulders and turned her back to face Das. She wrenched out of the man's grip but didn't try to move again.

Das glared at her. "You are home, Holiday. Your new home is with me. At least for right now."

And that statement wasn't ominous at all. "What are you talking about? I don't know you and I don't want to know you." She tried to turn again, but the man grabbed her coat and held her in place.

"You aren't going anywhere. Give me your cell phones." Das held out his hand.

Luke pulled his gun, bringing it halfway up. "I don't think so. We're both leaving."

The man holding her coat grabbed her hair below her knit hat and jabbed something hard in the small of her back, probably a gun. She squeaked. The men at the patio door pointed their rifles at them. Das shook his head slowly. "I don't think so. Cooperate, unless you want to see Holiday in pain."

"Understood." Luke gave his gun and cell phone to the van driver. The man patted him down, taking his wristwatch and a utility knife.

Holly didn't try to fight, just held her phone out. She whined, "Can't we all live in harmony?" The van driver patted her down. He was so busy feeling her up that he didn't check her coat pockets carefully, although he did find her big multitool. "Is this some sort of bizarre kidnapping scheme? I don't have much money."

"I don't need your pitiful salary." Das waved his drink dismissively, almost slopping liquid out of the glass. "You are here to fulfill the bargain your father made for you many years ago. Unfortunately for you, I no longer have need of a wife. You'll make an adequate slave."

All Das needed was a mustache to twirl. "Excuse me? I am a captain in the United States military. I am no one's slave. What century are you living in, sicko?"

"Hey, you told me you just wanted to talk to Holly. What in the world is going on here?" Luke took a step forward. The van driver waved a gun at him, and he stopped.

Luke's father said, "Lukas, shut up. We have no leverage here."

"Go pound sand. I should have never tried to save you." Luke's lip curled. He turned back to Das. "You said she wasn't going to be hurt."

Das snorted. "No, I said if she cooperated, she wouldn't be hurt. Let's test that theory." He smirked at her. "Holiday, take off your clothes. Now." He stalked across the room toward her.

Holly's fists clenched. Her nerves and bravado hardened into determination. "No."

The man behind her grabbed Holly's wrists tight, pulling her arms behind her. Das slapped her hard across the face, the force rocking her back into the man holding her.

Luke turned, raising his fists, but when the van driver pointed a pistol in his face, he stopped. Everything was going sideways. They were alone, and she was afraid.

"So much for harmony," Luke said loudly.

Das sneered at him. "Harmony is overrated. I think the Sevrasons need to have a father to son talk while I show Holiday her new role. Bring her." He walked away, entering a hallway to her right.

The man gripping Holly's arms forced her to follow Das. Luke stayed next to her.

Das stopped at the first door on the right. "Sevrasons, inside."

Luke reached over and squeezed her hand. He followed his father through the door but kept his gaze on hers until a man closed the door and stood in front of it.

Das entered the only door on the left side of the hall. Holly scanned the space. A large brass bed with nightstands on each side was on her left, with a door to a bathroom on the far side of the bed. A couch faced a TV screen on her right, and curtains were closed in the middle of the far wall, presumably covering a window.

"Over to the bed, Holiday." Das pointed.

The man marched her there. A metal chain with an open cuff at the end of it was bolted to the bottom of the bedpost at the foot of the bed.

"Take off your clothes." Das stood next to her, a twisted smile on his face.

"In front of all these people?" Her head rocked back from another slap.

"Now, or I cut them off you, and I won't be careful." He shrugged. "Your choice."

Holly returned to her earliest lesson—never show any emotion. She straightened to her full height, keeping her chin up and her face unemotional. She moved robotically and stared at the wall behind Das, so it would seem like she was looking through him. As she took off her boots and pants, she pressed the tracker/recorder on her leg and tried the female agent's approach. "I'm on my period. If I take off everything, you'll get stains." She grimaced. "Lots of clotting. Pretty nasty."

Das's face changed from lust to disgust. He slapped her again, knocking her to the ground. "Pick up the cuff, place it around your right ankle, and lock it."

The metal was cold in her hands. At the click of the lock around her ankle, she shuddered.

Das bent, grabbing her chin hard. "Think about where you are and what you are now, slave. There is no way out and nowhere to go, and I will not hesitate to hurt you." He surveyed her body. "You're too old for most of my clientele, but someone will pay for a military officer." His lip curled. "But if you continue to defy me, money means nothing." He pinched her chin, then shoved her back and walked away. The men with him followed, leaving her clothing in a pile beside her.

How did the feds miss that Das trafficked people? A metallic, scraping noise came from the other side of the door, probably a bolt or lock. That scraping noise should give her warning before they entered. She thought about everything Amy had shared about survival, resist, escape, and evasion training. Of course, Amy couldn't tell them everything, but she'd given them the basics. One of those was that the past wasn't important, only the present. Survive, resist, and escape—that mattered.

Holly waited, counting to sixty, then sixty more. Her face stinging, she pulled her long underwear top back on. The room was cold, and the clothing brought confidence. Or maybe just bravado. She took a handcuff key out of the snow pants, leaving the one on her leg in place. Listening intently for any sound from beyond the door, she inserted the key in the cuff lock. After trying several times, the lock finally opened.

Holly yanked the stiletto knife out of her jacket liner. Pulling up her sleeve, she cautiously stuck her forearm and dabbed blood on her panties, then hid the knife under the mattress in front of her. She slid the knife from her pants and put it under the mattress on the other side. Then she took the smaller knife from her long underwear pants and put it under a couch cushion. Keeping alert for any noise from the hall, she searched for a way out, peering behind the curtains first. There were boards—a shutter?—over the window, and no latches she could see. She slid the window open, hoping it wouldn't make any noise, then pushed on the boards.

They didn't give, but if she climbed on the windowsill, she might be able to kick it out. She gently closed the window and the curtains, then tiptoed to the bathroom.

There was a small bathroom window above the toilet. She closed the lid and stepped up. Nothing but a snowy landscape outside. The window was about two feet long by nine inches tall, and it swung outward on a hinge at the top, with a crank mechanism at the bottom. She'd have to remove the crank, but she could get through. Escape was worth losing a shirt or a little skin.

She glanced back at the door—better to do what she could while she was alert and relatively unharmed. Her stinging face was already changing to a painful throbbing. Pulling the mini-multitool they'd missed from her inside jacket pocket, she closed the window and unscrewed the latch mechanism from the window frame. She left the screws loosely in place so the latch wouldn't dangle. Das wasn't much taller than she was, so unless he looked closely, it would seem secure.

Should she escape now or later? It was still light, so it would be better to wait. If Das came back soon, she might regret her choice, but it was the smart play.

She barely turned on the water, so it wouldn't make noise, and drank from her hand. Despite hating the idea, she returned to the bed and refastened the shackle, shuddering. She hid the key under the mattress and pulled back the sheets to expose the mattress pad. Using the stiletto knife she'd hidden, she slowly sliced several long, narrow strips off the pad, making as little noise as possible, then hid them under the mattress. If, no, when she got the upper hand, she'd be ready to shackle him. It was her turn for an evil smile, despite the way her face ached with the movement.

She'd found a way out, hidden ways to defend herself, and had prepared to take Das out of commission. She was hydrated, so it was time for fuel. Pulling an energy bar from her coat pocket, she slowly ate, despite the additional pain. As she chewed, she cataloged items in the room that she could use as a weapon and memorized the layout. She'd be ready even in the dark.

Das must be used to victims, not survivors. They'd left her clothes and bought the menstrual period story. Her smile grew to a grin—they completely underestimated her. She was still in a lot of danger, but hopefully the FBI would roll in and she wouldn't have to do anything drastic. She finished the bar, put the wrapper under the nightstand, laid her pants out, curled up in her jacket and slipped into a meditation, ready for the next move. If the FBI didn't show before midnight, she'd rescue herself. And Luke, too.

Chapter 11

LUKE PACED THE SMALL room, his hands clenched at his sides to keep from hitting his idiot father. Holly could be suffering terrible things, and he couldn't do anything. Not with armed men outside the door.

"Lukas, please calm down." Father leaned against the door. "I can't take the stress."

Luke jerked away. "I don't care. I'm about two seconds away from killing you myself. I knew you'd gone bad, but trafficking? You are scum." He clenched his fists to keep from choking the piece of trash in front of him.

He held up both hands. "Lukas, please, I didn't know. Just sit, and I will tell you everything I do know."

"Fine. Talk." Luke sat on the twin bed closest to the window. Between the beds, a cheap nightstand held a clock but no lamp. Curtains covered a window large enough for him to get through, but it was covered with boards. Probably a shutter; brute force was noisy, but if that was the only way out, he'd take it. A door led to a small bathroom with a tiny window. But he needed Holly's condition and location before making any moves, although he was fairly certain she was across the hall.

They were in a spectacularly bad position. The helicopter must have taken the feds by surprise, and the sheriff's helicopter had come from Colorado Springs—it would have run out of fuel long before they arrived at the landing spot. The locators on them were small and, therefore, short range. He should have asked for the technical specifications. Das's people would have turned their phones off and removed the batteries, if not smashed them.

They had to self-rescue. Watching out the helicopter's window gave him an approximate location and direction to go when they broke out. Driving or walking wouldn't be easy, assuming he and Holly could escape.

First rule of captivity—no defeatist attitudes allowed. They *would* get out of here, and they *would* reach safety. He glared at his Father impatiently.

"Lukas, there was a reason I asked you to come back and join the firm. Not only is my health precarious, but Ravana Das had some very damaging evidence against me." He stepped forward, putting hands behind his back and spreading his legs—as if he was in command.

Luke snorted internally. The man commanded nothing but a boat on the river denial. "Real evidence or made up?" Not that he truly cared—his father had made his own bed, but he needed to know what was going on.

"Unfortunately, it's real. The majority our revenue comes from a certain political figure and that person is being investigated. That puts the firm in a spotlight, and me. Ravana Das can hide most of it, but I'm paying him a lot, and I had to help with his problem." He smiled. "Thank you for that. I truly appreciate you putting your father first."

Fury raging through his body, Luke lunged off the bed, hands reaching out for his father's neck, but he stopped when his knees hit the other bed. If his father had information, he needed it, and he couldn't reveal the FBI investigation. His father would use that information against all of them. "I'd never put you before Holly."

His father took a step back but kept the superior smile. "But you did. Obviously, I'm more important than any woman." He raised his chin.

Luke was happy to shatter his delusional world. "I'd put every woman in the world in front of you. You got yourself into this mess because you're a greedy slimeball. You can rot here for the rest of your life, and I won't care."

He glared, leaning forward in a menacing pose. "You'd better care. Das made sure you're going down with me!"

Luke snorted, then stared right back at his father. "Right. How is he doing that?"

"He has evidence that you have been working for my firm all along and emails and documents that tie you to the same political figures I'm tied to." He straightened and raised his chin again.

Luke sniffed. "Fake. Any competent investigator will see right through it. I've been deployed too much, I'm too low on the Air Force totem pole, and I've never been stationed in the right places." He held up his hand to stop his father's protest. "But I'll play along for now. I have no desire to get shot." He had to survive to rescue Holly and escape.

"That's all I ask, for now. I had no idea this would turn violent or that all these other people would be involved." He looked bewildered.

Luke shook his head. His father was a pitiful excuse for a human being. "You always think you're the smartest guy in the room." He marched to his father, grasping his shoulders and shoving him down on the bed. Then he bent over, glaring, and put one hand in the middle of the man's chest. "You are a selfish idiot." Luke thumped his father's chest, stomped into the bathroom, and closed the door, enjoying the sounds of indignant sputtering. Beating him to a pulp would be more satisfying, but he had to conserve his energy.

He used the facilities, then drank some water while exploring the small bathroom. The towel bars were thin, cheap metal and the toilet tank top too bulky. Plus, it would shatter after a single blow. The window was maybe a foot square—too small for him or Holly. He could pull out one of the stiletto knives, but using one successfully against two or more armed men was a long shot, even with the element of surprise. He drank more water. When he and Holly escaped, he had to be well hydrated. He needed a container because she might not have any water.

He leaned on the countertop and looked in the mirror, clenching the countertop so tight his hands hurt. If he pulled, he'd yank the whole thing off the wall. He could not think about what they might be doing to Holly. He couldn't afford to lose control. Survive and resist, then escape. That was all that mattered. Once he had his emotions back under control, he went back out.

His father sat up on the bed. "Did the great pilot come up with a plan?"

Luke didn't answer. He flopped back on the small bed, closed his eyes, and concentrated on his breathing. He had to rest his body, and that took putting his mind at ease. He could not think about Holly and what she might be enduring. He was in enemy territory, in the enemy's hands. He knew the drill, and he'd perform as trained even if it was against criminals, in the middle of America, rather than enemy combatants.

Patience. Observe. Analyze. Rest. Move decisively when you get, or make, the opportunity. Eat and drink when possible. Rest. He'd wait, then act.

Holly woke to a metallic scraping sound. She bounded to her feet, standing next to the bed.

Das entered, glaring. He pointed a wavering finger at her. "Take the shirt off."

"I was cold." She deliberately whined.

"I don't care. You will do as you are told." He pulled a pocket knife. "Take it off, or I cut it off of you."

She'd need the shirt when she escaped, and he might cut her. She pulled the shirt off, folded it, and dug in her jacket pocket, pulling out a tampon. "I need to use the restroom, or I can pee on the floor."

He slapped her across the face. "You will speak when you are spoken to. If you have a question, you will raise your hand." He unlocked the chain from the bedpost, then pulled it behind him, walking to the bathroom. She followed, moving her feet fast in small little steps so she wouldn't get yanked off her feet. He locked her chain to a loop bolted to the outside wall between the toilet and shower. "Stay." He laughed, leaving the bathroom without closing the door. His breath reeked of alcohol.

She'd used the toilet in front of a woman for random drug tests, so she closed her eyes, imagining that situation. The bedroom door slammed, and the lock scraped. She went, leaving the emergency tampon in place, and flushed the new one so the wrapper would be obvious in the garbage. Then she washed her hands and drank some more water. Dehydration was not her friend. She yanked and leaned on the chain, but it was solid.

Wrapping a towel around her shoulders, she closed the toilet lid and sat down. Then jerked in sudden realization—there could be surveillance. Cameras were tiny and cheap. But if they had any in the bedroom, they would have seen what she'd already done and taken her things. The FBI must be right about Das's underlings—none of them had current experience or they would have set up webcams. She'd been lucky, but she had to be more careful.

Since the feds hadn't shown up, she'd escape tonight. She knew where Luke was. As a pilot, he was trained in escape and evasion, so she'd take the chance of getting him out, too. She'd gotten away before and she'd do it again. She was a military officer, not a scared little girl. They had no idea who they were messing with. She sat on the bath mat, leaning against the counter, then used a yoga relaxation technique to rest.

The lock scraping sent Holly shooting to her feet. The van driver carried a bowl into the bathroom. She backed away, standing between the toilet and the tub. He set the bowl on the counter, then reached for her. She kicked with her unshackled foot, trying to hit between his legs. He twisted, and she hit his thigh instead, pushing him back.

He swore and punched her hard in the stomach. She stumbled backward against the wall, gasping for breath, but put her fists up. He limped out of the bathroom, muttering under his breath. After the lock on the bedroom door scraped, men shouted, hurling curses. After less than thirty seconds, they quieted.

When she could stand upright, Holly sniffed at the bowl and poked at it with the spoon. Rice, vegetables, and chicken in a very strong curry. They might have drugged it. She had a few more energy bars and she wasn't that hungry. She sat back on the floor, trying to remember how strong she was while her stomach throbbed along with her face.

She'd survived that blow, and she'd survive the next, then escape.

Chapter 12

HOLLY DROWSED ON THE bathroom floor with a cold washcloth across her face when the lock rattled. She rose, dropping the towels she'd draped around her for warmth on the counter when she spotted Das. As he walked across the bedroom, he wavered and stumbled. He entered the bathroom, unlocked the chain, and dragged her back to the bed, locking it to the bedpost. Inside, she cheered. She could probably light his breath with a match.

"Sleep on the floor." He climbed into the other side of the bed. "You have to earn bed privileges." His words slurred.

Relief and excitement almost made her jump for joy, but she bowed her head and sank to the floor. When Das turned out the light, she put her bra, long underwear top, and sweaters on, curled up on the snow pants, and pulled her jacket on top to keep warm. She rested, counting off the minutes, and waited for Das's breathing to change.

Snoring came from the bed, growing louder. Moving slowly, Holly put her jacket over her ankle to muffle any noise and worked the key. When she was free, she slid up next to the nightstand and unplugged the heavy brass lamp. Then she unscrewed the shade and the bulb and wrapped the cord around the top of the base.

She visualized her moves, preparing herself for success. Then she crept to Das's side of the bed, gripping the lamp where she'd wrapped the cord.

Das lay on his back, mouth open, snoring loud enough to wake the dead. She took a big breath, raised the lamp high on her right side and swung it down and across, fast, into his temple. She didn't want to kill him, but better him than her. He grunted and started to rise, so she hit him again.

He stayed down.

Putting the lamp down, she fished out the mattress pad strips she'd cut, tied his wrists to the headboard, gagged him, and fastened the shackle around his ankle. Then she tied his other ankle to the footboard. Smiling with grim triumph, she dressed, leaving her jacket and snow pants off. She retrieved the largest stiletto knife and padded to the bathroom, closing the door behind her.

She opened the window, letting the latch dangle free, grateful it didn't squeak. Standing on the toilet, she stuck her head out. She didn't see anyone, but it would have been difficult to spot a person in the dark. Pushing her jacket and pants through, she hoped Das's buddies didn't have night vision goggles. With a small jump, she landed on the windowsill, gasping at the pressure on her bruised stomach. With no time to waste, she wriggled out, dangling over the long drop. The snow would help cushion her fall. If she fell correctly. But she would.

Gravity took over, and she dropped. Her boots caught on the window ledge, slowing her, then she hit the ground. She let her arms collapse, rolling on her shoulder and over on to her feet. She couldn't help a gasp of pain when her shoulder hit, but at least she didn't scream. She'd have a bruise, but she was free.

She stood, peering into the darkness, hoping no one had heard her. After putting her pants and jacket back on, she walked around the house, staying close under the eaves to avoid the deep snow drifts. She kept her right fingers near the siding, in case she slipped, and rotated her shoulder. Sore, but no sharp pain, so she didn't break it.

Stopping at the corner, she peeked around it, then continued. Hopefully Luke was awake. Making a lot of noise to attract his attention wasn't an option.

LUKE

After some yelling from the living room, the van driver brought dinner, his passenger standing in the doorway with his pistol drawn. Luke ate the rice and curry mix, hoping it wasn't drugged, and most of his father's. A TV blared, with occasional laughter and scraping noises from the wall outside their room—their guard leaning and pacing. When nothing changed, Luke napped, setting a mental alarm for zero-one-hundred, since the clock radio was flashing 12:00. A thumping noise and laughter woke him. Sounded like drunks crashing into the walls. *Perfect.* They'd be split up, impaired, and easier to avoid and take out.

He yanked the top sheet off his bed, entered the bathroom, and drank water until he couldn't drink any more. After flushing the toilet, he ripped strips from the sheet. Returning, he put a washcloth over his father's mouth and a knee on his chest. "Stay quiet and still and I won't hurt you. If you move or scream or do anything but lie here, I will knock you out cold. I don't care if you die. Do you understand?" He made his voice even and unemotional, which should terrify his scumbag father.

His eyes wide, he nodded. Luke shoved a strip in his mouth and wrapped a strip around his head, gagging him, then tied his wrists and ankles securely to the bed. He whispered, "I will send someone for you. Don't make a sound or you're dead. Understood?" His father nodded frantically, the whites of his eyes showing. Excellent—terror would keep him quiet. "Don't think about betraying me. You're a traitor. I'll have no problem killing you." That wasn't quite true, but thinking about what might have happened to Holly enraged him enough to make the threat believable.

Luke put his snow pants and boots on, then opened the window slowly, hoping it wouldn't squeal. He had to figure out how to get the boards off. He pressed out, up, and down, but they didn't budge. Climbing on the bed and kicking it out would make too much noise, but he had no choice.

He froze at a crunching noise—footsteps in the snow, moving slowly. Shoot. Das had enough brains to set roving guards. The footsteps stopped in front of his window. He held his breath and listened.

A muffled brushing noise, followed by metal rattling on wood. A quiet exclamation of exasperation that was too high-pitched to be a man. "Holly?"

The noise stopped. "Luke?" a female voice hissed.

"Yes." Holly got away! She was amazing. He almost laughed with relief but held it back.

"Can you hold the shutter up? It's too heavy to hold and unfasten."

He forced his fingertips into the tiny cracks between the boards to hold the weight. "Got it." The fasteners scraped and squealed. He winced at every sound. Still, better than kicking it out.

"Last one," Holly whispered. It screeched, and he gripped the boards, his fingers cramping. "Down."

He tried to keep his grip and lower it, but it was heavy. It slipped off his fingertips. Holly grunted but lowered it without slamming it against the house. The thud into the snow seemed loud, but it wasn't. Luke put his coat on and wriggled out the window.

The full moon revealed a snow-covered landscape resembling a grainy black and white movie. Nothing moved except their breath, freezing in the frigid air. "Are you okay?"

Holly nodded.

He desperately wanted to pull her close and hold her forever, but danger surrounded them. He turned and closed the curtains, then slid the window shut. He could put the shutter back, but it might make too much noise. Better to leave while they could. "We'll check the driveway for cars. Maybe we can boost one." Holly nodded, so he turned and led the way toward the driveway. He placed each foot carefully to minimize the noise. At the front, the driveway had been plowed, but there were no vehicles. The garage was attached to the house. He'd rather break in, take a car, and disable the rest, but better they get away quickly than take the chance of getting caught. There were just too many men with guns. And they might have posted a sentry in the garage, plus garage doors were noisy. If they got caught in the garage while disabling vehicles, he'd be dead, and Holly would get badly beaten.

Luke pointed toward the road. Holly nodded and walked. Luke bent his head and spoke in a low tone. "Das?"

She grinned then winced. "Unconscious and tied up."

He grinned back. He wanted to hug her, but they had to move fast. When they got to the end of the driveway, he pointed the way out. "Great job. Are you sure you're okay? Any injuries?" That wince worried him. Das had hit her hard. He clenched his fists, wishing he had time to go back and return the favor.

Holly shook her head. "I'm fine. A few bruises, but nothing major."

He longed to pull her into his arms and kiss her, but time wasn't on their side. Besides, if she'd been assaulted, his touch might be unwelcome. "We'll stay on the road until sunrise unless we hear a vehicle. Then we'll go cross-country. Let's make tracks." He broke into a slow jog and counted his strides to get a rough distance. His breath fogged his face then blew away in the cold night air. Counting also kept him focused on escaping. He stopped every two hundred paces to listen for five seconds, then kept going.

He paid attention to Holly's breathing, but she never faltered or slowed, just kept moving next to him. They both slipped occasionally and had to keep their strides short because the road was slick and rough in places. They alternated jogging and walking for hours. Steep hills covered with snow and trees rose from both sides of the road, and there was no sign of life or other houses. Not that they'd dare risk trying to hide in anything nearby.

They'd have to move off the road soon. Luke didn't want to because moving through deep snow would be too slow. They finally passed the field where the helicopter had landed. It seemed so long ago, but it hadn't even been twenty-four hours.

An owl swooped close in front of them, making both of them jump. The raptor kept flying, so they kept moving. Finally, they came to a crossroads. Unfortunately, there wasn't a sign and there were no tracks on the other road. It hadn't been plowed, either. It probably led to a vacant piece of land or a Forest Service gate, and their footprints would be all too obvious.

Luke's stomach sank. The narrow mountain valley was too restrictive. They'd have to leave the road soon, or they'd get caught for sure. Decision time. "Let's take a break. We need to keep moving east, but I don't know how far. Let's move off the road." Luke walked into the deeper snow, testing each step before putting his full weight on it. A twisted ankle or knee would be deadly.

Behind a large fir, he brushed away the snow and sat. As Holly followed him, he held his right hand out and patted his lap with his left hand. "We need to share warmth now that we've stopped." But if she'd been assaulted, she might not want to touch him. "If you're okay with that."

She frowned but put her hand on his shoulder and sat in his lap. He wrapped his arms around her tight. The relief coursing through his veins made him lightheaded.

"Too tight!" she wheezed.

"Sorry." He loosened his arms, and she relaxed against his chest. "Are you okay? How did you get away? I'm so impressed."

"I'm fine. Bruised, but nothing worse." She lifted her hand to her face but didn't touch it.

"Thank God." He blew out a sigh of relief. "Will you tell me?"

"Sure." She shrugged and started. As she recited her story, Luke smothered his urge to go back and finish Das and the rest of them off. Remaining free was much more important.

"There are pilots who've been through survival training who wouldn't have done as well as you have. You stayed calm and positive and that's a huge part of the battle. You're so strong, so amazing." He pulled her close again but kept his arms loose. She didn't need pressure on her bruised body, and he didn't want to make her feel trapped. He couldn't see her face well enough to tell how badly she was hurt—the moonlight washed the color out.

She huffed. "We'll see how strong I am when we get going again. My stomach, shoulder, and face hurt, but it won't stop me. Are we moving off the road now?"

"We have too, soon. I know we're somewhere west of Leadville, but we're many miles from town and deep in the mountains. I'd like to stay on the road for another hour or so, but I don't want to take a chance that we'll get caught. And since the road is at the bottom of this narrow valley, leaving it means climbing up steep, untracked terrain, with deep snow. It's going to be extremely difficult. We also need to find somewhere to hide for the day. Maybe the FBI will find us through the trackers, but I'm sure these are short range, so we should plan on self-rescuing."

"Let's get going." She stood up.

He didn't want to let her go, but she was right; they needed to move. Luke shoved all the emotion into the back of his brain and concentrated on escape and evasion.

Back on the road, they alternated jogging and walking. Luke looked back every one hundred paces, watching for moving lights and surveying the hillsides surrounding them for hiding spots and paths, ready to run if necessary. As they trekked, a flat, snow-covered expanse appeared next to the road. It could be a meadow or a pond. Or both.

As the road continued, the meadow widened, then narrowed again. A steep, heavily treed ridge bordered the back side of the meadow. That hill would be a pain to get up, but the ridge looked like it might widen out and go in the right direction, which was down the mountain range and to the east. "Holly, hold up."

He found a few small pines and cut branches from the back of them with the stiletto from his pants seam. They jogged down the road another quarter of a mile. A line of bare trees crossed the flat expanse. "I think that's an irrigation ditch. We'll cross next to those trees to the hill. Walk behind the trees and try to stay in the wind-blown hollows as much as possible. I'll brush out our tracks behind us."

She nodded. "Good plan." She stepped into the deeper snow at the side, testing each step as he had. She was a quick study.

He followed her, turning back to wipe out their tracks. Depressions remained where they had walked, but it might be enough to keep their tracks from being noticed at vehicle speeds. Once they were next to the trees, they found wind-carved hollows as he'd predicted, saving them effort and time.

When they reached the densely treed hillside, he stashed the cut branches under some downed trees so they wouldn't be blown onto the open ground and give them away. The trees covering the hill were tall, skinny firs and pines, spaced two to ten feet apart, with lots of small branches, the lower branches bare. The snow was lumpy; probably a lot of fallen trees. There wasn't much underbrush, which made it easier for them to travel but also easier for anyone to see them.

Holly headed up the hill, pushing between two pines. Branches cracked.

"Holly, wait." She turned back to face him. "I don't know how much you know about winter hiking or hiking off trail, so please don't be insulted if I tell you something you know already."

"I won't be." She was calm and poised.

He smiled, irrationally proud of her. He didn't have anything to do with how she'd been trained, so his gratification was ridiculous. *Concentrate on the mission.* He cleared his throat. "Off a trail or road, safety beats speed, so test your foot placement before you put your full weight down. These snow mounds probably cover fallen trees, but we don't know how stable they are, how rotten they are, or how many layers there are under the snow. If you slip and fall, broken branches on those logs can stab you. Step over, not on, whenever you can. Also, staying dry is critical." He unzipped his coat, shivering when the cold air hit the base of his throat.

"If you get hot, open your jacket so the sweat can evaporate. It would be better to take it off and carry it rather than sweating through it. Don't let your feet get wet, either. Make sure your boot tops are tight, and your pants are tight over the boots, then the gaiters over that, if possible. Eating snow is normally a bad idea because it lowers your core body temperature. But we don't have any water and we'll be warm hiking up the hill, now would be a good time to eat snow and get a little fluid in. Don't go straight up the hill—try to zigzag across it. Takes more time, but it's less strenuous, and you're less likely to slip and fall."

Holly nodded, shoved a handful of snow in her mouth, and headed up the hill, diagonally. Luke swallowed a couple of handfuls, then followed her. She was so much lighter—she climbed over trees that collapsed under him with enough noise to wake the dead. But her legs were so short, going uphill meant wading through waist-deep snow. After following her for a short while, he tapped her on the shoulder. "Let me go first. My legs are longer."

She nodded. "I'll break trail on the flats."

They slipped and slid despite climbing diagonally. Each step was a huge effort, pushing through the deep, deep snow, putting a foot down, cautiously testing the stability, then dragging the trailing leg to the next step. When they finally reached the ridgeline, Luke called a halt. "Hey, let's rest a minute."

Holly found a snow-covered mound to sit on. He sat next to her, breathing hard, and grabbed some snow to eat. "We're going to have to be super careful going down this ridge. It's so steep, it will be too easy to slip. And since we don't have a map, we have no idea what the terrain is like. I'll warn you now that we may end up climbing back up at some point because we could run into a cliff."

She smiled but didn't look at him. "That's okay. I'd rather be out here with the possibility of falling off a cliff than be a victim." She huffed a laugh. "I don't think that awful old man thought his plan all the way through. Even shackled at the ankle, I can fight pretty good."

Luke's fists clenched. "He underestimated your determination by a long shot." He wanted to go back and pummel the man, but escape was far more important. He clamped down on the rage and terror, conserving his energy for later.

"I'm not the meek little girl my parents tried to raise." She grinned fiercely, more a baring of teeth than a smile.

Luke shared her grin. "No kidding—you're amazing. And before I forget, thanks for rescuing me. I was about to kick out that shutter, but I'm sure someone would have heard that."

"You're welcome. It would have been very noisy. Those latches were heavy duty." She shrugged. "Breaking you out was selfish; you're trained and I'm not. My chances are much better with you."

Luke laughed and couldn't help sliding an arm around her waist for a gentle hug, avoiding her bruised shoulder and stomach. "SERE training is pretty tough. I've had winter survival too, which should help. Plus, two people have better odds than someone alone—there's a big morale boost." He grimaced. "But we're not in a good spot, love. Traveling cross-country is hard, and in the high mountains, in the winter, with next to no gear? It's almost suicide. We've got to be really, really cautious. We have a couple of advantages." He shook his head, thinking about the soft-bellied men with big guns. "Those guys aren't likely to follow us through the woods. They aren't in good enough shape. But they can and will drive the roads continuously and watch for us. They could get that helo back, too, and that would be very bad, especially if they've got an infrared sensor, which they might for firefighting. Or a drone. Those are easy to get these days. That's why I want to hide during the day. We can build a shelter and put snow over it, so it looks like we're a bear in a den or something. Good thing the moon is near full, or we'd never have a chance."

"I have a small light on my keychain, but I don't know how long it'll last." She shrugged.

Luke turned toward her. "While we're here, what else do you have?" He dug his emergency supplies out.

"I have a couple of energy bars, a micro-tool, an extra packet of hand warmers, a tiny first-aid kit and another lighter." She pulled a shiny wrapped bar out of her pocket.

"Wow, I'm impressed. You're way better prepared than I am. I have a lighter and matches but no food." She was astonishing. He was the SERE graduate; he should have been more prepared. He'd been counting on the FBI's tech too much.

"You forget, I've been on the run before." She grimaced. "Why do you think I bring that backpack everywhere? I've got my passport, along with some gold and silver coins sewn in the liner, more food, and a plastic water container. I wish we could have looked for it, but I know we couldn't."

He couldn't believe how tough she was, always ready to pick up and go. "I'm amazed and kind of angry. You shouldn't have to live like that. I wish I'd known." He should have known, but he'd let his pride take over. "I'm sorry. I abandoned you, and even back then, I knew better than to believe my father about anything."

She shook her head. "It's more habit than anything else at this point. I thought I was safe in the military."

"You should be. This whole plan was ridiculously risky. The feds should have just charged Das and my father. Any competent investigator would have found more. I think Ness is looking for a big show to get promoted, and he used us." They shouldn't have gone along with the plan.

"No, this is better." Holly leaned away from him to look at him, and he released his hold. "They'll go down for abduction and assault with deadly weapons. Remember, you were the one who said the past didn't matter. The present does."

Holly was so calm, and it wasn't just an act. She was better at survival despite his extensive training—she had the right mental attitude. He stood. "If we're going to make those charges stick, we need to get going. It will take time to build a shelter. While we walk, look for stacked rocks with an overhang or trees that have fallen together. Something we can build a shelter under."

"Okay." She nodded and got up.

"Move slow. We can't afford to slip." The trees were thick on the steep ridge, giving them plenty of handholds, but there were a lot of deadfalls under the snow. They both slipped and fell, getting banged and bruised. Tree branches whipped their faces, and the rough trunks and sharp broken branches tore their clothes. Luke couldn't tell how far they'd gone or exactly where they were going because the trees were too big and too close together. With no other choice, they went down.

Then the trees disappeared. They stood on an exposed ridgeline of snow-covered rock that went a few more feet and then dropped off into sheer air.

Luke groaned. "This is what I was afraid of. We're cliffed out." He looked back up the ridge and then bent to either side. On his left, the road they'd taken away from the house glimmered silver far below. On his right, the hill had a gentler slope, but the trees were thicker. "Okay, we'll head back up but not all the way to the top.

We'll try to get down the north side." He pointed toward the right. "I don't see any cliffs."

Holly nodded and turned back up the hill. They climbed back up, using their footsteps for about thirty minutes and taking off their jackets on the way up. Luke's legs burned, and he panted. "Holly, let's take five."

"Okay." Holly leaned against a tree and pulled out an energy bar. She unwrapped it and broke it in half, handing him the larger half. He tried to take the smaller one, but she pulled it away. "You're bigger than I am. You need more calories than I do."

Luke snorted. "I don't think either of us is in danger of gaining weight on this trek."

She barked a laugh, then gnawed on the frozen energy bar. They traded bites of the bar with handfuls of snow. She tucked the wrapper into her jacket pocket. "My legs are burning. We've got to stretch before we sleep, or we won't be able to move after we get up." She leaned over, stretching her hamstrings.

Luke copied her. As he stretched, the burn didn't ease, but his muscles lengthened. "You're right. This is the hardest thing I've done for a long time." If he expected Holly to trust him, he had to share his feelings. "I wish you were safe at home, but being alone out here would be rough. I don't know how you did it all those years ago. I'm sorry I wasn't there for you."

"You can do amazing things when there are no real alternatives." Holly huffed. "Although, if I'd known just how tough those first couple of years would be, I wonder if I would have tried." She looked at her feet for a moment, then met his gaze. "You can quit apologizing. There's nothing to be sorry about. We were both stupid kids, but we lived." Her mouth twisted up on one side. "Succeeded, even."

She was right, but he'd been dumber by a long shot. "Are you sure? Because you have every right to hate me."

Holly gazed at the trees, then looked at him again. "I did. I felt betrayed by you and everyone else, but I've been putting all the blame on you, rather than on my family where it belongs. It was easier to blame you. You had it so easy, with your family's money and your charm and good looks."

"Like you don't have charm and good looks?" She didn't seem to realize how stunningly beautiful, graceful, and enchanting she was. He'd fallen under her spell.

She shrugged. "I'm considered attractive, but I don't have charm. I'm aloof and cold." She raised both eyebrows at him, then gave him a half smile. "Keeps the weirdos away."

"I don't find you to be aloof or cold, and you're devastatingly beautiful. Whoever told you that is an idiot." Maybe he still had a chance.

She grimaced. "Probably not. But I was wrong about you having it easy. Your family is just as bad as mine. You just hid it better than I did."

"No way." He couldn't keep back a laugh. "No one can hide like you can."

She raised her eyebrows again. "See, aloof and cold."

He shook his head. "No, it's hard to tell what you're really thinking. I never know unless you tell me. Fortunately, you don't have any problem telling me what you think, good or bad. Mostly bad." Luke laughed ruefully and looked to the north. "We need to get going. I don't know what time it is, but I'm betting it will be light soon, so we need a hiding spot."

She nodded. "Give me a second of privacy." She walked up the hill.

Another good idea and much easier for him. He turned away, unzipped, and let go against a tree to avoid a yellow spot.

Holly called, "Luke, come here, I've found something."

He walked up the hill, scanning for her. "I can't see you. Say something."

"Over here! To the north a bit."

Peering through and around the thick trees, he found her. He climbed, his legs burning and stomach growling like a bear. That bit of food hadn't done much but rouse his appetite. "What did you find?"

Holly waved her arm for him to follow. They walked around a stack of rocks jutting out of the hillside. A few feet later, she pointed. A large rock overhang created a sheltered spot about eight feet long, three feet wide, and maybe two feet high. They'd fit, but just barely. "Great job. I'll cut some green branches to sleep on if you can find some bigger branches that we can lean across the front to block the wind." All that rock should shield them from a heat sensor. It would probably block their trackers, too, but that was good. With no guarantee the feds were close, he'd rather not lead the bad guys right to them.

"Sure." She followed him back to the ridgeline.

Normally, he'd never cut living wood, but in a survival situation, all the usual rules went out the window. He gathered armfuls of small diameter branches to give them plenty of insulation. They couldn't risk a fire unless it snowed, hiding the smoke. Unless it got colder—they might not have a choice.

He cut boughs with the stiletto knife and carried several armloads to the shallow cave. Holly leaned sticks across the opening, and he wove larger green branches through them. Before the sun rose, they had a crude survival shelter. "I hope you're not too sweaty."

"Worried my stink will drive you out?" She grinned.

He laughed. "No, I'm sure I smell worse. I don't want you getting chilled when we stop."

"Right." She grimaced. "I tried to move slow. Dragging these branches is a little awkward."

"It's about to get even more awkward." He winked. "Let's use those toe and hand warmers. Retie your boots after you put the toe warmers on, so you can run if necessary, but keep them loose for better circulation. Button and zip everything, and put your hood up. You climb in first and make sure you've got enough branches to keep you up off the rock. Pull up extras for your head. Once you're settled, I'll climb in and curl around you to share body heat. Maybe we'll get some sleep." He rather doubted it, but they had to try.

"Okay." She bent and untied her boot laces.

He did the same, putting the toe warmers on and then sliding the hand warmers into his gloves.

She kneeled and wriggled into the shelter, then rustled around. "I think I'm set. Come on in."

He pulled his hood up and crawled inside, trying to not move the branches. He curled his body around Holly's, putting his left hand on her hip, and his right arm under her head, staying away from her bruised stomach and shoulder. The branches were lumpy, but they kept him off the cold rock. "Not the most comfortable bed I've ever had, but it's actually not the worst, either." He pulled her in tighter. Her head tucked below his chin and her body snuggled perfectly into his.

"Really? What was the worst?"

He chuckled. "During survival training, it was raining buckets. I couldn't find anything like this. I ended up sitting up against a big fir tree, trying to sleep. I wasn't very successful." He'd been so miserable.

"No one to share body heat?" She snickered.

"Nope, my wingman had already been captured. I made it through the night, then they got me the next morning. So, I was miserable, cold, and wet during POW resistance training." Of course, they'd all ended up wet, cold, and miserable; it was part of the experience.

"I wish I'd had your training. It would have come in handy." She shuddered.

He tightened his arms, hoping to comfort her, but he had to back that with words. "You've got to be kidding. You played those men perfectly. You're amazing." She was so brave.

"I thought it was a long shot, but it did work. It was still the worst experience of my life." She shuddered again.

"I'm sure it was. It sounded horrific." He really wanted to run back and kill every single one of them, starting with Das. But that would be stupid. He had to think about survival, not revenge, and keeping Holly safe. Including her emotional safety. "Am I making it worse by being this close?"

"No, no, you're fine. You put off a lot of heat—it feels good. I'm not comfortable, but I've slept in worse places too."

"Really? Where?" That was terrifying.

"Homeless shelters, buses, bus stops, doorways." She shrugged. "You don't really sleep because you're too worried."

"I can't imagine. I'm so sorry." He'd been such an idiot and had it so easy in comparison.

"Wasn't your fault. Water under the bridge."

He'd spend the rest of his life making sure she felt safe. "I'm not so sure, but we need to concentrate on today and get some sleep. Are your feet okay?"

"Yes, I'm fine."

She felt so good, so right in his arms. Exhaustion was a blessing in some ways. "If you need to roll over or get out, just elbow me. I'll probably roll over a lot, too. Branches over rock aren't particularly comfy."

Her body shook when she chuckled. "Try meditation. It might help." She breathed deeply and evenly. He matched her and counted sheep.

Someone was chopping wood. He jerked awake, then froze. That sound was a helicopter, but they had no way to know if it was the bad guys or good guys. He tried to peer out between the branches they'd laid over the opening, but the sunlight on the snow blinded him. Holly was behind him, gripping his jacket, pulling it tight. He put his hand over hers and squeezed gently. The chopper was far overhead, and by the fading sound of the rotor blades, it kept moving. Then it got louder again, returning, and then faded behind them. After a few minutes, the noise returned, but farther away.

He rolled over to talk. Holly looked up at the rock over their heads, then at him. "They're doing a standard grid search. Could be the good guys or the bad guys, but if it was the good guys, I think they would have picked up a signal from us. These transmitters are pretty low power though, so the rock might be blocking the signal. It's probably just as well because the bad guys could search for a signal too. We should probably pull them out."

"So, we just stay put?" Holly's shoulders rose.

He curled his gloved hands around hers. "It's the safest thing to do. If it's the feds, they can get the Army special forces unit on Carson to find us. It's a perfect training scenario." He forced a smile. He'd watch for the markings he'd been taught, but that was a long shot. He'd plan on a self-rescue.

"I guess we try to sleep." She shivered.

"Are you cold?" He wasn't comfortable, but he wasn't freezing.

"A little. I'm okay when you're behind me, but it's hard for me to stay close when we roll over. You're so much taller than I am." She shivered again.

He rolled onto his back, pulling her on top of him and holding her tight. She had so much less body mass than he did; of course she'd get cold easier. "Okay. I've got a plan. We're turning over at the same time, right?"

"Yeah. We have to." She huffed.

He rolled on to his side and let her go. "Take off your jacket." It was a little challenging in the tight space, but he got his jacket off and pulled off his outer fleece layer.

"You're kidding me, right?" Her shoulders jerked up towards her ears.

He had a long sleeve shirt and wool sweater, so he'd be fine. "Nope. Take it off, turn so your back is to my front, and then put your jacket on backwards." He wriggled into his jacket, leaving it unzipped, and loosened the cord tighteners at the hem.

"Okay." He helped her wriggle out of her coat and held it so she could pull it on backward.

Laying his jacket open, he pulled her close, keeping her jacket tight around her. He rolled to his back, so she lay on top of him, her back to his front. Then he zipped his jacket around them until it stopped and laid his fleece underneath his shoulder and rolled them on to it. He fastened the top of her coat snugly around her neck and upper back, so it would stay tight to her body and keep her warm. Then he tightened his hood and collar, keeping his jacket around her shoulders. Good thing she was tiny and his jacket a little too big. "Now, when I roll over, I'll take you with me, and you'll stay warm, and we'll both be warmer with the fleece underneath." His upper chest was a little cooler, but with her head next to him, he was warm enough.

"Good idea. Thanks."

"Sure, love. If it's too hard to breathe with the hood over your face, pull it under your head. Your hat and my chin should keep you warm enough. Try to sleep." With her head always on his bicep, his arm would probably fall asleep, so he'd have to turn more often, but that was a small price to pay to keep her warm.

"Okay. Thanks again." Her shivering lessened, then stopped, and she relaxed.

She fit perfectly up against him even with all the bulky clothes. Hopefully, she'd sleep. He'd try, but the sun was bright and he was too alert, listening for the crunch of snow under feet. After wiping the trail across the meadow, they'd left an obvious trail up the hillside. If Das figured out where they left the road, they'd be easy to follow, and they'd have a hard time escaping again.

Borrowing trouble was a bad idea. He'd done all he could. They were hidden. Holly was safe and warm in his arms. He needed rest, so he counted sheep again.

Chapter 13

HOLLY WOKE TO THE sound of her name. "Luke?" Her back was toasty warm and her front slightly cooler.

"Hey, sleepyhead. The daylight is fading, so we should get going." Luke's voice was low and rough.

His words vibrated through her chest. Poor Luke. He was probably exhausted because, while she'd been warm and snuggly, her head on his arm all night had to be uncomfortable. "Okay. Did you sleep at all?"

"Not as much as you did. But that's okay. I enjoyed holding you." He unzipped his coat.

She rolled away, mourning the loss of warmth and the feeling of safety. He wriggled out of the shelter. She followed, taking the hand he offered to help her up. As she stood, every joint ached, her muscles screamed, and her body protested, especially her stomach and her face. She took her jacket off and put it back on correctly, then rolled her shoulders and gently moved the rest of her body, trying to warm up. She didn't want to worry Luke. A patch of black remained on the dark green branches in their shelter—Luke's fleece. Stooping, she retrieved the jacket, wincing when her tight thigh muscles protested. She rose, returning the fleece jacket to Luke. "Do we leave the shelter here?"

Luke nodded. "In a war zone, I'd break it down, but I'm not worried about Das's guys finding it." He snorted. "If we're really stuck on this ridge, we might end up back in it tonight." He frowned. "Let's strip the trackers out of our gear and leave them here. Not only are they heavy, but if Das gets a helicopter, he could pick up the signal, too. Without knowing how close the feds are, it's not worth the risk."

She nodded and pulled her jacket back off, yanking the forearm guards out of it and the trackers out of the seams. They helped each other peel off the underarm trackers and leaned against the rocks to take off the calf trackers. Then they piled them in the middle of their bed and turned to leave.

Luke paused. "Before we get started, now's the time to take care of personal business. Then eat some snow if you're warm enough. We'll head out after that." He held up his forefinger. "Slowly. Very slowly. I don't know about you, but I hurt everywhere."

She hadn't fooled him. "Yeah, me too." She moved away, behind a couple of trees, groaning when her muscles protested squatting. After finishing, she ate some snow and climbed to join him, sitting on a rock. "I've got one more energy bar. May as well eat it now, rather than haul it around."

"Thanks. You don't have to share." He smiled.

"Like I'm going to sit here and eat in front of you." He shouldn't think so little of her.

"Holly, I didn't mean it like that." He frowned. "I'm grateful."

"I know." She handed him half, sat next to him, and ate, her stomach growling and rumbling, celebrating food. "I don't remember these tasting this good."

"They don't. You're just really hungry." He flashed a smile.

"Yeah, no kidding." They finished quickly and climbed slowly. Her legs ached and shook, protesting each step. Before she'd gotten ten yards, she unzipped her jacket and took off her hat.

About halfway back up the ridge, Luke headed down and across the hill to their right. Downhill wasn't any better. Even with trees to hang on to, she slipped and slid. And her short legs made everything harder.

At six foot plus, Luke stepped over a lot of the fallen logs, but she was all of five-two. She had to climb up, over, and down, and sometimes sideways. Too often, she'd end up standing on a wobbly log, and it would collapse or twist under her, crashing down. At least they didn't have to worry about the noise. None of those out of shape old men would be out here chasing them through the deep snow.

Luke helped her over the bigger obstacles, but it slowed them down. And he had to lead because it took her twice as long to break trail; she was literally waist deep at times. But they were in an ultra-marathon, not a sprint.

They edged diagonally down the hill, then turned and inched down and across the opposite direction, making their own switchbacks. After a couple of hours of this, they stopped to rest.

"I think down is harder than up. My legs, knees, and feet are killing me." Luke groaned, twisting his ankles.

"Yeah." Everything hurt. "I'm bruised from head to toe. I almost wish we'd flagged down that helo." She'd never been so beat up and exhausted. Never. She was starving, too. Even at the worst of times, she'd found a soup kitchen, a dollar for ramen noodles, or a food pantry.

"I'm dreaming about hamburgers and milkshakes." Luke sighed.

"Don't remind me." She wrapped her arms around her gurgling stomach. "I want fried chicken and a hot fudge sundae."

Luke groaned. "You are such a tease."

She laughed. "Come on flyboy, let's go."

"Okay, space cadet." He grinned.

"Hey, I'm in acquisitions, not space ops!" She laughed, not at all offended.

His brows rose. "Not for long, remember?"

She'd forgotten about her new job. "We'd better make it back in one piece. I don't want to miss out on the chance to be a real space cadet."

His smile faded. "Don't worry, I'll get you back."

She frowned. They'd make it by working together, but she wasn't going to start a fight. "We'll make it." She was absolutely positive. Not only were they both smart and strong, but Luke would risk everything for her. He'd turned his back on his own father for her. She'd do the same, but that was easy. Her father had sold her to the highest bidder—a truly evil man.

She followed Luke, putting one leg in front of the other and trying, but failing, to forget how much her body hurt. Her nose ran and her lips chapped, no matter how much lip balm she put on or snow she ate. As they plodded, she heard a dull, roaring sound, and it got louder. It could be a waterfall; the terrain was steep enough. The sound increased and sharpened—it was definitely water on rocks.

Luke stopped. She grabbed a tree trunk and looked down. Not a waterfall, but a steep, rocky gorge, water crashing along the bottom. Ice plastered the sides of the ravine and the surrounding trees, and icicles hung everywhere. It was dazzling even in moonlight; during the day, they'd be blinded. "Now where? We can't cross that!" She had to yell over the crashing river and the cracking of icicles breaking.

"No." He pointed to the right. "We'll follow the river. Hope there's no more cliffs."

She held up her gloved hands, crossing her fingers, then followed him. They moved away from the canyon and walked for a couple of hours. Finally, the terrain flattened, the trees grew farther apart, the river sound quieted, and the gorge gradually disappeared, leaving a wide river. The sides were still covered with ice, but a fall wouldn't be deadly. Fewer trees meant less deadfall to climb over, but there was more brush under the snow. They still slipped and slid, but the falls were usually cushioned by the snow and bushes. Gradually, they and the river turned toward the north.

Luke stopped and surveyed the area. "I think we should leave the river and head straight to the east. We should eventually run into a highway or a major road. Most of the highways in this area run north and south."

She nodded. "Okay, you're the expert. You were watching from the helicopter."

"You noticed?" He raised his eyebrows.

"You were definitely concentrating while you were looking out the window, not just sightseeing. I don't think most people would actually notice because your expression doesn't change. But you have a certain intensity."

His mouth twisted and he shrugged. "No one's ever mentioned that. I wonder if they don't see it or just haven't said anything. It seems like the kind of thing Amy would point out."

Holly laughed. "Yeah, that's totally her kind of observation. Sometimes, I think we're all just monkeys in her study zoo."

"Oh no, not monkeys." He chuckled. "Too many variables. Gears, maybe, or equations. She knows how they *should* be working and is completely confused when they do something different."

"You've totally nailed her." She chuckled. "I must be tired to use that phrase. Ugh."

Luke laughed and pulled her into a gentle hug, giving her time to back away. But she gratefully hugged him back. His words rumbled under her cheek. "I'm tired too. I promise we'll sleep in a comfy bed, take a hot shower, and get a great meal real soon now."

"Sure we will." She chuckled. They were in the middle of nowhere. "If you're going to keep that promise, we'd better get moving."

He released her and started forward. She followed, trying to stay in his footsteps. They slipped, slid, climbed, and fell for hours. Holly stumbled behind Luke in a daze of exhaustion and bruises.

She thumped into Luke's back.

"Oof." He jolted forward a step, then spun back, catching her upper arms. "Look ahead. I think our lives just got easier."

Holly leaned around him. The trees were less dense, and then they were gone. Power lines! Civilization couldn't be too far. Except those lines ran for miles and miles across the Rockies...

"High tension lines. I think I know where these go." A smile lightened Luke's grim expression. "We'll have to run if there's a helicopter or a small plane, but we'll be able to make better time under the lines. If we follow these east, we'll run into a highway."

"How do you know that? Do you spend your off-duty time studying maps?"

He shook his head. "No, I spend my on-duty time studying maps. I studied the area around Wilkerson pass, but we're a long way from there. Luckily, I've done high-altitude mountain training missions in the Leadville area before. Even circling up high, waiting for fighters, the wind shears can be pretty brutal. Whenever we plan a mission somewhere new, we study the maps and terrain carefully. Believe it or not, high tension power lines, even big ones like these, are really difficult to spot from the air at high speed." He turned a circle, surveying the surrounding terrain.

"Oh. I had no idea." She was so clueless. On her own, she'd have been recaptured almost immediately. "Glad you recognize this because I'm so lost."

"We all have different training." He grinned. "If we're ever trapped on a space station, I'll expect you to get us out." He hugged her quickly, then slogged toward the power lines.

As they came under the lines, Holly's happiness was tempered by exhaustion. The snow was beaten down by animal tracks, mostly deer, and fairly smooth underneath. Even though there were no tire tracks, they were clearly on a road of sorts.

The incessant hum of the lines overhead became annoying, but the easy travel was worth the irritation. They marched forward, grimly determined. Holly gratefully followed Luke, zoning out despite the need to watch for threats from the air. After what seemed like miles of snow crunching through the silvery landscape, she stumbled again but realized she'd been taking it easy. "Luke, let me take the lead. I've got to do my share."

Luke turned. "I'm fine. But we've both got to be alert now." He pointed to a glow over the mountains to the east. "It's getting light. I was hoping we'd hit the highway before daybreak, but no such luck. I have no idea how much farther we need to go. We need shelter. Look for a road crossing the lines. Maybe we'll find a cabin or at least not be sitting ducks under these lines. If you hear or see a helicopter, run for the trees." He strode onward.

At the faster pace, Holly had to stay alert. She searched for rock piles, or stacks of trees, but saw nothing but fields and hillsides with occasional groups of trees. They were in high desert, and the area was fairly barren.

"Hah!" Luke jogged ahead. A track crossed the lines, and he stopped in the middle of it, looking in both directions as she trudged in his wake.

"The good news is there's a road here." Luke spread his arms out. "The bad news is we have no idea where civilization is or if there's anything along this road that we can use. But since I don't see any shelter along the power lines, I think we should walk along this road to the south. It's downhill, too. Does that sound logical?"

"Sure. You're the expert here. And downhill sounds better than uphill." It was nice of him to ask, but she was too exhausted to remember how to breathe, let alone think.

They turned on to the tracks. Bushes and trees lined the road, the occasional gap revealing a snow-covered creek. Like the power line road, there weren't any tire marks or human footprints in the snow, but there were plenty of hoofprints, and other animal tracks, and the occasional remains of snow-machine tracks, probably created months ago. They slogged onward, looking for shelter. The trees disappeared, revealing a gigantic snow-covered expanse, the track running right through the middle. Small groups of tall pines dotted the meadow, but the area was mostly open and probably a mile long.

Luke stopped, scanning the meadow. "This isn't good. It's light enough to get a helo in the air. We'll have to listen carefully. If you hear anything, run for the nearest bunch of trees. That might be behind us, don't forget."

Holly nodded, saving her breath. They jogged, the crunch of snow sounding like thunder and the sky lightening every minute. At the first group of pines, they paused for a few breaths and then hurried to the next. At the third group, Luke grabbed her arm. "Holly, does that look like a building down there, behind the trees?"

She peered into the distance. "Yes, it does. Thank Vishnu." She put a hand over her heart.

They jogged side by side, then Luke suddenly stopped.

"What?"

He scowled, turning to look where they'd come from. "Our footprints. They're going to show. We can't wipe all of them out. It's just too far, and the snow is too firm. We'll have to hope the helo is too high and this place is too remote to be searched."

Holly's heart sank, but she agreed. There was no way they could go back and wipe out a half a mile of tracks.

"Why didn't I think of that!" He kicked a chunk of ice and sent it spinning down the track.

"Luke, you can't think of everything. You've done fantastic so far. Don't beat yourself up." She put a hand on his arm, hoping to reassure him. "If it was just me, I'd have collapsed beside a tree a couple of hours ago, if I'd made it that far. You've gotten us here, still in one piece. You've been scanning the sky for the past hour, so of course you weren't thinking about tracks. Besides, this snow is pretty well tracked up by animals already. Our footprints probably won't show up too badly. I can't believe how amazing you've been."

He flashed a smile at her, but it quickly morphed into a grim look of remorse when he glanced behind them. Then he broke into a jog and she followed. They reached the building, a ten by fifteen-foot log cabin. The timbers were gray with age, two or three falling apart, and there had to be at least a foot of pine needles on the roof. On the front door, a U-shaped bolt stuck through a hasp, rather than a padlock. Luke opened the latch and then the door, wincing at the squeal of rusty hinges. Standing in the doorway, they waited for their eyes to adjust to the gloom.

Near the door, there was a tiny wood table with a couple of log stools, with a very old, very rusty iron stove along the back wall. Near the stovepipe, two shelves held cans of food and pots. On their right, a square wooden box was attached to the wall. They left the door open, allowing the morning light to shine in. Dust covered everything, although not as thick as the pine straw on the roof. The air was stale and musty, like old animal nests, with a tang of moth balls as well.

"Holly, look at this." Luke picked up a piece of wood sitting on the shelf next to the canned goods. He angled it so the moonlight hit it. "It says, 'take what you need, please don't trash the place.' We just completely lucked out. Whoever owns this place has it stocked for emergencies." He smiled and his shoulders relaxed.

Holly peered at the shelves. "Look, there's a tiny LED lantern." She picked it up; it was just a bit longer than her hand. "It shouldn't show through the cracks, especially once the sun is shining. So it won't be obvious we're here if we keep the door closed." She turned it on.

Luke leaned over the stove. "Yes! Figured if they had canned goods here, they probably had a better stove than this rusty old thing." He thumped the metal top and pulled a plastic case from behind it. He put it on top of the stove and opened it. "Propane gas burner. We can melt some snow for drinking water and heat some cans, whatever they are. I'm going to gather snow and ice where it won't show up too badly. We probably need water worse than food." Luke grabbed the pot and headed outside.

Holly found a smaller pot, two metal bowls and two spoons on the shelf behind the cans. *Perfect.* The cans contained beef stew and and more beef stew. Her stomach rumbled happily at the idea of any food. Taking her prizes, she went outside to wipe the dust off in the snow. Using the micro-tool the thugs missed during their lewd pat-down from her pocket, she started the laborious process of opening a can with a tiny old-fashioned blade opener.

It could be worse—at least she had an opener, and she didn't see one on the shelf. How horrible would it be to not have one at all? All that food, and no way to open it. Sheer torture. She'd probably find a rock and bash it open. Her fingers aching, the lid separated from the can, and she sniffed. Beefy goodness wafted up—she certainly wasn't going to check the date. She dumped it in the small pot, filling it. One can at a time would keep them from overeating.

Luke returned and soon the stove was hissing with a bright blue flame. "Normally I'd be worried about running a gas stove inside, but since this place is far from airtight, I think we'll be fine." He put the snow-filled pot on the stove, then pulled a couple of mason jars off the shelf. "Looks like the lids kept most of the dust out of the jars. We can put the melted snow in these."

He went out to wipe the jars off, while Holly looked at the shelves again. Something gleamed behind the cans. She moved closer. Thin brown plastic squares. "Luke, we've even got MRE crackers to go with the stew!"

"Oh boy, Meals Ready to Eat. My favorite." His lip curled.

Holly smacked his arm lightly. "Come on. Before we found the stew, you would have been thrilled to have these!" She waved one under his nose.

He laughed. "You're right. And if we break them up into the stew, they'll be okay. Lots of carbs, which we need." He put the jars down on the table and crossed to the box on the wall. "This looks promising." He pulled out a large, dust covered plastic bag and took it to the door. He cracked the door, listened, and looked up. "We need to keep the dust to a minimum in the cabin. There are obviously mice here, and they carry hantavirus. The last thing we need is to get sick. I'll wipe it off." He took the package outside.

She swirled the melting snow. Luke returned, closing the door and unzipping the bag. He pulled out squares of folded plastic and olive drab material. Mothballs made Holly's nose wrinkle. "An air mattress. And a blanket! This is survival in style." He handed both to her, then carried the table and log rounds outside, wiping them in the snow. Then he brought a ball of snow inside and wiped the bed box. After throwing the snow out, he put the blanket on the table, then blew up the mattress.

Holly used her battered coat sleeves to grab the pot on the stove and poured the melted water into the jars. When Luke finished blowing up the mattress, she handed him a jar. They clinked glasses gently. "Cheers!" "Salud!"

Lukewarm, but it was liquid, and it gently showered the parched tissues of her throat, relieving the dryness wonderfully. It was the best water she'd ever had.

"Man, that's good." Luke put his glass down on the table. "Snow just doesn't cut it." They waited impatiently for the rest of the snow and ice to melt.

"Where did you get the snow from?" They needed to keep that area clean, so they could melt more.

"The ice is from icicles hanging from the roof and the snow is from behind the trees. I took off the top layer, then tried to scrape shallow troughs that will hopefully look like they were wind blown. I doubt anyone would notice from the air, anyway." He waggled his brows at her. "Also, I decided yellow snow will be on the north side of the cabin, so don't get water snow from there."

Her bladder protested. "Good idea. I should go do that." Holly listened at the door and looked up and around before she left the doorway. On the north side, she leaned against a nearby tree and relieved herself.

The mouth-watering aroma of beef stew hit her before she even got the cabin door open. Jars of water sat on the table and Luke stirred the stew. The smell filled the cabin and her stomach rumbled. Luke pointed at the pot. "If you stir, I'll go get more snow."

Holly stirred the stew carefully. The pot didn't fit on the burner very well, and the last thing she wanted to do was dump it. At least it had a handle. Between stirs, she opened one of the cracker packs and broke them into the bowls. Luke returned with a full pot of snow and a small fir branch, just as the stew was bubbling. She poured the stew out into the two bowls, then started opening another can while it cooled. The rich, meaty smell of the stew was making it hard to concentrate, and her hands were beat up and aching, so it was slow going.

"Here, let me." Luke held out a hand. "I've done this more than you have, I think." He finished opening the can and dumped it out into the pan.

They each spooned up a bite. Holly tried to chew slowly, knowing that eating too fast would just give her a stomachache, but it was so hard—she'd never been so hungry. The beefy taste exploded across her tongue, and she let out a ridiculously loud groan at the same time Luke did. She looked at him—his eyes were closed with a blissful expression.

"I think this is the very best thing I've ever eaten in my entire life." Luke licked his lips.

"It is." She nodded in agreement. "I've been hungry before, but never like this."

They kept eating. If she caught his eye, they'd both laugh. "I think we've officially reached the 'silly' stage of exhaustion." Holly took another spoonful.

Luke snorted and kept eating. He finished first, served the melted water, and put the second pot of stew on the stove.

"Luke, I hope you're planning on eating most of that one. I'm kind of full." Canned stew was filling.

"I wasn't, but I'll eat anything you don't. There are lots of cans, so eat all you want." A crease appeared between his brows.

She reassured him. "Remember, you probably weigh half again what I do, and you have a lot more muscle mass."

He gave her an ironically amused look. "Yeah, well, there is no way a can of stew will make up for the calories you've burned over the last twenty-four hours."

"True. I can probably eat a little more."

"We'll finish, sleep, then have more stew before we leave and take some of these cracker packets. Hopefully, we can find out who owns this place and repay them."

She nodded. "That would be nice. I suppose that even if there was paper and pencil here, we wouldn't dare leave a note."

He shook his head, his lips clamped together. "No, better not. I'm going to hide the stew cans and stir up the dust in here when we leave."

"Good idea." He really did think of everything. She was too tired to think of anything but sleep.

He dished out the second pot of stew and they ate methodically, without the laughter. Holly could hardly keep her eyes open. With full stomachs, they'd both hit the final exhaustion point.

Luke stood, stacking the stew pot and bowls together. "Tonight, or today I guess, since it is daytime, should be more comfortable and a lot warmer, inside, with a blanket. Still, make sure you've got everything on and zipped. We'd better take our boots off, so we don't blow out our mattress. But keep them near the bed, ready to go. I'll be back." He took the pot outside, probably to clean it.

Holly pulled her hat down, zipped up her jacket, and sat on the edge of the bed box to take off her boots. She slid onto the air mattress carefully, scooting to the far side.

The door opened and closed, and then the mattress rose under her when he sat, taking his boots off. "I'm glad this thing holds both of us. I wasn't entirely sure it would."

When his weight settled into the mattress, she bounced once. He wrapped his arms around her and pulled her into his body firmly, then arranged the thin wool Army blanket over them. It reeked of mothballs, but it was warm.

She wriggled back into his warmth and yawned.

"If you need to get up, just elbow me or crawl over me. Don't walk on this floor in stocking feet. If you get cold, wake me up, and we'll do the same thing we did last night." He yawned.

"It's much warmer, so I think I'll be okay." She yawned until she thought her head would split in two. She was so tired and achy and sore.

"I hope the water in the pot doesn't freeze solid. I'm not sure how much propane there is."

"We can always eat the cold stew if we have to." After a warm bowl, it would be disappointing, but she'd still be happy.

Luke chuckled. "By morning, or night or when we get up, I'll probably be hungry enough to do that."

"Warm food is such a luxury."

He snorted a little, and his chest rubbed gently against her back. "No kidding. Goodnight."

"Goodnight."

Even though they were nowhere near safety, the air mattress, her contented tummy, and the warmth and comfort of Luke's arms felt like safety. She fell asleep before she could start a meditation.

Chapter 14

HELICOPTER BLADES BEAT THE air into submission. Adrenaline flooded Holly's system, jerking her upright. At least she wasn't shivering with cold.

Next to her, Luke sat up, swinging his legs over the side. He leaned over to lace his boots. "We can run for the trees if they set down."

She glanced at his grim face, sliding next to him. He obviously thought the odds of making it were as low as she did. She laced her boots, then joined Luke near the door. Better to go down fighting than give up, no matter what the chances.

From the sound, the chopper hovered over the meadow. Then moved on, behind the cabin. After the sound faded, Luke opened the door a crack and peeked outside. "Nobody out there. Looks like we lucked out big time. Now that I'm up, I'm going to go vent a little fuel, unless you're desperate?" He raised his brows. She

shook her head. "Drink some water if it's still liquid."
He squeezed out the door.

Holly split the still-liquid water between the two jars
and drank hers, wishing she wore a watch. She usually
used her phone or a computer to tell time.

Luke returned, grinning. "A herd of elk must have
been in the meadow before the helo came—there are
tracks everywhere, including around the cabin. They
wiped out our footprints."

Relief let her blow out her breath. "That was lucky."
She opened the door, needing to relieve herself.

"Holly?" Luke held a small fir branch. "Take this, and
wipe out your footprints as you come back."

"Oh. Good idea." She left, closing the door behind her,
and surveyed the meadow. As Luke said, hoof prints
had thoroughly trampled the snow. Too bad they'd
missed seeing the herd. After she finished, she swept
her footsteps away, then latched the door. "Any idea
what time it is?"

"Mid-afternoon, I think." He grimaced, rolling
his shoulders. "Wish I'd seen the chopper. Law
enforcement markings are pretty obvious. My feet and
legs and every part of me would really appreciate a
ride." He stretched high, groaning and touching the roof
well before his full extension.

"Me too. Back to sleep?" She stretched too, bending to
put her hands on the tops of her feet.

"Nothing else to do, and I don't know about you,
but I'm taking any opportunity to get horizontal." Dark
circles stood out against his alabaster skin, making his
green eyes almost glow. The dark scruff on his sharp jaw
line increased his appeal rather than lessening it.

Luke was a temptation she didn't need but was too tired to resist. "Absolutely. Especially now that the adrenaline from our wakeup call is fading." As they curled together on the air mattress, Holly thought about how much worse everything could be and shuddered.

Luke pulled her in tighter. "Cold?"

She shivered. "Not really. Just thinking about what could have happened."

"Hey, survival situation rules—never think about the past, unless you can learn something from it that you need to survive now. Always be thinking ahead to your next move and what you need to do to stay alive. All positive thoughts, no negatives. And right now, that means sleeping."

"Yes, sir!" He was right. There would be time to think about all that later.

"That's better."

Did he kiss the top of her head? It was hard to tell through the hat and hood. She drifted off, feeling safe and warm.

Luke woke when Holly turned over, blinking to focus in the dim room. Time to get up, eat more stew, and get moving. "Holly?" She grumbled and pulled the blanket over her head. "Come on, honey, wake up." He shook her shoulder gently, but she still didn't wake. He'd let her rest; he could heat stew without her. He sat up, tucking the blanket around Holly.

As he bent over to tie his boots, he bit back a groan—despite the fairly comfy bed, good food, and much better sleep, his muscles ached and his feet were sore. Rising, he heated stew and crumbled crackers into their bowls. He'd never thought he'd be happy to have MRE crackers.

Cautiously searching the skies and the meadow, Luke left the cabin, collected more snow, and relieved himself. Back in the cabin, the rich scent of stewed beef filled the air, and his stomach rumbled. Plastic creaked—Holly sat up, scrubbing her hands through her hair. Her bedhead was an adorable ball of fluff, too soon hidden under her hat. "I figured food would wake you up when I couldn't."

"Hunger will do that." She put her boots on and joined him at the stove, stirring the stew. "This still smells really good. Surprising after two bowls yesterday, but I guess I'm still hungry enough that it doesn't matter."

The stew bubbled, so Luke took it off the stove and split it between the bowls, then put the snow on the stove to melt. He handed Holly her bowl, joining her at the table.

She chewed and swallowed. "Only one can this morning?"

Luke was sure he could eat more, but they should reach civilization soon. "I hate to wipe them out just in case someone else is in a bind."

She looked at the shelf and frowned at him. "There's five more cans, and more crackers."

"Good point. If we're going to eat, we should fill up." He alternated eating bites of stew with opening the next can. His beat up, swollen fingers made using the tiny can opener difficult. He lifted the water off the stove and put the stew on it, then poured the water into the jars. "Will you stir the stew while I put away the mattress?"

She swallowed a last spoonful. "Of course."

He let the air out of the mattress, taking it outside to fold it and put it back in the zippered plastic bag with the blanket. He placed the bag back in the bed box.

Holly dished the stew. "Good thing we're finished—I think this thing just ran out of fuel."

Luke pointed at the base of the ancient wood stove. "There's another can, but I'd rather leave it for the next unlucky person."

They ate quickly and drank most of the water, rinsing the pot and bowls with the remainder and drinking that too. Normally, bits of stew in water would be nasty, but liquid water was too important.

Holly grimaced. "Not the tastiest thing ever, but better than eating snow."

"True." They needed to clean up and get moving. "I'll wipe the cans, the pot, the bowls, and the spoons clean in the snow. Hopefully that will keep any predators from trying to break into the cabin. I'll hike back this summer to replace everything and pack out the garbage."

"Good idea. We can't haul it, that's for sure." Holly grimaced. She rearranged the remaining cans on the shelf, hiding the empty spots.

Luke wiped the kitchen items in the snow and stomped the cans flat. He used the fir branch to wipe out their tracks again and brought everything back to the cabin.

Holly slid the stove into the case, while he hid the cans inside the wood stove. They replaced the pots and bowls, then double-checked to make sure they hadn't left anything. Holly handed him two cracker packs. He stuffed them into his front jacket pockets. "Crack the door. I'll shield the light and turn it off when it's back on the shelf." He placed the tiny lantern on the shelf next to the cans.

The door squeaked and Luke turned off the light. Holly surveyed the area and the sky before she left the doorway, holding the door for him. He grabbed the fir bough and mostly closed the door with the branch still inside, then he held his breath and vigorously thwacked it against the floor. Hopefully, that would stir the dust and hide their footprints, or at least make them look older.

Pulling the branch out, he closed and secured the door, and they walked toward the next group of trees. Using the bough, he brushed out their tracks, biting back a groan when every muscle in his back protested his bent-over position. About a hundred yards from the cabin, he gratefully tossed the branch into the underbrush, and they trudged along the hoof print covered track.

Luke surveyed the surrounding mountains. "I'm not positive we're going the right way. We might be safer following the power lines to the highway. But I think there's fencing way down there." He pointed in front of them. "That means this cabin is on a ranch, so if we follow this road, we might end up at a house." Hopefully with a phone.

"But if Das found them first, we might be in bigger trouble." Holly's shoulders hunched.

"Safer than hitchhiking, though." If Das and his people were looking for them, it would be on the roads near that house they'd been taken to. "And what are the odds that Das would find this particular ranch in the middle of nowhere? If we find one, we'll look around, see if there are unusual vehicles for a cattle ranch. Any ranch should have a phone, and we can contact local law enforcement, who can get in touch with the FBI. I'm sure the FBI is talking to the locals now. They'd need people who know the area." Just saying the words caused his hopes to rise.

"Good points." She nodded. "I agree. We keep going on the road."

They left the meadow and passed through thick trees, then a smaller meadow, then more trees. The fencing Luke has spotted was an old, incomplete section that had been cut in multiple places. They continued plodding for hours. They still stumbled occasionally, but the road was much easier than the trackless wilderness. He wished for water, but hauling glass jars on a slick, icy track had seemed like a bad idea.

Holly grabbed his arm. "Luke, look. Is that a light?" She pointed to the left of the track.

A faint yellow glow glimmered up high through the thick tree tops. Hope rose. "It might be. Good eye." If they could reach a house, Holly would be safe.

They picked up the pace, but it didn't seem to get any closer. At least an hour later, they rounded a bend and found a metal gate, locked with a big padlock. Luke climbed up and over, Holly following him before he could offer her help.

The track widened and smoothed, tire and snowmachine tracks appearing. There must be people nearby. Luke shared a smile with Holly. Finally, the glimmer resolved into a big security light mounted high on a pole. The trees thinned, bordering a fenced pasture. A house, a barn, and a shed stood on the other side of the pasture.

Luke grabbed Holly around the waist and lifted her up. "We made it!" He pulled her tight against his chest, needing to share his excitement and relief. "Thank God we made it." She hugged him back, hard. He set her down when her arms loosened.

"I hope they have a phone." She raised her hands and face to the sky.

His joy remained, but he considered the homeowner's possible reaction to a knock on the door in the darkness. "I hope they don't meet us with a shotgun." They found the driveway, let themselves through the gate, and walked faster. As they got closer to the house, dogs barked. "Hope they aren't loose." A pickup truck, a small older SUV and a snow machine sat in front of the house. A tractor was sheltered in the shed beyond, and cattle jostled in a field behind the shed. The vehicles fit the house, and they were nothing like the beat up minivan Das had used.

"Or they're friendly." Holly shrugged. "I'll take a dog bite over Das, though."

The front porch light on the house lit, the door opened, and the outline of a person emerged, backlit by the porch light. They held a rifle or a shotgun at their side. "If you're here to steal something, you're out of luck!" yelled a deep male voice.

Luke stopped and yelled back. "We need your phone. We need to call the sheriff."

"All right, come on up. Keep your hands where I can see 'em."

They walked, hands up high, into the light. A woman's voice said, "My goodness, what in the world happened to you two? You look like you fell down a hill of razor blades. Come on up here."

They walked a little faster, keeping their hands in sight. As they neared the steps, the woman gasped. "You're the lost hikers they've been looking for! Your pictures have been on the news!"

Luke looked at Holly, she looked at him, and they both shrugged and chuckled. Holly nodded her head toward the woman. He took her cue to speak. "Ma'am, could we please use your phone?"

"Of course. Come on in. Don't worry about your boots. I've got dogs in here all the time." She turned and entered the house.

They followed her into a classic farm kitchen, the sharp scent of Pinesol lingering in the air and warm air thawing his face. A dark wood farmhouse table and chairs called to him; he wanted off his feet. But they had business first.

The woman crossed to the sink, pulling a phone off the windowsill and handing it to him. She wore a dark blue fleece jacket over sweatpants, and her smile lit the room. Her brown hair sparkled with silver, and freckles dotted her cheeks. "I'm Becky, and that is Matt. Don't worry, he's really a cream puff. Please sit down. You look like you might fall over any second." She gestured toward the table.

Matt didn't smile or put down his shotgun, but he did lean against the doorway and nod. He wasn't a tall man, or young, but he was solid. He definitely wasn't a cream puff—Luke certainly didn't want to get in a fight with him.

Luke pulled a chair out for Holly, and she collapsed into it. "Ma'am, this is Holly, and I'm Luke. Thank you for inviting us in." About to dial, he hesitated. "Ma'am, is there a non-emergency number for the sheriff, or should I just dial 911?"

Becky held her hand out, and he returned the phone. She dialed and handed it back to him.

"Thank you."

A female voice said, "Lake County Sheriff's Department, how may I help you?"

The relief loosened every muscle, and he plopped in the chair next to Holly. "This is Major Lukas Sevrason with Captain Holly Bose. I understand you've been looking for us?"

"Oh my gosh, yes. We've been looking the last two days. Where are you?" The female voice got higher and louder as she spoke.

Luke chuckled. "I don't actually know, but the very nice homeowner does. Hold on." He handed the phone back to Becky. "Could you please tell her where we are? I have no idea."

Becky took the phone. Matt laughed, then left the kitchen, taking the shotgun with him. Becky spoke rapidly, telling the woman their names and the name of the ranch with the address.

Becky handed the phone back to him, and the dispatcher spoke. "Major Sevrason, I'm sending a deputy out to pick you up. You're way out there, so it'll be at least forty-five minutes, maybe an hour. Becky tells me you can wait in her house, no problem. Is that okay?"

The crisis over, his whole body sagged. "That would be amazing. Can you contact the FBI?"

"They're the next call after I dispatch the deputy. We'll have you safe shortly."

"Great." He sighed with relief. "Thanks so much for your help."

"You're welcome. I'm just glad you're okay. Stay there and get warm."

He gave the phone to Becky. "Did she tell you it would be a while? I don't want to keep you up, so we can wait outside if you'd like." He didn't want to move, but bothering their saviors wasn't polite.

She put her hands on her hips and scowled. "Absolutely not. I won't hear of it. Besides, this is the most exciting thing to happen out here since a skunk got trapped in the calf barn. Now, what can I get you to drink? Water, coffee, a beer?" She turned back toward the refrigerator. Matt came back in, without the shotgun.

"Water would be perfect, Ma'am. Holly?"

"Water would be great. And could I use your bathroom? I'd love to wash my hands and face." Her expression reflected the longing in her voice.

"Of course. Come right this way." Becky pointed toward a doorway and bustled into the hall beyond. "Matt, please get a couple of glasses of water." Holly trailed, moving stiffly.

Matt glared, leaning across the table. "Did you give her those shiners?"

"No! That ass—" His brain kicked back into gear, and he slammed his mouth shut. "I can't tell you what happened without permission, but I definitely did not hit Holly. We both fell a lot on our way here, though." Holly's battered face sent fury raging through him. At least she'd gotten a bit of revenge.

Matt nodded, turned away, and got glasses of water. He started a pot of coffee. "May as well fix some. I'm sure the deputy won't say no to a cup after he drives all the way out here. And I'd be up in a couple more hours, anyway."

Luke drained the glass of water and took it to the sink, refilling it. "We appreciate your hospitality. It's been a rough couple of days." Luke washed his hands, then returned and sagged in the chair. Every muscle in his body screamed, and his feet felt like they'd been beaten with a cane.

Becky returned wearing jeans and a dark green sweatshirt. She pulled out a mixing bowl. "Now you sit right there, make yourself comfortable, and I'll make you two some pancakes. You must be starving."

Luke's stomach rumbled, but he tried not to show it. "I don't want to make work for you, Becky. Just sitting someplace warm and light is enough."

She pulled milk, eggs, and butter from her refrigerator. "It's no trouble."

Luke pulled the MRE crackers out of his pocket. "We had food and a comfortable place to sleep last night. I'm guessing it's due to your hospitality. Do you own the cabin up the road past the gate?" He put the crackers on the table.

Matt poured coffee for his wife. "We don't exactly own it; it's Forest Service land now. But my family built it back in the day, and we keep it stocked. We have grazing rights up there. It's a good shelter during thunderstorms."

Luke pulled out his wallet, which had miraculously remained with him, and put two twenty-dollar bills on the table. "We very much appreciate it. We ate some stew and crackers and burned through a can of propane. Do you think this will cover it?"

Matt waved. "Put your money back, son. We help each other out around here."

Luke nodded and smiled, leaving the bills on the table. "Thank you. But take this for a can opener, please. We had one on Holly's multitool, but others might not be so lucky. We didn't have a way to carry garbage, so I left the empty cans in the old wood stove. I tried to clean them with snow, but I know bears have a great sense of smell." The greasy goodness of bacon wafted through the air. His stomach rumbled again—loudly.

Matt smiled. "That's good enough for now. The bears are still sleeping. I'll take the snow machine and clean up. A can opener is a good idea, though." He paused, then frowned at Luke again. "How did you end up way out there? There's no hiking trails anywhere near that cabin."

Luke shrugged. He couldn't tell him the whole story, but Ness had agreed the case would be public, so he could share the general situation. "Sir, I can't tell you all the details, but we weren't hiking." He smiled ruefully. "We were helping the FBI with a case and things didn't exactly go as planned, so we ended up running. We've been hiking at night, and it hasn't been the easiest thing I've ever done."

Matt lifted the coffee pot and poured when Luke nodded. "I'd guess not. You both look pretty beat up."

That was an understatement. "Yeah, we fell a lot. But your cabin and food sure made last night much better than the night before. We were in a tiny cave for that one." He couldn't hold back a shudder.

Becky put a plate full of pancakes, eggs, and bacon in front of him. She placed a jug of maple syrup next to the plate. "Eat this and I'll make more."

Luke's mouth watered. He poured syrup, cut, and scooped up a big bite. The sweet flavor burst across his tongue. He groaned, involuntarily. "Ma'am, this is the best thing I've ever eaten." He shoveled another bite in his mouth. Heaven tasted like pancakes with maple syrup.

Holly returned and Becky set another plate down. "Sit down and eat. I don't want to hear another word from either of you until you've finished that."

Luke smiled at her, hoping his teeth weren't covered in egg and pancake. Holly chewed and sipped coffee. "Thank you so much. This is wonderful."

Luke finished his plate and politely refused seconds. "Do you mind if I use the bathroom?"

"Of course not." Becky pointed. "Right down the hall." She plated more food for Matt.

Luke used the facilities, then washed his face and hands, grateful for warm water. He couldn't wait for a shower, but he was five inches taller and twenty pounds lighter than Matt, so he'd have to put his dirty clothes back on. He'd be better off waiting. Back in the kitchen, he felt almost normal. "Ma'am, sir, thank you. I feel much, much better now."

"Stop thanking me." Becky waved a hand through the air in front of her. "It's nothing. More coffee?" She lifted the pot, pouring more for Holly.

Luke held his cup out. "Yes, thank you."

She filled his cup, then Matt's and hers. "Holly was telling us what she does in the military. What do you do?"

He told them about the life of a tanker pilot, along with deployment stories and some of the goofy things people did downrange.

Then the dogs barked. Matt rose. "Stay there." He left the kitchen and returned with the deputy sheriff. Between the bulky jacket, fleece hat, leather gloves, weapon belt, and heavy boots, it was hard to tell what he actually looked like, but he had a friendly smile. Matt motioned toward the man. "Holly, Luke, this is Deputy Rick Costa. He's been a deputy for a long time; knows the place like the back of his hand. He'll get you safely back to town."

Becky lifted the coffee pot. "Rick, do you want some coffee?"

He held out a travel mug. "Much appreciated. Thanks."

Luke and Holly thanked the couple, leaving their phone numbers. Then they followed the deputy outside, getting in the back seat of the sheriff's SUV.

Deputy Costa turned, looking at them through the security grate behind his seat. "Sorry you're stuck in the back like criminals. But I figure with food in you, all you're going to want to do is sleep, right?"

Holly was already yawning. Luke nodded, exhaustion weighing him down. "I hope you'll forgive us, but it's been a rough couple of days. Where are we headed?"

"Leadville. Get some sleep now because the FBI is waiting to debrief you." He turned around and put the vehicle in drive.

"Great." Luke scrubbed his hands across his face. Just what he wanted to do, talk to the FBI when he was exhausted. He yawned. The seat belt prevented him from holding Holly, but he grasped her hand, and she squeezed back. He put his head back and closed his eyes.

Chapter 15

COLD AIR HIT HER face. "Captain? Captain Bose?" Something grasped and shook her shoulder. She knocked the hand away. She didn't want to get up.

"She wakes slow," Luke said. "Give her a second."

Holly opened her eyes. She sat in a vehicle. The door was open, and a woman peered down at her. The woman's jacket was unzipped, revealing a badge and a gun.

Luke peered over the woman's shoulder. "Holly, we're at the Leadville Sheriff's Department. Come on. The FBI wants to debrief us."

That woke her up. She fumbled for the seat belt, her hand cramping when she pressed the latch. She swung her legs out and stood, muscles shaking and feet screaming. Bright security lights blinded her, but she was in a parking lot, surrounded by official vehicles. They were safe. Luke held out his hand and she grasped it. "Everything hurts so bad. I need a shower." She shuffled next to Luke like an ancient old woman.

"Yeah, so do I, but I don't think we're going to get one." Luke's voice was low and rough.

"Darn." They moved toward a door on the back of a two-story building.

Deputy Costa held the door for her. "Straight ahead down the hall to the door at the end."

Luke let go of her hand, nodding for her to enter. "Thanks for the ride, Deputy Costa. We appreciate it."

"No problem. Good luck."

Holly smiled and nodded at him, neck muscles protesting, and continued down the hallway. Special Agent Ness, along with about ten more people in civilian clothes, waited in a large room filled with long beige plastic tables, metal chairs along one side and a whiteboard at the front. Laptops, maps, and notepads were strewn across the tables, and a large screen displayed a map with a grid on it. They were led to a counter in the back and offered coffee, water, donuts, and pain killers. Holly took some of each.

Ness pointed at a chair in front of him. "I'm sure you're exhausted and just want to go home, but first we need to hear your version of events. Please hand your jackets to Agent Nelson. He'll download the recording devices while you talk."

"We didn't know if you were close, so we dumped the trackers in our first shelter. I'm not sure if the recorders are still in the jackets. If you give me a map, I'll show you the approximate location so you can retrieve them." Luke held up his hands and scowled. "But first, did you arrest those guys?"

Ness crossed his arms. "Yes, we raided the house at seven in the morning the day after they took you. Das is in the hospital with a concussion."

Holly gave a small fist pump. "Yes!" Luke grinned at her. She'd put up her hand for a high-five, but that would probably hurt both of them.

Ness cleared his throat. "We're fairly certain we got all of Das's helpers. Mr. Sevrason was very cooperative in identifying them." Ness seemed chagrined for a moment but quickly recovered his normal, non-committal look.

"I'm sure he's hoping it will help him get out of some of the charges." Luke grimaced and took off his jacket. Holly took hers off too, wrinkling her nose at the smell.

"I'm sure. Major, your father suffered a mild heart attack at some time in those twenty-four hours. He's getting the appropriate care." Ness paused, but Luke didn't say anything, probably because he was angry at his father. Ness continued. "By the time we found Das, you'd been gone for a while because we got nothing from your trackers. After the raid, we searched by helicopter but found nothing, and now I understand why, at least partially."

Luke nodded. Holly was sure he'd share their experience with Amy. Even though Amy didn't work at the SERE training school anymore, she had lots of friends there who'd love real feedback.

"Major, you'll be with Special Agent Rogers, back there." Ness pointed at a table with two men. "Captain, you can sit here."

Luke paused. "You're getting a medic for Holly, right?" Ness nodded. After another glare, Luke walked away.

Holly collapsed into the chair. After two more agents introduced themselves and got her permission to record the conversation, she told them everything that had happened. After an hour, a medic checked her over and pronounced she'd live. Then she told the story again, to the agent who'd been talking to Luke. After what seemed like hours, her throat was too hoarse to keep talking, despite plenty of water and tea. "I'm sure I've forgotten some stuff, but I'm exhausted, and I really need a shower, some fresh clothes, and some sleep." She winced a little at her whiny tone, but she was way past the point of caring.

The female agent stood. "Yes, Captain Bose, right now. We've got you hotel rooms down the street. Give me your sizes, including shoes. I'll find you something wearable." She pushed a piece of paper and pen across the table.

Holly wrote and then tried to stand, but her legs had locked. Using her arms, she pushed and eventually got on her screaming feet, stooped over like an ancient crone. "Everything hurts."

"I'm sure a hot shower will help. I know you got some food, but are you hungry?" Ness joined them, sounding slightly concerned. Probably because his career had just taken a hit, and he was hoping for a good word from her. From Luke's scowl, Ness was out of luck there.

"I can wait for morning. Or is it morning already?" In the windowless briefing room, she had lost track of time.

"Close. It's five. We'll let you sleep until ten, or until we can find something for you to wear, and then we'll take you to breakfast and then home." Ness's mouth twisted.

Luke joined her, taking her hand gently in his. She squeezed slightly and held on. After the escape and extended debrief, Luke seemed like her only friend.

Ness held his hand out toward the door. "I'm sorry I didn't lead with this, but thank you. You both did a very good job, and if you ever want to join the FBI, you're hired. Your testimony will put Das and company away. You will have to testify in person at some future time, unless they plead guilty." Luke held up his hand. Ness had the grace to look ashamed for a split second, then he shrugged. "Sorry, that can wait. Let's get you to the hotel." He strode down the hall in front of them.

They hobbled behind him, getting in the back of another black SUV, and stopped a couple of blocks later. Luke climbed out on his own, but when she tried to straighten her legs, they cramped painfully. The agents had to lift her out. On the sidewalk, she stretched, then the agents helped her into the lobby, one on each side. They crossed a beautiful marble floor, surrounded by gleaming dark wood walls and soaring ceilings with graceful chandeliers.

She should be wearing pearls and high heels, not a torn-to-shreds ski jacket and pants. But she was too tired to care.

After a short elevator ride and another shuffle, they reached their rooms; Luke's was next to hers. Holly declined more help, then slipped inside and locked the door, sighing with relief. The old-fashioned florals and fancy furnishings were pretty but wasted on her.

Dragging her aching feet across the room, she stripped everything off and left it in a pile on the bathroom floor. She never wanted to wear or even see any of it ever again, even if she had to leave wearing nothing but a towel.

She cautiously maneuvered into the shower, hissing a bit as the blessedly hot water hit her cuts, then shampooed, conditioned, and almost scrubbed her skin off. Once she finally felt clean, she stepped out of the shower and surveyed the vanity, relieved the basics were waiting. After running a comb through her hair, she brushed her teeth and slathered hotel lotion on her face and body.

Wrapping a fresh towel around her hair and another around her body, she climbed into bed and passed out.

Knocking woke her. Why would someone knock? She had a doorbell. Holly cracked her eyes open, then remembered. She wasn't home; she was in a hotel in Leadville. She rolled to the edge of the bed, every muscle, bone, and inch of skin hurting. "Coming!"

Her thighs felt like steel, her joints screamed, and she hissed in pain when her blistered feet hit the floor. Hobbling to the door, she cracked it and looked out. The female FBI agent held a bag out to her. "Thanks. And thank you for the toothbrush and comb."

"The hotel supplied those. Put your old clothes in the bag and we'll retrieve the tech and tools. I'm assuming you don't want those clothes back." She wrinkled her nose.

Holly matched her expression. "Oh no. I never want to see that stuff again. Or smell it."

The agent laughed, then sobered. "A half an hour enough?"

"Sure." Holly shuffled to the bathroom. Hopefully another hot shower would help. A little more than a half hour later, she stumbled into the lobby.

Luke joined her immediately. "Are you okay?"

She shrugged, then regretted it. "Under the circumstances, sure."

"Ready? Let's go." Two of the agents led the way out of the hotel and a block down the street to a diner.

Holly's muscles loosened slightly on the walk. They ate omelets, muffins, orange juice, coffee, and water, with a side of painkillers. After they finished, an unmarked black SUV pulled to the curb. Holly and Luke buckled up in the back of the Secret Service vehicle they'd started their adventure in.

Ness leaned inside, handing each of them a white plastic bag; hers was much larger than Luke's. "We recovered your phones and Captain Sevrason's weapon, plus the personal items you left in the vehicle and in your snow gear. We also found your shelter and retrieved the tech. I spoke with your respective commanders, and you are on medical leave until next Monday. In case you don't know, it's Tuesday night."

Luke pointed at his wrist. "How about my Breitling watch?"

Ness nodded. "It's there too."

"Good, it's been everywhere with me." He smiled at her. "I gave myself a graduation gift after pilot training."

Ness stepped back, closed the door, and thumped the roof once. They rolled down the street. Holly opened the bag, making sure her backpack was inside. Unzipping the front, she saw that her dead phone and passport were there, but the cash was gone. She felt the lining. The thugs had missed the silver and gold coins. She dropped the bag on the floor and put her head back, more than ready to go back to sleep.

Luke held his hand out, palm up. She curled her hand around his palm and relaxed when his closed around hers. Her perception had certainly changed. Luke was no longer the boy who'd betrayed her but a comrade-in-arms, a protector, and a compassionate, strong leader. But her reaction to the warmth of his hand meant he was more than those things. He'd become a true friend and was probably much, much more.

She'd have decide on a label later; she was too tired to think about anything but the comfort of safety and his hand on hers.

Chapter 16

AFTER NAPPING THE REST of the day and a restless night with too many nightmares, Holly woke near her normal time the next morning. It took her forever to crawl out of bed. She hobbled like an ancient crone to her bathroom, gritting her teeth against the pain, and turned the shower on.

Then she turned to the mirror. She'd avoided looking at the hotel; she hadn't wanted to know. Both sides of her face were mottled with black, blue, and purple topped with bright red whip marks from branches. Both of her eyes were black, too. Her hands were swollen and sore from grabbing trees and bushes to stay upright. Her legs looked like someone had beat her with a rod, and her stomach was painted with a big, multi-colored bruise, too. Her normal tan coloring didn't hide any of it, but Luke's pale skin would look even worse. And her poor feet had blisters on top of blisters. The medic had recommended leaving them intact and wearing slippers; popping them only invited infection.

But it could have been so much worse. She'd only needed antibiotic ointment. She smiled at the survivor in the mirror. She'd sent Das to the hospital with a concussion. He deserved worse, but that was out of her control.

She cautiously stepped into the shower and winced. All those tiny cuts stung. She stayed in the shower until the water started to run cold. She'd thought about a bath, but she wasn't sure she could get out on her own.

When she emerged from the shower, she could walk again. She wrapped gauze around her feet, put on soft slippers, and made coffee. While it brewed, she looked at her charged phone—twenty new texts, five new voicemails. Most of them were worried friends, or later, messages conveying happiness. The voicemails were from Colonel Haywood confirming her medical leave, an appointment with her doctor on Thursday, and an appointment with Mental Health too. Both Amy and Kristen had called, Kristen insisting she call when she woke. Luke had texted an hour ago, asking her to call, too.

She replied to most of the texts with an, "I'm fine, thanks, see you Monday." She called Colonel Haywood, but he was in a meeting. His secretary promised to pass on Holly's thanks to the colonel. She called Kristen, but it went to voicemail. She was probably in a meeting, too.

She sent a text to Luke.

> I'm awake, alive, and okay. How are you?

As she sipped her coffee and contemplated breakfast, her phone rang. She couldn't hold back a smile when Luke's name popped up.

"Hey, how are you feeling?" His rumbling voice brought a smile to her face.

"Sore, stiff, beat up, generally painful everywhere. You?"

"The same, but I'm happier about it. We're alive and free." He chuckled. "Are you doing anything today?"

The thought of moving made her snort. "Laying on the couch and moaning occasionally while I shovel chocolate in my mouth."

He sputtered a laugh. "I've got a better offer. How about a big breakfast, and then we'll sit in some hot springs? Plus, Amy and Chris are inbound. Group dinner tonight."

"That all sounds wonderful. Do we have enough time before dinner?" It was an incredibly thoughtful offer.

"Sure. If we're a little late for dinner, no one will mind."

Relaxing in unending hot water seemed like heaven on earth. "Okay, you're on."

"See you in twenty."

Holly tried to rush upstairs but could only hobble. She picked her most modest bikini, with yoga pants and a cute top over the suit, and put a towel in her bag. No reason to bother with makeup—it would melt off in the heat. She made it downstairs just in time for the doorbell to ring; she opened the door.

Luke's smile died, and he gently cupped her face, his hands warm and comforting. "You look like you went a couple of rounds with an MMA fighter and lost.

Does it hurt? I should have beat that guy to a pulp." He scowled.

She had no doubt that if Das was here, he'd be just that—pulp. "It looks worse than it feels. Ibuprofen helps."

His hands dropped and he smiled. "Traffic is a mess. So, instead of the hot springs, how about a massage and a sauna?"

"Sure. That sounds amazing, too." Heat in any form would feel marvelous.

"Good, because I already made reservations." He smiled. "Come on, let's go." He took her hand, rubbing a thumb across her palm, and led her out the door.

Holly shivered at the caress of his hand on hers. In the car, she snuggled into the heated leather seat. He'd preheated it for her.

"As much as I complain about this car, I think I'm going to miss it." He looked at the backup camera, his mirrors, then his surroundings. Then he pulled out.

She turned to look at him. "What are you talking about?"

"Didn't they tell you? I guess they wouldn't." He glanced at her. "The federal prosecutors are confiscating all of my father's assets, and one of those is this car. His company has been paying for it." He chuckled. "Actually, my company, but in name only. It's one of his assets." His grin turned to a grimace. "Not like I'm going to fight them on that."

That didn't seem fair. "Wow, nice way to repay you for your help."

He flashed a smile at her. "I can't complain. I've had a free car for several years now. Maybe they'd just let me pay it off? Nah, too much hassle. I'll buy something more practical for Colorado, something with all-wheel drive. I can afford it. Want to go car shopping with me?"

He had to be joking, right? "No. I hate car shopping. I'm horrible at it."

"But you'd make a great distraction. Any guy will be too busy drooling over you to bother haggling with me." He grinned.

She pointed at her face. "Especially right now, with the lovely black eyes and technicolor skin."

Luke laughed. "Trust me, you're still beautiful. But I suspect I'll have to deal with all kinds of folks trying to protect you from me."

She put a hand on his arm, where it rested on the console. "Luke, you didn't exactly walk away undamaged."

"No, but I don't look like I lost a fight." He frowned. Luke's face was covered with little cuts and whip marks like hers, but some of them were under his heavy black scruff, thick after just three days. He noticed her looking and smiled. "Figured I'd give my face a little time to heal before I try to shave, although that means it will be a bear when I do."

"Probably a good idea. Did they make doctor's appointments for you too? Mine are tomorrow."

"Mine are too." He nodded. "I think our appointments with mental health are back to back. They probably want to compare our stories and make sure I wasn't involved in any of your abuse."

She whipped her head around to stare at him, then clutched the back of her neck when pain shot down her back. She had to move more carefully. "Why would they think that?"

"I think they're just being cautious." He kept his eyes on the road and his tone was light.

"I'll set the story straight." Luke had protected her to the best of his ability. She'd have never made it through the Colorado wilderness on her own.

Luke parked at the restaurant, escorted her inside, and they were seated right away. He asked the server for two coffees and a large carafe of orange juice.

Holly read the menu, appreciating his thoughtfulness. "This place has the best orange juice, but I usually have a small glass."

"You could use the calories and the vitamins." He scanned her. "I've seen that shirt on you before, and it's not usually loose."

She was surprised he noticed. "Maybe we should market escaping across the wilderness in winter as a weight-loss scheme."

He chuckled. "You'd have to be a sadist to make that work."

She laughed, despite how it made her face hurt. He was funny and charming when he relaxed, and devastatingly handsome despite the red marking his face.

His expression sobered. "But seriously, you need to put some weight back on, or you'll blow away in the wind at Schriever Air Force Base."

Their server, an older blonde woman, set coffee and juice on the table in front of her. "Honey, unless he gave you those black eyes, this one is a keeper."

Her cheeks heated. "No, he helped me get away from that guy."

The server patted Luke's shoulder. "Good job." She took their order and left.

Holly cupped a hand around his prickly jaw. "You could use some calories too. The beard hides it, but your cheeks are pretty hollow."

"I know it. I had a protein shake earlier this morning and I'm hungry again." He rubbed his jaw gently into her palm like a cat, his beard rasping against her skin, making her shiver again.

"You must have been up a lot earlier than I was." She dropped her hand but not before he dropped a kiss on her palm. Heat spread through her whole body.

"You sleep more than I do. You're definitely harder to wake up, unless there's a helicopter involved." He smirked.

She shuddered. "I'll never sleep through that noise ever again."

"No, me either." He grimaced. "And the worst part is we could have been rescued that first morning."

"We had no way to know that. Hindsight being twenty-twenty, there are some things we and the FBI should have done a little differently." A lot of things, actually.

He scowled. "Yeah, like not doing it at all."

"Are you seriously telling me, 'I told you so'!" So much for her grateful and happy mood.

"No, but..." He tilted his head.

She held up her hand, then winced when her shoulder protested. "Don't even go there. With any luck, Das will never make it out of prison."

Luke shook his head. "I doubt he'll get that much time, Holly. But he'll get enough that you shouldn't have to worry about him again. You realize we're both going to have to testify here and in Washington DC?"

"Maybe he'll cut a deal." She hoped so. Her new satellite operations job meant she'd be working rotating shifts. Scheduling time off for that wouldn't make her any friends. At least it should be official duty, not leave.

"Maybe. I'm sure my father will. If he'd sell out his son, he'll certainly sell out Das." He scowled at the table.

Holly put a hand on his arm. "Betrayal by family is the worst. I'm sorry, Luke."

He turned toward her, his scowl turning sad. "You would know."

"Yeah." She sighed. Thinking about her family, especially her father, always brought a mix of anger, betrayal, and sorrow. Still, it could have been worse. They might have succeeded. She'd be living in constant fear, with kids to protect. But she wouldn't have stayed with an abusive man. Not after living with what her mother went through.

The server brought omelets, bacon, and biscuits. The smell of browned butter and crispy bacon was irresistible, and Holly's mood got better with every bite. She was fairly certain Luke felt the same because both of them ate without speaking. He finished his meal and about a quarter of hers.

Holly sipped coffee. "Every time I eat, I think, 'that's the best thing I've ever eaten,' but this time, I think it's true." She smoothed her hands over her bruised and slightly swollen tummy.

"Yeah, I wonder if I'll ever get past that point. Probably won't take as long as I'd like it to." He glanced at his watch. "Are you ready? We'll be a little early, but the receptionist said they weren't busy this afternoon and they were flexible."

"Sure, let's go." A little pampering would be very welcome. It was a lovely gift.

They arrived quickly and entered the spa. Typical new age instrumental music, a subtle lemony scent, and soft carpet combined with natural colors and plants to provide a calm, relaxing environment. The atmosphere worked its magic, making Holly smiled.

The gorgeous receptionist, her bright white teeth contrasting with her dark skin and burgundy lips, stood. "Welcome. You must be Luke and Holly."

"Yes, we are." Luke nodded. "We're a little early. Is that a problem?"

"Not at all." She shook her head. "You can stay in the sauna." She tilted her head toward a hallway on Holly's left. "Come this way."

They followed her, the humidity increasing and subtle scent strengthening. "The men's changing room is down there, women's here. There are lockers with keys, robes and sauna wraps by the lockers, and sandals as well. We recommend you shower first. I'll meet you on the other side and escort you to your sauna in fifteen minutes, if that's enough time."

"Perfect." Holly nodded and turned into the changing room. She showered and found the door on the other side. Outside, Luke chatted with the receptionist. His powerful legs were sexy despite the black and blue bruises vivid on his pale skin.

"Ready?" Her smile flashed. "Follow me." She led them to a redwood door marked with a number one. "Here you are. There's drinking water, towels, and a cold shower if you want to alternate cold and heat. Just relax." She turned away. "I'll get you when your massage therapists are ready."

They thanked her again, grabbed water bottles, hung their robes, and entered the sauna. Redwood boards lined the small compartment, and the scent of cedar wafted on the hot air. A heat element and water bucket stood at the back, with benches on both sides. It would fit six close friends, four easily, and was spacious for two.

Holly relaxed on the wood bench. In seconds, the heat penetrated and relaxed her body, even if breathing was a little challenging until she got used to it. "Oh, wow, this is fantastic."

Luke sat next to her and rested his feet on the other bench. She was envious—hers weren't long enough. She was also trying, very hard, not to stare at his amazing body, set off by the short sauna wrap. He was so gorgeous, even bruised black and blue, with solid shoulders flowing into cut pecs. A sprinkling of black hair arrowed down across eight-pack abs and disappeared beneath the wrap. And his legs were solid muscle.

"Usually I get too hot, fast, but today I'll love every minute of it. I ran my hot water tank empty last night." He put his head back.

"You should have taken a bath." Luke Sevrason in a tub of hot water, green eyes beckoning…heat rose in Holly's cheeks and chest.

He shook his head. "I've only got a shower. Normally, it doesn't matter, but last night it would have been perfect. That's why I wanted to hit the hot springs." He shrugged. "But it wasn't to be." He glanced at her legs and frowned. "If you want to put your feet up on the wall, you can lay down and put your head on my lap."

"I don't think that's a good idea." That kind of intimacy was dangerous. She'd forgiven him before their adventure, but she still wasn't sure about a relationship. Their careers were so different and had few military locations in common. And she knew making serious decisions in her current state of physical and emotional exhaustion was a bad idea.

He patted his leg. "Why not? This is a public place. I'm just offering a pillow. Relax."

She considered his generous offer. Putting her legs up would feel good. She slid down and turned, carefully putting her head just above his knee. After a minute, she relaxed, enjoying the lightness in her feet and legs. He stroked her hair. Holly closed her eyes.

A quiet knock sounded, and she sat up, Luke's hand sliding off her head and down her back. "Careful."

"Holly and Luke? We're ready for your massages, if you're ready."

Luke called, "Be right out." He gazed at her, his eyes soft and warm, a small smile on his face. "Ready?"

Holly rose slowly, missing the warmth and comfort of his hand. "Yes."

Luke opened the door. The receptionist said, "Careful coming out. Some people get a little dizzy with the temperature change."

Holly stepped out and shivered when the cool air hit her hot skin. Luke followed, resting his big, strong hands warm on her waist.

The receptionist smiled. "Everyone okay?"

They both nodded. "Okay, this way." The receptionist led them into a room labeled massage. A man stood by one massage table, a woman by the other, with a screen between them. "This is Katy and Rob, and they'll discuss your choices with you before you get started."

Rob, a medium-height Hispanic man, dark hair styled in a faux-hawk with very broad shoulders under his spa-logo polo shirt, waved. "The first question is, do either of you have an issue with a male massage therapist?" They both said no, and Holly was a little surprised to hear that from Luke.

Luke said, "Some women can't press hard enough for me."

Katy, a tall, willowy redhead with light blue eyes, nodded. "Okay, Holly, you're with me. But to clarify, you need a recovery massage, correct?"

Luke nodded. "Yes, we just finished up a very challenging twenty-two-mile trek through the snow, and we fell a lot." He waved a hand at his body. "We're both pretty beat up."

Holly was shocked. "We did twenty-two miles?"

He turned to her, nodding with his lips clamped. "Seven were on the road, and the three at the end were on that track, but we did twelve miles of untracked cross-country."

"Wow, no wonder I feel like this." She rubbed the back of her neck.

"Yep, there are SEALs who'd have a hard time doing that." He turned back to Katy and Rob. "Sorry, you were saying?"

Katy scanned her from head to toe. "How about a hot-rock massage? Let us know if specific areas are tight, and if they're not too bruised, we can work those a little harder."

"That sounds perfect for me." Luke nodded.

Katy pointed. "Holly, you'll be on the left, and Luke on the right. You can take off as much or as little as you like. We'll start face down, so slide under the sheet with your head in the rest." She and Rob left.

With the screen between them, Holly didn't have any problem taking everything off before sliding under the sheet.

"Everyone set?" Rob asked.

Holly raised her voice. "Yes, come in."

Rob folded the screen back. Katy rubbed her hands together, then picked up a shiny black rock. "If anything is uncomfortable, please let us know."

Katy placed the warm stone on Holly's back. After that, she was too busy enjoying the sensations to do more than moan in pleasure.

When they were done, Katy wiped oil from her back. "Stay there until you feel like getting up; there's no rush. Please rise slowly, or you could get dizzy. Drink plenty of water today to help flush your system. It was our pleasure serving you today."

Holly wasn't sure she could get up—every muscle had relaxed. "Thank you both so much." After more pleasantries, Rob rolled the screen back in place, then he and Katy left. Holly sighed, sat up, and put on her robe. "Wow, that was amazing. I feel so much better." She slid off the bench. Her feet still hurt, and the rest of her body ached, but much less.

"Agreed. I think this was a better choice than the hot springs, although I would have liked to see you in a swimsuit. But a towel is just as good. Do you want anything else while we're here? Manicure?" His arm appeared from behind the screen, his hand out, palm up.

She joined him and slid her hand into his. "This was more than enough. You are going to let me pay for half, right?"

"Sorry, it's already paid for, tips and all. Did it when I made the appointment." He smiled. "Tell you what, next time we end up running for our lives, you can treat me to the spa." He turned toward her and winked.

"Funny guy." He was so thoughtful and generous.

He smirked. "Ready?" He led her to the door and opened it, holding her hand as they returned to the locker rooms. "Take your time. I'll meet you out front."

She let her hand slide from his, regretting the loss of his comforting grasp. "Thank you so much. This was just what I needed." Words were good, but actions meant more. She reached up, slid her hand behind his neck, and tugged his head down, pressing her lips to his, then releasing him. After she stepped back, he smiled, then stepped backward to the men's locker room, holding her gaze. She watched until the door closed, then entered the women's locker and fanned her face. All that heat in his expression—she probably needed a cold shower. She hugged the feeling close while she washed, enjoying the warm water and lemon-scented scrub.

After she dressed, she joined Luke in the lobby. He helped her into his vehicle and drove to his house, holding her hand almost the entire way. He pulled into the carport and hopped out.

As Holly opened the door, her stomach rumbled. "I can't believe I'm hungry again."

He smiled down and offered his hand to help her out of the car. "I know. I'm starving. Chris knows how tough our trek was. They'll have lots of food." He led her up the stairs and held the door open for her. Kristen, Amy, and Chris gathered around them, offering hugs and sympathy. Rex bounced around like a puppy.

After a few minutes, Amy whistled. "Hey! There's food in the kitchen. Go get some. Holly and Luke need to eat, and the living room is more comfortable than the entry."

Holly chuckled along with everyone else, then followed Amy's instructions. Holly loaded her plate, then plopped on the couch.

Kristen sat next to her. "Holy Fajitas, Holly! I don't think I've ever seen you eat that much."

"I know. It's ridiculous, isn't it?" She shook her head. "We ate a huge breakfast late this morning, and I'm starving again." Luke sat next to her, with a plate piled higher than hers.

Amy put a glass of water and a beer in front of her, with a second set for Luke. "We'll let you eat, and then we want to hear the whole story. Luke, you owe the

SERE school a case or three of beer. If the FBI couldn't find you, the training was obviously excellent."

Luke swallowed a mouthful of food. "No kidding. Although Holly did great, and she hasn't had anything but the basic survive and resist briefing." He smiled proudly at her. "My boss called this morning to check on me. He'd planned a squadron training scenario for the day after we self-rescued. The guys were a little disappointed they didn't get to show up the feds."

Amy raised her beer toward him. "I'd bet you'll be briefing the SERE school and probably every flying squadron in the USAF. First truly successful SERE we've had in a long time."

"I suppose, but it wasn't exactly against an enemy." Luke shrugged.

"Close enough. You evaded the bad guys, the feds, and the state cops. That's an amazing accomplishment." Chris raised his beer bottle and clinked it against Luke's.

They ate while Amy and Chris told them what they'd been doing over the last few months. Luke got another plate of food. After she finished eating, Holly told them the story, Luke interjecting occasionally.

"So now what?" Chris asked.

Kristen handed fancy chocolate cupcakes to everyone. Holly savored the rich, dark chocolate and sugary goodness.

Luke put down his half-finished cupcake. "Das, his co-conspirators, and my father have been formally charged. Their homes were raided, and I heard they freed several trafficking survivors. They've found written records of more and are freeing them, too.

They're seizing all of Father's assets to pay for his fraud. I'm fairly certain he'll make a deal to testify against Das." He snorted. "He was willing to sell me down the river, so he'll definitely sell out Das."

Holly squeezed his leg. "And they're taking Luke's car too, since his father paid for it."

"That sucks. That's a primo car." Kristen put a second cupcake in front of Luke. "Here's a consolation prize."

He shrugged one shoulder. "I don't need it. I've got an SUV."

Kristen sat down. "What are you doing with your week off, other than sleeping and eating?"

Holly grimaced. "Tomorrow we're both seeing physical and psychological doctors. I don't think either will do much for me, but I guess you never know."

Kristen raised a brow and smirked. "What did you two do today?"

She was fishing. Holly smirked back at her. "I made it out of bed, which was by no means a sure thing." Everyone laughed, but with a grim edge. "Everything hurt so bad. All my muscles were in knots, and I'm cut and bruised everywhere." Even after the massage and drugs, the aches and pains were returning.

"Those shiners are pretty obvious, even with your darker skin tone." Chris pointed at her face.

Holly grimaced but immediately stopped because that movement hurt. "Once I got out of bed, Luke took me to breakfast and then to a spa for a sauna and hot rock massage. I feel so much better." She squeezed his hand and smiled at him.

Luke grinned. "It was enlightened self-interest. I wanted to go, but there's no way I'm showing up at a spa all by myself."

"What else do you have planned this week?" Amy asked. "Now that we know you're safe, we're headed back. Chris is saving his leave for his retirement."

"Smart. I'm sleeping a lot." Luke shrugged. "Not in the mood to go snowboarding, that's for sure."

Holly agreed with him, but living in Colorado, she needed to replace her winter clothing. "I need new clothes. The feds gave us the jackets and pants, but the rest of it was mine and it's trashed."

Amy groaned. "I hate shopping. But there are end of season sales. Maybe you should hit the outlet mall."

Holly matched her groan. "Normally, I order everything, but you're right. And if I don't find what I need there, I can go to Denver."

"If you don't mind, I'll go with you. I could use a fashion adviser." Luke leaned against her shoulder for a moment.

She snorted. "Right, Mr. Designer Suit."

"You noticed, so it was worth the money." He shrugged. "But my father paid a personal shopper to pick all those fancy clothes out. No more of that, either."

Chris snorted. "You don't need that stuff, anyway." He stood and gathered plates. "We've got a long drive tomorrow, so we're heading to bed, sorry." Amy joined him, also yawning.

Holly rose, Kristen and Luke joining her. They put up the few leftovers and cleaned. Everyone gathered for goodbye hugs, then Chris, Amy, and Rex disappeared into the guest room.

Kristen grabbed her purse and keys. "Holly, I'll drive you home." She winked. "Take your time while I warm up the car." She closed the door, leaving Holly alone with Luke.

Luke took her hands in his. "I know we don't have to pretend anymore, but our relationship was never fake for me. Can we talk about it?" He gazed intently into her eyes.

Holly couldn't say no. She didn't want to say no but wasn't sure she was entirely ready for a solid yes, either. She nodded, biting her lip. "Let's talk. But not tonight." She rose on her tiptoes and dropped a quick kiss on his soft lips. "Good night."

"Good night." He watched until she got in Kristen's car.

Kristen put her car in drive. "Looks like things are going better."

Holly nodded. "Yes, but there's still something that's holding me back." He still seemed too good to be true. Or he was setting her up for a fall. There had to be a catch, because she didn't get the big wins.

Kristen sniffed. "Girl, give yourself a break. You've had a tough time. You need to heal. Take advantage of those doctors and the time off. Relax. Sleep. Eat. Then date the man. You don't need to marry him tomorrow."

Holly laughed, relief bubbling through her. "You're right. I'm jumping the gun. Thanks."

"If you have trouble sleeping, call me anytime, day or night." She drove through the quiet town. "Or call Luke." Her brows waggled. "He might have just what you need to sleep like the dead."

Holly couldn't hold back a giggle at Kristen's insinuation. "I'm definitely not doing that." But she wondered what it would be like to come home to a man who loved her, rather than an empty, cold house.

Chapter 17

HOLLY WAS DONE. THE poking, the prodding, and the never-ending questions had ended in a full-out bawling breakdown in the therapist's office. An abduction, assault, and an escape through the wilderness couldn't make her cry, but talking about it had. She wanted to go home, take a bath, and drink a glass of wine. Or maybe two. The whole bottle might make her feel better. She dabbed her eyes and left the bathroom.

Luke, wearing a flightsuit, leaned against the wall outside, looking cool and professional. "Do you want to get some dinner?"

Maybe Luke's therapist had gone easier on him. Or he was more resilient than she was. Suddenly, the noise and bustle of normal people surrounding them was unbearable. Holly strode for the front door. "No, I just want to go home." And not think about any of her experiences ever again.

He nodded. "I understand. Are we still on for tomorrow? And if so, what time shall I pick you up?"

She'd say never, except living in Colorado without winter gear seemed stupid. Especially after their recent trek. "Ten?"

Luke followed her to her car. "I'll see you then." He bent slightly to look into her eyes. "Are you sure you're okay? If you need to talk, or just have someone around, I'd love to be there for you." He stepped closer, holding out his arms.

She opened the car door and stepped away from him. "I'm fine. I just need to be alone." They were in uniform. Besides that, if he hugged her, she'd break down again. She needed her house, her bed, and her things.

He swallowed hard. "Okay. I'll see you tomorrow."

Holly pulled into her driveway without remembering the drive. She kept reliving those horrible hours, chained to the bed, with men threatening her. And after her breakdown, the therapist insisted on seeing her every week for the foreseeable future. She'd have to talk about it again and again, bringing it all back and making it more real than it was while it happened. She'd probably have to talk about her childhood, too.

She let herself into her house, locked the door, then searched the entire house, including under the bed and the inside closets. Only then did she start the water and pour a glass of wine. In the bath, she put her head back and closed her eyes.

Intellectually, therapy was a good thing, necessary even. But she really wanted to forget the whole thing and never, ever think about it again.

LUKE

Luke watched Holly drive away, then walked to his car. She'd looked haunted and exhausted, and all he wanted to do was hold her close and protect her. He knew he was pushing for too much, too soon, but he'd never stopped loving her, even when he'd thought she was married. Knowing she was alone and needed support, but wouldn't take help, was difficult to accept. Her face and body all screamed that she was in deep emotional pain. Even if she didn't want to talk about it, he desperately wanted to hold her and care for her. And if he was completely honest, he needed the comfort, too. He drove home and trudged up the stairs to his too-quiet apartment.

He opened a beer and plopped on the couch. He'd rather be in that cold cave with her than sit comfortably by himself. He had it so bad.

Maybe being around any man was too much for Holly. She'd survived a terrible experience, one that so many women endured; expecting her to turn to him for comfort was ridiculous. Picking up his phone, he asked Kristen to check in on Holly later. At least he could do that much for her, even if she wouldn't let him do anything else.

She'd agreed to meet him tomorrow, so she hadn't shut him out entirely. He had to be grateful for the small things, to be happy with any small part of her that she was willing to share. Pushing for more would only make her run. Patience had never been his strong point—his privileged upbringing had never encouraged that practice—but for Holly, he'd do anything.

Even leave her alone—forever, if she asked. But he hoped for more. A lot more.

The next morning, Luke woke early and ate ravenously, then tapped his fingers impatiently on the couch cushions. He had hours left to burn before he could pick her up. Sitting and brooding did nothing except make him more impatient, so he'd do something useful. He loaded the washer and cleaned the bathroom but kept looking at his watch. The expensive watch should make time go faster on command. He laughed out loud at his ridiculous thoughts, the sound echoing oddly in the bathroom, and went back to scrubbing.

Finally, his calendar notification went off. He drove to her house, parked, and jogged to her door. She opened it, smiling. Her beauty stunned him, despite the horrible bruises, the black eyes, and the tiny lines of pain radiating from her eyes. He ushered her carefully into his car and they drove north. "Did you have breakfast?" He didn't want to go shopping. He wanted to take her home. Instead, he gripped the wheel tighter and kept his attention on the traffic.

"Yes. I can't face an outlet mall without food and coffee. Besides, I was starving again when I woke up. I wonder when I'll stop feeling like an eating machine?" She smirked and shrugged.

He had to keep it light, so he didn't scare her away. "When you're ten pounds heavier than you were before our adventure."

She thumped his shoulder. For a tiny thing, she packed a wallop. "That's not funny. Ten pounds on me means buying new clothes." Despite her claim, she smiled.

"You have more muscle now and muscle weighs more." She was gorgeous despite the bruised face. She'd become stronger and that would help her fight more effectively, too. Not that he'd leave her to fight on her own, or fairly. He'd bullied the feds into fast-tracking him for a concealed carry license. They thought they'd swept up all of Das's co-conspirators, but he wasn't so sure. The cold metal weapon against his lower back was comforting.

"Good point. Still, I should be slowing down soon. I hope." She shrugged.

He grinned. "I figure I'm good for at least another week or so of extreme chowing." He'd been in pretty good shape before their wilderness trek, but his thighs strained the seams of these jeans, and the waist was loose.

She laughed, and he joined her. Making her laugh was one of his favorite things to do. She didn't have enough joy in her life. Every laugh transformed her from beautiful to stunning. She stunned him, anyway.

She didn't seem to realize how much her every word and gesture meant to him. Or maybe she didn't care.

But he knew that wasn't true. Besides, even if it was, it didn't matter. He'd be there for her no matter what.

He parked at the outlet mall and sighed. He hated shopping. He'd miss having a personal shopper, but he didn't need fancy clothes. "Once more into the breach, dear friends!"

"Come on, it won't be that bad. Quit being a baby!" Holly smirked and got out of the car.

To his surprise, it wasn't that bad. They found a ski and board shop and got great gear at a decent price. She talked him into a slate blue jacket, rather than his normal black, and in turn, he talked her into a raspberry plaid that looked fabulous against her skin. Her normal skin tone, not the technicolor camouflage pattern she current sported.

Then, since they were there, they window shopped and tried on clothes that neither one would ever wear just for a laugh. On their way to lunch, they passed a lingerie shop. He had no trouble picturing her in some of those little pieces of lace and silk. But Holly had been objectified enough; she didn't need that from him.

During lunch, Luke wracked his brains for ways to extend their non-date. Leaving the restaurant, he spotted a theater. "Want to see a movie?" Maybe a date-like activity would help his cause.

"That sounds perfect." She knocked her shoulder into his arm. "I've done enough walking today."

"Me too." Luke pulled up the theater schedule on his phone. "There's an action thriller with a couple surviving in the wilderness,"—he snorted—"an over-the-top comedy, or an animated kids' movie. Which one?"

Holly leaned close to peer at his phone. "I've had enough survival stories. That comedian isn't my favorite." She smiled up at him. "How about the cartoon? It's a weekday, so there shouldn't be very many kids, and this production company makes good films for everyone."

"Why not?" Luke led her to the theater, bought tickets and snacks, and found perfect seats in the almost deserted theater. He settled into his seat and put the popcorn between them. He'd rather hold her hand, but she had to make the first moves. She'd been pressured too much by too many people.

Kids 'movies had definitely improved, but he got more joy out of watching Holly's reactions than the action on the screen. She even took his hand during the final scene. He'd have watched anything to have her small hand nestled in his.

After the movie, Luke retrieved his car while Holly used the bathroom. He pulled up front, hopped out, and settled her into the passenger seat, then got on the freeway south. "I hope you had fun today."

"I did. Thanks for coming along. Shopping is better with someone else." She flashed a smile at him. "And the movie was good. I like it when the princess rescues herself, instead of waiting for some prince."

He grinned. "Reminds me of another princess who rescued herself."

She shot a confused frown at him. "I'm not a princess."

"You are to me." But he was no prince. Even the wealth that had made so many women chase him was gone. Add in the fact that his father would soon be a convicted criminal, and he'd be lucky to still have friends. A relationship seemed impossible. Fortunately, he knew Holly didn't care about his money.

Holly's stomach rumbled. "I can't believe I'm starving again. We just had a huge tub of popcorn!"

"Quit complaining. We'll be watching what we eat soon enough." He'd never counted calories but usually kept his diet on the healthier side, with lots of veggies and lean meat.

"Too true." She turned and frowned at him. "Not that you have to worry, do you?"

He shook his head. "Not much. But that will change. My father put on quite a bit of weight after forty."

She sniffed. "I won't have that long."

He shook his head. So many women had a twisted view of their bodies. "You're in great shape, and you normally eat like a bird."

"My sisters tell a different story, especially after they had kids. I'm sure I'll be in the same boat." Her expression seemed unusually sad.

He'd better tread cautiously, even if the idea caused a swell of hope and happiness in his soul. "Is that something you want to do?"

"Not yet, but yes, I'd like to have kids someday. You?" She gave him some serious side eye and bit her lip.

"Maybe not quite yet, but I don't want to be a senior citizen when they're graduating high school either." He laughed. He didn't want to scare her off, but having kids with her would be a dream come true. The longing surprised him, but the more he considered it, the more he wanted that. But only with Holly.

Her hands twisted together in her lap. "I'm kind of worried, though. I had terrible role models. My mom was more like a servant than a wife. My father wasn't a nice man. The only kid he cared about was my brother." Her shoulders rose to her ears. "I'm just not sure I'll be a good mom."

Luke snorted. Her fears, while understandable, were ludicrous. "Are you kidding me? You share so much love and have amazing determination. You'll be a great mom." She'd survived so much, persevered and succeeded against the odds. She couldn't be any less than wonderful.

She blushed brightly enough to see through the bruises. "Thanks." She bit her lip and swallowed hard. "I think you'd be a great father, too."

"Thanks." He glanced at her pink cheeks. "Despite my father, I had some good role models. Our housekeeper and driver in DC had a couple of kids who were older than me by about a decade. Mrs. Medvedev, Nana, treated me like I was hers, at least as much as she could. And Papa M taught me how to work on cars, and unplug toilets, and all those other things you're supposed to learn from your dad." His father would never lower himself to do manual labor of any kind. With his father in jail, Luke needed to check on Nana and Papa. They might be in a tough spot, and they'd be too proud to ask him for help.

She tilted her head and smiled slightly. "I always wondered how you ended up with a set of morals and good manners. Most of our classmates were entitled jerks."

That was more than true. "I got lucky. Nana didn't put up with lies or laziness. She made me do chores for my allowance. I don't think Father knew, but I don't think he cared either." His father was distant at best and absent most of the time.

"We all did chores but no allowance. Anything we needed had to come from Mom's tiny budget. I think the first new clothes I ever got was our school uniform." She snorted. "But only that first year. Then I had to ask the graduating seniors for theirs and tailor them myself and haunt second-hand stores for everything else."

Luke frowned. "I knew you were on scholarship, but I didn't know you were poor."

She scowled. "My father made a decent living, but every penny went to him and my brother, not to the 'useless' women who kept them fed and comfortable. I remember Mother begging for money, but he'd tell her to shut up." Her tone was very cold and bitter. "I can't believe he gambled everything away."

Luke would like to smack the man, hard, but he couldn't. "Is your mom going to be okay?"

"Yes." She blew out a sigh. "May sent an email. Once Mother saw a real doctor, her issues were easily taken care of. Didn't even cost that much." Her smile showed her relief.

"That's excellent." Luke pulled into Holly's driveway, got out and opened her door, then escorted her to her front door. "How about dinner tomorrow?" He was too nervous to smile.

She turned to face him, frowning. "Dinner? Why? We don't have to look like a couple anymore."

Luke recruited his courage. "It was never an act for me, Holly. I want this second chance more than anything."

She stared at him for what seemed like forever. "Only if I get to pay this time. Non-negotiable."

He shrugged. "Fine. I have no problem with that." If he got her time and attention, he didn't care what it took.

"Where and when?" Her brows almost met on the bridge of her nose.

He couldn't kiss her, no matter how much he wanted to. "You pick. This is your date." He smiled and held up his hands in surrender. If she needed to be in control, he'd give her the yoke, no problem.

She nodded slowly. "Okay, I'll pick you up at seven. We'll have barbeque. I think I could stand one more night of extreme chowing."

"I'll see you then. Can't wait." Luke bent down and kissed her cheek. Her light scent teased his senses, and he wanted to pull her into his arms and never stop kissing her. But it was too soon for that. She had to make the first move. He waited for her door to lock, then made his lonely drive home.

Holly twisted her hands together. She never should have agreed to another date. Give Lukas Sevrason an inch and he'd take a mile. Once again, she'd be waiting every minute of the day to see him, sad at the least little frown, happy only if he was happy. But she wasn't that person anymore. For the last decade, she'd had no family to rely on but also no one to hold her back. She did what was best for her, what she wanted to do, and was responsible for her own happiness. She didn't have to worry about someone else's feelings, needs, or wishes. She and Kristen supported each other, but they didn't exert control. While it would be nice to have a significant other, she wasn't sure she wanted to deal with everything else that came with a relationship.

Men had controlled and constrained so much of her life.

But she couldn't just ignore Luke or move or employ any of the other normal avoidance techniques. First, the military decided where she lived and for how long. Second, she wasn't giving up her friendship with Amy, which meant being friends with Chris, too, and Luke was his best friend. He'd be around, and her ability to resist him was minimal.

She put her head back and sighed. Third, Luke really was a great guy, and without him, she might still be in Das's clutches. Not only that, but he'd treated her as a team member, even though he had a lot more training, and logically, he should have just taken charge. And he'd been grateful she rescued him from the house, not dismissive of her efforts like some men.

If she was really, really honest with herself, she wasn't sure she wanted to resist Luke. She'd felt so much safer after she'd gotten him out of that house—sure, part of it was he knew more about escape than she did, but the other part had just wanted him there, with her. He was reliable and trustworthy and loyal and gorgeous on top of that, with a hard body that didn't quit.

Plus, they'd both been betrayed by their fathers—the very people who should have protected them.

Holly went upstairs and got ready for bed. Sliding under the covers, she remembered how safe she'd felt, even in that freezing, miserable cave, snuggled up against Luke. And how cold and lonely her life was without him.

Chapter 18

HOLLY PULLED UP IN front of Luke's beautiful old house in downtown Colorado Springs. She'd love to live nearby. Sometimes the traffic was horrible, and the Colorado College parties or downtown street celebrations got out of hand, but the side streets were quiet. The area was filled with vintage houses in gorgeous condition, big shade trees, and tiny parks. She trotted up the stairs to his top-floor apartment, admiring the woodwork and painted-lady colors. She knocked, suddenly nervous.

Luke answered the door. They both wore jeans and button-down shirts, but he looked like a movie star, while she'd fit into any basic office. Her heart pounded with nerves. "Hey, ready to go?"

"Sure. Let me grab my jacket." He locked up and they trotted down the stairs.

They got in her car and she drove to the restaurant. She struggled to find a neutral conversation starter. "Are you still starving?"

Luke held up his hand, tilting it back and forth. "The edge has dulled. I don't have to eat every minute of the day, just every third minute." He chuckled. "You?"

She nodded. "I'm in the same boat. I'm definitely ready for barbeque tonight."

He turned in his seat, running his gaze down her body. "Your clothes look a little looser than they did before, but that's probably muscle. You look great, not like you just escaped from the cast of 'Survivor—Colorado Backcountry, the Deliverance Edition'."

She laughed. With her bruises turning yellow and green, her face looked worse. But it didn't hurt as much. "Thanks, I think."

"You're always beautiful." He squeezed her hand resting on the gear shift.

Despite knowing he was wrong, the ridiculous statement made her shiver, her emotions swirling. But they'd arrived, so she pulled into the restaurant parking lot and walked next to him to the front door. Luke held the door for her, and the fantastic scent of smoked meat washed over them. Holly's stomach growled. Loudly.

Luke laughed and she scowled at him. He held up both hands. "Hey, mine growled too. Just not quite so...emphatically."

She held back a laugh and followed the hostess to a table. They both ordered sweet tea and full racks of baby back ribs with all the fixings. "I'm sure I won't be able to eat all of it, but leftovers are always good." She sipped tea, the sugary liquid refreshing, rather than cloying.

Luke raised his glass and tapped it against hers. "I'll have no problem finishing. I can probably eat whatever you leave, if you want. I remember doing that a lot back in high school. Your lunches were much better than the school's."

Her nose wrinkled, remembering those stressful days, worrying about everything. "I couldn't eat too much or I wouldn't fit in my school uniform. I didn't have any money for a new one." She'd been grateful for the stretchy material, while the rich girls complained about it being cheap.

He laughed. "You've never watched your weight. You eat like a bird."

She was half his size and didn't need that much food. "I eat plenty. I have a pretty high metabolism, and right now, it's through the roof."

The server brought their food, and they both ate silently, enjoying the delicious meat, corn bread, and beans. After her stomach stopped growling, Holly struggled again with a neutral conversation topic. She settled on the obvious. "Have you recovered?"

Luke nodded but shrugged slightly. "I'm banged up, but my muscles feel good. I'll do a light workout tomorrow. You?" He licked sauce off his fingers.

Distracted, she tried to remember what he'd asked. "Uh, the same. I thought I'd go for an easy run-walk in the Garden of the Gods. It's pretty this time of year and there are no tourists." Running wasn't her favorite exercise, but a gorgeous location made it easier.

He grinned. "Great idea. I'll meet you there if you want."

Holly scoffed. "I'm sure you run much faster than I do."

"Probably not right now." He shrugged. "If my heart rate gets too low, I can throw in some sprints or run backwards." He raised his brows. "But I'm betting you're not slow."

She couldn't help bragging. "I broke the ROTC field training obstacle course record, but I was younger and had more incentive."

His brow wrinkled and his head tilted. "What incentive was that?"

Sometimes it seemed like her whole adult life was nothing but one desperate struggle after another. "Distinguished Graduate. That meant I'd get a full-ride scholarship for my last two years. It was the only way I could stay in school." She'd hardly slept that entire month, determined to do everything perfectly.

"That's a good reason." He nodded. "But you're in great shape. Especially after our trek."

She shook her head. "That was all endurance. Running is different."

He frowned and sat back. "Look, if you'd rather run by yourself, then just tell me. But please take pepper spray with you."

She held up her hands, palms out. "You're welcome to come along. It won't be enough of a workout for you, though." His reminder made her grimace. Running in a park by herself did seem a little riskier than it had before their operation gone wrong.

He leaned forward. "A recovery run is all I'm after." He chuckled. "I'm happy walking briskly instead of hobbling."

"Funny, I didn't notice any hobbling in the parking lot." She'd definitely been paying attention because

Luke Sevrason was breathtaking. From the envious glances, every other woman in the restaurant agreed.

He laughed. "Male ego. I can't hobble in front of someone I'm trying to impress."

He was impressive enough already. Holly took a huge bit of coleslaw, giving herself time to think. "Why are you trying to impress me, when I've been nothing but discouraging?"

He leaned forward, capturing her gaze. "There were a few times when you were downright encouraging." Luke's voice was low and resonated through her belly.

She stared at him for a few moments, trying to catch her breath. Which was ridiculous. She was acting like a little girl again. She slammed her fork on the table. "You didn't answer the question."

"Holly, you've asked me this same question several times, and every time I answer, you don't seem to believe what I say." He reached across the red and white checked tablecloth, took her greasy, sauce-covered hand in his, and ran his thumb across her palm. "I don't think I'll answer anymore. Not with words, anyway." He leaned over, kissed the palm of her hand, then let it slide from his slowly. His smile was barely there and his gaze focused on her mouth.

Her palm tingled, his caress electrifying her entire body; she couldn't breathe. She finally managed to break his stare and shoveled some beans in her mouth. But all she wanted to do was kiss him and forget about the rest of the world. After eating another bite, she got the courage to look up again.

He'd returned to eating but gazed intently at her while he chewed, and her breathless state returned. She gave up trying to eat and asked for a box. When he finished, he let her pay and drive him home. He kissed her cheek, then bounded from her car and up his stairs, waving at the top before he went inside.

She drove home in a dazed and confused state, unsure how to react. Clearly, he wanted her, physically at least. But that was nothing new. Men approached her all the time; she should be dismissing him as just another selfish jerk. But he wasn't. He'd definitely proven that. Still, something held her back from accepting his words. Her reactions made no sense.

After tossing and turning most of the night, she got up, determined to put Luke out of her mind. She'd see what he meant soon enough, or she wouldn't.

After dressing, Holly drove to the Garden of the Gods, her stomach tumbling with nerves. She should turn around and go to the gym on base. Then she wouldn't have to deal with Luke, his smoldering good looks, or his actions. She parked but didn't see his car there. She was a little early, or maybe he overslept. She dismissed her concerns. She wouldn't worry about him. She'd take care of herself, like she always did. Relying on others was a recipe for disaster and heartache.

She swung into her normal warmup routine. Her muscles were still stiff from their trek; she'd need extra time. Not that she minded; the park was gorgeous. The beautiful spires of red rock reached for the sky, glowing in the morning sun, inspiring her to reach high too.

She made a last-minute check of her car key—secure in the pocket of her leggings—and jumped when Luke's voice rang out behind her. "Morning, sunshine!"

She spun on her heel. Luke rode toward her on a bicycle-built-for-two, with a helmet dangling from the second set of handle bars. She laughed. "What is this?"

"What does it look like?" He gave her a silly grin and swept his hand across the bike handlebars.

"I know what it is, but what are you doing with it?" His smile was contagious, and she couldn't hold back a laugh.

He stopped next to her. "You were right. Even for a recovery run, we'd be at different speeds. But if we ride together, there's no problem."

"That's...very thoughtful of you, Luke." Such a considerate and generous idea.

He hopped off the bike and placed the second helmet on her head, fastening the buckle, then kissing her cheek. He pushed the bicycle handlebars toward her, his signature scent overcoming the crisp mountain air. "You're in charge, so you get the front. We can go as far as you want to." His lips rose in a slight smile and his eyes captured hers.

She'd barely warmed up, but sweat broke out across her chest, and her breathless state returned. She broke eye contact and shook off her state. "Right. Let's make the loop around the park, and then we'll see how much farther we feel like going. Where did you get the bike?" She adjusted the front seat to the lowest point.

"Manitou Springs. It's just a short ride from here and we can get breakfast after, if you'd like." He held the bike steady, standing so close that his breath warmed her neck.

Grasping the front handlebars, she hoped her movement covered the shiver down her spine. "Sure.

Ready?" She straddled the bike and looked over her shoulder.

He winked. "Always ready for you."

Holly faced forward, feeling heat rise in her cheeks, and put her foot on the top pedal. She'd ignore his comments and focus on the exercise. "We'll go on three. One, two, three." She pushed down on the pedal and sat, then pedaled steadily. The sensation was a little odd but not that much different from a single-person bike. Her gear shifts were a bit rough on the way up the first hill, but she got smoother as they gained speed on the downhill side.

"Whoo-hoo! Look maw, no hands!" Luke whooped as they sped down the hill.

Holly put the brakes on to make the turn at the bottom but had to cut the corner enough to stay upright. "Whoa!" Fortunately, there wasn't any traffic, and she managed to keep some of the momentum for the next hill. They climbed and swooped and the miles flew by. Before she was ready, they'd returned to the parking lot. She pulled to a stop behind her car, grinning. "That was fun. Go again, or is that too much?"

"It's a blast. Let's go." He pointed at the road, grinning.

She dismounted. "I think you're in front this time."

"You're in command." He smiled slightly. "But I like having your six."

Her wind-stung cheeks heated again. "No, it's your turn in front."

He dismounted and, grasping the front handlebar, slid behind her, his body brushing hers, caging her in.

"Whatever makes you happy." He let go of the back handlebar.

She stepped back to the second seat, flustered by his nearness but paradoxically missing his warmth. He counted off, and she pushed down on the pedal and hopped on. The seat was a little high for her; she should have adjusted it. She'd have to stand and pedal on the hills, then coast on the downhills.

The front seat was way too low for Luke. He stood to power up the hill, and the pretty red rocks faded in comparison to the view in front of her. Tight black bike shorts couldn't hide his powerful glutes and legs, flexing as he pedaled, and his t-shirt was equally revealing, showcasing rock-solid shoulders. The Garden might be for the gods, but the man in front of her had a body worth worshiping.

They reached the top and rolled down, the pedals churning faster than she was comfortable with. She hopped up on the seat. Luke was moving much faster—they weren't going to make the corner at the bottom! "Are you trying to crash?"

He laughed and whooped. Luke took the perfect line around the corner, leaning the bike to stay upright, and they made it halfway up the next hill before she had to pedal again. When they coasted into the parking lot, her heartbeat pounded. She hopped off, stomping up to confront him. "Are you trying to kill us?"

He grinned. "That was fun! There was no danger. Pilot, remember? Managing momentum and turn radius is what I do." He swooped his hands in front of his body, one following the other. "I can crank 'em around like nobody else." He shot his wrist like a fighter pilot.

"You fly a huge tanker, not a little fighter." She doubted he was pulling high g-forces on a regular basis.

He shrugged. "Only because of my father. I scored high enough in pilot training to get fighters, but it wasn't a good idea. Too much conflict of interest." Despite that sobering reminder, he grinned. "Another loop, or do you want breakfast?"

His happiness was contagious, but not enough to risk death. She mock-frowned at him. "As fun as that was, I think I need something in my stomach." Her annoyance had settled her previous nerves, and hunger made her stomach growl.

"Hop on." He jerked his head at the back seat. "We'll take the bike back, grab breakfast at the cafe next door, and then I'll drive you back here."

"Or you can commit suicide by asphalt by yourself and I'll meet you at the cafe." She tried to look down her nose at him but was having trouble holding back her amusement tinged with a bit of healthy fear.

He stepped off the bike, holding the handlebar. "Or you can get in front. The seat's a little low for me and I like the view from the back. I'll tell you where to go." The corners of his mouth turned up slowly.

Her entire body heated. She took the bars from him, stepping close to the bike to avoid brushing against his Lycra-clad body. "Hope you had good scores in navigation, too." He laughed and she hopped back on.

As they peddled, he directed her to the bike shop, leaning far enough forward to speak into her ear. Despite the breeze from their speed through the cool air, his breath made her shiver. They dropped the bike and helmets off, thanked the staff, stretched, and then walked to the café next door. Inside, the scent of buttery pastries and rich, dark coffee made her stomach rumble. The tall interior walls resembled an ancient building in Italy or France, the warm colors and rough texture making the space seem cozy and intimate. The big glass case was jammed with colorful muffins, cookies, and pastries, the selection almost overwhelming.

After they ordered, he sipped coffee. "What's on your agenda tomorrow?"

Returning to work wasn't going to be fun. "Ugh. I've got a week's worth of email to wade through before the weekly status meeting. Then I've got to figure out how a permanent change of station works when I'm not physically moving. I'm sure they're used to it around here, but I've never done it."

He shrugged. "With Peterson, Schriever, and the Air Force Academy all in Colorado Springs, I'm sure they've got a checklist."

She grimaced. Checklists were great until something unexpected happened. "I'm sure it will be a bigger pain than it should be."

He huffed. "Isn't it always?"

"True." Their breakfast arrived. "What does your Monday hold?" She took a bite of apricot pastry and almost moaned at the delicious, buttery sweet flavor.

He sighed. "I've got a week of email, too, and we might have a deployment warning order for the unit. I'll pull out the training plan, brush it up, and make sure I've got people to teach everything and places to hold the training." He shrugged. "Fortunately, or unfortunately, depending on your point of view, most of us have done this plenty of times before. It's pretty much engraved in my bones. But working with the Army makes it entirely different and more challenging."

Her stomach dropped to her feet. "Are you going?" With all the horrible things going on in the world, there was no telling where Luke might end up. But it would probably be in the Middle East. Nothing was safe over there.

"Almost certainly." He nodded sharply. "I'm the most senior officer who hasn't deployed with the unit."

"But you deployed last year. You've been here less than six months." It shouldn't be his turn to go, not yet. Plus, they had too much unfinished business.

He shook his head. "Doesn't matter. New unit, my clock resets." He shrugged, clearly unconcerned by the idea. "Besides, the warning order is probably for six months from now, which means I'll have more than a year in the states before deployment." He sipped coffee, his green eyes fastened on hers. "Are you going to miss me?"

Their server brought the check. Holly pulled her eyes away from his.

"Honey, I'll be happy to miss you, if you'll show me what I'm missing." She winked, turned over the check, and scrawled something on it, then put it on the table. The pretty blonde turned, sauntering away with a hip-thrusting walk.

Luke scowled after the woman but managed to grab the check first. "My turn. You bought last night."

She scoffed. "You just want her phone number."

He laughed. "Not when I have yours." He glanced at the check, put cash in the folder, and dropped it on the table. He escorted her out of the restaurant with his hand on her back. "I've never spent any time here. Want to show me around?" He gazed at the surrounding streets.

She blinked up at him, a little surprised he'd want to do anything so touristy. But if he was deploying soon, she certainly wasn't going to pass up the chance to spend time with him. "Sure. Manitou is a funky little town with some really great artists. Let's go uphill first, then come back down to your car."

"Sounds good." He smiled and held out his hand.

She bit her lip but slid her hand into his. They explored tourist traps and fine art shops and tasted the mineral springs, laughing at the faces they both made at the taste. Each time they left a shop, he held out his hand, asking for hers. He leaned close, asking her opinion on art pieces, and brushed a hand over her shoulder as he passed behind her. The bright colors of Manitou faded in comparison to the joy sparking in her heart.

Hours passed and then they were back at his vehicle. He closed the door behind her, then drove back to the park, parking next to her car. She turned toward him. "Thanks, that was fun."

"That was my line." He reached out and ran his finger along her jawline. "Looking at the silly and sublime was a blast. We should do it again when more shops are open."

Her shoulders rose with his gentle caress, and she struggled to concentrate on what he said, rather than focusing on his lips. "Sundays are a little quiet. But less crowded."

"Having the shops all to ourselves was nice." He smiled slightly. "I'd really like to go to that Moroccan restaurant someday with you." He scanned her length, spreading heat across her body. "Would you wear a sari?"

She sucked in a desperate breath, trying to remember why being with Luke was a bad idea. "I don't have any. Left with just the clothes on my back, remember?"

He frowned. "You wore one for graduation, didn't you?"

And there was the reminder. Luke appearing with that gorgeous woman on his arm, betraying her completely. "It didn't make it." She'd never wanted to wear a sari ever again.

"That's too bad." He caressed her cheek with his thumb. "I'd always wondered what it would be like to unwind that present."

She jerked away. A second reminder—Luke didn't want her, he wanted the fantasy, just like every other man.

His tiny smile turned to a frown. "Holly—"

Her phone rang, and she dove into her legging pocket. Saved by Kristen. "Hey, Kristen, what's up?"

"Are you up for a mani-pedi this afternoon? I've got tentative reservations if I can confirm in the next few minutes."

Anything but staying with Luke. "I'm not home, but if I've got time to get a shower, sure."

"Yeah, you've got an hour and a half."

Just enough time to drive across town, far, far away. "Perfect, count me in. I'll pick you up."

"Great. See you then." The call ended.

She opened the door and didn't look back. "Thanks, Luke, the ride was fun. Breakfast was great. Got to go." She got into her car and didn't look at him until she backed out of her parking spot. Luke's head rested against the seat and his eyes were closed. His expression looked pinched, like he was in pain. Her stomach and her mood soured.

Maybe being saved wasn't such a good thing after all.

"Holly. Holly!" Kristen shook her shoulder.

"Huh?" Kristen glared. Holly sighed. She was a bad friend. "Sorry, lost in thought."

"About what?" Kristen's glare turned to a frown. "Never mind. I know that look." She smirked and put the back of her hand to her forehead. "That's your 'what I am going to do about the incredibly hot and thoughtful man who wants me more than anything' look."

Holly scowled. "He doesn't want me. He wants the idea of me. The 'me' back in high school. The exotic fantasy girl who never stood up for herself and did everything he wanted immediately."

Kristen returned her scowl. "Really? I don't think so. From everything you told me, he treated you like a partner during your escape. And that was after you rescued him. A lot of guys would have totally overreacted to that by being domineering jerks. But he wasn't, was he?" She tilted her head and raised her eyebrows. "Well? Was he?"

"No." He'd led, but collaboratively, and never treated her like she was less than he was. But that was in unusual circumstances; life or death. She had to pull her weight or die.

"And what has he done since then? He's gotten you a massage, gone shopping with you, taken you to a movie, dinner—" She gestured dramatically.

The list of thoughtful things Luke had done made her feel petty. "Hey, I paid for dinner!"

"But only because you insisted. And you were out with him this morning, weren't you?" Kristen poked her shoulder. "What did you do today?"

"We rode the Garden of the Gods on a two-person bike he rented. Then we had breakfast and toured Manitou Springs." And she'd barely said thank you. She was a terrible, ungrateful person.

Kristen gave her another skeptical assessing look. "And do you think Luke Sevrason would bum around Manitou Springs on his own? Or ride a bike around the Garden?" Her mouth flattened.

Holly's stomach dropped. "No." He did all that just for her.

Kristen glared. "If anyone had done anything even a tenth that romantic for me, you couldn't pry me off of him with a ten-thousand-mile screwdriver." She raised her eyes and hands to the ceiling, shaking her hands. "What is wrong with you?"

Kristen's exclamation had drawn every eye in the small shop, and every one of them wore puzzled expressions. Holly dropped her head to her hands, trying to hide.

"Look, Holly." Kristen put a hand on her shoulder and lowered her volume. "I understand that it's hard for you to trust any man. And Luke's actions in high school were awful. But high school was a long time ago. You've both changed and grown." Kristen put her fingers under her chin and pushed, so Holly had to look at her. "I'm absolutely sure that man loves you."

Despite the hope that rose with Kristen's words, Holly shook her head. "It's not him, it's me. He is trustworthy, I know that. Love? Maybe. But the real problem is I'm terrified of losing my independence. I've fought hard to get here. I don't want to give anything up." Love had never been worth the cost. She'd loved her parents, and they sold her. She'd loved Luke, and he dropped her in the cruelest way possible.

Kristen sat back and crossed her arms. "Answer me this, then. Why did you break him out? You could have left him there. You didn't need him. Getting him out only slowed you down."

Holly shook her head. "He had all that training. I got out on my own, but staying free was an entirely different thing." Amy had told them enough about escape and evasion to know that.

"Really?" Kristen raised a brow and cocked her head. "You couldn't have knocked in a few more heads and stolen a car?" The nail techs at their feet looked at them with shocked faces. Kristen motioned impatiently at their feet. "They were bad guys, okay?" Their heads dropped, but they were clearly listening hard.

Fortunately, Kristen already had the details, so Holly could keep the conversation generic. "That would have been much more dangerous." They might have been older men, but they weren't weak, and they had numbers. And guns.

"But you went and got him first, right? Didn't look around at all, did you, Miss Independence?" Her chin came up and her mouth clamped together.

Holly looked away, squirming. The nail tech made an exasperated sound. Holly froze. "That's true. I didn't."

"Think about that for a minute. And think about this." She paused, pursing her lips and then twisting them. "If you really can't trust him, ever, then tell him that. He needs to know it's hopeless, done and over, so somebody else can have him. He's too great a guy to be by himself the rest of his life. And you're too great a person to be alone too, but if that's what it takes for you to feel safe?" She shrugged. "Better to be safe and lonely, then scared with someone."

The thought of Luke with another woman—like the beautiful restaurant server—made her heart plummet to her feet and jealousy course through her veins. She clenched her fists tight to her chest, and as Kristen asked, really thought about telling Luke to walk away. Facing him, telling him it was over, and she'd never be able to love him—but that was a lie.

She loved him completely, whether he loved her or not. The chance of his betrayal was far less than the pain of losing him. Or losing herself. "Just cut my heart out and stomp on it already."

"If that's what it takes...." Kristen's tone was hard and unforgiving.

Holly wasn't just hurting herself; she was hurting all of her friends, and Luke most of all. She didn't want to cause anyone pain, especially Luke. He'd been hurt enough, by his family and by her. "No, you're right. Like usual. You were right before. I have to get over my fear and let go." She gulped. "Trust. But that's easier said than done." Her stomach tossed queasily.

"I can think of one way to do it." Kristen smiled and waggled her brows.

"What's that?" Holly knew that expression—danger loomed ahead.

She huffed. "Jump in with both feet. Easing in doesn't work. Half the time, you give up before you get all the way wet."

"And how do you suggest I do that?" Holly wasn't sure she wanted to know. Kristen's ideas could be wild.

Kristen gave her a wicked smile. "Well," she drawled, "when we're finished here, we're going shopping."

Two hours later, Holly wore a new, drop-dead sexy, fire engine red wrap dress, sky-high stiletto heels, her hair and makeup were perfect, and her credit cards blazed a fiery death. Kristen texted Luke; he was at home, doing laundry.

Holly wasn't sure she was ready, but the thought of Luke with another woman made her fists clench with rage and her heart shrivel. Kristen was right. She couldn't let fear hold her back or she'd lose him forever.

She drove to Luke's house and parked, her stomach in knots and her hands shaking. She had to find some courage. She'd faced down an evil fiend and trekked through the wilderness. Telling Luke that she loved him should be easy. But it wasn't.

She'd do it anyway, even if it seemed harder than confronting that horrible man. She got out of the car and balanced on her new heels. They were far too high for someone who mostly wore combat boots. She tiptoed up the steps and knocked. Footsteps tapped across the hardwood floor. Strange—those sounded like high heels, not a man's shoes.

The door opened, and she was face-to-chest with a woman. A beautiful, tall woman. A little older, but her blonde hair cascaded in perfect beachy waves, her porcelain skin glowed, and eyeliner and subtle shadow made her blue eyes stand out. The woman was everything Holly wasn't.

Oh. Holly was too late. He'd given up and moved on. The way he'd looked in the car wasn't despair, it was resolve. Her stomach dropped to the bottom of her feet, impaled by the spike heels of her shoes.

"Yes?" the woman asked. "Can I help you?"

Luke's voice sounded from inside. "Who is it? Kristen asked me if I was home."

"Are you Kristen?" The woman looked Holly up and down, frowning.

"No. No, I'm not. And since Luke is obviously busy, I'll be on my way." She turned and trod down the stairs. Hopefully, she'd make it to her car before Luke got to the door. But why would he bother? He had a gorgeous, tall blonde, just as she'd predicted.

"Hey, wait. I'm sure Lukas wants to talk to you!"

She sped her steps and walked to her car, with her head high and her face calm, white noise roaring in her ears, barely holding back tears. Never let emotions show, just as her mother taught her. Finally, she reached the safety of her car and opened the door. A hand clamped on her shoulder. She turned, swinging with her car keys sticking out of her clenched fist.

Luke jumped back. "Holly, wait."

She stopped. Calm, cool, collected. She wouldn't cry. "Why? I can see that you're busy."

"I'm never too busy for you." He took a half-step back and looked at her. "Wow, you look beautiful. Are you going out on a date?" A frown creased his brow.

"No." She shook her head. "I'll see you later." She turned blindly back to the car. She was losing the battle with her tears. She had to leave before he saw.

"Hey, wait." His hand came down on her right shoulder, rubbing gently. "What did you want?"

"Never mind. It was stupid. I'll see you next week." She bit the words out in short, choppy sentences to keep from sobbing and looked up at the sky to keep the tears from falling.

His other hand landed on her left shoulder, and he caressed both, massaging gently. Her stomach lurched—impalement by high heel was obviously not healthy. His breath wafted across her ear. "Holly...I sincerely doubt you wanted something stupid from me." His voice was soft and warm. "You've never asked me for anything. If it's in my power to give, I will. Anything at all."

"I think it's too late for that. Just let me go." She pulled against his hold, desperate to get in the car before the tears fell.

"Please don't ask me to do that." But his hands released. "I will, but I don't want to. Not ever."

Holly stopped pulling away, lulled by his voice, then remembered the blonde. She stiffened and lurched a step forward, then spun to confront him. "I don't share, so you'd better, or one of these stupid high heels is going through your foot!"

He frowned so hard his brows almost met between his eyes. "Share? What are you talking about?" His eyes widened and his mouth dropped open. "You thought—no, no, no." He held out his hands, palms out. "The woman upstairs is my father's fourth ex-wife, Lindsay. She's driving back to Montana with my half-sister, Susan. They're crashing in my spare room for the night."

Holly's stomach lurched again, heat flooded her cheeks, and her eyes shut. She desperately wanted to sink through the pavement and disappear rather than face the embarrassment. Maybe she could get into the car and drive away before he fully realized why she was there.

"Wait a minute. Kristen obviously texted for you, not herself, and here you are all dressed up." His tone lowered to a rumble. "It's too late to go out for anything but a drink, and you don't drink and drive, ever." He took her hands in his. "Did you get dressed up for me?

Because if you did, my step-mother just went from mostly nice to truly wicked."

Holly stood there with her eyes clamped shut, her heart trying to pound out of her chest, and heat scorching her from head to foot. Her mouth was open, but she couldn't get a word out, and even if she could, she didn't know what to say.

He let go of her left hand and traced her jawline with a finger. "Holly...say something, please? I really, hope you wore this for me, because if you didn't, I'm going to have to kill someone, and then I'll end up in prison. I don't think I'll do very well in there." His fingertip rasped against her cheek. "Please say something?"

"I don't know what to say. I'm so embarrassed and confused and—" She was wailing. She never wailed. But her calm, cool control was gone. Conflicting emotions stormed through her, locking her in place.

Luke cupped his hands around her chin, lifting it so she had to meet his gaze. "Then I'll say something. You are absolutely drop-dead beautiful. But no matter how you look or what you wear, I'll always love you more than anybody or anything." Then he bent slowly, never dropping eye contact until he was so close she could feel her eyes start to cross, and brought his mouth down on hers.

His words finally penetrated her embarrassment-fried brain. He loved her. She threw her arms around his neck and pressed her body to his, kissing him back with all the love in her heart. She lost herself in the press of his soft lips and firm body against hers, twining her tongue with his, the heat of embarrassment changing to the heat of need.

A car horn blared and she jumped. Luke jolted, then pulled her close again, his firm arms holding her close. "Was all this for me?" His hands ran up and down her back, both soothing and scorching.

Her heart soared and she smiled. Time to be brave. "Yes, it was. It is. Kristen smacked me between the eyes with some truth today and knocked some sense into my head. Then she made me buy all of this so I could channel enough of her personality to come over here and jump in with both feet, instead of pussy-footing around in the shallows like I have been doing."

"I'm not sure I quite understand that metaphor, but I don't care." Luke grinned, then grimaced. "What I do care about is not having an empty apartment. Of all the rotten timing."

She slid her hands down his solid chest. "I can wear this dress again."

He pulled her in tight and growled in her ear. "But I don't want you to wear the dress."

She held him close but, under the circumstances, had to laugh. "I don't think there's a different choice right now."

He released his arms slightly and smiled ruefully at her. "True. We're not seventeen anymore. We can muster a little self-control." He let go but kept her hand in his. "Let's take a moment, then we'll go upstairs. You can meet Lindsay, and maybe Susan if she's not in bed yet." He grimaced. "You can help me tell Lindsay what happened and that she needs her attorney again."

"Oh, no. He's not paying child support?" She winced. That poor woman.

"He was, plus health insurance." He sighed. "Susan needs lots of very expensive therapy and medical care. That's why I was in Montana last summer. I knew visiting them would lure my father to come out. For some reason, poor Susan thinks he's the most wonderful man in the world." He shook his head. "They're both on his company's insurance and it's about to disappear. I'll do what I can, but I don't have that kind of money anymore, either."

"I'll help you, but you'll have to make it up to me." Although, her family was likely to be worse. She'd bet that several of them would be asking for help soon.

He smiled down at her wickedly. "Now that, I can promise to do. Very thoroughly."

Holly grinned at him, her heart singing with joy. "Before we go up."

He pulled her into his arms again. "Yes?"

She put her hands around his face. "I love you, too. More than anybody or anything."

His arms closed around her tight, his soft lips met hers, and her cares dropped away. Nothing mattered except Luke Sevrason.

Chapter 19

AT LUNCH ON MONDAY, Kristen interrogated her unmercifully, wanting every detail. After Holly told her story, Kristen grinned. "I told you he loved you, didn't I?"

"Yes, you did. You were right. You're always right." Holly laughed. She'd tell Kristen that for the rest of her life.

Kristen looked at the ceiling and raised both arms high. "Yes, yes I am. Finally, I can tell all the women asking for introductions that Luke is taken, not in the middle of a culturally driven courting ritual."

"What?" Holly wasn't sure she'd heard Kristen correctly.

She grinned. "You would not believe how many texts, visits, and phone calls I got every time Luke sashayed in here. Monday afternoons were torture. I've told so many women that Luke was head over heels in love with the ice queen of space, but some of them didn't care. So, I made some stuff up." Kristen rolled her eyes and sputtered laughter. "If someone asks you a weird question about Luke doing this or that for you, just nod and smile. Got it?"

"Glad my heartache could provide some amusement for you." Holly mock-glowered at Kristen.

Kristen smirked. "I could have done worse, you know. I could have made those introductions."

Holly held up her hands in surrender, then bowed. "Okay, you win. Thank you, Kristen, oh goddess of love, for spinning ridiculous stories so you wouldn't get bored enough to start introducing Luke to all your other friends. I do appreciate it."

"You should, darn it." She shook her head, puppy dog sad look on her face.

"I promise to do the same for you someday."

Kristen wrinkled her nose. "I'll hold you to that."

A man with slightly geeky glasses caught Holly's eye. "How about now?" She stood up and waved. "Colonel Lee! Hey, come join us!" He stared at her without any expression, so she kept smiling and waving him over. He finally nodded and walked toward them. "There. First installment of repayment, waiting out the frown of a stubborn lieutenant colonel." Then Colonel Lee looked at his phone, at her, back at his phone, and at her again. That didn't seem like a positive reaction.

Kristen giggled. "Thanks, Holly. I knew you'd be worth the effort."

Holly's phone buzzed on the table.

> Meeting today at regular time and place. Ness.

Her stomach clenched. "Now what?"

Colonel Lee stopped in front of her. "Captain Bose, the FBI just pulled my conference room again. What's going on? I thought this was over."

Holly shook her head. "I have no idea, sir. Just got notified myself. This is not what I needed today."

"Me either. Now I've got to find another room for my briefing." His mouth twisted in distaste.

Holly winced. "Sorry, sir. Maybe you can put us in a different one?"

He shook his head. "No. They need room for twenty people."

"That doesn't sound good. I'm glad I didn't leave the building for lunch." Her whole body tightened with tension, and she wrapped her arms around her waist.

Lee's lips flattened in a frown. "I'm sure if there was an active threat, they'd have told you."

"Maybe. Anyway, I'm sorry about messing up your schedule." Holly smiled at him. "Join us anyway?"

"Sorry. I've got to go." Lee returned to the serving line and got a to-go box.

"I'm sure it's nothing." Kristen stood and gathered her tray.

"I hope so." But Holly's stomach didn't think so.

LUKE

Luke entered the conference room, hoping to catch Holly alone before the meeting, but had no such luck. Everyone had shown up early for the latest in the

Bose-Sevrason saga. At least they'd left a seat next to Holly for him. When he pulled it out, smiling down at her, she looked up with a frown, then her face lit up with happiness. Whatever news the FBI shared, he was the luckiest guy in the universe. He sat and squeezed her hand under the table. "How was your Monday?"

She shrugged. "As expected, except for this." She glanced around the room, worry pinching her expression.

Special Agent Ness strode to the head of the room. "I'm sure all of you are surprised to see us back here again, and it's not a pleasure cruise for us, so let's get to it." He spit out the words, clearly unhappy to be there. His ambitions had bitten him badly. He'd been officially reprimanded for endangering untrained personnel.

Luke couldn't find one iota of sympathy for the man—and he trusted him even less. He shouldn't still be in charge.

"As you all know, Mr. Sevrason, Mr. Das and Mr. Das's co-conspirators were all charged with the appropriate crimes, and all of them posted bond and were placed on house arrest in exchange for giving up their passport and wearing electronic monitors." His lips clamped and twisted momentarily. "Unfortunately, Mr. Das cut his monitor off and disappeared. We can't find him. We speculate that he is coming here for a second try at Captain Bose. You'd have thought he'd have learned his lesson from the hospital stay last time, but you never know." He frowned at Holly.

Luke glared. It wasn't Holly's fault the guy was obsessed or that Ness's inadequate plans fell apart.

"Major, Captain, you are once again under surveillance. Normally, we'd simply confine you to base. But since Mr. Das had base access and knows too much about how the military works, that's not sufficient. We've found agents who look similar to you. They will take over your civilian lives, and we'll put the two of you in protective custody." He grimaced. "We've got a safe house. We'll take you to work each morning and back each day. If you have an off-base requirement, please let us know and we'll arrange it. Make a list of the things you'll need from your homes for the next week. We'll have your stand-ins pick it up tonight and deliver it tomorrow. You'll just have to make do with what you have for tonight." He stared at them.

Luke glared in return. Victim blaming was ridiculous; survivor blaming was worse.

"If you have no idea where he is, isn't this overreacting a bit?" Holly asked.

"Better safe than sorry. We made mistakes last time. I prefer not to repeat them." His pinched face said just how hard that admission was to make.

Luke still wasn't sympathetic. Ness brought it all on himself. Luke wasn't trusting him with Holly's safety. "I want our weapons tonight. No excuses. If not, we'll take our chances without you." He had to protect Holly without relying on these idiots. If they had to, they'd load up and go somewhere. Both of their supervisors would agree. Mikells would probably invite them to his home.

Ness's lips clamped together for a moment, then he nodded. "Agreed. If you have to shoot, please be aware of your surroundings and ensure a safe shot."

Luke kept his volume low, just for Holly. "Thanks, I'd never have thought of that on my own. Not like I didn't do that every day downrange."

"He's talking to me, not you, Luke." Holly's lips brushed his ear.

"I think you know that too," he stage-whispered. He raised his voice. "Where are you looking? Das must have lots of contacts across the United States because of his job."

"Yes, but all official contacts have been told his access and clearances were pulled due to criminal charges. We know he frequented strip clubs and other similar businesses and met with the owners of those clubs in many cities, but we're not aware of any real friends anywhere." He cleared his throat. "The comments he made about you, Captain Bose, made us curious, and we started digging. After you ran in high school, he decided to find an obedient girl. He returned to India and had so little trouble that he decided it would make a good business. Poor girls, and boys, are lured with promises of American spouses and jobs and then they ended up not only being prostitutes but also working in small businesses, usually in very bad conditions. We've taken down his sex-trafficking organization, but there may be family members or other associates we've missed. Das enforced silence viciously." He cleared his throat again. "But that doesn't help us find him."

"Maybe he broke into another house up in the mountains." Holly jerked her head to the west.

"We're looking at that possibility. We've put out bulletins to every FBI office, military base, and police department across the country. He may have escaped to

Mexico or Canada or got on a ship." He shook his head. "We just don't know and don't want to put the two of you in any extra danger."

"Got it." She nodded sharply. "Can I get my things from my office?"

"Go ahead." Ness nodded back. "And please inform your boss. You too, Major."

Luke nodded at him but stood. "I'll come with you, Holly." He didn't want to let her out of his sight.

"Okay." She smiled at him. He was turning into a teenage girl—one smile from her, and he was ridiculously happy. They took the stairs to her cubicle, two agents shadowing them. Holly pointed at her chair. "Wait here. I'm going to check with Alice and see if the colonel is available. If not, I'll write him an email." The female agent followed her down the hall.

He looked around her bland, beige cubicle after she left. No family photos, naturally. There was one of Holly, Amy, and Kristen at some official function in their mess dress. He looked closer and smiled. The female formal wear wasn't that attractive, but the three of them together were stunning. In another picture, the three wore casual summer clothes, and the next was Chris and Amy's wedding photo with all of them. On the left side of the desk, their ski trip photo stood by itself. That trip had been fun. Hopefully next time, they'd be the ones cutting out early to "rest."

But they had to get through the new threat first. He couldn't believe the courts let Das out of jail at all. By the nature of the evil, a human trafficker had connections to smugglers. Das could easily be on his way out of the country. But Luke agreed with Ness's suspicions. Das might be unstable enough to risk his current freedom for revenge. No way that guy was getting anywhere near Holly. If Luke had the opportunity, he'd be a missing person no one missed.

"I talked to the colonel," Holly said, and he jumped. He'd been so lost in his rage he hadn't heard her. That was dangerous—his situational awareness had to be perfect to keep her safe. "He's just happy I'll be coming to work. Do you need to let your boss know?"

He struggled to speak. "I'll call on the ride to the safe house. He'll feel the same as your boss."

"Okay, let's go." Holly took her jacket off the back of her chair and her purse from a drawer.

They walked down the stairs, gave their keys to the agents, and were escorted to the VIP parking entrance. They got in the back of an SUV with dark, mirrored windows. The walk let him regain control of his emotions and focus on the situation.

"Geez, I feel like a celebrity." Holly snorted. "Using the General's entrance, riding in the back with blacked-out windows, protection detail shadowing us, the whole nine yards."

"No champagne. Celebrities get drinks." He'd shoved the rage back and put himself firmly back into downrange mode—head on a swivel, looking for threats.

"That's okay, I've got you." Holly put her hand on his.

"Yes, you do." He clenched her hand.

The agent driving cleared her throat. "Is pizza okay for dinner, or do you want something else?" The woman was medium everything—height, build, skin tone, dark brown hair in a very short, almost men's style cut. But she drove like a pro—checking the mirrors and their surroundings, with her gloved hands at ten and two.

"Pizza's fine for tonight, but not every night." He preferred healthier items when possible. "If this lasts longer than a couple of days, we'll need a grocery run."

"Just give us a list. We'll get whatever you want. The house has a well-equipped kitchen." The woman's voice was very level and matter-of-fact; a stone-cold agent.

"If you've got to be locked down, it should be in luxurious conditions." Luke snorted.

"You've had more experience with that kind of thing than I have, Major."

He glared at her in the rear-view mirror. "I live on my salary, not my father's criminal enterprises."

"Major, it was a statement of fact, not an accusation. I'll try to be more careful." Her voice was even blander.

"Sorry, I over-reacted." He took in a deep breath and let it out slowly. "I thought this was over, and now here we are again. I want to keep Holly safe. She's been through enough." He tried to moderate his breathing and corral his emotions.

"Keeping both of you safe is our mission. We won't fail."

Holly squeezed his hand, hard. "Luke, I'm fine, and I'll be fine. They'll catch him sooner or later. I sincerely doubt he's stupid enough to come after me after I bashed his head in. Maybe he's after you."

His free hand clenched. "If I could only be so lucky. I'd like to get a few shots in for what he did to you." He locked his rage down again.

"He's probably in Mexico, and not anywhere near here." Holly waved toward the window.

"It's pretty likely, Captain. But we'll act as if he's right outside." The agent's attention was clearly on her driving, not their conversation.

"By the way, Special Agent...?" Holly trailed off.

"Sorry I didn't introduce myself. White."

"If they didn't tell you, Das is a really heavy smoker—it's a dead giveaway." Holly wrinkled her nose. "That's how I knew he was stalking me in the parking lot at Building One—that horrible, heavy, stale cigarette smell, from unfiltered cigarettes. You don't smell that much on base."

"Thank you, Captain Bose, that's very helpful. Scent is key at night." White nodded.

"Anything I can do. Please feel free to call me Holly."

In the face of Holly's positivity, he couldn't be rude. Besides, White acted like a pro. "And I'm Luke. Happy to help as well, but complaining is a soldier's duty, you know."

"No problem. It's what we all do. Especially on babysitting duty. No offense to you personally, but it's not fun."

"I can see that. Especially when your protectee knows enough to be dangerous." Holly laughed.

"Hey, we're dangerously good." Luke knocked his shoulder into Holly's. "Made it out of that place on our own, evaded capture, self-rescued, the whole shooting match." The SERE school asked him to be a guest speaker for their next class.

She gripped his hand hard. "Don't get cocky, Luke. He won't underestimate us this time."

Luke disagreed. "I think he will. He's just like my father. Thinks he's the smartest guy in the room and then can't figure out why things went wrong."

"Could go either way. It's always safer to overestimate the enemy's capabilities." White's voice was still deadpan.

"One more question, Special Agent White," Holly said.

"Go ahead."

"Do you care if Luke and I share a room?" Holly's tone was unemotional.

Luke blinked. He'd planned to sleep on her floor or in front of the door if she didn't want him in her room at night. He hadn't thought to ask the agents.

"Not at all. It will actually make things easier for us because this place has only one easily secured room. We'll put you in there, Captain Bose."

"Good." She squeezed his hand again.

He'd planned on sneaking into her room later, but this would be a lot easier, and smarter. He didn't want to get shot—friendly fire wasn't. He wasn't sure if Holly's preemptive question had anything to do with their relationship, though. They'd have to talk about it because he had to know what she was thinking to avoid any misunderstandings that would set them back.

They wound up the foothills, deep into the expensive Cheyenne Mountain Estates. The houses got bigger and fancier, but in a range of clashing styles, from classic timber-frame to Spanish colonial to brick edifices that looked like they belonged in the deep South. Finally, they pulled into a garage in a large, but comparatively unassuming, wood-sided house with a bland brown on brown paint scheme. An older house, probably built before the area was subdivided.

Agent White turned toward them. "Please wait until the garage door is down."

The door closed, and he hopped out, then held out a hand for Holly. They both turned to face White.

White wore a dark blue pantsuit that was a size too big. Probably hiding the weapons she carried. Her voice was medium too, but flat, as was her look. All work and no play, which was fine with him—all the better to keep Holly safe.

White turned away and spoke over her shoulder, walking to the door at the back of the garage. "I'll give you the tour and security plan on our way in. We keep all exterior doors and windows locked at all times." In the doorway, she turned back and held out her hand. "The front door code is 4545, but please don't leave without informing us, unless it's an emergency situation. We'll have at least one on duty agent outside and one inside, twenty-four-seven."

They entered a large living room with beige walls, medium brown carpeting, and a fairly low ceiling. Unobtrusive western-style prints in wood frames hung on the walls, along with a big flat screen. SA White continued her lecture. "Keep the drapes drawn. As you can see, there's a small workout area here and a TV area, with a wet bar and small fridge. Feel free to use it all. Here's your suite." She opened the door to a bedroom but didn't step in. "Bed, bath through the door there, closet, TV. If you'll drop your bags, I'll show you the rest of the place."

Holly left her purse and backpack, then they followed White up the stairs. She pointed as she spoke. "Living room, kitchen, powder room, and laundry. Feel free to use these." More beige walls, brown carpeting, brown upholstery on a big sectional. SA White pointed at the back of the house and at a staircase. "There's a master suite on this level; our team lead is using it. He's sleeping right now because he likes to take the night shift. Upstairs are four bedrooms for the rest of us."

The kitchen had black granite tile countertops with older-style medium oak cabinets above and below. White picked up a pair of tactical headsets, holding them out. "Here are comm units for both of you. We don't expect you to wear them all the time. If we need you to wear them, you'll hear a loud, beeping tone. Major Sevrason, since you already have one, your call sign is Revlon. Captain Bose, yours is Kali." She looked inquiringly at Holly. "Unless that's offensive?"

Holly shook her head. "Not to me."

White nodded sharply. "We'll also ring your phones, so program something recognizable for our numbers."

"The theme from Hawaii 5-O?" Luke joked.

"Whatever lets you recognize it, Major. Questions?" She stared at them without expression.

Confirmed—White had no sense of humor. "When is your shift change, and do you brief at that time?" Luke asked.

"Zero-six and eighteen hundred. And yes, that's when we'll brief. Do you plan to attend?" Her brows rose a millimeter.

He shook his head. "Not regularly. I just like to know because things usually go wrong at shift change."

"True." She nodded once. "Other questions?"

"No, thanks." Holly shook her head.

"Are either of you allergic to anything?" Both of them shook their heads no. "Food preferences, especially pizza?"

Luke directed her to Holly. "I prefer pepperoni or combos or something with meat, but I'll eat just about anything except jalapenos. They're just wrong on pizza."

"I'm with her." He could take or leave jalapenos, but the rest was spot on.

"Good. I'll order. I imagine it will be forty-five minutes or so, if you want to get settled. We got you basic toiletries for tonight. If you need something, please let me know."

Luke smiled and nodded. "Thanks. We'll be back up in forty-five or so."

They trotted downstairs, comm sets in hand, and entered their room. Like the rest of the house, it was shades of beige with brown carpet and oak furniture. After checking over their accommodations and the rest of the basement, Luke flopped on the bed, which was probably a queen. More than enough room for them. "This mattress is pretty decent. And we're the only ones down here." Anticipation fizzed in his body.

"I noticed." She stood in front of the dresser, playing with the earrings she'd just taken out.

Something wasn't right. He peeled off the mattress and wrapped his arms around Holly, his front to her back. She leaned into him, so she wasn't nervous about him. In the mirror above the dresser, she looked so tiny and fragile next to him. But she wasn't. She was steel and whipcord, rolled in determination and courage. "Are you okay?"

"Yeah, just…" Her eyes were a little too wide, and she licked her lips.

He smiled and squeezed gently. "A little nervous?" She fit so perfectly against him. He wanted her with every fiber of his being, but he wouldn't push her. She'd been forced into too much in her life. Plus, they had a real threat to deal with. Being lost in each other with that kind of evil on the loose was a bad idea.

"Yes. You too?" A smile flickered.

"It may not be manly to say so, but yeah." He shrugged. "But we're just sleeping next to each other. Just like the cabin, only more comfortable. We're on a mission, not a vacation."

She relaxed into his body, and her warm, spicy scent, reminiscent of chai tea, soothed his soul. He put his cheek against her soft, thick hair and rubbed gently, like a cat. If only he could purr. He took in a breath and loosened his arms, even though he never wanted to let her go. "If we don't make it upstairs for dinner, Special Agent White will probably come looking for us."

She wrinkled her nose, adorably. "You're probably right. It would interfere with the mission not to have us adequately fueled."

"She is a little uptight, isn't she?" He stepped back but captured her hand in his.

"Just a bit. You'll win her over." She giggled.

"Or you will." Very few people could withstand Holly when she set out to charm them. "Let's go."

They ate pizza while White made phone calls. Luke was pleasantly surprised when another agent delivered not only their weapons, but a fresh uniform for the next day and sweats to sleep in. After changing, they settled on the bed to watch a British murder mystery. Holly fell asleep before the first break, so he moved her under the covers and kissed her forehead. She smiled and turned on her side.

After the show finished, Luke turned everything off, made sure his weapon, shoes, and communications headset were arranged for fast retrieval, and slid into the bed next to Holly, turning his back to her. He longed to hold her tight, like he did in the wilderness, but keeping her safe was his mission. He settled into the bed and counted sheep.

Luke woke and blinked in the darkness, smelling cinnamon. Holly snuggled into the curve of his body, and he pulled her closer. The love of his life, back where she belonged. If he'd been smarter back in high school, he could have held her every night for the last decade. But that time hadn't been wasted. They'd both changed and grown; their relationship would be entirely different without the time apart.

Besides, the past was gone; only their future mattered. First, he'd keep her safe, then hopefully, she'd accept his ring. But whether she did or not, he loved her and she loved him, and that was all that mattered.

He listened, trying to decide if a noise had woken him. After hearing nothing more, he wrapped his arms around her a little tighter and settled back to sleep, happy and grateful they were safe, alive, and together.

Chapter 20

HOLLY SETTLED INTO BED next to Luke, carefully not touching him. A week had passed with no sign of Das. Every morning, an FBI agent dropped off Luke at work on Fort Carson, and his stand-in would ride back to the safe house, leaving his car on base. Holly was driven to the VIP entrance at Space Force headquarters, trading places with her stand-in. Both stand-ins slept the day at the safe house, then watched for Das each night.

Her work hadn't changed, but as Luke's unit prepared for deployment, his hours got longer. She spent some of the extra time at the gym after work, then met Luke at the safe house. She made dinner while he worked out, then they'd watch TV, read, or surf social media. They'd sleep and do it all over again.

Holly missed Luke every minute they were apart, and he seemed to feel the same. He never passed up an opportunity to hold her, kiss her, and tell her he loved her, but neither of them took it any farther. They were both waiting for things to go wrong, and the FBI agents surrounding them left no illusion of privacy.

Even though she'd be doing approximately the same things at her house, she longed for her own bed and the comfort of her things. At least there she could go out for a walk or get together with Kristen. Or move ahead with Luke. Luke obviously felt the same restlessness, spending time in the small house gym while she did yoga.

The weekend had dragged. Two full days with Luke would normally be wonderful. But they were trapped in the bland, brown house in a holding pattern. The safe house felt more and more like a prison.

No one had seen Das. The agents seemed more on edge, rather than less. Special Agent Ness was particularly unhappy, but fortunately, they didn't see much of him in person. Holly was actually looking forward to Monday, but only because she'd get out of the house.

Sunday evening, they watched two more episodes of their murder mystery and went to bed. Loud beeping woke her with a jerk. She sat up, the covers falling away. "What is that?"

"It's the FBI comm link. Quick, grab it." Luke turned a light on.

She shoved the headset into place. "Revlon, Kali? Report." The voice was Special Agent White.

"Revlon." Luke had gotten his on quickly, while she fumbled.

If she remembered correctly, the microphone was voice activated. "Kali."

"There's action at Kali's house. Stand by, I'll patch you in."

"The mechanical room and the back of the garage are scorched. The car has sustained some damage. I don't know how much. They won't let me back in the house yet. I haven't seen anyone matching the target's description." The woman snapped out her words.

"Shiva Overwatch, have you spotted the target?"

"Negative, Control. No sign on any camera."

"Keep a close watch. This could be a distraction for an abduction. Break, break. Tanker, have you seen any sign of the target?"

"Negative."

"Tanker Overwatch, same question."

"Negative, Control."

"Understood. Maintain watch."

Luke rolled away from her and sat up. "Get your shoes on, Holly."

He was right. She had to be ready. She slid her trainers on and picked up her gun.

"Black Watch, any sign of target?"

"Negative, Control. All quiet."

"Copy. All stations, stay alert. Shiva, text your questions to Kali."

Holly picked up her phone. A text came in from an unknown number.

Call USAA in the morning. I'll bring the fire department and police reports.

That was smart. While the special agent could impersonate her at a distance, up close was a different story.

"Control, Shiva. I don't anticipate further action until morning. Will Kali be present for the fire marshal's inspection?"

"Will analyze risk and get back to you. Kali, who would you call if your car was inoperative?"

Holly considered the answer. Kristen would have been her first call before she finally got together with Luke. "Revlon or Lake."

"Tanker, pick up Shiva. Stay at Tanker's tonight. Shiva Overwatch, stay in place and watch for further action. All stations, stay alert. Retrieving both subjects at one time may be the target's plan. Float, after Shiva and Tanker are inside Revlon's apartment, stake out the Lake apartment. Break, break. Kali, Revlon, will let you know more in the morning. You're clear to drop off."

Grateful the FBI was taking the possibility of a threat to Kristen into account, Holly took off her headset. "Now we both have to go car shopping." She probably should have replaced her car a year ago.

"Misery loves company." He snorted.

She untied her shoes, toeing them off. "I'm definitely not miserable in your company." Going to sleep with all the adrenaline running in her system seemed impossible. But settling next to Luke would help.

He slid into the bed, pulling her in tight. "Me, either. Sweet dreams, Kali."

"Sweet dreams, Rev." She snuggled back into the curve of his body. With him near, her dreams were always sweet.

The next morning, Special Agent White drove the rough road to Luke's workplace on Fort Carson, swerving around the worst of the holes. "Captain Bose, the fire marshal will be at your house this morning at ten. Call your property manager and USAA and tell them to talk to the fire marshal, as you are currently unavailable due to military requirements. That way, you aren't at risk, and Shiva doesn't have to act as you in the daylight."

"I'll give it a shot." Her property managers did as little as possible.

"We'll intervene if we have to, but since only the car and contents are yours, we have no interest in the property."

"Did everything end up smoky?" Hopefully she wouldn't have go through all the cleaning that Amy had done.

"They caught it early. Your car was mostly cosmetic damage."

Holly grimaced. "It's an old car; they'll probably just total it. I probably should have replaced it already." She hadn't wanted to spend the money because she was always waiting for the other shoe to drop. More than one shoe had thudded thunderously to the ground, but she didn't have to run anymore, so she'd make the investment.

"Major Sevrason, after I drop you off, I'll drop Captain Bose, then I'll come back to Fort Carson for Tanker, since he's taking Shiva to Peterson first." She pulled up in front of Luke's unit.

"Good plan. See you this evening." Luke unbuckled, slid over, and kissed her passionately, totally ignoring White. "Love you."

Holly released her grip around his neck. "Love you too. See you tonight."

He got out and trotted to the large, industrial-style metal building he worked in. It held not only offices for his unit, but garage space for Humvees and other large equipment their mission required.

SA White drove away, heading for the Fort Carson north gate. Holly pulled out her phone, checking the weather. Her body jolted against the seat belt when White suddenly turned left and accelerated. "What happened?"

White squealed around two more corners, Holly white-knuckling the door handle. They were returning to Luke's building. Back on the straight road, White tossed a comm headset at Holly. "Trouble. Put that on."

Holly secured the set on her head, then returned her phone to her pocket, grateful she wore a combat uniform rather than blues.

"Control to all, status?" Ness snapped the words.

"White to Control. Kali secure in vehicle, on comms. En route to Revlon's work location."

"Tanker and Shiva en route to Revlon's from Peterson. ETA twenty minutes." A woman's voice; must be her impersonator, Shiva.

"White, Control. First priority is Kali's safety. Second is Revlon's. Third is everyone else on scene. Post security notified of hostage situation. You are on-scene command until I arrive. ETA twenty-five minutes."

"Copy, Control. Security here is contract, not military, correct?" White didn't sound happy about that fact.

"Affirmative. Trying to contact proper command element now."

Holly leaned forward between the seats. "White, what happened?"

She tapped her earpiece, turning off her mic. "Revlon walked into an ambush. Das is there. He's got two hostages. He's taken shots at Revlon and the unit commander. Revlon's trying to get Das to release the hostages in exchange for himself, but Das is threatening to kill them if he doesn't just give himself up. Do you know if they have a weapons locker there?"

"I don't think so." Dread pooled low in her stomach. Luke would sacrifice himself in a heartbeat for someone else, but especially a unit member.

"I'd prefer to resolve this situation before post security arrives. Civilians will make it complex." White's tone remained her normal, flat, matter-of-fact briefing voice. "Good thing Revlon had the sense to contact us before he did anything else."

Holly gritted her teeth and took White's cue. She'd focus on the situation now, deal with her feelings later. "Do you have a weapon for me?" She wasn't leaving Luke to fight on his own.

"There's a locker in the trunk. You stay in the back seat. I'll get you one. In the meantime, I'll give you my backup." White bent over while continuing to drive at high-speed across the rough, bumpy road. She handed a small semi-automatic back to Holly. "No safety. There's a round in the chamber."

Holly took the matte-black weapon, pulling back the action part way to check that it was loaded. "Ruger LCP, just like mine." Holly gripped it firmly, her forefinger outside the trigger guard, and pointed it toward the floorboard, sighting down the barrel.

They skidded to a stop a block away and across the street from Luke's building. "Control, White outside Revlon's location."

"White, Post on lockdown. All agents outside of Post coming in on code, but having trouble with the traffic. Need to get Revlon on comms. Unit member will let you in the north side door. Revlon and unit members unarmed but wearing combat gear."

"Copy. Arming Kali and Revlon."

"Concur."

"Kali, watch my back while I get weapons and a vest for you. Stay in the vehicle, watch out the window. We'll wait for the north door to open, then you sprint on my six."

"Copy." Holly lowered her window partway, her heart pounding while she gripped the small pistol tight.

White surveyed the area with a hand on her weapon. She opened the door, slid out of the car, ran to the back, and opened the hatch.

Holly searched their surroundings, but nothing moved. White brought Holly a bullet resistant vest and then handed her a larger semi-auto pistol with two full extra magazines. "It's a .40 cal. Action is like the military issue pistol but has a bigger kick. It's locked and loaded, safety on." White tapped the lever on the side.

Holly gave White her LCP back, and she slid it into her ankle holster. Holly put the vest on and placed the extra magazines in her left thigh pocket. The side door opened, and they ran, heads turning, looking for threats. White wore another weapon in a holster at the small of her back.

A man in full combat gear except a rifle cracked open the door. "Special Agent White?"

"Yes." She held up her identification.

The man scanned her ID, then turned and jogged along a narrow hallway to the left. They followed. Holly's heart beat double time, and she gripped the gun tighter.

The man spoke in a low tone. "The tango is in the commander's office. The office is in the back-right corner of a large, open room with two rows of those old-school metal desks. There's no back exit. The office has glass windows all around the top half, standard office walls on the bottom. Shades on the windows are closed. Tango has two of our guys in the office, one wounded. We don't know how bad, but the other one is keeping pressure on it, so it can't be good."

"No weapons locker in this building?" SA White asked, evidently confirming what she'd been told.

"No, or he'd be dead already. Army won't let us keep our weapons here." The man's voice was fierce, and Holly couldn't blame him.

"Post security should be showing up soon," White said.

"Great, more good news." There was nothing but sarcasm in his tone.

They trotted through a large, open garage filled with shipping containers and military vehicles, then down another short hallway that opened to a long, narrow room. Two rows of desks faced away from them; she could see two full desks and two partials. The room must continue beyond their line of sight. The two rows of desks were separated by an aisle, with narrower gaps between the desks and the outer walls of the rooms. The desks were huge, bulky things of dull gray and green metal, with matching chairs in front of each desk. Those desks probably stopped bullets a lot better than her office cubicle would.

Luke sat on his heels, back flat against the hallway wall on her right, closest to the room. Relief coursed through Holly—he was safe and alive. Three other military members crouched next to him. They all wore full combat gear with vests, helmets, and empty holsters. Holly couldn't see Das or the office—it must be at the end of the row of desks.

"Kali, stay here." White pointed behind the men. She walked past the men and crouched next to Luke, pushing the man next to Luke back. She handed Luke a headset, and he put it on, then replaced his helmet. White pulled the weapon at the small of her back and handed that and an extra magazine to Luke. "Revlon's on comms and armed," White said.

Holly stayed at the end of the row of men, ready to move forward and fire. The man White had pushed back turned to look at her. From the rank, he must be Luke's boss, Lieutenant Colonel Mikells.

"Any changes?" Ness asked.

"No. I'll try again." Luke turned toward the room, staying low, shielded by the hallway wall and the desks. "Mr. Das. Send the sergeants to the doorway, I'll come out, and we'll make the swap."

"No, you come in or I kill one of them now!" Das's voice was rough and harsh.

"You know that isn't going to happen, Mr. Das." Luke remained calm. "This is a combat unit. We will not give you an additional hostage for nothing."

SA White leaned closer to Luke and whispered in his ear—the one not encumbered with a comm unit. Then she crawled past him on her elbows and toes, so low that her vest almost dragged on the ground. She turned into the narrow gap between the walls and the desk, disappearing around the corner into the room. The men crouched next to Luke moved closer to him again.

Luke stood, remaining behind the hallway wall. "Mr. Das, at least let the wounded man go. If he dies, you're headed to death row. Do you really want that? For some stranger? Don't you at least want revenge on me?"

Holly closed her eyes for a second, terrified for all of them. Then she closed the gap between her and the last man in line. If shooting started, she'd do her best to bring that man down.

A thud resounded, like something had been kicked. Silence rang, then Das yelled, "Send someone to drag him out."

"No." Luke's voice was adamant. "Sergeant Zest brings him out. I'll trade for both of them or nothing."

"Fine." The exasperation and fury were clear in his voice.

Ness said, "Major Sevrason—"

"Shut up, Ness. You're not in command here." Luke clicked his mic off.

Holly moved closer and stood, peering around the men's armored bodies, ready to run or shoot. Two rows of five big metal desks filled the room. At the far end of the room, glass windows were shielded by beige mini-blinds; in the middle, a single door, half-glass with the same closed mini-blinds. The door opened halfway. A man's head and camo-covered shoulders appeared above the desk. He must be kneeling on the mottled-brown linoleum floor. Das couldn't be seen.

Das yelled. "Come out, Sevrason. No guns, hands up. You cross in the middle. One iffy move, and I kill them both, then you."

"Fine, I'm coming." Luke crouched and handed his weapon and magazine to his boss, then pointed low, at the right-hand wall. Luke whispered something in the man's ear, while removing his empty thigh holster.

Colonel Mikells, his dark olive skin barely showing below a desert-camo combat helmet, dropped down on his belly. Luke duck-walked out into the room between the rows of desks, the darker-skinned man using him as cover to low-crawl across the room. Holly wanted to scream and pull Luke back, but she didn't. He was doing the right thing.

The remaining two men moved closer to the room. Holly followed, wiping her sweating hands on her uniform. She stood slightly behind and to the side of the men, where she could see the room, and pointed her pistol at the ceiling, keeping her finger off the trigger.

Luke stopped in the middle of the room, his hands in the air above the desks. Colonel Mikells kept crawling between the desks, getting nearer to the office. SA White must be doing the same thing along the closer wall, which Holly couldn't see.

Luke shot to his feet, turning in a circle, then crouched again. "You can see I'm unarmed. Send the sergeants out. We'll make the swap."

"Go." Das practically snarled the words.

A man in a combat uniform, presumably Sergeant Zest, half-carried another man. The wounded man's arm draped over Zest's shoulder, a strip of reddened material tied around his thigh. Blood stained the area around the makeshift bandage and both men's hands.

"Start walking," Das snarled. "Slowly, or I'll put a bullet in both your backs and then take out Sevrason."

The sergeants stepped forward together. The injured man hopped on his good leg, leaning hard on Zest, his face pale and strained. Luke stood and walked toward them. As they got closer, Luke made hand gestures to the sergeants down low on his left side. Presumably, Das couldn't see what Luke was doing. Sergeant Zest mouthed "copy," and the injured man gave him a tiny, sharp nod.

Relief let her heart rate slow; Luke had a plan. She closed her eyes for a split-second. Of course he had a plan.

As the men came face to face, they dove behind the desks to both sides. Gunfire rang, making her wince for a split second. Then she pointed her pistol toward the office door. If she saw Das, he was a dead man.

On the left side of the room, White sprang to her feet, fire blasting from her weapon, and she ran toward the office door. Mikells did the same. Holly raised her pistol again.

Before White entered the office, she glanced at Mikells. He reloaded and nodded at White. They moved simultaneously to either side of the doorway. White ducked her head into the office and pulled back. She raised her weapon to the ceiling. "Cease fire. Cease fire. Target is down. Repeat, target is down." Then she entered the office, weapon aimed down, presumably at Das.

Holly lowered her gun and followed the men in front of her into the room. Mikells followed Special Agent White into the office, keeping his weapon pointed down as well.

When she got closer, she could see Das lying on the floor in a pool of blood. White nodded at the man standing behind her, stepped over to Das, and kicked the weapon, a semi-auto pistol lying on Das's hand, away, then checked Das's pulse. "Target is neutralized." Then she slapped cuffs on him and cut away his shirt, balling it up and pressing it to his shoulder.

Guess Das wasn't dead. Holly would normally be happy that a human being continued living, but even bleeding on the floor, Das made her skin crawl.

"Control copies. Notifying Post Security. Security and medical team outside if someone can let them in." Ness didn't sound happy. "White, you'll remain in command. I'll meet Das at the hospital."

"Copy." White didn't move.

Holly grabbed the arm of the closest man. "There's a medical team outside. Can you go let them in?" Both men jumped and ran back down the hallway. She joined Luke, who crouched next to the wounded man.

Another man in combat gear dropped a field medical kit next to the injured man. He shoved desks away from the wounded man. "I've got him."

Luke yielded his place to the medic, grabbed Holly's hand, and pulled her away. Holly shoved her gun in her thigh pocket, yanked off the comm unit, then wrapped her arms around Luke and squeezed him hard. Their protective vests clashed, but she didn't care.

His arms closed around her, holding her firmly and stroking her hair and back soothingly. "I'm okay. Nothing hit me." He pulled his comm unit off, too.

She hung on tighter, trying to control her trembling. She leaned back just enough to see Luke's face, gripping the sides of his tactical vest. "I know. I love you!"

He smiled down at her. "I love you, too."

Voices bellowed, ordering everyone to put their weapons down. White's voice rang out over the thunder of feet and jangle of metal from the security officers' belts and the rattle of a medical gurney. Holly couldn't see her beyond the tsunami of black-clad people. "Stop! Federal crime scene. Put those weapons up." A chorus of protests and questions followed. She yelled. "I'm Special Agent White of the FBI and this is my scene. Stay back. Yes, he's alive. Get another ambulance. Now!"

"I'm Lieutenant Colonel John Mikkels, and this is my squadron." The man's voice boomed—he was loud enough to cross a parade field. "Back off and secure those weapons. Now! FBI's scene, and my unit, my building, and my command. If you don't like it, I don't care."

Luke muttered, "You go, sir! Rent-a-cops all think they're Wyatt Earp."

"Sevrason, you okay?" Colonel Mikkels asked in a slightly quieter tone.

"Yes, sir. I'm fine, not a scratch." Luke's arms tightened around her. She buried her head into his chest despite the hard vest and plastered herself against him.

"Good. Parker, get Jefferson stable, then bring the med kit here. Sevrason, escort these fine people out of my building. The rest of you, guard the doors. Don't let anyone in unless they're medical, full bird or higher, or more FBI."

"Yes, sir!" Voices rang from various points around the room.

Luke dropped a kiss on Holly's forehead, pulled out of her arms, pointed at a desk, and walked over to the vociferously protesting security people. He smiled at them, spoke quietly but authoritatively, and began herding them out. The medical team loaded Jefferson on the gurney and left.

Holly smiled, watching him charm the angry security people. She walked to the desk he'd pointed to and sat down. The picture from their group ski trip was the only one on his desk.

"Kali, you okay?" White called from her post in the office.

Holly chuckled. "I'm fine. I'll just hang here." She rolled her shoulders and neck, releasing the tension.

Lieutenant Colonel Mikkels strode to her, waving her to stay seated. He sat with one hip on the desk. "You're the woman this guy was all excited about?"

"Yes, sir, that's me. Holly Bose." She held out her hand, and he shook it firmly.

He was a bit shorter than Luke, his dark brown hair threaded with silver through his widow's peak and intense dark brown eyes that looked her up and down, clinically, with a bit of a scowl. "I'm sure you're glad this is over." He spoke in a low baritone, and the words were clipped—a command voice.

"Yes, sir. Is the sergeant going to be okay? I feel terrible he got caught in the crossfire."

He frowned. "He should be fine. Bullet went through the meaty part of his thigh and didn't hit a main artery." He slashed his hand horizontally through the air in front of him. "Don't feel bad. Das was the responsible party who made all the bad choices. You just got caught in the crossfire yourself. And thanks for rescuing Sevrason. I'd hate to have to break in another Chief of Training." His mouth curved on one side in a half-smile.

Holly smiled. "You're welcome, sir. I'm sure he would have gotten himself out without too much difficulty." Talking to Luke's boss reminded her that she was very late for work, and she almost laughed at that thought. "Sir, I should call my boss and let him know what happened. He's got to be wondering why I'm not there yet."

"Don't let me stop you." He got up and took a step back toward his office, then turned around and came back, leaning over the desk toward her. "Do you happen to know if the special agent there is from here or DC?" His volume was much quieter.

White hadn't shared any personal details with them. "Sorry, sir, no idea. Why?"

"It's nothing. Thanks." He strode back to his office and talked to White. As she watched, they shook hands, chatted a bit, and then White laughed. Even Luke had never managed to get a laugh out of her.

Holly called her office and explained to Colonel Haywood what happened. He told her to finish up with the FBI and if any of the day was left, to take the rest of it off and check out her house and car. Then the rest of the FBI agents arrived, Das was taken away handcuffed to a gurney, and the debriefing started. At least her part of the story was quick and easy.

After she finished, one of the sergeants showed her where the squadron snack bar was, so she got a drink and a snack for herself and Luke. He smiled and nodded but continued his debriefing.

White leaned against the office wall, just outside the door, Mikkels on the other side of the doorway. "Ma'am, can I get you something to drink or eat from the snack bar? Colonel Mikkels?"

Colonel Mikkels shook his head. "Thanks, but I've got a fridge here." He pointed into the office.

White held up her hand, blocking him from entering. "The crime scene team won't want the scene disturbed any more than it is now."

He reared his head back in surprise and scowled. "Why? The guy's alive. One of us got him with a Bureau weapon. Don't think they're going to need a lot of brains to figure this one out."

"Protocol. Don't mess with the protocol." The corners of her lips rose slightly.

"Fine." He turned back toward Holly with an ironic grimace and a heavy sigh. "Captain, a cola would be appreciated. Stephanie, how about you?"

"Cola as well, thanks." White nodded.

Holly walked away, somewhat bemused. Even Luke couldn't charm a first name out of Special Agent White in a week and Colonel Mikkels got it in under an hour? Maybe they were bonding over the bad guy. She shuddered. But something good should come out of the mess.

She got their drinks, then returned to Luke's desk, trying to forget the grisly conversation Mikkels and White were having, comparing death scenes, evidently. While smiling and laughing. She shook her head in disbelief. It just proved that everyone had a soulmate.

While she waited for Luke, she called her insurance company. As she finished her conversation, Luke returned, dangling his car keys.

"Let's pick up our stuff from the safe house. Then we'll check out the damage on your place. Sound like a plan?"

She rose, walking by his side in the middle of the office. "With one small modification, sure." Her heart pounded, but with anticipation, not fear.

"What's that?" He smiled at her.

She stopped. Luke's hair stood on end from his hands running through it, and his shirt was soaked with sweat from the bullet resistant vest. But he was the sexiest man she'd ever known. "Let's stop at your place before mine. We can celebrate being alive."

He laughed and grabbed her hand, guiding her through the door. "I'm all for that. Here's to being alive!"

Chapter 21

Epilogue

Six months later

HOLLY TRIED TO MAINTAIN her emotionless facade, but she was failing miserably. Then she remembered that was okay. She and Luke struggled to overcome their "hide your emotions at all costs" upbringing, especially under stress, but counseling helped both of them. She tried to memorize Luke's gorgeous face and let the teardrops fall to the hard tarmac of Peterson Field beneath her feet. A hundred feet away, a C-17 cargo jet waited to take the squadron to Spain. From there, they'd go to an undisclosed location, but it was probably in the Middle East.

"Hey, it's only a few months." Luke wiped her teardrops away with his thumbs.

"I know, but the last few have been so good! I don't want it to end." Since Holly's house had been heavily damaged by the fire Das set, she'd gotten out of the lease and moved in with Luke. Many of their coworkers thought they were moving too fast, but their friends knew better—they'd been together longer than anyone, including Holly herself, had thought. Their shared danger and survival brought them together, but love kept them going every day.

He smiled softly at her. "It's not an ending. It's just another adventure. It'll be over before you know it."

She buried her head in his chest. "I know. But I'll miss you every minute."

He wrapped his arms around her. "I'll miss you too. We'll take a trip when I get back to celebrate, right?"

"Something to look forward to." She looked up at him, trying to smile, and he wiped her tears away again.

"And here's something else to look forward to." He dropped his arms and stepped back, reaching into his desert-tan flight suit leg pocket. Kristen, Amy, and Chris stood at their side, Chris aiming his phone at them.

Luke got down on one knee and held a small box up to her, the lid open, something sparkling inside. "Holly, will you marry me?"

They'd talked about getting married but in general terms. He grinned, probably at her astonishment. "Yes! Of course I will!" As he stood up, she threw her body into his, making him stumble. Then he caught her and brought his lips to hers. The world disappeared, then clapping and hollering penetrated her hazy brain. She released her death grip on him but didn't let go.

Luke laughed. "Do you want to actually wear this, or shall I take it back?" He held the glittering ring high.

"Of course I'll wear it!" Her smile stretched, hurting her cheeks. But she didn't care.

"I wasn't sure, since you didn't even look at it." He slid it on her finger.

She glanced at the gorgeous diamond, but she didn't care about the ring. "It's beautiful, Luke. I love you." She wanted to memorize this moment, her heart swelling in her chest with love.

"I love you." Luke lifted her for a kiss.

"Sevrason, let's go!" a man bellowed, breaking them apart.

She fisted his flightsuit zipper tab, pulling him back in. "Stay safe over there. Come back to me."

"I will. You be careful, too." He dropped a quick kiss on her lips, then turned and ran for the plane. He was the last one to board and waved at her from the hatchway.

As the door closed, she blew him a kiss and he caught it, mouthing, "I love you!"

Kristen yelled over the sound of the jet engines spooling up. "I just love happy beginnings!"

"Me too!" Holly waved at the big jet taxiing away. "Me too." They might be physically separated, but nothing could break them apart. Evil men, wild wilderness, and crazy schedules had tested them, but they'd survived and thrived. A deployment was a tiny blip in the lifetime of happiness to come.

Want to know more about Special Agent White and Lieutenant Colonel Mikkels? Sign up for my newsletter! There's no spam, and I won't sell your information to anyone, ever. First, you'll get "Bitter Roots," the prequel short story to the complete, four-book Bitterroot Montana Veterans romantic suspense series. Then, once I finish writing it, you'll get the free short story "A Different Kind of Date." John Mikkels falls hard for Stephanie White—he's freefalling without a parachute or a plan.

Saved by the Guardian, Kristen and Jason's story, is next!

Author's Note and Acknowledgments

WHILE THIS STORY IS completely fictional, trafficking in human beings is a real problem, and it happens everywhere, including the so-called civilized nations. Evil people of every nation profit from horrific slavery. Children are targeted, but women and men from all walks of life get trapped into a terrifying life of forced sex and hard labor. Many victims are drugged, adding addiction to their burdens.

It takes all of us to end this abuse. If you see something suspicious, say something.

How to Fight Human Trafficking

- **Learn the Signs:** Educate yourself to recognize potential trafficking situations. Check out polarisproject.org

- **Report Suspicious Activity:** Call the National Human Trafficking Hotline at 1-888-373-7888 or text 233733 (U.S.).

- **Support Survivors:** Donate to or volunteer with organizations that provide resources, safe housing, and job training for survivors.

- **Advocate for Policy Changes:** Support legislation that combats trafficking and protects victims.

Thank you.

I also want to note that the Sevrason Aerospace fraud—shipping fees in the thousands for tiny parts—is taken from real life. The contractor was convicted in 2007 of defrauding the government for $20 million over a nine-year period and was sentenced to six years in prison after pleading guilty. In addition, the bribery of a Congressman is also taken from real life. Randy "Duke" Cunnigham was a legitimate war hero. Then he betrayed his oath to the Constitution, and was sent to prison for it.

Sadly, there are many, many similar cases, and often, they directly harm military members.

Acknowledgments

Thank you to everyone who reads, buys and reviews my books! I appreciate your time and hard earned money.

Thank you also to all the usual suspects—you're awesome! Sorry I didn't list you all out this time—I rushed, getting this book out for the Fundraiser for Freedom.

Anne M. Scott Biography

After twenty years in the US Air Force, Anne M. Scott traded her sword for a pen. Well, a laptop. She writes about strong women and men, love that grows slowly in small western towns, with suspense, action and adventure, and anything more than kisses behind closed doors.

Anne is lucky to live, hike, and ski in the Bitterroot Mountains of Montana. On the rare occasions she leaves, Anne volunteers with Team Rubicon, a veteran-led disaster response organization. She also writes exciting science fiction as AM Scott and hopeful post-apocalyptic fiction as part of D.C. Layton with Mike Kraus.

Check out her closed-door, slow-build Montana romances at: https://www.amscottwrites.com/romance/ and signup for her newsletter at:
https://subscribepage.io/eXAcUR
https://BookHip.com/TQGCATB for a free ebook. Buy direct and save!
https://payhip.com/AMScott/collection/bitterroot-mo

ntana-veterans-seriesUse code DIRECT10 for 10% off at my store!

You can find her on most social media, although she's on Instagram more often than anywhere else:

Facebook: https://www.facebook.com/AnneMScottAuthor

Instagram: https://www.instagram.com/annemscott_author/

Threads: @annemscott_author

Bluesky: amscottwrites.bsky.social (combined account for Anne and AM)

Email: romance@amscottwrites.com

Website: https://amscottwrites.com/romance

I love to hear from readers! If you find errors, please let me know at the email address above. I'm on all the normal social media, but somewhat irregularly, so if you ask a question or make a comment, please don't be offended if I don't immediately reply. I'm particularly difficult to contact when I'm on Team Rubicon operations or out backpacking—cellphone towers don't exist in disaster zones or the wilderness!

Also By Anne M. Scott

Strong women and men overcome hardship, survive danger and find love in the beautiful town of Marcus, deep in the Bitterroot Valley of Montana.
Small town, closed-door military veteran romance, with suspense, action and adventure awaits in the Bitterroot Montana Veterans series!
Free e-Book, *Bitter Roots*:
https://BookHip.com/TQGCATB
Bitter Haven: https://books2read.com/BitterHaven
Bitter Retreat: https://books2read.com/BitterRetreat
Bitter Sweet:
https://books2read.com/BitterSweetMarcus
Bitter Past: https://books2read.com/BitterPast

Join the active duty heroes and heroines of the Wild Blue Yonder Hearts! Every story comes with a strong military hero, a determined military heroine, plus action, adventure, adversity, and danger with anything more than kisses behind closed doors. Fly away into the Wild Blue Yonder today!

Saved by the Airman:
https://books2read.com/SavedByTheAirman